The Knightsbridge Crowd

MARIANA DE' CARLI

Published by SLKY World
© Copyright 2024 Mariana De' Carli

All rights reserved. This book or parts thereof may not be reproduced in any form, stored in any retrieval system, or transmitted in any form by any means—electronic, mechanical, photocopy, recording, or otherwise—without prior written permission of the publisher, except as provided by United States of America copyright law.

IBSN: 979-8-9921355-2-7 (Hardcover)
ISBN: 979-8-9921355-0-3 (Paperback)
IBSN: 979-8-9921355-1-0 (Ebook)

Disclaimer:
1. Portions of this book are works of fiction. Any references to historical events, real people, or real places are used fictitiously. Other names, characters, places and events are products of the author's imagination, and any resemblances to actual events or places or persons, living or dead, is entirely coincidental.
2. Portions of this book are works of nonfiction. Certain names, places and identifying characteristics have been changed.

Cover design and interior formatting by Qamber Designs.
Edited by Dani Edwards of Scott Editorials. Proofread by Emma Willims of Scott
Editorials.

First printing edition in 2024.

SLKY World Press
Orlando, Florida
www.slky.world

www.marianadecarli.com

To my dearest Silky, for always listening to my stories

"Humanity is not perfect in any fashion; no more in the case of evil than in that of good. The criminal has his virtues, just as the honest man has his weaknesses."

-Les Liaisons dangereuses, *Pierre Choderlos de Laclos*

CHAPTER ONE

The Ground Rules

'Everyone knows there are only three types of people in Knightsbridge,' Allegra declared confidently through her perfectly shaped smile.

'The new rich, the formerly rich, and the almost rich.'

I erupted into a smirk, assuming she had forgotten something, and replied, 'What about the old money?'

Her face instantly displayed her fleeting interest in the topic before closing the conversation: 'Don't be ridiculous; they left this part of town a long time ago.'

It had certainly been an oversight on my part that I would be able to understand the pecking order in this part of South West London, particularly when I sat firmly in the unmentioned category of wishing I was rich. I was part of a curious group of people who just about made it to the right school due to concessions and sacrifices made by my hardworking parents. They had aspired for me to enjoy the best education their salaries could afford, which had the unintended consequence of me growing up in a rank of society often inaccessible to our tax bracket. It would never be lost on me that my role was that of a mere observer rather than a participant in all that happens between Hyde Park Corner and Brompton Road.

At that point, I realised it had been months since our last coffee at Harrods. Allegra and I had been distanced by spending the summer in dramatically different ways. Much like the other socialites with well-known European surnames, her summer had been spent in a weekly destination hopping calendar along the different Rivieras from the Aegean to the Mediterranean. Despite this, her flawless skin had no hint of a tan, with only a slightly more apparent tone of her freckles providing a glimpse of a seaside vacation.

Throughout the two-decade-long friendship we maintained to date, Allegra di Pienza had never changed her signature look. Long, luscious waves in her dark chocolate-coloured hair complimented her large almond-shaped eyes. Her British and Italian mixed heritage came together to form a combination of continental mystique with characteristically English features. The locks were professionally coiffed three times a week to ensure they maintained their bouncy appearance. In all these years, I had never seen her leave the house without her signature black, winged eyeliner. Our university colleagues often compared her to a vintage beauty that would appear as a siren in an Italian 1960s movie.

After taking the first sip of her dark chocolate mocha, Allegra shared another of her great truths that made you feel like everyone should know about it.

'September is truly the most underrated month of the year, Paze. The city is buzzing with everyone coming back from their summer homes, people packing up to move away, and we finally get some new blood to take their place.'

'Finally, something we can both agree on. Speaking of which, my summer internship has materialised into a formal job offer. As of this coming Monday, I'm officially a journalist in training!'

Allegra jumped up in excitement and pulled me in for a warm, congratulatory embrace.

'I'm genuinely so proud of you! I'm sure I will be ringing you up to write positive stories on my upcoming store when you're running the press and my fashion empire finally kicks off.'

Her ability to make you feel like the only person in the room who mattered always made me forget all the distractions that, at times, made me question our relatability. At the end of the day, I could sense her sincere happiness at seeing my modest success, and it made me feel at ease.

'I can promise to always be fair to you.' That sounded like a better compromise. Nobody was subject to only positive press, so I couldn't offer her unconditional bias. The best I could do was act with integrity.

'How's your project going? Are you the proud owner of an online fashion business yet?'

'It's in the works; I shortlisted potential investor partners from France but ended up distracted with holidays. I should get back to my business plan. That's the one thing I can actually control.'

There was a noticeable hint of annoyance in her voice, but I also knew better than to solicit information that had been deliberately kept from me.

'Can't your parents back your store?'

'Where's the fun in that? Besides, this way, I can still technically call myself a self-made woman.'

The irony was not lost on Allegra that many heirs around town loved to proclaim themselves struggling entrepreneurs allegedly bootstrapping their start-ups from the ground up. It certainly helped if that ground was Carrara marble. Regardless of her self-awareness, she still shared their deeply rooted need to prove that they could exist in a realm not created exclusively by their hyphenated surnames. It's always been fascinating to me that those with significant springboards due to wealth and connections persistently tried to convince others, and themselves, that they would survive without them, whilst the rest of us wondered what it would be like to have that dilemma at all.

We rushed through the last sips of coffee before it was decided that a woman in possession of a new job offer must be in dire need of a sophisticated office wardrobe. I hadn't planned to spend an afternoon shopping nor a part of my savings in the most traditional department store in town, but then again, Allegra had mastered the art of persuasion before I had learned how to read. I convinced myself that I had earned the right to treat myself after a gruelling summer of being an overworked intern. As I pulled out my credit card to pay for the graphite grey wool suit that I had tried on in the dimly lit changing rooms, the saleswoman pushed back the card to my side of the cashier.

With a cheeky wink, she exclaimed,

'Miss Allegra has taken care of it.'

I decided to walk home from Knightsbridge and absorb the change of the season from late summer into autumn as I made my way west through Brompton Road. The leafy green trees that lined the side streets around the garden squares had started to display tones of yellow. I walked past the traditional souvenir stores that seemed to disappear into a row of coffee shops with outdoor seating for people-watching.

One of the most comforting parts of that walk was the assurance that year after year, the same familiar faces would be sitting on the external terraces. I offered a sympathetic smile and nod to the strangers whose names I never stopped to ask but had grown to recognise. I learned throughout the years, the customary etiquette around Knightsbridge was a polite but distant salute that was courteous but shy of showing too much interest. Despite the apparent coldness, the reassurance of always sharing that fleeting acknowledgement with the same strangers felt like a constant in a city that was so fluid. It was almost as if Knightsbridge existed as a small village within London with its own rules and pace.

I continued on my footpath back to my apartment, passing by the opulent Brompton Oratory on my right side. Perhaps it was nostalgia for my Catholic upbringing, but I always felt like I would eventually go inside one day. There were rumours that masses were still held in Latin there, catering to purists who held on dearly to the most traditional form of worship. In the previous years of living in the city, I had yet to find the right occasion to visit. At the time, peeking through the grand wooden doors at the glistening gold altar into what was surely one of the most underrated Churches in London would suffice. The most I could offer at that moment was to move my right hand from top to bottom, then from left to right, signalling an invisible cross as a sign of respect while crossing the road to the next block of monumental buildings that descended into the neighbouring South Kensington.

That time of the year, the trees had started to neatly blend in with the palette of painted details on building facades in tones of gold and beige. I had established somewhat of a personal ritual where I'd stop on the corner between the Victoria & Albert Museum and the Natural History Museum, parted only by the aptly named Exhibition Road. A flurry of tourists seemed to merge with the groups of visiting students looking to access the museum lawn that would, in winter, convert into the ice-skating rink.

I purposely slowed down to avoid the incoming herd of people marching their way past me onto their sightseeing destinations. Between beanies, baseball caps, and exotic-coloured hair, I spotted a distinguishable platinum blonde bob fashioned with a cascade of loose waves at the end. As

I approached, the familiar blue-eyed vamp was my close university friend, Mila. Her undeniably Russian beauty had always stood out with a bright red lipstick contrasting with her otherwise monochromatic look of a crisp black trench coat and white turtleneck. The mysterious smell of Mila's leather-based perfume reached my nose before our faces touched for a cheek-to-cheek kiss.

'Well, hello gorgeous, I can't believe I haven't seen you all summer!' Mila exclaimed excitedly in her characteristic international school accent that was neither fully British nor American but could, at times, be both in the same sentence.

I had missed our near-daily conversation before responsibilities turned us into busy adults. Unlike Allegra and me, we hadn't known each other since childhood, but Mila became an important confidant during our three years at King's College. She had many times been the voice of reason for both Allegra and me through heartaches and the emotional roller coaster of attending a competitive degree. The casual run-in gave me a sense of security as I had previously feared adult civilian life would drift us apart.

'How was Monaco?' I asked with the eagerness of living vicariously via my glamorous friend but also knowing she was too blasé to ever share anything too juicy.

'Allegra has made a new enemy. Or maybe she's become someone's enemy. It all sounded very theatrical.'

'She did seem focused on her personal philosophies of societal order today.'

'Well, something tells me that the social guerrilla is about to descend on K-Town.'

I chuckled at the thought of seeing Allegra running with her platform wedges and a balaclava on her face, terrorising some poor soul around Cadogan Square. As entertaining as that imagery was, this battle was most likely going to be fought in a much more vicious manner. One thing I learned from my time spent at Dainter International Girls' School was that type of warfare would be carried out in condescending stares, guest list sabotage, and the eventual, ever-so-subtle yet very carefully worded confrontation of the opponent. The face-to-face moment would certainly take place in an appropriate environment, a quiet back table in one of the cafes inside Harrods. Yet the finale would only be the final piece in an extended season of preparation where sides would be taken, and numbers would be blocked to avoid misplaced loyalties.

'Any idea on what could have disturbed our friend's peace of mind?'

'Nobody with more than five friends ever has peace of mind.' She paused for a minute, reflecting on her own wisdom. 'As dramatic as Allegra usually is, all we've seen this summer is how many different ways people are willing to sell their souls to make it into the crowd.'

As I said my goodbye to Mila with an affectionate hug, I continued walking home as the hotels started to display fewer Michelin guide stars and more neon signs indicating vacancy. Some brutalist concrete emerged in stark contrast with the Victorian and Edwardian houses that lined up the more homogenous blocks of South Kensington.

The spirit of cosmopolitan London started seeping in after crossing Gloucester Road, with a mix of glass facades and stucco-front flat buildings opposite an unexpected high rise. I crossed the road to continue west via the residential garden squares that would, in a few more steps, take me to the front of my white-painted flat building at Collingham Place. I ran up the crimson carpet, reaching the second floor with my heart speeding from my lack of fitness. I opened the door that led straight into my living room, which was also incidentally my bedroom and kitchen, all neatly packed into twenty-eight square metres. Every night, I came home to a slight sense of claustrophobia. I reminded myself that being that close to the action was all worth it.

Kicking off faux-suede ankle boots, I collapsed into my mauve sofa with my legs sticking out to the couch arm. I pulled out my phone while my legs playfully lounged on the ceiling-to-floor mirrored wardrobe from IKEA, which the landlord had managed to squeeze into the place. The photos taken earlier that day with Allegra had already been filtered and posted to her Instagram account. Remembering the unexpected revelations made by Mila, I started to scroll through the posts of the last few weeks in search of any hint that could reveal the brewing rivalry between Allegra and a new fiend.

The only noticeable fact was the mysterious absence of Axwell from all the holiday snaps on her feed. Considering their penchant for public displays of matching glamour, it was odd that Allegra had decided not to have her significant other in any summer photos. But then again, their relationship had only just been made official a few months back at Allegra's birthday bash in May, and by high society standards, it was not unusual for pairings to remain unannounced online for a while.

Much to my own disappointment, discretion was still the main rule in engaging in any type of dispute uptown, so I'd have to arrange for another rendezvous if I wanted to learn anything further. I collected myself and made my way to my kitchenette hot pot. With one month to go before my first paycheck, it was time to carefully meal prep for a week of taking my own lunch to work. Turning up the volume on the Boiler Room playlist, I decided to make a pink penne with chicken recipe with a hint of vodka. Hearing about the potential antics of my friends was a pleasant escape from the anxiety of taking my first steps in my professional career over the next few days.

I was very immersed in Knightsbridge despite the fact that I didn't live there.

CHAPTER TWO
We All Have Bosses

My alarm went off at six o'clock in the morning, and the sound seemed to bounce continuously from the naked walls to the metallic bunk bed frame. I was already awakened by my anxiety-induced throbbing heart but had chosen to lay lazily in bed, enjoying the warmth of the soft duvet. The blinds covering the window next to the bed frame prevented any hint of sun from seeping through into the room. I sat myself up on the bed and wiggled in reverse in order to lower my body from the top bunk via the grey hanging staircase.

On the lower storey of my bed ensemble was a meticulously organised home office with a desk, some storage space, and many decorative items collected over my twenty-four years. The set-up allowed for some escapism from the reality of living in an overpriced, urban sardine can. It felt ironic to spend four years as an undergraduate waiting to finally leave student accommodation just to continue living in equally cramped conditions, only it was not subsidised by the university. The expected immediate break between life as a student and adulthood seemed to increasingly look like a prolonged transition, for which the length would rely heavily on my ability to make adequate decisions as opportunities presented themselves.

For the first day working at Sizzle Media, I had laid out the brand-new suit selected in the last shopping trip to Harrods. With the outfit of the day pre-arranged on the sofa from the night before, there was time to enjoy a leisurely breakfast in my tiny office-turned-eating area. That critical morning, my choice of breakfast consisted of a brown flatbread wrap, a generous spread of Sainsbury's caramelised onion hummus topped with chicken mortadella slices, and edam cheese. That had been ritualistically perfected for years to accompany a morning cup of homemade latte, and the consistency of starting any significant new step in life with the same meal had a soothing effect.

Having felt the caffeine kick in, I rushed through applying a tinted face oil that gave my skin an illusionary tanned glow. The no-makeup makeup look was on trend, which gave me the perfect excuse to limit the amount of priming needed to fit in at my workplace. The main goal for that day was to settle into the office ambience without calling too much attention to myself from the get-go. To break off the seriousness of a suit, I completed my outfit of the day with sleek white trainers and pulled my shoulder-length hair into a casual ponytail topped with a 90s-style black velvet scrunchie. My clothes were often tasked with masking my internal discomfort with starting anything new.

The bus journey to work was an unexpected morning highlight. Having taken advantage of getting out of bed early, I jumped on the route Seventy-Four bus, which would take me from home to work via one of the most scenic drives in London. I had studied it obsessively before the first day in an attempt to familiarise myself with what would be the new normal for years to come.

I journeyed through the glistening buildings of Knightsbridge eastwards and stopped by the sumptuous gates of Hyde Park. There, I changed buses to upwards on Park Lane, where the early rising Mayfair residents were making their way over to the park for a jog. Staring out at the Dorchester Hotel, I synchronised my music selection with the setting by playing a house remix of Vivaldi's Winter. Much like the hotel, that was a song that could be naughtied with a little update or savoured as the classic it was meant to be.

The bus carried along to Oxford Street whilst I tried to distract the growing anticipation about the day ahead. Out of the window, the crowd walking past in a rush of morning commute hurried past each other in a caffeinated frenzy. It felt safe to observe from my seat, using the time to imagine their backstories as a way to keep myself from crumbling in nervousness. A fresh-faced woman with red hair, probably in her mid-thirties, clutching a slightly weathered brown bag. She looked like a secretary in her pencil skirt, probably too busy tending to her toddler in the morning to worry about makeup before rushing out to work. I wondered if that's what I'd become eventually, after years of taking this same route. I certainly hoped not.

I arrived at Charlotte Street in Bloomsbury with renewed anxiousness mixed with excitement at the thought that it would be the place where I would spend most of my time every day. The feeling of arriving at the office as a full-time employee was very different from my first day as an intern, working at the secondary adjacent building that housed all the contract workers. The permanent role was at the headquarters, with all its grandeur and chic ambience. Immediately as I walked through the front doors, I saw an unmistakable Jean Michel Basquiat painting that set the tone for what was to come further inside: Sizzle Media was a place where the cool factor was just as important as the price tag.

As I stood admiring the main entrance, I heard a deep voice from behind me. I jumped in surprise and turned red in embarrassment before the man who had walked up behind me started to talk.

'Paisley Taylor, welcome to Sizzle Media. I'm Nathan, the content lead for your team. Didn't mean to startle. I recognised you from the picture on the badge I printed,' he said as he pulled out my employee access card from his leather backpack.

'Paze will do. My parents met in art school; ironically, I truly dislike paisley print.'

Nathan broke into excessively loud laughter, calling the attention of the reception staff and once again sending my cheeks into a vivid shade of pink.

'Sorry that I wasn't around to interview you before you joined us permanently. I've been on assignment this summer covering hotspots for our features section.'

'I think I was the only person in London through July and August, apart from tourists.'

'They don't count,' Nathan said while breaking into cartoonish giggles.

He seemed friendly, even if he had an obnoxiously loud laugh. The content lead would be my direct manager as a newbie journalist for the Sizzle Media online portal. It was reassuring to have had a casual encounter at the door that felt as natural as one could be in front of a multi-million-pound painting. My biggest fear on the way in was walking through the large glass doors at the entrance and feeling utterly out of place, like an imposter who didn't deserve to be there. That was a feeling that clung to me in important situations, but none of them had been quite as intense as this morning.

Nathan guided me through the security turnstiles that opened with our employee cards. Walking past an elevator that seemed to be corded off to the general public, we made our way up the elegant recommissioned-wood staircases that led us straight into the digital publication floor. There were several ornate desks, clearly rescued from antique shops and given a new life with a coat of fresh varnish. Instead of stale white cubicles, employees had gorgeous wood-crafted stations that were equally unique and mismatched. The style was chaotic but worked well in embodying the creative mind. Without knowledge of the place housing Britain's most progressive digital hubs, a visitor would probably believe they had stepped into a 19th-century publisher with all the retro typing machines used as adornments. Then, upon closer inspection, they would see that pop culture accents broke the vintage feel.

'Here's us, the content team. Say hi to Paze, everyone, and please be nice. Let's not scare her off on day one; let's wait until day five at least,' Nathan declared to a group of co-workers sitting in rows near each other, with two unoccupied tables at the end. I responded with a coy smile as I set up my stuff on the empty desk pointed out by Nathan. Everyone around looked too immersed in their own mornings to notice much about me.

The exception to that was a young woman who walked towards me with purpose. She had on a very tight black dress that showed her sculpted curves, which were complemented by noticeably tall stiletto heels. Her deep olive tan harmoniously blended with her green eyes and stood out in contrast to her waist-long liquorice-coloured hair. That was the most confident walk I had ever seen in a twenty-something-year-old.

'I'm Celine, the office manager and executive assistant to the CEO. Welcome to your new home,' she said while extending a hand for a firm handshake.

'Oh, that's nice, I'm Paze. I'm part of Nathan's team,' I responded while examining her face for signs of familiarity. I had definitely seen her before, but I couldn't pinpoint where. Unfortunately, I couldn't discern if she had been at my job interview or perhaps someone I came across while working as an intern, so I tried to look at Nathan as a cue for her to move on to her next morning task. She also seemed to examine every part of me in great detail.

The feeling of potential prior contact was mutual, but at the same time, I tried to convince myself that I would have certainly remembered her with that assertive stomp. Her accent was indiscernible; there was a twinge of French, but she had a decidedly British intonation. Perhaps she was another of us confused international school kids that fit neither here nor there. Apart from the sense of previous acquaintance, I felt slightly intimidated by her presence as someone who clearly knew too much about everything that happened in this office. I made a mental note to keep myself on her good side.

Her mobile phone rang as she was about to continue our introduction, so she diverted her attention to the caller, waving goodbye as she walked away. I took the opportunity to search for Nathan, who had since sped in front of us to where a small group of employees stood clutching morning coffee mugs.

As I was about to make myself comfortable on the desk, Nathan got up suddenly and announced that we were five minutes away from a team meeting to define which stories would be covered this week on our portal. That was one of the most awaited moments as I would finally find out what would be assigned to me. Just as we started making the rounds covering the different columns and topics, Celine rushed off at full speed, trying to balance herself on her shoes and heading over to the lift that had been unavailable downstairs.

I turned to Nathan and discreetly asked, 'Is she okay?'

Nathan responded mid-smirk. 'Florence must be back from New York. Celine won't risk her stilettos for anyone who isn't the boss.' His tone clearly demonstrated his disapproval of Celine's differentiated dedication to Sizzle co-founder Florence Moray, which, based on the disconnect between his sarcastic smile and words, told me there might have been some prior tension between those two.

I hadn't met Florence yet, but everyone knew about her reputation as one of the most successful women in the media business. In a sector where women were often pressured to be ruthless in order to be respected, our CEO had gained a reputation for being empathetic and maintaining one of the highest employee retention rates in the city. Working in close proximity to her meant being mentored by an industry legend. Her hands-on leadership inspired many MBA courses and was one of the main reasons I had accepted the gruelling internship opportunity to get my foot through the door.

'Do I get to see her sometime?' I couldn't help but ask since finding out we were standing within a few stories of each other.

'You've got to earn that privilege. Cheeky, aren't you, on your first day?' Nathan snarked in a half-serious, half-joking voice.

I stared into the lift as the doors closed behind Celine, watching her go to the place I clearly wanted to visit one day. In preparation for my original job interview, I had already read her biography and copiously watched her public speaking engagements to learn as much as possible about Florence's success story. Unlike most people I come across, Florence was a true rag to riches, and she publicly celebrated her family's working class roots as a key part of her drive. Over the course of a few decades, she became the name nobody could avoid, but she was still frustrated with finding that after shattering every glass ceiling, there was another one above it.

Florence had risen through the ranks at a time when women had been told they should be grateful to have an editorial role in publications. Owning or investing in a media company was still very much a white man's game, yet she was having none of it. That was what made her my idol, biggest career inspiration, and ultimate boss. These were the invisible power dynamics that weren't typically covered in the aforementioned mainstream media that, in her view, was only concerned with performative equality.

In many ways, Florence understood that in order to change narratives, there would need to be a woman at the real top—so high up that nobody could pull a story for calling out the men who had been too often protected by their pals in the right circles.

Sizzle Media was founded as a student publication at first, and its main aim was to simply tell stories in an ethical and impartial way. Most of what she wrote herself in the early days were exposes that shone an uncomfortable spotlight on stories that other places had been too afraid to cover. An independent journalist at heart, in business, integrity trumped everything else. The company would eventually become a fully-fledged empire with several magazines, online portals, a TV station, and even an events department that promoted seminars teaching business "the Florence way".

Surely, there had been critics who attempted to interject her efforts to disrupt the status quo, but the team at Sizzle never shied away from an aggressive response exposing privileges and biases. That was particularly true when Florence underwent a public divorce from a House of Lords member, leading to the separation of written word as Sizzle Media and the television portfolio. Her ex-husband had rebranded the TV business as Sizzle Reality, dedicated solely to unscripted television, typically of questionable calibre. It was stressful, yet it only pushed her more to go beyond. It was that very fiery essence that had motivated me to finish my university degree in hopes of one day also becoming a thought-provoker with a platform.

'Don't daydream too much; you've got to crawl before you climb to the fifth floor,' cautioned Nathan, making eye contact and tilting his head to where the rest of the team sat. I suppose everyone else might have had my same dreams.

'I know, I'm just really excited to be here. I studied journalism so I could create something meaningful, just like she did,' I answered with authentic enthusiasm.

'Yes, didn't we all? But here I am debating on whether a piece on how to choose the best revenge dress should make it into the landing page or if we should just add another quiz.' Nathan responded with a clear resignation that presumably would come to everyone after a few humbling years in the industry.

'I always wondered how those quizzes were selected.'

'Well, you're about to find out; that's where everyone here starts. Your first assignment is to come up with snazzy quizzes that drive traffic in some of our key demographics. We need to be in touch with our university students as much as our more mature readers.'

I tried not to show my disappointment at the news that I wouldn't actually be writing any articles. Also, as much as it looked easy, they didn't exactly teach you at university how to craft short quizzes that could appeal to both a teenager and a pensioner. In fact, the whole concept of driving traffic was something completely overlooked throughout my degree. The focus was almost entirely on substance, whereas having an audience seemed to be an afterthought to most professors on the course. My stomach started curling again with the thought that the starter task could be too left field for me. Like every other student, I had also wasted hours on those online quizzes, and still, I had never thought of them as the work of anyone specifically.

As I made my way back to my assigned desk and prepared to finally start work, my phone vibrated with a new message.

Allegra

> Hey! Any chance you know a Sara Gram?

The name was certainly familiar, but not one I associated with an actual acquaintance. I opened Instagram to search for Sara, and upon coming across her profile, I remembered exactly how I knew her. Far too many of my friends seemed to have run-ins with Sara, which seemed so coincidental it was almost suspicious. I messaged Allegra back after the discovery.

> **Me**
> Yes, she keeps coming up time and time again.

The response invoked a nearly instant ring of the phone. I quickly looked around for the nearest toilets, from where I could answer her with a little more privacy than the open space office.

'Do tell,' said Allegra in an imposing inflection.

'Well, every so often, someone drops her name in the context of some sort of boy drama. I heard she once tried to get Mila's ex-boyfriend's phone number in front of her.'

Hearing the words come out of my mouth, I instantly regretted sharing, as Mila was very private about her affairs.

Allegra's voice changed from inquisitive to sarcastic as she responded with, 'You don't say!'

Despite knowing I shouldn't, I couldn't stop myself from sharing further. 'I heard Mansour mention once that his cousin flew her out to Dubai. It sounded like a lot of fun till his watch was gone.'

Sounding more upbeat, Allegra concluded, 'Love this. Well, I'm sure you've got much more important work things to do. Have a fab first day!'

Before she could disconnect, I asked, 'Wait a minute before you go. What's with the sudden interest in Sara?'

'Oh, I'm sure you've heard about my summer inconvenience. No matter where I went, this petulant woman came, too. More details next time we meet, don't want you to get fired on your first day for always being on the phone.'

THE KNIGHTSBRIDGE CROWD

In agreement, we said our goodbyes with our usual Italian *ciao*. The call's revelations were far too interesting to be ignored. After my last encounter with Mila, the thought of what, or rather who could have rattled Allegra during the summer was a recurring thought. Without a doubt, our next meet-up would be filled with details about the exact moment when Sara had crossed the invisible line of civility into the territory of "troublemaker".

The possibilities of what could have gone wrong were endless, and with limited places that were socially acceptable to be patronised in summer, there was a direct increase in the odds for Knightsbridge elite to be found in the presence of the *quasi*-elite. Wishing to avoid someone in the sunshine season could be very tricky unless, of course, you're willing to sacrifice the most significant events of the calendar—something Allegra would never do.

I tried to redirect my focus on my work as I had to come up with my very first quiz to be published in this week's content sprint. Perhaps there was something in that intrigue that could inspire good quality content for the site. Sipping my takeaway cold brew that had been brought in especially to encourage creativity, my mind raced through the events of the last few days for inspiration on something that could be broad enough for a general audience.

An idea suddenly sprung to mind that the quiz could centre around helping a reader discover their movie nemesis based on a selection of preferred summer destinations. People generally love thinking of personalities in binary terms, the good and the bad, which easily translate into the hero and the villain. Most unsettling, we all seemed to know that a villain lurked inside us all, so any test that invoked our inner antihero had the potential to draw significant attention. I figured that if I could channel my distractions into material for work, it would actually go pretty well.

After a rough design plan of how the first content push could look, it was time to populate the document with fancy images to anchor a potential audience. Few people knew summer hotspots like me. After all, I had spent half of my life listening in on conversations from people who actually went to those places. With a little bit of effort, I could combine memories from trips to visit college friends on the continent with all the titbits of unofficial reviews provided by the crowd. I remembered the late-night call by Allegra about how every man who flirted with her in Monaco was basically a friend of her father or the father of a friend. The quiz would have a real insider feel, which could've given me an edge despite how small the task seemed at first.

Consumed by my work, the hours passed without me having noticed. It was only when colleagues started asking if I ate at lunch that I realised it was already late afternoon. Pre-packed lunch allowed me to continue perfecting my post without needing to walk away from my desk for more than a short break the whole day.

As the clock approached five in the evening, Nathan looked over from his desk and asked, 'How's the first quiz going?'

'Great, just about to finish putting the shareable version together. It's about how your summer destinations can tell you who your archetypal movie nemesis is,' I finally responded confidently for the first time since meeting him earlier.

'Oh, I like it. Are we thinking Maleficent or more like Regina George?' Nathan said while slightly increasing his pitch to emulate a Californian accent.

Breaking into a proud smile, I said, 'Actually, I thought of more cult-classics like Agent Smith in The Matrix.'

'There is no spoon. I like it. Very original. Push it out. By the way, you've got a one-quiz-a-day policy this week,' he said as he got up to start packing up for the night.

My smile quickly dissipated into shock, mouth fully open.

'That's intense. I've just managed to come up with the first one.'

Nathan shrugged, indifferent to the clear concern showing across my face.

'We all have bosses, Paze. Do something out of the box, and maybe you'll be one step closer to that meaningful journalism carrot.'

I hope so. I can't imagine how it would look if I were stuck writing such trivial pieces after years of training for this job. Thankfully, my self-pity party was short-lived with an incoming notification:

Allegra

> Dinner tonight, we're taking her down. Planning starts immediately.

I wasn't a fan of takedowns, but then again, better to be on the right side of the action.

CHAPTER THREE
Keep Your Enemies Closer

Allegra had suggested we meet at Andalus Restaurant, around the corner from a casino hotel tower and across the street from Knightsbridge underground station. Apart from the impending dramatics that were surely going to dominate the evening, I was looking forward to tucking into a Lebanese feast of vermicelli rice and *shish taouk* with a generous side of freshly made chilli and garlic sauces. In all honesty, I would have gone for the food alone, but nothing could beat a dinner with a sideshow of an upper-class feud as much as I hated joining in on pettiness.

The choice of location was no coincidence, nor was it purely based on a culinary preference. For Allegra, there was a deep sense of comfort in the familiarity of the environment, which had been there for decades without much change to the decor. Few things were as important to her as consistency. On my arrival, I found her perched on the last table near the window, neatly tucked inside the restaurant for privacy but ultimately close enough to the street to eye anyone relevant passing by Seville Street.

'You're finally here!' she said whilst simultaneously blowing two air kisses.

I quickly sat down so I could catch my breath after having decided to walk from my apartment, a journey that had taken me thirty minutes of brisk movement. The moment I walked inside, I instantly regretted not stopping on the way to top up my perfume as I became intoxicated with the scent of Arabian Oud. I placed the vintage Gucci bag my mother had picked out as a graduation gift from a thrift store in Covent Garden on the chair next to Allegra's jewel-toned Bottega Veneta oversized clutch. She glanced over to see my accessory and nodded with a smile, a clear sign of fashion approval.

When I settled in the seat directly opposite her, I noticed that her relaxed disposition had changed into the clearest depiction of contempt. Even without uttering a word, it was possible to notice her look had fixated on something taking place on the street through the windows behind me. Her half-smile, unmatched by eyes of disapproval, had clearly been in response to spotting an undesirable guest amongst the sea of regulars. Still keen to maintain composure, I focused on her, awaiting a cue on what should happen next.

'Allegra lowered her gaze towards the right side, using her eyes to point in the direction I should look. After a gentle turn of my head came an admission in a discreet, low tone. 'She's here.'

I quickly scanned the street outside and stopped on a tall woman with an athletic, immaculately tanned body peeking from a white bodycon dress only moderately covered by a loose suede trench coat. Sara's physical attributes were impressive enough to distract a Knightsbridge newbie into believing her Amazonian proportions were sufficient to excite an audience in this part of town. However, as a more seasoned near insider, it was impossible to overlook the fact that her distressed Miu Miu handbag had seen better days. I chuckled, thinking to myself that her tote was more travelled than I was.

Allegra had decided that Sara, whilst a regular in the scene, was *persona non grata* in any social occurrence over which she had minimal influence. Admittedly, that was a sentiment shared by most people I had met on that side of Hyde Park. If asked why she had descended into social disrepute, the reasons varied from the shallowest to tales of contentious altercations. For Allegra, she had mentioned her suspicions of Sara before dinner with her long winding origin story that alternated between Mediterranean and Scandinavian, with sometimes a mix being offered as an explanation. Then, there was the question of her lineage, which had originally been touted with noble connections, only for a quick Google search to suggest that her nobility was within a shady family business context rather than peerage.

Despite the seriousness of possibly having unsavoury sources of money, on its own, it was not sufficiently offensive in certain circles to develop such a reputation. The final *goutte* in the saga of being or not being high society was Sara's penchant for finding herself in affectionate situations with men of the crowd, regardless of their relationship status. Whilst she wasn't the first to decide that a wealthy man was always fair game, it was her being unfazed every time she was caught that was most infuriating to the 'ladies who lunch'.

Allegra snapped after my prolonged glare with an intriguing declaration, 'I can't fathom what possesses her to still show her face around here after what happened this summer.'

I moved my body back to face Allegra fully as a sign of my willing participation as a listener.

'What happened in the summer? I feel like I missed much of the action by staying in town,' I replied honestly as I briefly remembered my decision to postpone any holidays in favour of improving my chances at postgraduate employment at a magazine by working pro-bono for eight long weeks at Sizzle's back office.

'I'll let Mansour fill you in on the latest. Look, he's just coming now to join us,' she concluded while pointing at the door.

As soon as Allegra finished her sentence, a short-framed figure walked rapidly through the door and hurried over to our table. Mansour had a sense of fashion that matched his outgoing personality. His military-style jacket with sharply padded shoulders seemed to give him height above his stature, which he carried confidently in a pair of slightly heeled men's trainers. Raised with frequent trips to his London home, he acted like our very own Middle East correspondent in a bureau of gossip about how the members of the scene behaved whilst they thought no one was watching overseas.

'My two favourite co-conspirators looking the part; that's why we're friends,' he exclaimed while quickly rating both of our outfits mentally after eyeing us from head to toe.

'We never disappoint, Habibi,' I joked as the tension of the moments before his arrival dispersed into the musky airwaves.

Before anyone else could sideline the conversation, I jumped in with, 'So, is someone going to tell me why we're going to be hating Sara this Autumn?'

'Well, in my defence, I had no real issue with her until I got to Ibiza for Mila's birthday celebration. She had warned me in the past not to associate with that woman, but you know me and how I like to give people a chance to show me their true selves.'

Based on the information divulged thus far, once again, Allegra's trusting nature had let her down. I found it particularly difficult to empathise since half of Knightsbridge seemed to have a problem with the same person. It would have been wiser to simply stay away.

Allegra continued after a brief pause. 'So, I didn't mind if she came along to the party we were organising back at the villa. First, she walks in and goes straight to the men without saying a word to the hosts. Then, at the after party, she was deeply concerned that not enough men at the table meant she'd be forced to pay—something she would rather be tortured than do.'

Even though the story hadn't ended, I could already pick on several of the reasons behind Allegra's evident disdain. There were few things that upset Allegra quite as much as a woman who believed beauty and youth were a tradable currency. Had Sara remained quiet, Allegra would have gladly paid the entirety of the bill, but there was something particularly offensive to her in women who treated male company like a walking ATM. I had always thought it stemmed from a lifetime of protecting her brothers from such potential. Nevertheless, it was a belief deeply rooted in her that it was more respectable to offer than to assume.

Mansour took Allegra's pause as an opportunity to jump in.

'That's only the beginning, Paze. At some point between the afterparty and the way home, she ran off with Axwell. As in, *Allegra's* Axwell.' Mansour had shared just as Allegra distracted herself from the story by following Sara with her eyes.

I couldn't help but ponder on whether that was just the stereotypical woman-versus-woman-over-the-affection-of-a-man fight that had already tired out over a decade ago. I recalled leaving school in the early 2010s, optimistic that the world had finally listened to Chimamanda Ngozi Adichie's plea that we compete for careers, not for the affection of men. The Queen herself had included that quote in one of her most significant contributions of the last decade. By Queen, of course, I meant Beyoncé, and by contribution, I was thinking of her 2013 hit Flawless, which I often listened to while hyping myself in the morning before taking the bus to work.

I couldn't help but rattle the discussion with an interjection. 'So, this is about how things ended with Axwell?'

The comment went through Allegra's ears and almost instantly arched the unbotoxed part of her eyebrows. Clearly, I had struck a nerve, which, in all honesty, had been my intention. We had spent the last few years arguing with professors at university over the misconceptions of female relationships as portrayed in the media. Both of us were well-versed in malignant ways by which rivalries play into long-existing stereotypes of the emotion-driven woman who acts hysterical while consumed with lifestyle envy. As a true friend, I felt it was my obligation to ensure that we, too, would not descend into the girl-fights-over-boy fantasy.

'Au contraire, my friend. This isn't about men at all. Quite frankly, she did me a huge favour taking off the dead weight that was Axwell with his party boy antics.'

'Then do enlighten me,' I responded in confusion.

Pacing her next words with a discrete lick of the lips, she continued her explanation, alternating eye contact between Mansour and me.

'This is a much bigger issue. Sara is someone without boundaries; she'll do anything to get what she wants and doesn't care who will get hurt in the way. My objection to her is the question of stopping someone who is willing to take everything away if it suits her without consideration at all for anyone else. I simply cannot sit idly as she weeds her way around people I care about, hurts them, and then discards them like pieces in a chess game.'

The declaration seemed to emerge from a place of vulnerability. Allegra rested her chin on her left hand. Her eyes had a sad twinge, looking lower than their usual spark. It was a rare sight behind layers of walls built by Allegra in order to self-preserve in a cut-throat society. She seemed threatened by Sara, but there was also a part of it that was driven by her instinctively protective nature. In a sense, her intentions were an honourable attempt to safeguard everyone from someone she genuinely felt could disrupt the otherwise very close circle.

Before I could respond, Allegra continued, 'Then, there's the question of loyalty. I tried to understand her perspective as an outsider without the backing of either a well-established family or a bank account large enough to avoid people asking questions. Unlike most people in the crowd, I never discriminated against her on the basis of her flimsy story of how she pays her bills here in London.'

Her tone was so convincing that an innocent bystander would be fooled to think that retaining a minimum sense of non-discriminatory behaviour due to social class was something truly magnanimous. In all honesty, to her, it probably was an attitude to be commemorated since far too many folks were so heavily embroiled in their own social conventions that it was shocking that there was any time to do anything meaningful. In the world of Allegra di Pienza, the honour of not being shunned by her was something not to be taken lightly as it was, for many people, including myself, a ticket into a far more glamorous existence than previously available.

Looking straight at Mansour, Allegra questioned, 'So, how does she repay my generosity?'

Keen to participate in the inquisition of Sara Gram, Mansour responded firmly, 'With betrayal. It wasn't enough to be invited out. She took advantage of a discussion between Axwell and Allegra to give him a taste of her warm hospitality on the side of the road.'

'On the side of the road?' I accidentally repeated the comment, slightly incredulous at the lack of modesty. But then again, what happens in Ibiza usually stays in Ibiza. Unless, of course, what's happening involves the romantic partner of one of London's most well-known socialites.

'Yes, Habibi, just like that in front of any car passing by, including ours. I think she wanted to get caught. You know she's one of those people who doesn't just do the deed but needs people to find out it happened. I told you how she stole my cousin's watch in Dubai after that bank holiday trip, right? Do you know how we found out?' Mansour, ever the instigator, continued, adding fuel to the fire.

I shook my head, bracing for yet another turn in this increasingly interesting emergence of an opponent worthy of my best friend's wrath.

'She posted a picture of herself wearing it on Instagram. Blocked him first, of course. But it took all of five minutes for the screenshot to make the rounds. Fahad couldn't press charges because his family would strictly reprimand him if they knew he had been with a girl out there. Or with a girl at all. Convenient, isn't it? Stealing from the person who could never let it get out.'

I couldn't help but participate in the conversation. 'Honestly, that's awful. Fahad is the best of us; he probably didn't even see it coming.'

Allegra purposely closed and opened her eyes, prolonging the pause.

'No, he didn't Paze. Axwell is one thing, the club table whore who's seen his share of things. If someone pulls one over on him, well done her. But Fahad? Or Mila? Or you? That's not happening on my watch, excuse the pun.'

Mansour responded with a friendly slap on Allegra's arm while exclaiming, 'Hey! What about me?'

Breaking into the first laugh of the entire lunch, Allegra responded, 'You can more than fend for yourself, darling. My sympathy is with anyone who tries to come up against you.'

The three of us broke into loud laughter, knowing very well that it was absolutely true. There had been roles established in our circle of friends, and everyone knew that Allegra and Manosur were like two peas in a drama pod. It was their notorious tough skin that made them naturally gravitate towards the role of gatekeepers, protectors of the peace, and, ultimately, the ones to drive out any unwanted intruders.

Since meeting on the first day of orientation at King's College during freshers week, the bond between Allegra and Mansour had been unbreakable. From early on, it became obvious that despite growing up in very different environments, their families were quite similar in the way that they reared the ultimate social butterflies. Etiquette came naturally to both; they knew the right things to say and how to look their best while saying it. All of the rules that I had painstakingly learned at school in order to merely fit in seemed to occur spontaneously in the two of them. A part of me was always jealous of how effortlessly the two existed in a state of constant cool factor.

Returning my focus to the Levantine feast on the table, I nearly forgot about the ongoing drama. I was about to bite into the complimentary baklava brought by the waiter when Mansour jolted forward in his chair.

'Do you remember who introduced Sara to my unlucky cousin?'

Allegra and I both looked at him intently while prompting our answers with a nod.

'It was Caetano. Remember that model-looking Spanish guy who befriended Fahad in Marbella?'

Alas, that did ring a bell. Fahad was the complete opposite of Mansour in every way possible. While Mansour was a city boy who loved the glitz of Sloane Street, Fahad preferred the quietness of Greenwich, where he'd lived during his studies. He had held on tight to many of the traditions that Mansour eagerly forgot the second his plane would arrive at Heathrow. One such great Arab tradition was vacationing in Marbella when the weather was too unbearably hot to return home.

I replied to Mansour's comment, curious as to where his train of thought would lead us next,

'I do remember that. I was studying Spanish in Malaga that summer and passed by to see you guys. Everyone seemed so snobby there; much preferred my good old student town.'

'In my defence, I always said nothing good ever happens in Marbella,' he replied while giving his characteristic raised brow stare, a cue that my own experience was not relevant to where he was trying to get to here.

He continued. 'I had seen this statuesque man around before, he's always at Fashion Week. We've never been super close, but we've shared a drink or two at Annabel's before. Caetano is always everywhere you look, but you're not sure why.'

The worst thing was, I knew exactly what he meant. One of the main features of the high society circles was that, in reality, it was much more like Dante's *Inferno*, with many layers and peculiarities as you went closer to the epicentre.

At the wider edges of the circles were people whose lives were entirely dedicated to penetrating another layer of the strata that separated them from insiders. Those people were no less part of the crowd. After all, should you hold a party in Knightsbridge with only true belongers, you'd have about five attendees. The outliers usually appeared in every hotspot, but nobody could pinpoint who invited them. Nevertheless, they relentlessly attended anything and everything that ever had more than three people in attendance—usually to populate their social media with carefully selected photos showing to their own outliers that they'd made it. Or at least that they were faking until they really made it.

Allegra jumped in, keen to hear more. 'Yes, we all know Caetano. Relevance?'

'Well, as you know, my parents made me make a pit stop in Marbella en route to Ibiza last year. I went to pay my respects to Fahad's parents at their humble abode.'

I couldn't help but smile at Mansour describing his cousin's eye-watering waterfront villa in near proximity to Marbella's golden mile of restaurants as a "humble abode". Resisting all temptation to mention anything, I let him conclude his story.

'He invited me to lunch at El Chiringuito, which I thought was for two, but out of nowhere came Caetano. Fahad was keen to impress me with his new acquaintance since I've always tortured him about needing to make new friends in London.'

Allegra was growing impatient and asked, 'Let me guess, you weren't too impressed?'

'He was quite witty, actually. Meeting him over lunch made me realise he's far more intelligent when he's sober. I was so distracted by the conversation that I missed the part where Fahad starts fawning over a girl in a V-shaped, nearly see-through bathing suit. When I caught wind of what he was looking at, I noticed how her movements were slow and deliberate. I'm not even into that type of thing, but I nearly dropped my food while waiting for her to take off her towel fully.'

'I speak for both of us when I say spare us the male gaze of it all.' Again, I felt compelled not to let the conversation enter into territories I wasn't about to support.

'Well, Caetano is always aware of everything, so he offered to introduce Fahad to his good friend Sara Gram. An offer he was in no position to refuse.' Mansour made sure to emphasise the last part to absolve Fahad of any maliciousness.

'The intrigue takes an unexpected turn!' I contributed, earnestly curious as to how it would play into brewing controversy. On the other hand, I started to piece the information together and form a picture of Mansour's own resentment towards Sara. His cousin was a shy and mostly pious young adult who, due to his own convictions, lacked the experience to deal with a seasoned social climber. He must have mistaken her interest in his status for affection, only to later come to terms with being a pawn in her game.

Mansour elaborated further. 'Fahad couldn't take his eyes off her golden body. He confessed to me later that night that she was like the real-life version of one of those Sports Illustrated magazine models that had been hidden in our bedroom as kids. It was the first crush that I knew of, so I wasn't about to give him the wake-up call.'

'So, did he ask her out on a date?' I elicited.

'He was way too nervous for something that was official. He had Caetano serve as messenger and arranged for her to meet him at a beach club the next day. Fahad is so cute; he booked out all the cabanas so they could have some privacy.'

'And so, did it end in smooches?' Allegra questioned while sipping on some coffee, but she was also already aware of the answer to her rhetorical question.

'She didn't even show up! Sara sent a message via Caetano that she didn't show up to meet unknown men.'

I could imagine Fahad's face of disappointment at hearing the news, with his small, rounded eyes looking more rounded than ever.

'Turns out my cousin is a little Don Juan. He went out to Puerto Banus and bought a Cartier Love Bracelet. He signed a card and had it sent via Caetano, who at this point was a very willing participant in the whole thing.'

'Cute gesture, terrible taste.' Allegra was nearly as unimpressed at the choice of jewel as she was at the choice of company. I had heard the impassioned speech she made about how the Kardashians ruined perfectly nice pieces by stacking them as if they were the Live Strong plastic bracelets of 2006. As a general rule of thumb, if a woman from Calabasas with a vocal fry would wear it, then Allegra would have no place for it in her closet.

'Well, terrible taste in both shopping and women. Of course, she leapt at the opportunity once she could properly assess the agreeableness of the credit limit. The rest of the days in Marbella I had to play nice with them as they were inseparable.'

Teasingly winking at Mansour, Allegra said, 'Well, don't you deserve a Nobel Peace Prize.'

I was more intrigued as to how the relationship evolved between a much more conservative Fahad and a far more liberally raised Sara. Mansour replied to my query with a lot of sass.

'Well, honey, it was the gig of the century for her. All he did was take her to places, but we all know he's not touching anyone till marriage. She was literally being paid to just exist.'

Continuing with the same judgmental tone, he said, 'Her summer went from working at a shop in Puerto Banus to having more caviar for lunch than Mila's parents—and they produce it.'

'The more important question is, are you still friendly with Caetano?' Allegra was beginning to see where the conversation could favour her own endeavours.

Mansour let out an eerily enormous smile, 'I'm friendly with everyone.'

'He seems to know a lot more about Sara than we do, which could be convenient. Do you know if he's back in town?' Allegra, who had clearly formed a plan, reshaped her shoulders into a confident posture while speaking. She no longer resembled the withdrawn person who had first sat in that same place.

'Everyone's back in town. You know the best way to attract these sorts of people is to throw a party. They always come,' Mansour responded, fully aware of what he was propositioning.

Looking mischievously at Mansour, Allegra dropped her final verdict of the day. 'Well, I'm now throwing a party to commemorate the new season. Will you be a doll and let Caetano know he's finally on my guest list?'

The grin of approval was always a sign that my two friends were more like twins with telepathic capacity to reach each other's scheming minds.

While signalling the waiter for the bill, Mansour declared, 'As the saying goes, keep your friends close and your enemies closer.'

The dice had been rolled, and shortly, the invitations would be sent. In printed monogrammed paper, of course. I had spent the last few days vigorously checking my mailbox for a delivery containing the personalised invite that would grant me access to the event that would set off the autumn social calendar. Even though it was irrational to imagine that I wouldn't be invited to an Allegra-hosted affair, there was still always an uneasy anticipation that would brew up with unwelcome thoughts of whether this would be the first time that I wouldn't be a part of it all.

The nervousness of awaiting the delivery, combined with the understanding that this event could be considered Allegra's first move against her newest foe, made it difficult to focus on anything else other than my inner circle. In her rush to prepare for the party, her texts had gone quiet, but the rest of the group remained active in their frequent updates of public sightings and pairings involving those on the other side of the fence. True friends always keep tabs on whoever isn't following the ground rules.

I had little to contribute as I was firmly involved with my onboarding process at work. As happened far too frequently, I was more of a consumer and encourager than an instigator. The increasingly sarcastic and judgemental tone of messages was a good escape from my reality of trying to create engaging content for Sizzle's online portal.

But then, midday on Friday, a courier came to drop off at work a package that needed to be signed for personally by me. I tried to disguise my clear excitement with a fast-paced walk that didn't quite materialise into a sprint. In front of the reception, I offered my signature in exchange for what was surely my ticket into another round of high society mischief.

I opened the small envelope, which had my name written in elegant calligraphy on the front. As I pulled out the card inside, I saw the Di Pienza family crest embossed in matte gold, followed by immaculately written words:

> *Miss Allegra Di Pienza requests the honour of your presence at her turning of the season evening gathering. Attire: Formal.*

It was an antiquated method, but nevertheless, it made you feel special every time. Before I had a chance to read the final lines, I noticed Nathan standing behind me, prying on the content of the letter.

'How do you know Allegra di Pienza?' he inquired with a surprised expression.

'We went to school together. We're old mates.'

'Look at you, Ms Knightsbridge; I had no idea you were such a posh one.' His tone was more one of judgment than compliment.

'I'm not at all; I'm just friends with some of them,' I said, defending myself and creating some distance with my words.

'Well, you have to cover it for the portal; I'm bumping you up to your first story.'

I was so ecstatic that I nearly forgot how much Allegra despised social columns.

'I'd need to check with her first; she's usually not into these things.'

'Aren't you her good friend? Make it work.' *And he made it clear he meant it.*

CHAPTER FOUR
Everyone Goes to Le Rosey

One of the things that was most certain about Allegra was that she would deeply study any social opponent. It was essential for her to understand the background story, what they were after, and how far they'd be willing to go to reach it. That had always been her *modus operandi* in executing a flawless high-society war. As such, the war that was waged between Allegra and Sara meant that the latter was soon to find herself as the subject of interest. The freshly delivered invitations had only just reached their recipients, and they were already the most desired envelope in town.

With all the excitement, the week had passed in a flash, and I found myself unpacking my Friday lunch when I was suddenly summoned.

Allegra

> Meet me and Mila for a coffee at 6pm sharp at Leena's on Motcomb.

Unwilling to miss out on the action, I confirmed that I'd go straight to Motcomb Street for an impromptu after-work rendezvous, where the planning of Allegra's party would be discussed. The tone was direct; I could read the tension through the lines of the WhatsApp text. It was just the energy boost I needed to get through the end of an otherwise uneventful afternoon at Sizzle.

I wondered if any new information had already been uncovered. *Had there been a confrontation since we last spoke? Surely not,* I thought to myself, *otherwise, it would have made its way to me already.* Observing the environment around the office, where everyone was too preoccupied with their own deadlines to realise my idleness, I started to count down the hours to being released back into my natural habitat. The workday had started like any other should, but surely there would be some unintended entertainment.

Looking back at the content planning dashboard on the project management software, I couldn't help but wish that work was as exciting as the hours after it. It had only been a few weeks in the role, yet my creativity in churning out content for the website had already started to struggle. The idea of creating personality tests to define how a selection of questions could tell a complete stranger their preference in 90's movies for weeks on end seemed far more appealing on paper than in reality. Worse yet, the only chance presented thus far to escape the mind-numbing task relied on being able to cover Allegra's party for Sizzle. I had yet to muster the courage to ask her for permission, although the planned coffee catch-up presented a great opportunity to ease in the request.

The original plan of crafting meaningful journalism pieces had been put aside in favour of a consistent paycheque. Besides, the role I had was my way into an organisation with far more interesting divisions that did create genuinely hard-hitting articles. None of my family worked in the field, so nepotistic hiring was out of the picture. That thought was just another reminder of the chasms between my schoolmates and me. My personal connections were far too precious for me to burden with my struggles as a budding journalist, so I had to resort to applying for an internship the old-fashioned way and gradually work my way to the top.

The thought of directly using my friends as a theme for an article was something I was still grappling with. It didn't feel right, but I also wouldn't be the first person who needed to rely on their friendships to get ahead. I pushed away the thought, reassuring myself with the notion that I wouldn't actually do anything without their express consent. In a sense, if they agreed, they would be an active part of what I was doing, so it was very different to people who disingenuously build relationships for the sake of their own advancement. I was proposing something totally different; they would know of my intentions upfront and would be in presumed control at all times.

The reliable stomp of Celine's heels sounded like a school bell, releasing me from monotony. Since I had barely worked for the final hours of the day, I was more than ready to rush out as soon as I saw her walking in my direction. I purposely kept my eyes locked on the floor in order to avoid eye contact with anyone who may unleash a sudden onslaught of small talk. My tactic was successful and allowed me to board the first passing bus quickly, heading to the seats in the back where I would be able to discreetly retouch my makeup before the meet-up.

I was so focused on the task at hand that I hadn't noticed Celine had boarded the same bus until I looked to the side and noticed her sitting across the aisle from me. Offering a polite Londoner smile, signalling that I acknowledged her but had no wish for verbal interaction, I pulled a makeup pouch from my handbag. As I applied a layer of highlighter to my upper cheek, Celine asked, 'Where you headed? Date night?'

Restraining my urge to ignore her, I replied while holding up my mirror and brush to my face, 'Not at all. Meeting my girlfriends in Knightsbridge for some coffee. They're always dolled up.'

'That's cute; I'm heading that way, too. I'm staying there at the moment.'

That was unexpected. I hadn't quite placed Celine as a local, but then again, that would explain where I had seen her before. One thing I knew about London for certain, though, was that often things were not as they seemed.

'Whereabouts do you live?'

'I'm staying on Sloane Street. You should pass by for a drink afterwards; let's call it a girl's night.'

I continued applying makeup using a mascara wand to both elongate my eyelashes and hide the confusion as to how Celine managed to live in one of Knightsbridge's most expensive streets. I wondered if she came from money but did the job to keep herself busy before settling into a more conventionally wealthy life.

'That would be lovely. I'll let you know once I'm ready to graduate from espresso to Negroni.'

Her offer was a surprise. I had yet to socialise with anyone else at Sizzle outside of work, so I found it genuinely appealing to potentially befriend one of my floor mates. More importantly, she was one of the few that had a direct line to Florence Moray. Since starting work, my closest interaction with her was strictly via company town halls, where she delivered flawless motivational addresses to make the entry levels like me believe we were a direct part of the group's strategy.

I didn't see how the quizzes that I was constrained to producing offered any value to anyone. I couldn't wait to meaningfully contribute to the business. One of the biggest lessons I learned from my years in an elite school was that decreasing the distance between yourself and your end goal wasn't going to come from patiently waiting to be recognised in a crowd. You always had to find a way to get the right person's attention.

With the plans for later set in place, I finished applying my face paint while Celine tucked in her AirPods, signing off on our interaction. The next half hour of the ride passed in a flash as I attempted to reorganise myself into a presentable state. When the bus finally reached the stop right outside of the Knightsbridge tube station, Celine and I both exited, exchanging waves. I continued walking over from the bus stop near Knightsbridge station towards Belgravia as the chaotic main roads slowly diluted into the quietude of residential streets.

The streets leading to Motcomb weren't sleepy per se, but there was no doubt a change of air once you crossed the first large garden square off Sloane Street. Instead of being store-lined with multiple lanes of vehicles, your eyes were met with lush shades of green carefully tucked into resident-only fencing. The cars were silent, there were fewer pedestrians, and usually, those walking around had a reason to be there rather than the combination of businesspeople, tourists, and shoppers of the uppermost parts of the area.

It was easy to spot my friends as I approached the cafe; they were laughing loudly as they sat on the veranda, enjoying the still-pleasant weather. Both Allegra and Mila had their signature change-of-season coats, each in their characteristic black and red, respectively. Whether it was a conscious decision or not, their personalities were represented in their usual hues. Allegra's closet was largely dressed in black, with occasional tons of gold. Her choice of outfit was usually classical luxury with an air of mystery. Only on very specific deliberate occasions would she steer far from her regular choice. In contrast, Mila always wore bright clothes that brought a much-needed light-hearted tone. Allegra opened the conversation abruptly as soon as I sat down.

'I have important matters to discuss. My event planner is on standby.'

'We're all ears,' I responded, speaking on behalf of Mila.

'I'm cutting the guestlist off at 120; it's a number I like.'

Mind you, a party catered for one twenty was already quite intense for me. The ability to please all attendees simultaneously was a talent not to be overlooked. On a good day, I could manage our small quartet, but there was more than one occasion where I much preferred a one-to-one catch-up. To be unanimously seen as a great host was far more challenging altogether when the audience was pompously discerning. Overall, such occasions required hosts with the tact of a diplomat wrapped in carefully selected couture.

Mila jumped in with a critical question. 'Who's in and who's out?'

At that point, Allegra pulled out her leather-covered Hermes daily planner and opened it to a page containing a handwritten list of names. There were people who would pay good money for access to her proverbial little black book; it was essentially a who's who of London's elite. It was also a consistent list. The first half of the names would never change, apart from an eventual replacement by the next generation of same-surnamed people. The margin of newness was confined to the second half, whose addition or removal to the most relevant circle in town would rely heavily on their own behaviour. Those sixty lines were disputed territory, and for some people, all bets were off when their position in the list was at stake.

Running her eyes up and down the piece of the paper, Mila pointed at line twenty-one and said, 'Alexandra Wolf is still in Germany, forgot to mention it, but she asked me to let you know she won't be coming.'

'That's one more slot open, in that case. I'll leave it like that for now in case I need to make a last-minute addition.'

Allegra flipped the page to a checklist of tasks that needed to be completed before she could fully hand over the party to her planner. The requirements for the event were too specific for her to fully entrust it to someone else. No risks would be taken in order to ensure that the right people were impressed and equally intimated.

'Mila, I need your caviar supplier.'

'Consider it done; I've also ordered a crate of Belle Epoque for you. That's my contribution.'

'*Merci*, that's lovely!'

'Onto flowers, strictly white aromatic. What do you think, Paze?'

Before I could muster an answer, a tall, thin man approached us with a slow-paced walk. His cardigan was beautifully matched with his camel moccasins. Despite the dimming sunlight of the September afternoon, his eyes were concealed behind large-framed shades. The flamboyant gait was matched with an equally over-the-top expression of affection when greeting us. I hadn't met him yet, but the lack of concern from the others in the group meant he was someone I should have known.

'Allegra darling, thank you for inviting me to your party. Shall I bring the cigars for later?'

The comment was met with the least honest type of laughter.

'Caetano, dear, it's a pleasure. I've heard so much about you from Mansour. Thought it was time for us to get to know each other better.'

I quickly assimilated the name and meaning of that very strategic invitation. He had walked into Allegra's trap like a fish to a net under the illusion of swimming freely. The only reason I couldn't actually foster any feelings of sympathy was that I assumed he, too, had his own agenda. There were rarely innocent bystanders in such games, and the fact that he just happened to know where to find Allegra informed me that he'd certainly done his homework.

'I can never remember where we first met. Did you also board in Surrey?'

'No darling, not me. I went to Le Rosey—'

'Did you? I hadn't heard you went there,' Mila interjected.

'Well, everyone goes to Le Rosey; it's hard to keep track.'

The hilarity of it was that Mila had, in fact, gone to Le Rosey, Switzerland's well-known boarding school refuge for the young and restless with deep pockets. She had, of course, not confessed in the conversation, which I assumed was part of a strategy to elicit more than to participate. The fish entangles himself in the net without the fisherman needing to do much.

He continued. 'One thing, I haven't seen a plus-one option on the party RSVP. Is it strictly nominal?'

'Yes, I tend to only extend the accompanying invitation to those whose partners I am acquainted with, but perhaps it's someone already on the general list.'

'A friend of mine asked to come as she'd heard about the party from all our mutual friends. She's actually an old colleague of mine from Le Rosey; you know Sara Gram, right?'

The audacity of the comment nearly made me choke on my chocolate biscuit. With all the rumours going around about the summer escapades, it would be nearly impossible for someone close to the action to not have heard anything at all. On the other hand, it was going exactly as Allegra had planned.

'We've crossed paths. I wasn't aware she had studied in Switzerland,' Allegra replied with hints of sarcasm.

'I would have certainly remembered her on campus,' Mila retorted, looking directly at Caetano for a reaction.

Realising his mistake in not properly assessing the potential discovery of his lie, his body moved in discomfort into a pose with hands firmly placed on the hips in mocked confidence. I could see him mentally readjusting his story to fit for purpose.

'It's probably because we are a few grades above you. It makes sense.'

The best way to sustain a false origin story was to find someone else in equal need of legitimisation who's willing to corroborate the lie. Hence, ladies and gentlemen, we came across the boarding school fraud. The choice of school was as important as the act itself. It was key to steer clear of anything niche enough that if you ran into genuine alumni, they could have outed the imposter. The best option to be believed was to go with something very well-known to the mainstream audience, Swiss and with a rotation of incomers and expelled rebels. Maybe they were just the wallflower in a sea of protagonists. Le Rosey would probably be ideal.

Sensing the tension increase in the environment, Allegra put a decided end to the story with a final comment.

'Unfortunately, the numbers are all accounted for; I'm sure we'll have the opportunity to socialise with her at a later date.'

'That's alright, at least one of us will get the honour to enjoy some drinks *chez* Allegra.'

The ensuing goodbyes were as disingenuous as the initial hellos. That was purely a convention that must be followed as none of us had any real affection for him. The three of us waited carefully to ensure he had walked past the end of the cobbled street before making any comments on the interaction.

Mila opened up the floor for commentary.

'Well, that was something, wasn't it?'

'We now know what they pretend to be. I'd be curious to know what they really are behind it all,' responded Allegra.

Deciding to, for once, have the final say, I jumped in with my sentencing.

'In the end, do we know much about who anyone is behind it all?'

Silence ensued for a few seconds while they thought about my comment, only to move on to checking their phones for updates on the party affairs. Perhaps my contribution was too deep for an afternoon of more trivial affairs. I conceded that I was going to be denied a response, so I finished my coffee and decided it was time to move on to my second appointment of the evening. After catching up with my personal friends, it was time to dedicate myself to closing in on my work relationships.

I headed West on Lowndes Square towards the Sloane Street address Celine had shared. After I reached her street, I walked past the enticing storefronts that make up one of London's most exclusive shopping districts. My pace always slowed down as I peeked in to see the latest fashion trends that I looked forward to wearing as soon as they hit the fast-fashion shops. The creativity of the merchandisers who worked with the Sloane Street shops had always challenged to appeal to both the overseas buyers looking for cutting-edge facades and the old-time residents who preferred to preserve the sanctity of classical luxury. As much as I enjoyed thrifting in the vintage designer outlets of Covent Garden, I always told myself that one day, I, too, would enter through the marbled entrances like one of them.

The building I was looking for was nestled between stores selling impossibly expensive diamonds. An antique-looking gate hid a small fountain from the street view. Inside, there was a small cobble path into a dimly lit building with classically decorated red carpeting and oak accents. I had passed that street many times without noticing the hidden gem behind the unassuming gate, which, despite the recent trends of more minimalist decorated lobbies, had stood strong as a reminder of a far more decadent past era.

The long hallway eventually came to an end, where I found the door corresponding to the apartment number Celine had provided. She opened the door dressed in a comfortable sweatpants ensemble with her hair tied up in a bun, a departure from her usual overdone style. After greeting me with two cheek kisses, she let me into the apartment and sat me in the living room while she whisked off to the kitchen to concoct the cocktails for the evening. I sat there thinking about how the week had led to spending time with both old and new friends.

'You're sure you want a Negroni, right?' screamed Celine from the closed kitchen room a couple of doors down.

As I got up to move closer and reply, I noticed that despite the large number of picture frames in the pad, not one of them contained Celine. They were mostly old photographs, poorly preserved from overexposure to light. I assumed they must have been family heirlooms, but noticeably, the figures in the photos were very different to her in terms of looks. As my eyes scanned the room, the living room seemed to have been unchanged for quite a few decades as it lacked any new technology. I figured it must have been a family property, one that probably wasn't used much.

Rattling noises started coming from the other room. I walked into the kitchen and found Celine opening all the cabinets as if she were unsure of where the cocktail cups were kept.

'Do you want me to help you look for it?'

'It's fine; I just never have people over. Sit back on the sofa, will be there in a minute.' That made sense; it was probably a family property, and she might have been shy about inviting anyone over until it had been cleaned out. It's also not common for people in big cities to shy away from home gatherings unless, of course, you're Allegra and have a team of helpers to put it all together.

In the few steps that it took for me to walk back to the sofa, I passed by a stack of unopened mail. A quick glance was enough for me to realise they were all addressed to Lord Thurrington, a name I most certainly recognised. He had been a co-founder at Sizzle Media and was the previous husband of Florence Moray. Their high-profile divorce had swarmed all over the media for the last few years, with huge speculation over the splitting of their media empire. He had since dedicated most of his time to growing an empire of companies across all sectors.

The big question was, why did Celine live in Lord Thurrington's apartment? There was no trace of him around, but it didn't mean he hadn't been there prior to my arrival. It was perhaps the biggest revelation of the evening. It left me with the conundrum of who I could share it with and who could give me context without spilling my prying.

Just as I was about to text our group chat, Celine finally emerged with the drinks and offered a toast. 'To us, girls who go after what we want.'

CHAPTER FIVE
The Unboxing Campaign

Like any self-respecting socialite, Allegra dedicated her pre-event days to preparing for a public appearance. Make no mistake: that was a process that was carefully crafted with the help of the top fitness and wellness experts in town. It had been two weeks since we'd last seen each other, but I had been kept regularly updated with her progress thanks to a slew of texts. It had been an endless supply of photographs of overly green meals and selfies in workout gear.

In the meantime, I had shied away from most of my friends in favour of enrolling in a company-sponsored story-writing boot camp, something Nathan had organised for me to join despite being new to the business. I didn't need much convincing, but he still felt it necessary to reiterate that it could be a great opportunity for me to see if I was cut out for that job. I was keen to show my appreciation for him, so I promised an invitation to Allegra's evening of fun. Nathan also didn't need much convincing, but I still felt it necessary to remind him that it would be his chance to rub shoulders with some of the people he had written about previously. However, it was still a social invitation, and privacy should be respected.

After successfully spending time immersed in honing my craft, I was more amenable to participating in the usual Knightsbridge mischief. It was twenty-four hours before everyone descended into chaos, which meant that I had the moral duty to stand guard around Allegra as she grappled with last-minute consternations. She had already messaged me multiple times; the last one requested my presence after work at her gym. There was no time to lose. Conversations would be held in conjunction with other errands. In that case, that meant a last-minute fitness stretch, which would consist of her whining at her personal trainer, followed by a dip in the metallic floored pool of the Carlton Hotel.

Certainly, like Allegra di Pienza wouldn't be caught at your high street gym facility, she was also too discerning to join the hyped-up members-only clubs of the area, where overpaid bankers typically spent their wellness stipend. It was far more on brand for her to work out at a hotel, where her gym mates would constantly change, only a select few knew you could get a subscription. Besides the appeal of being able to peacefully train away from the prying eyes of other residents, the place itself was a refuge within the city. From the pool, the floor-to-ceiling windows allowed for panoramic views of the green garden squares of Knightsbridge.

As soon as I walked in, I spotted Allegra already in her black one-piece bathing suit in the pool. I made my way over and sat myself in the nearest sun lounger. As soon as she saw me, she swam quickly, eventually stopping on the edge of the pool.

'I've missed you! How was the course?' She sounded full of energy as she continued stretching her legs inside the pool while we conversed.

'It was amazing; I missed being able to focus completely on one thing. That's probably what I miss most about university.'

'Not the parties?'

'We're still partying. Tomorrow night is a point in case.'

I found that to be the perfect segway into a conversation I had skirted around over text, where it would have been difficult to properly assess Allegra's body language.

'There's something I've got to ask. Please be honest and tell me if it's totally inappropriate.'

'Yes?'

Allegra looked at me, pushing her eyebrow upwards to show her curiosity.

'My team at Sizzle asked me if I could cover your party for our social column. If you were to agree, I promise I'd keep it very discreet, and nobody would even notice me.'

'Come on, Paze, of course it's fine! You're not real media anyways; you're my friend.'

The comment was both harsh and true at the same time. It made me flinch slightly, but I hid it behind a grateful smile. The work I was doing was certainly not the media that would expose anything unwanted, and as a friend, I was going to be far more cautious than an unknown face behind a blog. That was a small victory. It would certainly put me in a much better standing inside Sizzle.

'One more thing. Can I bring my boss Nathan as my plus one?'

Her eyes looked up at the seeing, almost producing an involuntary roll. I could tell she didn't want to oblige but might do so out of politeness.

'As long as he plays nice.'

'You've got my word!'

We smiled at each other, sealing the agreement with friendly terms.

'All this planning and exercising makes me hungry. Let's head to the lobby restaurant for a quick lunch?' Allegra said as she slid towards the pool steps, and I handed her a towel.

'Definitely, but I need to get back to the office, so make it quick. I can't wait for you to do your full hair and glam.'

Allegra dismissed my comment, waving a flippant hand.

'It's just lunch. I'm going to wash off the chlorine quickly and put something fast on. Can you grab us a table? Meet you down there in less than ten minutes.'

I headed down the hall and took the wood-panelled lift to the reception. The hotel had a combination of business travellers and dolled women looking to meet them. With my oversized poncho over a baggy pair of jeans, it was almost as if someone had thrown me in there accidentally. As I walked over to the host and requested a table for two, I could sense the tone of surprise in his voice, clearly wondering how I had ended up there. Looking around the room, I was one of the few women, and even more peculiarly, I wasn't dressed to impress at all.

Soon after, Allegra came through the front entrance of the restaurant, but unlike the case with me, everyone was very accommodating to her presence. We still looked very out of place, but Allegra seemed completely unbothered by it. I felt very out of place, and I made a mental note to order something fast so I could leave soon after. She had dressed in a comfortable off-duty ensemble, a blush pink cashmere jumper and beige trousers. The look was understated chic, sending the message that she didn't need much effort to look prim.

We overheard some of the chitchat on the nearby tables and chuckled at the impassioned discussion between a foreign dignitary and his aide over the menu. His French accent was accentuated, making him speak louder so the aide could fully comprehend his frustration.

After a few minutes of us quietly laughing while looking at each other, I commented between sips of sparkling water.

'To think some of the world's future rulers sit here to debate if the chicken cream soup is more of an appetiser or side dish is somewhat horrifying.'

Allegra nodded, collapsed onto a comfortable silk sofa, and ordered her food to recover from her session of avoiding any real exercise. Suddenly, from the corner of the room, Axwell emerged carrying a large orange Hermes shopping bag. The great villain of the summer, her ex-boyfriend and major cause of social embarrassment made eye contact with us.

I noticed he looked uncharacteristically well put together in a lightweight blazer over a pair of dark-washed jeans. It was a change from his usual scruffy, clearly hungover look that was so mismatched it looked like the closet had thrown up on him. Even his unruly locks were gelled up in a neat, old Park Lane boy style that would have made his mother proud.

He calmly marched towards our table while proudly holding the large shopping bag with his right forearm. I looked at Allegra, who remained contained as she poured more water into a tall glass. *Could she really be calm in a moment like this?*

Axwell stopped in front of our table like an aristocratic statue, looking down at us from the height of his six-foot-tall stature. In a grand gesture, he presented a peace offering that could perhaps be key in brokering a new relationship. It was a carefully orchestrated unboxing campaign, very deliberately organised in full public view. Incidentally, so had the incident that had also ended their relationship. Regardless of what was in the wrappings, I could see Allegra's face shift from lacking emotion to a discrete look of approval.

The large bag was sealed with an elegant brown bow engraved with the brand's logo. Allegra opened through the layers of white satiny paper and eventually reached the leather surface below the white wrapping paper. The *terre*-coloured Togo Kelly bag was a sight to be enjoyed. Her eyes glazed over the elegantly selected colour palette, eventually looking up to Axel, still in silence. He had impressed the recipient. It was an exquisite sight. It was apparent to both Allegra and me that he must have gone to extreme lengths to get a hold of a Kelly in London. The thought of Axwell scrambling to find a gift that would impress even the least impressionable woman in town made me open my lips into a subtle smile.

The gift was bold, but it seemed to work. Allegra let out a contained smirk, which was matched by Axwell's own grin. That was the high society equivalent of begging for someone to take you back. The lack of words would have made most people uncomfortable, but I knew the two of them well enough to understand that their communication reached far beyond verbal.

The silence was broken as Allegra moved her eyes from the handbag to Axwell.

'Thank you, the colour is very special.'

'I had my mother's buyer sneak me past the podium list. It had to be yours.'

Of course he did. Axwell may have looked scruffy on the best of days, but he was every inch the posh heir. While he mostly chose to ignore conventions on a daily basis, he was well-versed in them enough to use his manners when it mattered most. That was precisely why all of our friends saw him as such a threat; he was capable of switching on and off the man that Allegra thought she wanted when it was convenient.

'You know my forgiveness is not for sale, right?'

'I wouldn't expect it to be, but it doesn't mean I can't spoil you while you think about whether you'll forgive me.'

'A person must first apologise before being forgiven; there's no mercy for those who don't repent.'

'I'm not going to beg.'

Allegra crossed her arms across her chest, but it didn't match her facial expression. That remained neutral.

'Then you won't get anything.'

As she said that, her head shook, mimicking how a young child would react when being told they wouldn't get access to their favourite toy.

'Fine, I'm sorry. I want you back. In fact, I need you back.'

'And what makes you think you deserve me?'

Her expression started to change from neutral to playful, with a pressed lip to show for it.

'I don't. I've been horrendous to you, but you always push me to be better. I want to be better for you.'

I could have sworn my eyes rolled at the words coming out of his mouth, but luckily, I realised that had only happened in my head. It was completely contradictory how Allegra was perfectly capable of seeing through most people and yet could not identify the insincerity in his voice. I wasn't even sure that she truly had feelings for him, but the challenge of transforming someone as messy as Axwell into a presentable member of society was enough of a thrill to keep her interested.

'Thank you for your offer. I think we should continue this conversation later in a quieter setting.'

Allegra moved quickly and triumphantly, holding her trophy towards the hotel doors, confident in her successful assertion of dominance. The afternoon drizzle had kicked in while we were engaged in our lunchtime theatrics. Seeing my face contort at the possibility of spending an afternoon in wet clothes, the doorman pulled a red umbrella from a cleverly hidden metal umbrella rack. I was grateful for quick thinking that ultimately saved my hair from unnecessary frizzing.

'I will ask Allegra to park in front of the door so I can return it.'

He responded with a gentle smile. 'You may keep it, ma'am.'

Such a pleasant man. The service there came at a price, but one that was very much worth it. I told myself that I'd surely return to offer a nice tip one day once my finances were more substantial. At that moment, I was just grateful I had a friend who could drive me back to the office without needing to overspend on rideshares. With the time spent indulging in Knightsbridge, my lunch hour had long passed and taking public transport would set me back another hour.

The clock had just about struck 2pm when I entered through my office door. Nathan was already hovering around my desk, wondering if I would return from my lunch break. He was keen to discuss the performance of my latest content piece for the magazine's website, a quiz that ambitiously sought to guess the London district you should choose based on your favourite dishes. I could tell he was equally curious about the status of the invite that had been promised to him as a quid pro quo for believing in me.

'That was quite a long lunch—' He suddenly stopped mid-sentence and stared at the elaborate wooden umbrella handle in my hand. 'Fancy little thing! Where did you get that?' He had just finished the last syllable before letting out a loud gasp. 'Oh wow, Carlton Tower! Were you visiting a sugar daddy?'

I couldn't help but burst into laughter. Between the sassy tone and the absurd suggestion that I'd be patient enough to tolerate someone due to a financial arrangement, I nearly produced a snort. It also made me wonder how he'd thought making such an assumption was appropriate at work.

'Allegra was doing the final chop to the guestlist, as you do. In good news, you made the cut!'

Nathan let out a screech, which I expected to be closely followed by an air jump. Luckily, he saved us both from embarrassment.

'I can't wait for all the sarcastic stare-downs and couture.'

'Hey, they're actually not that bad. Plus, Allegra would be caught dead before she had a guest feel uncomfortable.'

Nathan didn't seem convinced. It was pretty clear his attendance was a field trip into high society land in search of any faux pas that could yield him something to gossip about with others.

'This story is growing. Do we need a photography team to go with you?'

I understood his excitement. After all, that was one of the most elusive socialites in town. However, Allegra had entrusted me to maintain decorum, so I couldn't afford to show up with a full entourage, which could compromise Allegra's trust in my ability to keep things unintrusive.

I responded in a calm but confident tone. 'It would be too invasive with the guests. Not everyone is aware that we're covering it.'

Not one to let things go, Nathan ended the conversation. 'I hope they're as loyal as you are to their secrets.'

Me too.

CHAPTER SIX
An Unwanted Guest

I left work and headed straight to a beauty salon on the way home. It was not a day for a home blow-dry; the look was that of a 90s supermodel with a modern twist. Time quickly passed as my hair was pulled, discreetly lacquered, and left looking effortlessly full of volume before I was ready to go back to my apartment. That evening was not the usual night out with friends; it was a chance to enter London's busiest social season on the right foot.

At home, my long black silk slip dress had been left on the sofa, ready to be paired with a faux leather coat and strappy sandals. It didn't take long for me to shower and start a makeup routine in varying tones of gold. In less than three hours, I underwent my very own swan makeover from workweek exhaustion to the belle of the ball. Not bad, given Allegra had taken the full week to prepare herself with the added luxury of committing to her work as much or as little as she pleased. *Adult life wasn't going too bad for me.*

Since I was technically on the clock, I ordered an Uber that would later be billed back to Sizzle as a work expense. I took advantage of the car ride to capture the perfect selfie that would inform my soon-to-be growing number of social media followers that I was on my way to Allegra's glamorous affair. Being seen to be going to an event is nearly as important as the event itself.

The party was set to start at 10 pm, a little late for London tastes but just right for a mixed crowd of local and international jet setters. The two shiny black doors of Allegra's Belgravia townhouse were closely guarded by two security guards hired by her event planner for the occasion. I stood for a short moment before being let into the checkered floor marble entrance. A large mirror accompanied me as I walked past the staircase, through to the large dining room that opened towards the orangery and terrace. There were three different environments, which all flowed into each other, with guests distributed around the generously sized area.

Catering staff were passing around with glasses of champagne and fancy, mostly fish-based, canapes. There was always something glamorous about canapes made with exotically named food that you can't quite picture in your mind but which taste like they cost more than your monthly food budget. I grabbed a flute of bubbly on my way in as I walked slowly, nodding at the known faces in the crowd as

I passed them during my survey of the ambience. I found Nathan perched by a flower arrangement, seemingly taking in the glitz around him. He spotted me and waved over, which made me pace towards him.

'Oh, hello there!'

'Well, you look fab!' I said mid-air kisses. Nathan did look the part, wearing a vintage Loro Piana jacket that was every inch the mid-60s old-money aesthetic that I was sure he'd seen Allegra would approve of.

'It's a find from a trip to Covent Garden; it probably belonged to someone's dad here.' I laughed, but I also knew he was probably right. 'So where is she?'

'Who? Allegra?'

'No, the Queen. Obviously, Allegra.'

'She's never at parties when they first start, not even her own. Much like royalty, she only graces us with her presence once the room is full.'

Nathan raised his brows while simultaneously pouting so as to show his approval. He moved his own glass of champagne towards mine and muttered, 'Well, I'll drink to that.'

The room continued to fill up with the steady arrival of the season's couture-laden guests. The fall palette of colours made the glistening antique chandeliers in the room revert back to a demure shade of light. All shades of terracotta made an appearance in different textures, from sequin to cashmere. The heels of the guests, in all variations from kitten to the men's Cuban squares, made a vibrant noise against the cold marble floors. In contrast, lush antique carpets surrounded the furniture, which was elegantly placed to invite guests to converse. Every element of the salons in use had been arranged to captivate visitors and hold their interest throughout the evening.

One of my favourite parts of any Allegra party was the feeling that, for a short moment, a melange of different people that I didn't see elsewhere were also in that room. Her cousins who lived in different European countries, our college friends who had left since graduation, and the occasional wildcard outsider all converged, making the conversations more vibrant. The range of accents audible from any one conversation made it clear that the guest list was as rich in geographical diversity as the enrolment list in any top boarding school. As I walked through the different interconnected galleries of the ground floor leading out to the generous garden in the back, I recognised some faces and wondered if others would make it back on the guest list next time around.

'Miss Paisley, you come over here right now!' I heard a high-pitched Southern USA accent. I looked behind me to see a tanned blonde in kitten heels that matched perfectly her deep purple velvet handbag.

'Ava! It's been way too long; I thought we lost you to Miami forever.'

I could nearly hear Nathan's thoughts demanding an introduction.

'By the way, this is Nathan—my manager at Sizzle Media. Nathan, this is Ava Beauregard.'

She extended her delicate, porcelain hand to Nathan, who became visibly enthralled by the enormous ruby cocktail ring on her middle finger.

'My oh my, Allegra let you bring a journalist to her inner sanctum.'

He finally let go of her hand and instead grabbed a champagne glass from a tray carried by a passing waiter. I jumped in, worried that he may be stumped for words following her comment.

'I'm also a journalist, and I don't bite.'

'I meant a real journalist, sweetie.'

In any other scenario, I would have been offended, but I had gotten used to Ava's teasing. It was a part of her Southern charm, and a part of me loved her authenticity in a sea of pompousness. Having her around would lighten the mood if your ears could get used to listening at a few octaves louder than necessary for indoor speaking. She had attended Dainter with both Allegra and me as an exchange student from Texas. While many of our peers found her too peculiar in a sleepy countryside setting, we both enjoyed her spontaneity. *I wish we had kept closer in touch.*

'Trust me, this one is on the come-up,' Nathan responded while giving me a proud look. I had his trust, which confirmed that bringing him into my world was the right move.

'I'm sure she will. She kept us all guessing what she'd do next.' Turning to me, she continued, 'You need to come visit. I just got the new place in Miami, and it needs a good welcome party.'

Very tempting, if only I could afford holidays at this point.

'I'm going to need to prove myself to Nathan a little more before I can ask for days off.'

'Don't be a stranger!' Ava said before moving towards the banquet table.

We continued scouting the perimeter for familiar faces. There were several friends of Allegra's who I only knew from social columns or the odd well-known celebrity who had come as the plus-one of an established society figure. As a general rule, Allegra wasn't too fond of people frequently seen in tabloids, especially those with no particular talent. I always found that quite intriguing since the rule was easily waived if you had the right family tree.

Nathan turned to me as I scanned the room. 'I'm going out on my own for a bit, see what kind of embroidered hand towels they have in this kind of joint.'

'Don't get yourself into any kind of trouble.'

'Fine, I won't bite the rich people. See you later, Lady Paze.'

He does make these events far more enjoyable; I should bring him more often. It was refreshing to be able to mock all of which simultaneously fascinated and irritated me without being reproached by people who took it all too seriously.

I found a corner next to the hedge wall at the back of the garden from where I could see all the action while enjoying the crisp air. The bubbles from the flute of champagne in my hand went quickly to my head, causing the terraced garden lights to seem just a little less defined.

Once all of the guests had arrived, it was time for the hostess to finally make an appearance. Much like a queen, Allegra would only ever arrive after everyone was there. I moved slowly towards the inner rooms as I knew she would expect to see me and our other close friends as she made her way down from the residential quarters upstairs. I caught a glimpse of Mila's back as she stood against a marble column in view of the stone steps.

'Good evening, gorgeous,' I said while side-hugging her with an air kiss that would otherwise land on her cheek.

'Aren't you sight? The working girl city chic look suits you well.'

'Well, thank you! Have you seen her today yet?'

'No, but she has said she's up to something.'

I saw a spectre of black matte leather heels slowly descending from the top of the staircase. I looked up to see Allegra making her way down in an antique gold statuesque dress and heard the room fall into a murmur. That time, it wasn't the enormous flawless diamond earrings and necklace set. Although she did have jewellery so sparkly it was visible from the floor below, it was a far less convincing accessory that caused jaws to drop to the floor.

Standing strongly on her left side was Axwell, walking down with her with an arm offered in support of his leading lady. It was an unexpected sight given the recent scandal and polemic breakup, which, of course, everyone in the room was perfectly aware of at that point. At the same time, Allegra displayed an expression of satisfaction in announcing to all that she had at least won the battle. There may have been differences in the weeks prior, but whatever conversation entailed after the reencounter had clearly convinced Allegra that things would be better.

Having had the privilege of being at the moment of the grand gesture, I was perhaps less shocked that Allegra had decided to stand by her man. I was concerned for my friend, but ultimately, it was her choice—not that it stopped anyone in the room from whispering.

Waving at me from the edge of the dinner table, which was being used to display the fixed banquet, I spotted Mansour. We locked eyes as I moved closer to him, keen to hear what he was clearly needing to tell me based on his vigorous waving.

'Well, this wasn't on the run sheet.'

I hadn't had the time to discuss the events that had taken place earlier, which would have certainly provided more context for how we had gotten to the evening's reveal. Things sometimes moved so fast in those circles that you had the feeling that a single day was six months in everyone else's world. I hinted at what took place, giving my two cents on the matter.

'For better or for worse, he's a man who knows how to make a public entrance.'

Mansour pressed his lips harshly together, crossing his arms before responding.

'I've seen him making one too many of those recently. I don't like him for Allegra.'

'It's not up to us, Habibi. Unfortunately, we can't control who our friends date.'

Growing agitated with both the sight of Axwell and the conversation, Mansour moved his hand up in the air in protest.

'Since when?'

I laughed loudly, and from behind Mansour, a chuckle responded to our conversation, which was clearly louder than we had intended. She was a petite, attractive brunette dressed in a two-piece ensemble skirt and top in shiny lurex. He turned around to unveil who had emitted the obviously feminine sound. Her deep brown eyes locked with Mansour's as she offered a coy smile, slightly embarrassed about having uninvitedly participated in our conversation.

'You're new! I'm Mansour, and this is Paze.'

'Ameerah, it's a pleasure.' Hearing her name, Mansour's eyes lit up, realising that the woman encounter could have been a compatriot.

'Saudi?' he asked directly.

'I grew up in Kuwait, but I've been in London for a while.'

'That's awesome. Where did you study?'

She continued picking out delicacies from the buffet before responding to Mansour. She seemed unfazed by his attention.

'It's a small design university; you probably don't know it.'

'No way, I'm just launching my own fashion line.'

Mansour was clearly interested, but just as he was about to continue, I was instantly distracted by an even more unexpected appearance that entered my line of sight. From the corner of the room, I could see Alexandra Wolf emerge from behind Allegra despite having declined the RSVP. More interesting was that walking in next to her, holding onto her forearm, was unwanted guest number 121. Sara Gram had weaselled her way into the event, likely taking advantage of Alexandra's ignorance of the recent occurrences.

He noticed my intent stare, moving my head to grab a better glimpse. Noticing what I was looking at, Mansour touched my arm to acknowledge the impending drama. No words were needed to explain that we needed to rush to Allegra's side.

Excusing myself from the new acquaintance, I picked up my pace to quickly make my way to the entry foyer, hoping that I wouldn't trip on my heels. I looked back and noticed Mansour hadn't been as quick but held out a phone in his hand with a large smile. *Had he managed to get Ameerah's number? Smooth, Mansour.*

Approaching the host, I stopped a few feet away and tried to look busy checking the flowers for their freshness. I was within distance to hear everything without making it look too obvious. Mansour joined me in the faux task while using my shoulder as a perch for his head to get a better look at the incoming menace.

Allegra launched a welcoming smile towards the pair while offering her cheek to Alexandra. She said, 'I thought you were still in Germany; great to have you!'

'Thank you very much. You've got a lovely house. I hope you don't mind that I've brought a friend. She's been so kind in helping me select an art piece at the Harrods art gallery, so I couldn't cut the conversation short.'

'Not at all, welcome Sara.'

'You two know each other?'

'Barely. Do make yourselves comfortable.' Allegra's tone was stone cold, hiding any hint of emotion behind rehearsed pleasantries.

Unable to stay silent, Sara joined in the conversation to make everyone even more aware of her presence.

'Allegra, I'd be able to tell this is your house from afar. It has your essence.'

'It's been in the family for a while; it's reliable and longstanding,' she said, looking longingly at an approaching Axwell, who slowed his pace as he recognised his summer escapade.

'If only all things could be as longstanding as houses,' Sara said while laughing loudly, wanting everyone to notice her.

The sheer insult of it. Luckily for Sara, Allegra would never insult a guest on her property, no matter how inconvenient their comments. Instead, she fixed Axwell's collar as he greeted the guests with an awkward halfwave. I jumped into the conversation in an attempt to reduce the growing tension.

'The essential things should be longstanding. Friendships, jewellery, careers.'

Alexandra analysed my contribution, placing a hand on her cheek before responding, questioning my contribution.

'Not love?'

'I'll tell you once I'm really in love,' Allegra responded, poking fun at herself and using humour to deflect her discomfort while simultaneously coming across as a gracious host.

Axwell laughed and walked off to chase a waiter who passed with a silver tray filled with all shapes of drink glasses. Taking notice of him leaving hearing distance, Sara looked at Allegra and asked,

'So, would you consider Axwell fair game since you're not in love with him?'

'I don't believe in trapping people against their will. Besides, if it were ever a game, I'd be winning, anyway.'

Allegra turned around on her heels, cutting off any opportunity for a reply. Instead, she searched for Axwell, who just emerged from the nearby salon with two glasses of champagne. He handed her the drink with a kiss and used one arm to grab her waist and possessively showcase his affection. *She must be quite pleased.*

The party simmered and diluted until it was just our inner circle left behind. I hadn't noticed until the room emptied that Nathan had disappeared at some point in the evening without saying goodbye. I made a mental note to remind him of his rudeness the next workday, potentially using that to get into some meatier coverage.

A post-event ritual we had developed throughout the years was lying on the sofas of Allegra's house while discussing the best moments of the night. We removed our shoes and used each other as human pillows as we lay casually surrounded by used glasses that would soon be cleared by the morning staff. Allegra chose to forgo her usual protocol by lying in reverse on a chaise lounge with her legs lifted by the taller side of the furniture while her head rested on a well-stuffed silk Versace pillow.

She kicked off the evening debriefing session. 'So, let's see what we've achieved tonight: Mansour met a girl, Axwell and I shocked everyone, Paze made her debut as a journalist, and Mila… ate caviar? There had to be something more exciting that happened to you.'

'I kept everyone sane, you know me. I'm more of a henchwoman than a showstopper,' Mila responded with a cheeky smile that suggested she always let out less than what actually happened.

Mansour sat up to face Allegra, and I could see in his eyes that he was bubbling with the need to mention the unmentionable. 'Can we discuss Sara and her complete lack of tact?'

'I'd rather not,' Allegra responded sarcastically.

'How could we not? She shows up uninvited, then directly confronts you in front of your invitees. Thankfully, she had the decency to leave early,' Mansour snarked.

'Can't we just make her go away? I feel like we've given this woman more timeshare of our minds than she deserves,' I interjected.

Mila jumped in with her usual wisdom: 'My guess is that she'll go away—they always do, and someone new will take her place. There's a spinning wheel of distractions that's constantly giving us excuses to behave poorly with each other.'

Allegra turned her head slightly towards the sofa we all shared and said, 'Today wasn't her day, but it will come. It always does.'

Our friendly gathering was inconveniently interrupted when a clearly drunk Axwell walked in, and we all rolled our eyes. Allegra may have been forgiving, but none of us were prepared to have him join the sofa afterparty just like that. Besides, I wasn't fully convinced that the sudden act of leniency towards our inebriated friend wasn't a calculated act of self-preservation.

'I'm exhausted. How do you guys have the energy to do this after being busy for a whole evening?' he said whilst holding a bottle of gin by the neck. His sweaty demeanour and dilated pupils gave us all a hint that it wasn't just alcohol running through his dramatically pulsating veins. I felt sorry for the staff that would have to scrub clean the white residue from his frequent toilet visits during the party.

He was one of the few people capable of making a perfectly pleasant activity seem like an arduous chore, which, considering his lack of actual employment, was probably the most work he had done in months. Axwell was still a budding DJ/promoter/guru/serial entrepreneur—essentially an untalented brat bankrolled by a trust fund.

Sensing the silence in the room since his arrival, he decided to start a conversation with us.

'I need another holiday to detox from people.'

Allegra looked over and said, 'I need to be in Paris to interview a potential co-founder for my store. Want to come?'

'Paris isn't usually my place, but with you, it could be.'

My shoulders lifted up, automatically reacting to the cringe I was witnessing. I had vowed to keep myself from judging Axwell as he was my best friend's boyfriend, but his pickup lines were as awful as you'd expect with someone who needs to hyphenate his job title as much as he did. There was no human way to exert the feeling of embarrassment on behalf of someone in greater intensity than what I felt at that moment.

To avoid having to listen to any more of that, I announced my departure, which was instantly followed by Mansour and Mila. Once we stood outside the house, with the thick wood door safeguarding our privacy, the three of us broke into childlike laughter. *It was just like the old days.*

CHAPTER SEVEN

Not all that glitters is oil

With Allegra jetted off with Axwell for a romantic escape, I would be able to truly focus on the essentials. I had in my possession the only photos of an eventful night with the most sought-after socialites in town. I was given *carte blanche* by Allegra to put together the coverage for Sizzle. The story behind a high society party may not have been the most complex piece, but nevertheless, it was significant for me as another step towards success. The key part of the task at hand would be to ensure nothing but a light-hearted, complimentary article was written, preserving the ongoing disputes to the confines of the walls they took place in. At the surface level and to most of our readers, that was nothing more than another evening of fashion and wealth, but of course, to everyone there, it was so much more.

Order had been restored. Allegra had forgiven a major indiscretion by her summer boyfriend. At the same time, it had also become abundantly clear that her opponent was not one to disappear into the background. Nathan had also been friendlier than ever to me, starting off the week with an offer to buy me lunch on the way in as a means to amend his noticed sudden absence from the party. It seemed things were falling in their rightful place at last.

The Sizzle Media office had several corners from where I could quietly pour into my work. I would be able to enjoy a good playlist while jotting away the details of the who's-who in attendance. I moved my laptop to an empty spot on the co-working converted banquet table next to the kitchen area. A quiet day in the office was looming, and I was ready for it after a weekend of high social energy.

'Heeey girl.' I heard the high-pitched voice through my earphones, making me turn around to see Celine standing behind me. I begrudgingly moved my ear protection against the world at an impossibly slow pace before speaking.

'Morning, Celine! How's everything?'

'Fab. How about we do another girl's night next weekend?' Her smile was unsettling, particularly when I couldn't stop thinking of the fact that she had some sort of secret connection to the ex-husband of the woman in charge of my future.

'I think I'll pass; I've had a pretty hectic last few days. It's time for some recharge.'

I wasn't even lying that time around. Since I was *sans* glamorous best friend this week, I planned to enjoy my time alone and take care of myself. *For once.*

'Too bad, I've got a good link up for getting into Scarlett's tonight.'

As much as I was curious to know more about how Celine was gaining access to one of the most exclusive private member clubs in Mayfair, every interaction with her felt like a liability. At the same time, I neither wanted to be her friend nor her enemy.

'How about we plan this better once I've submitted my article? Message you later?'

Feeling victorious, Celine winked at me and walked away with her typical model saunter. Satisfied with the interaction, I could return to the work, which would inch me a step closer to actual journalistic coverage. Gulping a mouthful of water, I settled into my seat and split the screen on my laptop between my note-taking software and the web version of my phone's instant messenger.

Somewhere on the other side of town, Mansour was forwarding me live updates from his exchanges with Ameerah. The two had been inseparable since Saturday night, and I was starting to get concerned that he was too involved. There was a zero to a hundred pace to their brewing relationship that didn't feel fit for longevity. In the span of less than a week, they had already had all three meals together, watched a movie, and even gone off to Mansour's Surrey retreat for a spa day. His schedule had become completely populated by all things Ameerah. It was also making me a little bit jealous since our group was quickly coupling up. *At least I have work to keep me company.*

A quick vibration on my phone let me know that Nathan would need to take a rain check on lunch. I saw through the glass separating my inner sanctum from the main office frenzy that he was heading out the door with Florence in tow. The closer he was to our commander-in-chief, the more likely I was to have free access to her, which didn't directly involve Celine and her towering heels.

The thought of how awkward it would be if Mila also found a love interest and I ended up becoming the group singleton popped up in my mind. I caught myself off guard in a session of self-pity while staring at my computer screen, waiting for words to magically roll onto the keyboard. I sat at the office of the media group I always dreamed of, and instead of putting together a well-written piece, I was focused on what everyone else was doing. *You're not this person.*

I pulled out my phone, but that time, there would be no mindless scrolling through social media or being sucked into a mindless conversation about my friend's latest conquest. My fingers moved quickly to the food delivery app I used most, and I put together a shopping card of motivation for the afternoon, my characteristic hummus wrap ingredients, a six-pack of Red Bull light, and a Snickers bar to amp up the creative juices needed to finish the story. Pulling my hair into a messy bun, I turned my focus to the laptop while I waited for sustenance to arrive. It was my time to shine.

The week carried me straight into Friday morning without much of a break from the mundane. Once I finished writing, editing, and publishing my first article, it was time to set out on a new content planning sprint around my impending column. I had developed a flow of feeding the website quizzes in between obsessing with the metrics showcasing the popularity of each one of them. It became apparent rather quickly that the life of a professional journalist was akin to being at sea: periods of calm followed by trying to survive a storm, only to find yourself back in the cycle once you've managed to make it through another week. I had the hottest story in town the week before, but who's to say I would be able to keep it up with both my readers and editors? I felt pressured to top my first success, afraid that it would be forgotten as a one-hit wonder if I didn't.

Nathan came buzzing in to gather all his ducklings for a meeting as we prepared to find out more about what he had in mind for us next. There was a certain cadence about him that was particularly perky. He presented his ideas to us on the regularly scheduled material, emphasising the different sections allocated to each one and seemingly skipping over any assigned work for me.

'Well then, my lovelies, back to work.'

'What about me? What should I focus on next week?' I was genuinely curious as to why I had been singled out amongst the team.

'Ah, Paze, I've got something more confidential for you to work on. Let's sit somewhere private,' he said as he lured me into an empty office.

My heart raced with the excitement of once again being tasked with an actual story and not just feeding the quirky features. I was convinced the website statistics that I had recently learned to harness were feeding a previously unknown interest in the analytics that could quantify how popular was every individual content piece published. It would be a beneficial break to interject with a new story to work on.

Nathan broke the silence in the office while looking more serious than usual. 'Florence is interested in profiling someone who was in your party coverage.'

'That's great news! She actually saw my work?'

'She did. She always comments on what she read in our morning editor meetings. Speaking of which, I was thoroughly impressed with the chat I had with Alexandra Wolf. I suggested to Florence she could yield interest as an up-and-coming businesswoman.'

I tried not to showcase my bias against running a story on yet another nepo baby with moderate success. It had always been mind-blowing as a consumer of mainstream media how editors were continuously trying to promote articles when they didn't evoke any positive emotions in the readers. Instead of honesty, I chose employment.

'Sounds great, Nathan; I can definitely muster up a profile. Any information on what her business premise is?'

Nathan sighed in relief. 'I thought you might not be too interested since she hinted at the party about ongoing tension with your dear Allegra.'

'Not at all, work is work. Besides that, if she was on the list, then it can't be that bad.'

'Well, in that case, I will leave it in your hands. Can't wait to hear more about how she was inspired to build the app that will change the art world forever.'

I couldn't tell if he was sarcastic or really had been convinced by Alexandra. Either way, I would have to gently inform my best friend that someone was about to outshine her. I had always imagined that Allegra was going to be my first business profile. Luckily, I would have a few more days to find the most diplomatic way to break the news.

I left the office in a state of both annoyance on the subject of choice and simultaneously relief of not needing to return to the minor tasks of the previous days. When I made it back to my handbag, I noticed four missed calls from Mansour.

Dialling back immediately, I heard him answer the phone in a few seconds and launch into a statement: 'She committed the cardinal sin.'

I wondered how Ameerah could have, in such a short time span, already so dropped in Mansour's esteem.

'I asked her what she wants to do with her life, and she says she won't work because her dad is in oil.'

I cringed just hearing that over the phone. Every time someone says, "My family is in oil," an olive tree falls in the Middle East in solidarity with the blatant lie. You would think that by that point, people would have googled the business of commodities before starting to attach themselves to a sector that had always been heavily state-owned and regulated. It was an amateur move, usually too easy to dismantle. I never understood why people still used that line when it never once ended well. I'd think they would soon branch out their fiction to something less obvious; maybe an orange planting magnate would be less conspicuous.

In Mansour's own words, 'Almost nobody is really in oil, and if they are, then you'd know them. We'd know about them; they would be written about in political opinion pieces or, at the very least, a Forbes feature. I've looked into it, and nothing comes up.'

Only very few families had ever secured any meaningful private contracts in the business of petroleum, yet a large number of scammers would shamelessly claim wealth they didn't have, usually by adding a surname that wasn't their own.

'If you're in oil and I've never heard of you, the closest you've been to oil is that olive variety at your local Waitrose.'

Mansour was fascinated with the entangling of those who spoke too much with their own web of deceit. He carefully planned the unmasking ceremony, as he would call it, in the same way one prepares for their wedding. The guests who would witness the debacle would be chosen by their individual attributes, such as a capacity for spreading rumours, excelling in maintaining a chronic look of displeasure and, of course, a penchant for snarky yet discreet commentary. At the head of the table, Mansour needed a power player to complete his chess dining table.

'I'm going to need local backup to make the scene truly spectacular.' One thing I had learned from spending too much time with my *khaleeji* friends was that "local" was one with ancestral roots based in the country being discussed. To all of us used to the term, it was clearly a person with social and historical understanding enough to unmask a pretender.

'Do you think it's truly necessary at this point? This sounds like it wasn't mean-spirited.'

Mansour ignored my counterpoint and continued describing his plans. 'Someone young enough to accept the invitation but who will be offended enough by the deception to ensure that today is the last time Ameerah claims to be the First Lady of oil.'

'Fine, don't listen to me, but I do think you're going overboard here.'

'I assure you I am not. There were several red flags in the last few days. She asked me to drop her off in a random location, nowhere near Regents Park—where she said she lived.'

'Have you spent too much time in London Mansour? Even a total outsider like myself knows that she probably doesn't want to be seen with you, so her family don't start asking when they're meeting your folks.' Having gone to school with many Middle Eastern heirs back at Dainter, I was well-versed in the need to keep things under wraps until one was ready to make a lifetime commitment.

'Valid, except that I had to reset my GPS, so I stopped further down the road. I saw her get into a flat block above Tesco. If we go back to the original claim, either way, she shouldn't be living there. She didn't specify that her father works for a company. She made it intentionally ambiguous to suggest ownership.'

In his defence, it was vague, and no oil heir lives above Tesco.

'I am starting to worry about your overall sanity here reading so much into this.'

'Ms. Paze, since when doesn't grammar matter to you, of all people? Our resident journalist thinks word choice does not matter.' I could hear Mansour's grin through the fun in his tone of voice. The one thing I knew about him beyond any doubt was that nothing would deter him once he was motivated to prove a point. Little did Ameerah know that even a comma could be used as evidence against her in the court of high society standards.

'I concede, it did sound odd. Any other information I should know before passing my verdict?'

'Well, there is another strange item on the list. I tried to speak to her in Arabic; let's just say her proficiency level was "I once smoked sheesha on Edgware Road, and I liked it."'

I let out a loud laugh, temporarily forgetting where I was and the lack of privacy at work.

'Did she pull the "*shway shway, habibi*" when you asked her if she spoke Arabic?'

If there's one thing I learned from Mansour, it was that every girl with her name engraved in an Arabic necklace in Dubai repeated that phrase, and made every native speaker cringe a little inside.

'You know the deal. Don't worry, we will have fun with this one. Tonight, we have dinner at Le Poulet Gourmet and unmask the imposter. See you at 7:45!'

Nothing said weekend mood like some old-fashioned drama and showdown. It was the energy boost I needed to close off my workday. I had yet to take up Celine on her offer earlier in the week, but that had just moved to the second plan of importance. I had a takedown to witness, and as they say, *better her than me.*

The table was set for eight o'clock, which gave us a fifteen-minute advantage to settle at the table before the guest of honour arrived. Mansour was dropped off by his driver with an immaculately dressed plus-one, who I recognised as a regular fixture at his dinner parties. His ally was Loujain, a designer-clad fitness guru turned influencer who had a perfect American accent from spending her college years studying in Los Angeles.

Mansour took the lead to the reservation desk, ushering us through within less than a minute of arrival. The perks of being a regular didn't go unnoticed. We walked in a joint stride like a coven, looking for sacrificial prey. Disrobing our warm wear on the heavy wood seats, we looked at each other, preparing our synchrony to defend our friend.

An unsuspecting Ameerah arrived and greeted Mansour with a warm hug. Loujain extended a confident hand for Ameerah to shake while analysing the loose caramel-coloured curls that fell to the side of her toned arms displayed in a cutout neoprene top.

'Remember me from Allegra's autumn party?' she asked with a friendly smile as she moved to greet me last. It was an odd question, given my proximity to her new beau, but then again, perhaps my name hadn't come up in conversation. I felt compelled to change that perception.

'Absolutely, Mansour hasn't stopped talking about you.' I thought that might do the trick to convince her to tread lightly.

A sense of guilt fell upon me as I was aware that that was by no means a friendly encounter in the making. I made a mental note to fight her corner if I felt she was worthy, but that would depend on her own actions. I felt tension brewing in my stomach as Mansour ordered a plethora of dishes for the table. His eyes had a deeper tone than usual, which, along with his asymmetrical smirk, let me know he considered the battle won even before the tirade started.

As his mouth started to open while holding a mocktail in his hand, I averted my eyes to the cocktail menu as a means to showcase I was only half supportive of what was inevitably going to ensue.

'We're all gathered here today to celebrate the marriage of Ameerah and the truth.'

Both Loujain and I locked eyes and psyched a nervous swallow while Ameerah remained completely unphased by the provocation. Clearly, we were both far more nervous than the two parties involved.

I gave Mansour a stern look and uttered his name, trying to hint at him to stop in his tracks before his nasty streak got the best of him.

'It turns out that you aren't exactly the oil heiress you alluded to being,' he said, nearly laughing, the words spilling out of him.

'The concept of heiress is really rather fluid, isn't it? Not that I'd use those words myself, but yes, my father is in oil,' she countered with unwavering confidence.

'Yet we both know you aren't an oil heiress. There aren't many of them, and at least one of us would know you.'

Even if the accusation wasn't pointed at me, I lowered myself in the chair and grabbed the water glass placed in front of me.

'I technically never lied. My father was in oil. He was an engineer; for many years, he worked in Kuwait and directed a large production facility,' Ameerah contested while placing both elbows on the table, bringing her hands together in defiance of common etiquette.

'You misled me, saying you didn't need to work. How can you deny that you paraded as an heiress when that's literally what you said to me?' His voice matched hers in increased irritation. The tension oddly made me less nervous and more entertained.

Not one to be outdone, Ameerah looked him in the eye while pointing her index finger at him. 'You wanted to be deceived. Or rather, you wanted to believe to be deceived so that you could humiliate me to make yourself feel better, or shall I say superior?'

In all honesty, that was the first time I ever saw Mansour speechless. Worst of all, it was also the first time someone held a mirror up to him and made him face himself. He'd never been a man of apologies, but I didn't see another way out of the current corner.

'Ahh...' Just as he was about to retort, Ameerah pulled the linen napkin from her lap and placed it dramatically on the table. She rose from her chair, collected her belongings, and looked down at us with disdain.

'Well, this has been an interesting evening. I will head out and leave all of you to talk about me behind my back where you belong. See you around.'

The display of honest emotion was so refreshing. Mansour was ultimately my close friend, but I had to recognise he could be a handful. It was a tiny, feisty woman who ultimately gave him something to be concerned with. Still in shock, Mansour tilted his head while longingly watching Ameerah leave.

I broke the silence, still confused about how the evening had transpired. 'I'm still confused about how she lives in London, and isn't a millionaire heiress but doesn't work. If anyone figures it out, though, sign me up.'

The rest of the table broke into silly laughter at my comment. Mansour finally recomposed himself and called over a waiter to take our order. After ordering for all three of us, he finally opened up.

'I think I'm in love.' It was unexpected, but then again, nothing makes a billionaire as interested as when he can't get something.

Loujain jumped in. 'I'm not sure she's ever speaking to you again. Can't we just find you a nice girl back home once you're ready to settle down?'

'No, no, no. It's Ameerah or nothing. Nobody talks to me like that... I need her.'

Well, that was a new sentiment for him. Had it been known that a talking down was all it took for Mansour, highly eligible bachelor of Knightsbridge, to fall, many would have probably tried before that night. Admittedly, there was a naturality from which the interaction emerged that didn't make it seem like something intentional.

The rest of the meal was uneventful, apart from both Loujain and me having to prevent Mansour from texting Ameerah. We both considered a phone confiscation to avoid further embarrassment, but alas, we settled with him leaving it within sight from where we could protect his integrity with our judging eyes every time he made a swift movement towards the device.

As we were leaving, both Mansour and I had our phones light up with simultaneous notifications.

> Allegra
>
> I'm back in town sans Axwell. Tell you more tomorrow.

We all looked at each other, wondering what could have possibly happened when things had seemed fairly settled between the two of them. *Or rather, who had happened.*

CHAPTER EIGHT

Fairies, Dior and Godmothers

No alarm clock works better than a hint of incoming drama the previous night. The morning sun finally showed hints, and I even considered going for a morning stroll as a means of passing the time until it was deemed an acceptable time to call a friend. The urge to experiment with fitness quickly left my body and was instead replaced with a far more pressing need for my signature breakfast wrap. The adrenaline would be soothed by food rather than exercise.

The morning rain was motivation enough to use the Uber account my parents had generously linked to their card for emergencies. Between the light sleep and the possibility of getting soaked, I was sure they would understand why I needed extra help getting to work. On the way in, I greeted Nathan while holding my laptop case and water thermal under my arms as a signal that I was in a rush rather than in a chatty mood. I mouthed to him as I left his side that I was heading to an important meeting.

I took my laptop to one of the meeting rooms where I booked a meeting called 'Paris Catch-up'. It wasn't entirely deceptive; something would surely come up that could inspire a new article. The meeting room walls were soundproof, providing the discretion needed for me to get the latest updates on what had caused the completely expected fall from grace of Knightsbridge's most obvious bad boy.

I kicked off the conversation with a reassuring tone. 'I'm here for you. Tell me what happened.'

Allegra cleared her throat and said, 'Axwell kept turning up to the hotel drunk at all times. He seems more interested in hanging out with famous DJs than businesspeople.'

She paused, but I remained silent, not wanting to make matters worse by passing judgment on the fact that Axwell had done exactly what he always did. It wasn't my place, but that didn't stop my mind from mentally going off on her.

'It was odd. He kept trying to make me feel bad for dedicating myself to the business but also criticising me for not being a serious businesswoman.'

I remained guarded with my feelings. It was a time to hear her purge herself of a long overdue hanger-on.

'I know you're silent because you never approved of him,' she continued, demanding a reaction from me. I was inevitably cornered into sharing a speck of opinion on the matter.

'You know, one of the things that I love most about you is both your best quality and your biggest downfall. You always want to see the best in people.' I started with a soothing truth before continuing to a far harsher reality. 'The explanation for him trying to constantly bring you down is his unwavering feeling of inferiority next to a woman who has it all.'

I could hear Allegra let out a sweet, innocent laugh. She knew it was true, and being a glass-half-full person was often how she described herself to people when they first met. It was her general lightness that made even the strongest hater choose to interact with civility when it came to her. Her charisma and surnames were a lethal combination that Axwell couldn't manipulate into submission.

'Thank you for that. I never want to stop believing we all have something good to offer. I just realised that I outgrew Axwell,' she chimed in, even then being gentle to her detractor.

'Well, he is more of a liability than an asset at this point.' I offered my insight, not trying to point out the obvious but also taking a subtle jab at his general persona.

'I completely agree. Being associated with stories in gossip pages isn't a good look for someone scouting for a serious business partner. My angel investor suggested I formally cut him out.'

I'm glad it didn't have to be me who said it to her. I pulled from memory things that made me admire Florence as inspiration for my newly single friend.

'A businesswoman uses her intuition in all aspects of life. I knew you would make the right move.'

Allegra knew exactly what she wanted. Axwell belonged to the past, and she was too focused on building her future. I merely stated the facts. She agreed with a hum before continuing.

'Besides, he outlived his purpose. I can't stick around for another scandalous break-up. It's better to leave things in the way and timing that I chose.' There was also that, every so often, she would remind us that every relationship in her life would serve a purpose. *I wondered what my purpose was in her life.*

'Good choice. I'm glad to see you taking this so seriously.'

'I can't afford to lose. My family will never stop telling me that they knew I wouldn't make it. I want to show them I'm so much more than they think.'

I had immense respect for Allegra's cut-throat approach to her new venture. So often, people get distracted and lose sight of their ultimate target. Knowing when to cut loose that which is holding you back is one of the most important power moves for anyone who wants to sit at the top. It reminded me of a pending topic that I had been avoiding telling her mid-trip.

'On that note, I've been asked to do my very first profile feature.'

'Gosh, that's exciting!'

'I know, and to start off, I'll be profiling a woman in business, which is definitely a cherry on top.'

'What? Oh no, you didn't have to! Of course, I love the idea; it would be great for my brand to get this kind of exposure.'

I took what was likely the loudest gulp in telephonic history.

'It was actually a personal request from Nathan that we kickstart the series with Alexandra Wolf.'

'Why? What is she even doing that's relevant?'

Her inflection was higher pitched than usual, revealing her discomfort at the choice.

'Apparently, she's just returned from Germany with significant backers for a direct-to-consumer fine art app.'

'I see. Well, that's good for her.'

I could hear Allegra's disappointment. I hated myself for bursting her balloon, but the truth was that her business was still lacking professional gravitas. In the world of heirs and heiresses, ideas were a dime a dozen, but only those with true business acumen made it past the initial twenty-four months. It was easier to make bold decisions with Daddy's money.

'I wish it had been you; I didn't get much of a choice in the matter.'

'I know, darling. I'm sure you would do something if it were in your power.'

Truthfully, I was relieved for once that I was powerful enough to make that decision. I also didn't think the conversation could get much more discouraging, so I made up a convincing excuse about needing to wrap up some last errands for the day before I could head her way for a proper catch-up.

Taking advantage of a quiet space, I sat with the task at hand and a blank email draft in sight. I still had to reach out to Alexandra for an interview.

Email subject line: Profile for Sizzle's website

It must have been barely a blink of an eye before I had a response in my mailbox. Instead of a meeting date or time, I had a list of FAQs that had been long prepared and ready to circulate with all details of her business and curated profile—the parts which she wished for people to actually know, of course.

It was shocking to see her level of precision and command. I completely understood why Nathan had admired Alexandra. Her demeanour could be cold in the social sphere, but her professionalism was unrivalled by anyone else in our circle, clearly. While most of my friends would struggle to put together a mission statement for their companies without the support of a handsomely paid consultant brought on by their parents to ring-fence their investments, Alexandra was both coherent and precise. Attached to the email was even a high-resolution black and white photo of her wearing a crisp pale shirt. This woman was intentional in everything she did.

With my task made easy, I would be able to finish the profile in record time. The opportunity had fallen into my lap at precisely the right time to impress Nathan. I appreciated him coming to my defence, however unrequested, during the conversation with Ava at Allegra's soiree. However, I was far from making my mark at Sizzle. As a newbie, I would have quite a while to go before I could get the space to write the things I was truly passionate about—even if I wasn't entirely sure yet what those were.

I left the office at 9pm but resolved that I had just completed an entire article from beginning to end in a matter of a few short hours. Despite the long workday, my mood was of complete satisfaction rather than exhaustion. *I had a real article out that I could be proud of. This was good.*

The next morning, I made my way back to the building that was quickly becoming more of a home to me than my apartment. The Sizzle Media sign that hung at the door of the office building entrance had started to lose its novelty and gave way instead to comfort. Even the receptionist had begun asking me how things were going.

Barely a few moments after settling in the content team corner, Nathan came over to my desk with an expression that couldn't hide his intention to ask me to do something for him. I had learned in the few weeks of being there that he would hurry towards you with the largest possible smile and hands in the air as if he was ready to break into a jazz routine. The faster the cadence of his hips, the larger the request was bound to be.

'So, since you've done such a great job on the event side of the website, I think we should permanently station you as our resident social columnist.'

My face gave away the combination of shock and rush of excitement that I had at once. It was my very first promotion. A thought of fear came into my body as I did not want to get boxed in as someone who purely reported back on the adventures and misadventures of the rich and sometimes famous. On the other hand, rent day was coming up and sinking my teeth deeper into Sizzle Media meant living in London. A less desirable role was better than none at all.

'Since you're taking over, I need you to come up with a calendar of things you'll be covering weekly and monthly.'

'How will I get into all the events? Do we get invites?'

'Check with our press release team; they get all the corporate stuff. But for the social gatherings, I expect you to manage like you always have.'

'What do you mean?' I asked, raising an eyebrow of uncertainty at where this conversation was headed.

'Befriending the right people, of course.'

There was a growing sense of dread since I had chosen to cover my friends as content for the website that I could start over-relying on them to continue climbing in my professional career. Worse, the closer I tried to separate the two worlds, the more difficult it became as Nathan grew increasingly interested in my personal life.

'I will make your life a little easier. Your first event is the Heart of Diamond Charity Ball. We also get invites as Florence is on the Foundation Board.'

My ear perked up hearing that as a part of the upcoming assignment, I would be coming in close contact with the boss. Chances like that were seldom granted; it was not something I was in a position to let pass without doing everything possible to have a meaningful interaction with her.

'Out of curiosity, why is the ball called the Heart of Diamond?'

'The family that started the foundation, the Guptas, are a diamond trader dynasty. They have been in the business for four generations and are generous philanthropists.'

'Interesting. I'll try to look out for them when I do the coverage. When is it again?'

'Tonight. Sorry for the late notice! You've got the day today to be prepared. I've given you a head start by sending you a list of our available photographers for tonight.'

I looked at Nathan in visible shock. A day was barely enough time to process that I was finally a real guest and not a plus one or friend of someone's, but I would also need to put together a look that would adequately fit the part I was about to play. It was also a large-scale society event outside the typical controlled environment that I had gotten accustomed to being around Allegra. I was headed to a new room full of eyes to judge me.

I dialled Mansour in a panic. It was the time to rally my troops. I needed to enlist all the help I could gather to ensure my first official appearance was both memorable and appropriate.

When he finally answered the phone, I started off with some politeness.

'How are you holding up?'

With a clearly saddened voice, he replied, 'Not great. I'm both avoiding the places she could be at but also wishing I would randomly bump into her.'

I thought that was my cue for a change of topic. 'Well, allow me to cheer you up. I'm going to be covering the Heart of Diamond Charity Ball for Sizzle.'

I heard a screech followed by an, 'Oh my gosh! I can't believe you're finally coming with us this year.'

'I'm thinking of asking Allegra to borrow a dress.'

'Don't tell Allegra, but we all know Mila has the best fashion sense out of all of us.'

He had a point. While I would always go to Allegra for strategy, it was always going to be Mila who had the cutting-edge couture. As a regular front-rower at any fashion week that mattered, her closet was somewhat of a fashion archive in its own right. Luckily for me, she was always happy to allow me to borrow, after she'd exhausted a trend of course.

After a short message exchange, I got the final confirmation I'd been hoping for:

Mila

> I've got just the dress for you.

The brewing excitement made me release a discreet squeal. I looked around, slightly embarrassed by my reaction. Luckily the only person to notice was Celine, midway to the lift to the upper floors. She turned towards me and started smiling to signal an interaction was imminent.

'What was that, Paze, someone interesting texting you?'

'As a matter of fact, yes! My friend Mila is lending me a gown for the Heart of Diamond Charity ball tonight. Speaking of which, I'm on assignment, and it's my first story as a permanent employee.'

Celine threw her arms around me and brought me in for a close hug.

'Congrats! I'm so happy for you.' Her smile opened up with warmth, and it seemed to be based on true emotion.

'You're not getting rid of me anytime soon, it seems,' I said while moving my brows upwards.

'Wasn't planning on it. You're one of the few people here with an interesting life.' As much as I wanted to disagree, I had yet to have a conversation with Nathan that wasn't about food.

'I'm going to love you and leave you. I still have a couture dress to pick up and a ball to attend.' I couldn't believe the words rolling out of my mouth in a non-ironic way. Still, it was a work function, so it wasn't as frivolous as it sounded.

With two air kisses, I managed to depart from Celine and finally made my way to the exit of the building. I had only a few precious hours to stop by Mila's house in Trevor Square before preparing myself for the evening from both a personal and professional perspective.

I arrived at the glossy black door outside Mila's three-story townhouse. When I knocked, instead of hearing a feminine voice greet me, I was surprised by a squeal similar to the one previously sounding through the phone at my office.

'Mansour! You're here!'

'You think I'd really miss out on all this action? Never! Besides, this is a huge day for you.'

Despite his exterior seeming piercing at times, in his heart, Mansour was a great friend. It must not have always been easy for him to be the only male friend in our chaotic group, but he always reassured us that growing up in a family of five sisters as the only son had prepared him for that role his entire life.

Inside Mila's house was a world as artful as her personality. The entry hall of the early 19th-century home had been modernised with mirrored walls that created an infinity effect. Within a few steps into the drawing room, there were quirky and colourful pieces of art displayed across the cream walls. There were hints of her latest visit to Art Basel Miami everywhere you looked. I sat on a purple velvet chaise that faced a white wood staircase from where Mila would emerge at any moment.

'I'm coming down, dress and all!' I heard her squeal enthusiastically as I saw a garment being held underneath a dust cover, seemingly weighing down a struggling Mila as she tried walking down the steps without tripping.

Mansour rushed to her aide and pulled the hanger to take the gown down from the side of the handrail. 'I've got this. I need both of you in perfect form tonight as my two dates.'

'I don't know about you, Mila, but I'm definitely nobody's date tonight. It's strictly a business function.'

'Nobody needs this level of dress for a business function. This is your big night to shine, and we all know it,' Mila said with an inviting smile.

'Unless, of course, you'd like a pantsuit instead for your strictly business nonsense,' Mansour teased, knowing full well that I very much did want to not have everyone guess whose plus one I was for once.

'Alright, alright. Tonight is a big deal for me, and I love that we can do this together. Now, can I see the dress?'

Almost as if they had been rehearsing it all afternoon, they both opened different sides of the dust cover simultaneously. The classic silhouette clinched at the waist, expanding into a layered crinoline skirt in baby blue. I could recognise the signature Dior look anywhere, and that one was particularly iconic as a dress of choice for many starlets and royals in the many iterations since it was originally created by Mr Dior nearly a hundred years prior.

I held the dress on the hanger over my clothes to see myself in the mirror. Wearing Mila's Dior dress made me feel a different kind of beautiful. For one night, at least, I'd be unavoidable. I couldn't resist the urge to twirl like a young debutante.

'Mila, you're basically like my fairy godmother,' I said while still incredulous as to how I had spent an entire life without that dress.

'Bring her back in one piece, and don't do anything I wouldn't do.' It sounded like a fair trade-off for look the best that I ever had.

I made a note to be on my best behaviour tonight, or at least try my hardest to be.

CHAPTER NINE

*Work and Play,
Play and Work*

The hours before the ball passed by as if time had been sped up thrice the normal rate. In the blink of an eye, I found myself once again using my emergency Uber account to make my way to Allegra's place in order for us to arrive together in her far more suitable chauffeur-driven Bentley Mulsanne. It was unanimously decided in my friend group that one could simply not combine couture and ride-share in one sentence, let alone in one evening at society's most exclusive ball.

It was also a big night for Allegra, her first venture back into a major outing as a newly single woman. Not that it phased her at all; if anything, shedding the dead weight gave her a renewed glow. Nevertheless, in moments like that, there was nothing quite as coherent to her new status as walking in alongside her friends rather than missing a function to sulk over a man.

As she walked out to greet me, herself wearing a romantic Valentino long red dress, she looked at my outfit with clear admiration. 'You look impeccable, Paze!'

'Look who's talking. You're absolutely glowing,' I complimented her truthfully.

'Ready to take on the town?' she said as she grabbed me by the arm, and we started making our way into the back seat of her ride.

I didn't quite answer her question; rather, I deflected by singing along with the music in the car. *Am I ready? Do I know what this new chapter would entail?* My mind was miles away from the sounds that made our bodies dance effortlessly. There were many unanswered questions that kept me wondering whether I should be worried about the path I was taking or if I should've simply enjoyed that path without concerning myself with queries that I lacked the foresight to understand.

The ride to the Pall Mall was short. Instead of talking, Allegra blasted the stereo to the sound of Solomun's latest remix. We danced in our seats with our hands in the air as if we were two teenagers on our way to a school prom. We stopped only momentarily to snap hugging selfies, which we both posted to our social media. I was high on life.

As our driver stopped, I spotted Mansour and Mila standing together at the beginning of the red carpet that led to the main door of the palatial building housing a gilded ballroom. All the surrounding buildings, much like that one, were home to some of London's most exclusive members-only clubs. Once the realm of men alone, it had been more recently opened to both genders and international patrons of political influence.

'Oh, hello there!' An excited Mansour paced over to us, offering me his arm as I descended.

After positioning me next to Mila, he went back a step to help Allegra. When she set foot out of the car, I could see her face transform from my best friend into the uber socialite everyone who led the gossip pages would recognise. With every step into the main gallery, her chin seemed to elongate further until she was nearly looking down at all of us. She was radiant. Her bouncy curls flowed down from her shoulders while her eyes looked smouldering in a golden brown smoky look with a gentle liner that pulled them upwards.

I walked right behind them with Mila, who had opted for a delicate lavender lace gown with a high turtleneck. Our group truly looked invincible. Everyone was dressed to the nines in their couture. It was the epitome of years of dress rehearsal, waiting for a chance for all of us to shine equally. *I was finally one of them.*

The first person I recognised near the entrance to the main ballroom was Celine, who was presumably there to support Florence. Instead of a ball gown, she was wearing a black pencil skirt suit and holding several phones. She waved at me as I made my way in whilst capturing every part of my outfit with a mental camera scanning up and down.

'Paze! You look incredible.'

'Thanks to this crew over here; they're my personal glam squad.' I pointed to my friends with my head as we formed a circle around her. She nudged me with her arm before speaking.

'Aren't you going to introduce us?'

'Of course, this is Celine Moulin—my co-worker at Sizzle. And these are Allegra di Pienza, Mansour Nasser, and Mila Popova.'

There was barely a chance to extend a hand before an attendant asked me for my name. The usher next to her informed me, 'Miss Paisley Taylor-Jones, I will accompany you to your table. You're sitting with the corporate sponsors.'

'Is Florence Moray there?'

'No, she's with the board members at the head table.'

It became apparent very quickly that I would be sat away from my friends and anyone of interest. The event team escorted my friends to their respective chairs while I waved at them with an expression of 'Please don't leave me behind!'

Allegra blew an air kiss with a wink of acknowledgement as she walked off. I walked solo towards the back of the ballroom, where those who worked for organisations deemed worthy enough to sponsor but not to make the pages of the press were exiled. I mentally mapped out the room in the process, taking note of all the faces I recognised and that would be duly mentioned in my coverage of the event.

As I arrived at the remaining edge of the ballroom, I spotted a coy Sara Gram sitting next to a much older gentleman. With his face turned towards her while whispering into her ear, I couldn't make sense of his identity. Instead, my eyes quickly turned to finding a place where I could pry into the evening's happenings from a safe distance. I quickly found an empty seat at a nearly full table and settled into it, collecting my dress so as to not disturb the neighbouring attendee. It took me a minute to get appropriately positioned before my eyes met with a dark-haired, hazel-eyed man.

He stretched his hand to the side to shake mine and said, 'Philip Bex, nice to meet you.'

'Paze, it's a pleasure,' I responded, taking a minute to notice that I had found a seat next to an extremely attractive and well-dressed man.

'So which company set you up for this?'

'Sizzle Media. We're donors, but I'm actually here to cover the ball for the social column.'

It felt good saying that. It was probably the first time in my life that I felt I truly belonged. I wasn't there as someone's plus one; I was there representing an institution. One that I worked for in a position I had worked hard to reach.

'I'm filling in for my stepdad. He's out of town, so I got emotionally blackmailed into coming. He's way too proud as a sponsor to let a ticket go to waste.'

I chuckled a little too hard, considering the comment was only moderately funny. I guess it's easier to laugh when the sight is so pleasing to the eyes with his broad shoulders and dimpled smile. I reached out an arm to a waiter passing next to our table. The conversation was about to get sprinkled with prosecco bubbles.

'Are you from London?' I took it as a compliment that he thought I was a busy city girl.

'Not at all, I'm from Surrey. Born and bred.' My voice had gone slightly high-pitched. I took a sip from the flute while maintaining eye contact.

'Seriously? Me too, I'm from Cobham,' he said, letting out a surprised laugh.

'Epsom. Can we call each other neighbours, Philip?'

'I guess we should gang up on these city folks. Also, everyone just calls me Bex.'

That little word 'we' sounded sweet coming from him. I smiled mischievously while noticing how his rugged nose fit so perfectly with the structured cheekbones that made him look like a man who both knew his wine but also played rugby in school.

Food started to be quickly brought in and placed in front of us while we made small talk about the unknown shapes and textures that emerged on porcelain plates in front of us. There wasn't much of a reason to interact with the other people at our table, who mostly stuck to their phones and photographed the ambience. I suddenly remembered I hadn't seen my photographer since I arrived, and discreetly pulled out my phone from my bag to send him a message.

Me

> Hey! I'm all the way in the back. Let's take some photos after dinner?

He quickly responded while I toyed with my hair, hoping that Bex was watching.

Photographer

> On it. I've taken some red carpet shots but will come find you after dessert for some more.

Me

> There's a table next to mine with an older man and a young woman in bright pink strapless. Please confirm his name and take pictures for coverage.

I wouldn't have been able to stare for too long, she'd probably have recognised me if I had. Besides, my eyes were firmly set on Bex instead. That didn't mean I couldn't get someone to get the scoop on my behalf. That's what colleagues were for, after all.

Just as soon as I laid my phone next to my water glass, an elegantly dressed woman in her mid-20s wearing a bright yellow frock similar to my own borrowed couture took the stage on the other side of the ballroom and started speaking into a microphone.

'Good evening, ladies and gentlemen. For those of you whom I've not yet had the pleasure to meet, I'm Nisha Gupta, and it's a great pleasure to welcome you to the Heart of Diamond Charity Ball.'

Bex whispered to me, bringing his body close enough to mine so that I'd be the only one to hear his take.

'Apparently, she's the granddaughter of the founding partner in Gupta Stones. Most people have diamonds on them that can be traced back to them.'

I pulled my head in closer to his ear to respond. I was close enough to feel the heat of his skin touch mine.

'Do you know if she's working in the family business? I'm profiling some of the next-generation magnates for work.'

'I hope she is. I'd hate to see another one of these promising young women from prominent families fated into the family foundation in order to make way for male offspring in the boardroom,' he responded with a disapproving tone.

'Is that really a thing? Sounds depressing,' I said, with a little shock, considering how my own group was very fortunate to have parents who supported their endeavours.

'Yeah, I've seen way too much of it. I'm more into the finance side, and we often see female members pushed to the side after they complete their studies, ever so discreetly.' He sounded almost resigned to the fact that it happens quite frequently.

'She's got to be in for the long run, though, if she's running the show tonight,' I added, with growing interest in our evening's host.

'I guess we'll find out in time. Or rather, you can find out and I can read about it via your column.' There was a charming way his smile opened as he said *my* column.

By that point, I was spoon-deep into my crème brûlée when I saw my photographer approaching us. I gulped the remaining prosecco from my flute, knowing it would probably be my final drink for the evening.

'Right, Bex, duty calls. Will be back in a bit.'

His lips pressed into a discreet frown. He looked disappointed to see me leave.

'Good luck, and see you around.'

I directed my photographer around the room, capturing photos of the usual suspects plus a few new faces that had worn unique outfits. I checked his camera for photos and found that he had only captured Sara on her own, proudly posing as if anyone was truly interested in her being spread across a society page. I asked him inquisitively, 'How come her date isn't pictured?'

'He didn't want to be photographed with her, even specifically asked me to delete the previous snap,' he replied with a sigh of irritation at having been confronted for doing his job.

'Did he offer us his name?' I pried, more curious for personal reasons than professional ones.

'No, but I caught a glimpse of his place card, and I recognised him from the top 100 CEO feature we did last year. He's a big shot.'

Interesting. I noted mentally that I'd need to dig up the edit from our online archives and see if he could recognise the culprit from a line-up of successful men with a taste for keeping younger company. Some time must have passed by doing laps around the round banqueting tables. As I searched and failed to find Bex, my point of reference to find my table, I realised he had already left. That was also my cue to leave, as I had finished my work and needed to go find my ride home.

Once I comfortably sat in Allegra's car again, I opened my clutch bag to find my compact mirror and check the state of my makeup. I instantly noticed that the main occupant of the bag, my iPhone, was missing. I looked around my skirt and panicked as if I were to find it magically under layers of fabric. It quickly proved unfruitful.

The only person who had sat with me all night was Bex. I considered it was more honourable to just buy a new device than contact a man first after spending the night flirting away with him. My cheeks turned red at the humiliating thought, but I couldn't afford to do that on a new starter salary. I bit my lip, thinking of how I'd need to sleuth through social media accounts to find him the next morning and hopefully keep my dignity in the process.

Like in all urban fairytales, I quickly unravelled after the ball into a hungover mess. A full day of work followed by flowing drinks had turned out to be a bad idea for someone still new to the realities of work-drink balance. My feet hurt from wearing shoes that had been made as a torture device, a punishment against feminine vanity. I spent the day lounging in different spots of my cube-shaped apartment while wearing a comforting fluffy pyjama set. My main activity for the day would be using the work laptop to find Philip Bex online. With a side of greasy comfort food.

Luckily for me, last night's Philip Bex was the first result to appear on Google. As it turned out, the Surrey boy was also a journalist, but unlike me, he'd already made it to editor for Financial News. I stared at my screen as his black and white LinkedIn photo appeared on the top results alongside his job title, and I instantly felt a rush of warmness reach my cheeks. I was enticed to click through and see what other parts of his life were available to the public. I read out loud the words on his profile tagline.

Editor at the United Kingdom's most influential financial news source. Living in London, a city that is really many in one.

A man after my own heart. I'd always felt that there was something particular about the way Londoners organise themselves in neighbourhoods with such distinctive characteristics. In some manners, it may have seemed to non-locals as a clique meant to exclude, but I'd never seen it that way. I also found comfort in the idea that if you searched wide enough, there was a community in London for everyone with similarly minded people who became, in many ways, an extension of yourself as you navigated adulthood.

It was fascinating how much we would relate if we ever went on a proper date. *Am I being a little creepy? Snap out of it!* I would just need to remind myself not to let out how much I had already fawned over his profile.

Scrolling down to the education section, I chuckled at the fact that he went to University College London. Of course, a bit of school rivalry is always fun; the UCL vs Kings topic was quite tongue-in-cheek when it comes to competitiveness, as long as they admit we're slightly better, that is.

My daydreaming of conversations came to a halt as a request came through from Philip Bex to be added as a contact on LinkedIn. *I forgot to switch on Private Mode to avoid him seeing me browsing his page!* I was mortified that I had looked like a bit of a stalker by lurking on his profile mere hours after casually meeting at the gala. At least he had the decency to reciprocate by adding me, sparing the embarrassment of a one-sided interest. As soon as I accepted his request, a message popped up along with the infamous green circle signifying he was currently online:

> Bex
>
> Hi, Paze; it was nice meeting you last night. You ended up forgetting your phone at the table. I've got it with me.

That was a relief. The last expense I needed now that I was considering moving into a better apartment was a new iPhone. Besides, I wouldn't have minded meeting Philip again under less formal circumstances. We exchanged pleasantries the night before, but we were both understandably guarded, as it turned out we both usually stood on the inquisitive side of conversation. I took a deep breath and prepared to send out an uncharacteristically bold message:

> Me
>
> Thanks. You're fun for a UCL boy. How about I buy a coffee as a reward for keeping my phone safe?

I closed my eyes as I hit send as if that would minimise the effect of the potential rejection I had just set myself up for. It wasn't my usual method to entice a man into sharing a drink, albeit a non-alcoholic one. I felt every heartbeat in the next moments as he presumably wrote his response.

Bex

> Cheeky, I like it. How about 5pm today? I can't imagine you'll survive any longer without it.

The worst part of it was that he was completely right. I had just had the most significant night of my career and my own personal debut as the type of journalist who gets invited to events. Yet, without my phone, I had limited means of telling anyone about it or even running a sanity check with my friends about the look I selected to wear later to coffee. I made a mental note to play it safe with a classic white jacket, a teal silk top, and some tight black jeans. It was both business and fun, which would avoid the pressure of turning up looking like it was a date.

Me

> I can't. You caught me. Is Earl's Court too far from you? There are some places down the road from the station.

I decided it would be best to stick to somewhere near me, far away from the prying eyes of my friends and their friends.

Bex

> That's perfect, I live in Barons Court. Won't take me long, call you when I reach.

Such an unexpected turn that he lived nearby. It also made perfect sense that he would live in one of the areas of London that most resembled Surrey. I had once seen flats to rent on the Queens Court grounds that faced the manicured lawns of the tennis club. The place was close enough to the hustle and bustle yet still slightly disconnected from the madness. That was just the sort of place I'd like to call home once I managed to escape my sardine box.

I squeezed myself out of bed and down the bunk bed stairs, shaking off the laziness that had consumed me since my Cinderella experience. The first glimpse in the mirror confirmed my fears that I had since morphed into a raccoon in urgent need of skincare. The rendezvous wasn't a formal date per se, but that didn't imply that I shouldn't, or rather wouldn't, make an effort. With the face mask cooling in the minibar, I would be able to depuff my face in a few hours. There was work to be done, and time was of the essence.

CHAPTER TEN
Fast Cars, Fast Dates

The pavement leading from Collingham to Earls Court wasn't particularly even. However, it didn't mean that I would be turning up in flats; I had opted instead for black suede mules with a flirty, thin heel. My hair was down and slightly messy, but it went along with a deliberately smudged smoky-eye. I had added a hint of teal to the corner of my eyes, which matched my top and gave the look an air of dangerous fun. It was all a stark contrast to my true personality, someone who much prefers to listen to stories of how others had fun over tea, but it was too soon to scare him off with my grandmotherly ways.

As soon as I arrived, I saw Bex, his back turned, peeking into a café, presumably searching for a free table. Standing tall, his physique was far more impressive from that angle. I could get a sense of his strong shoulders through the fitted navy cardigan neatly draped over a tight white shirt. He must have sensed my eyes on his back as he turned around instinctively and released a shy but warm smile that revealed the unforgettable pair of dimples from the night we met.

'Mr Bex, have you been waiting long for me?' I was in a flirty mood, and he was looking dangerously cute.

'You couldn't have gotten here faster if I had said I'm holding your most precious possession for ransom. Oh wait… I am.' He smiled broadly with a cheeky tongue slightly sticking through his front teeth.

We had barely sat at the table, and I already knew more about him than many of the people I had spent most of my time with over the last few years. He had grown up with two sisters who were both living abroad with their partners. He visited his parents every bank holiday and woke up for a daily swim, a little too early for my taste. Everything about him screamed disregard for the walls and protocols people usually have around going on a first date. I liked it.

Hours passed like they were minutes. I had not felt the urge to check my phone, even when going to the bathroom every so often. Meeting him had been completely unexpected but had also consumed my interest. We tried every dessert on the menu until the waiter eventually let us know the cafe was closing to clean up before the next meal service.

When we both stood up to leave after the parting of the bill, Bex looked at me with his lips in an upward grin. I could sense from his experience that our afternoon had not fully satiated him, so he blurted out:

'Do you want to watch a movie?'

'Sure… when?' I tried to add a bit of mystery to all my words by enunciating a little slower than usual.

'Now. I love movies; do you have other plans?'

'Not really.' It didn't take more than a second to know I wasn't ready to end the date anytime soon.

'Will you go on a second date with me?'

'How does that count as a second date if we're still on the first one?'

'My invitation was strictly for coffee. A new date starts the second we cross that door. It's like a portal to the future—to the second date.'

It wasn't the best line, and had it come out of any other man's mouth, I could have laughed. Instead, I let out a coy smile and took his hand so we could leave together.

'Do you want me to order the car?' I offered while sizing up his casual getup and observing his perfectly polished brogues.

'No, I've parked down the road. Don't worry, you won't have to walk much on those things.' He gestured with his feet towards my heels.

We stopped after a few more steps, where a pristine, white Aston Martin was parallel parked on the side of the road. I tried to hide my surprise at his choice of car, particularly one that was not typically associated with a salaried employee at a minor publication.

'Before you ask, it's my stepfather's ride. I'm merely the custodian since they're never here in London.' He fidgeted with his hair while talking, which I noted as uncharacteristic nervousness despite the otherwise laidback day.

'Good to know; I was about to take you for one of those city guys with a disgustingly high bonus.'

'Trust me, if I was, it wouldn't be cars I'd be buying. I'd start with getting my own place, where I don't have to be reminded of the man my mum ran off to Monaco with one Christmas and never came back.'

There was pain in his voice when he spoke about his family. Most of my friends would keep things like that private, afraid that it could be used against them as leverage. Philip was different; he was raw emotion. I want to keep him always like this. I also decided not to pry at the moment. He had shared enough, considering we had just met.

Bex turned on the car and instantly blushed as his previous playlist started blasting. He had clearly planned on concealing his interest in Y2K hip hop for a little while longer, but the autoplay feature on his iPhone let him down. Our eyes met as his cheeks turned a shade similar to pink lady apples.

'I know this amazing indie cinema in Hampstead. Up for a drive out of this area?'

'That sounds awesome. I don't know much up there.' It was sadly true; I hadn't explored much beyond the student areas in my uni years and then stuck mostly to where my friends lived afterwards.

'It's okay. I won't hold it against you that your whole life seems to rotate around Kensington and Knightsbridge,' he replied cheekily, taking his first jab at me. I may have had it coming after spending a significant part of the afternoon name-dropping my usual haunts.

'Alright, alright. I do realise there's life outside of SW7. I'm technically an SW5 postcode myself.'

The rest of the ride was focused on how many of the song lyrics he actually knew. I wanted to ask him about his work. Even though we were only a few years apart, he had clearly risen in the ranks quickly. I wasn't ready to let him know how much I had read into his online presence just yet. I took advantage of the journey to check the messages popping on my screen from every single one of my friends, who had clearly worried about my lack of online messages for hours.

Mansour

> Are you up yet?

Allegra

> Did you see who was there last night?

Mila

> How did the dress hold up?

Nathan

> I need to know EVERYTHING!

Celine

> Girl, we need to talk about last night.

The inadvertent effects of the weeks prior started to become noticeable. People were becoming interested in talking about me, not just to me. I didn't have the time to go into details with everyone, so I decided to ignore Nathan till working hours and got back the rest with a simple broadcast:

On a date, speak soon!

Admittedly, I knew more messages would ensue, but there was some satisfaction to be obtained from the mischief of getting them all speculating about what I was up to. I put my phone safely back in my handbag and smiled to myself, giving Bex a side glance that probably looked unnecessarily devious. I then sank into the luscious leather seats as my body gravitated towards him while he hummed to the songs on the speaker.

He glanced away from the windscreen as he pulled the handbrake up and said, 'You know what? I thought you looked like a celebrity at the gala, but I like this Paze better.'

I responded with a deep smile that concluded with flushed cheeks that were most likely visibly through the carefully laid coats of liquid highlighter. I decided I needed a swift subject change before became too mortified to interact any further. 'Come on, I checked timings on the way, and we're going to be late for the comedy flick.'

At the cinema, we laughed together at the silly commercials on screen, preluding that year's Christmas day releases. We looked at each other for one second too long, and I started to feel the heat accumulating on my cheeks. Before I could overthink how embarrassed I was feeling about blushing, he placed a hand on my neck and gently pulled me towards him until our lips melted together.

Instead of pulling away, I gave in to the kiss for what felt like several minutes. When we finally pulled back, I sank into my seat, comfortably resting my head on his upper arm. It felt intimate; it felt right.

The 115 minutes of film passed quickly with an occasional peck that made my nose crinkle. When it finally came to an end, we got up and stood outside the venue, his hand on my hip, bringing me closer. He grabbed my hand to walk towards the car, where he placed his back to the hood while pulling me in for a hug.

'I'm kind of not ready for this date to end,' Bex said to me while moving himself up to sit on the hood itself.

'Do you know what? Me neither. I'd be up for a club tonight.' I could feel excitement brewing as if we were preparing for a student night again back at university.

'That would do. West End?' he suggested, giving me an opening to take charge of the rest of the plans.

'Let me check what's good tonight,' I replied, diverting my attention to my phone as I pulled it out.

I posted to our group chat:

Me

Anyone up for clubbing with us tonight?

Allegra

I'm in. I can book us at Rogue Club. Table's under my name, see you there!

The Rogue Club was one of London's hardest-to-join members' clubs, which meant, of course, Allegra was a member. Nestled on the upper part of Knightsbridge, it was housed on the ground level of an elegant luxury hotel facing Hyde Park. As Allegra's guests, we would arrive and seamlessly walk straight to her table. There were no crowds, no queues, no waiting out in the cold, and not even an entry fee. The whole experience was completely different to a regular night out. Luckily, I hadn't had one of those in years.

'Allegra has got us a table at Rogue's,' I proudly declared.

'As in the members' club? Seriously?' He seemed both confused and slightly impressed.

'Going to a members' club is almost like hosting a house party at this point. We literally know everyone there.' I realised almost immediately how pompous that sounded.

'Sure, Miss Knightsbridge. Let's check out your stomping ground,' Bex said as he leapt from the hood of the car and got into the driving seat.

Once we were both seated in the car, Bex sped through the green streets until we started seeing more densely packed flat blocks. In less than half an hour, we were back on my side of town and making our way into the club via a deep red carpet that led through a gold-framed door. We were led straight into the main room, where the hostess showed us to a small circular table where a bottle of champagne sat atop an ice bucket. I poured a glass for Bex and me as I pulled him a little closer to the rhythm of the electronic dance music blasting.

'I'm not going to lie, this is more fun than I expected,' he whispered in my ear as I placed an arm around his shoulder.

'There's Allegra!' I said, spotting her at a distance as she made her way through the ornate wood frame that connected the main club room to the entry hall. My full attention shifted to my incoming friend and what I could decipher of her intentions based on her ensemble.

I could see her wearing a short lingerie-inspired mini dress in midnight blue with beige lace accents. The dress was delicate but sensual, perfectly complimented by a micro Fendi bag and thin nude-coloured heels. Her hair was placed in a high ponytail that let us all know she was there to play. Even her signature eyeliner was more fun than usual, with some added gold sparkle for good measure.

As soon as she arrived at the table, Allegra caught the attention of a familiar muscled blonde who stood tall at the table next to us. He was always known as the bad boy from the school next door when we were younger. Since then, he had been obsessed with finding a reason to get close to Allegra during her periods in between relationships. There was the negative side of always seeing the same people when going out.

'Hey Allegra, single looks good on you,' I heard his call even through the music as he made no effort to conceal his clear interest in my friend.

Instead of speaking back to him, she just winked at him and continued to greet me with a hug. She whispered into my ear, 'I need all the details later! He's super cute.' We both giggled, and she moved over to introduce herself to my date.

'Allegra, it's a pleasure.'

Extending a slightly awkward hand, he responded, 'Philip, but everyone calls me by my surname. Bex.'

I smiled, pulled Allegra in by her arm, and told Bex, 'She's my best friend in the whole world.'

'So, you're the one I should really work to impress?' he said, using the thin expression lines in his brows to emphasise how seriously he took the task.

'Oh, absolutely. If I decide you're not good to have around, then you're not lasting very long here,' Allegra commented with a hint of sarcasm.

We were interrupted by an enthusiastic Georgie Carter making his way to our table, clearly not satisfied with the earlier wink. He had sex appeal; it was undeniable. He was the Knightsbridge guy who looked good in a suit but could probably throw a punch if someone got too close to him in a club. Georgie was also atypically well-dressed for a man his age, yet his shirts were just a little too tailored to show off his toned biceps. He seemed to have spent far too long in boarding school, which probably led him astray at some point and created the rugged edge that was so distinguishable.

'Hey, gorgeous. If this was a proper club, I'd buy you a drink or ask you to dance.'

Allegra seemed in the mood to entertain his advances as she bothered to dignify it with a response. 'So, what can you offer me instead?'

He took a step closer to her and said, 'A night you won't forget.'

I leaned in closer to Bex and whispered, 'I wish the music was a little bit louder so I wouldn't need to hear the worst pick-up lines ever.'

He laughed at me and reverted the judgement. 'Aren't you glad you're on a date with a journalist? We're meant to be a little bit better with words.'

Valid point. My thing was more the nerdy guys than the muscles. I was surprised Allegra was even remotely attracted to George. The rebound is often worse than the original version. The problem with the situation was that Axwell was already pretty low when it came to most dating criteria. He wasn't prone to loyalty, lacked humility, and, despite the love bombing grand gestures, was something of a walking red flag. Judging by the way she was smiling at her suitor, the pattern of attraction with Allegra and red flags seemed far from finished.

From the view we had of the door, I noticed another familiar figure walking in. None other than Sara Gram herself made her way in, holding on to Caetano's arm as they made their way to a table on the opposite side of the dance floor. I was certain neither of them were members, so I wondered whose guest list they had made it onto.

Even though Allegra was mid-conversation with Georgie, I used my eyes to direct her to my line of sight. The art of communicating without words was something we had perfected through years of needing to say things in the least appropriate of places. I successfully stole her attention away from the toned arms close to her, which I knew thanks to an immediate change in her expression and pouting of her lips.

In a matter of seconds, Allegra very deliberately placed her hand near Georgie's neck and ran it down his right arm all the way to the drink he was holding. Locking eyes with him, she took a seductive sip of his vodka mixer. He had his back turned to the dancefloor and was none the wiser to the story developing around him. In the clear view of the table opposite, the scene caught the attention of the precise two people for which it was intended.

Bex looked at me, confused. 'I can't tell what's going on, but something is going on, right?'

I pulled him slightly away from our table mates and said, 'There's a lot to catch up on. I usually just observe and avoid getting involved.'

Both Caetano and Sara marched towards our table, visibly enticed by the possibility of material for future gossip. My instinct kicked in, and I started dancing to the rhythm, using my body to invite Bex to avoid the inevitable by making ourselves busy. I still stayed close enough to hear the interaction but far enough so that I could pretend I hadn't.

Caetano waved at Allegra, who responded by extending a hand over Georgie's shoulder while he tilted himself slightly to see if he recognised the new arrivals.

I could hear Sara as she loudly greeted him. 'Georgie, long time! Can you believe I lost your number since we met that time in Marbella?'

Not one to fluster, he responded without moving himself from his proximity to Allegra. 'I lent you my phone when you were stuck outside Nikki Beach. It didn't cross my mind to save it.'

The boldness of Sara's moves never ceased to amaze me. Neither did Allegra's ability to pretend she didn't exist as she stole Georgie's attention back by also starting to dance. It may have disturbed her peace in another scenario, but there was no provocation that was about to prevent her from having fun.

'Well, you can save it now if you'd like,' she added while Caetano gave her a stunned look. He may have been her friend, but it seemed even he couldn't believe the words coming from her mouth. Good news for him, his clear displeasure would surely win him some points for continuing to stay on Allegra's guest list.

Turning himself around to face her, Georgie pulled Allegra's arms around his waist. 'I'd rather not, thanks.'

'Ouch, that's gotta burn,' Bex said while pulling a face at me.

Fuelled by liquid courage, I hung myself from his shoulder so I could speak directly into his ear. 'Probably does, but guess who's getting lucky tonight? Georgie boy.'

Bex reciprocated my closeness by moving his own hand down my back until it nested around my waist. I could feel his body's warmth on my skin as his shirt had been rolled up with the rising temperature of an evening spent in liquor and dance. He moved his lips closer to my neck, which made my hairs stand with the vibration of his voice.

'He might not be the only one.'

CHAPTER ELEVEN

Fashion Week, Fashion Peak

I woke up in the comfort of my home, satisfied that yesterday's bad ideas of what could have happened didn't materialise into today's regret. After a full-steam-ahead day, I felt that I needed to slow down before things crashed between Bex and me. I had always been the first to criticise fast-burn situationships, so I wasn't ready to start biting my tongue just yet. Instead, I would focus on Bex detox while prioritising all things comfort.

I rubbed my hands on my face and saw last night's makeup coat the skin on my palms. Tones of iridescent cheek highlighter mixed with walnut-coloured eyeliner were a pleasant reminder of a night well spent. My body was still tangled up in a mixture of pillows and duvet while I rolled around in a college hoodie that had served as pyjamas after we called it in at 4am. I arguably smelled even worse than I felt.

Moving over to the side of my mattress, I found my phone, which must have been there since I fell asleep the night before. It was already two o'clock in the afternoon, and my Sunday hadn't even started. The only course of action that could happen was the hunt for the perfect hangover sandwich. Thanks to one too many student nights over the last few years, I knew just the place that had a sufficient amount of grease and a very pleasant view.

I poured water on my body almost too quickly to qualify for a full shower and immediately dressed in baggy jeans, a faded charcoal t-shirt, my trusted trench coat, and sunglasses that would seem out of place for the season. I'd risk being confused for a tourist wearing dark shades in near winter rather than admit defeat to the state of post-alcoholic bliss.

I sent out a text to the group chat to see who was interested in a twelve-foot baguette with a side of the previous night's gossip.

Me

> Ciao! Anyone not eaten yet? Passing by the Sandwich Shop up on Kensington, then heading out to the park. Food with a view?

Allegra

> YES! I still smell of what I think is cologne but can't be sure. Be there in 20.

The intrigue. As per her message, she had been so deep in cologne it had taken a concerted effort to remove. It wasn't entirely surprising that our needs ended in different paths. Allegra had spent the last hours before I decided to call it a night dancing far too close to Georgie. She was having fun, and I wasn't about to judge a woman for wanting to have fun without any other intentions. I had bid her farewell with a peck on the cheek when it was time for me to turn into a pumpkin, but that didn't mean she, too, had to leave things to the imagination just because I had.

> Mila
>
> I need to be in on this. Just because I don't enjoy the action doesn't mean I don't want to hear every bit of it. See you there!

It would be good to check our decisions with the one sane friend in our group. I had just spent the most eventful forty-eight hours of my adult life between my social debut and meeting the first man to pique my curiosity since entering graduate life. There certainly was a sense that things had been on a fast track since the end of summer, which was both exhilarating and frightening.

I hadn't the time to ponder too much on the growing unease that, sooner or later, my spout of recently found good luck was bound to subside. In the meantime, I had a sandwich to attend to and friends who could calm my nerves. I rushed down the stairs of my building with the last remaining bit of energy I could muster.

On the walk towards the upper part of Kensington, my headphones kept the street noises from distracting me. I typically found it quite comical to walk down a glistening historical brick block of flats while listening to the obscenely worded anthems we had heard on the dance floor a few hours before. A slightly wicked smile took over my lips as I thought of how close I had been dancing to Bex. Detox day.

Just before I could get trapped in more thoughts, I was spotted by my friends waiting outside our favourite struggle-morning spot. I crossed the street and collapsed into a trio hug as we could barely contain ourselves from falling into a state of laughter.

Mila took the lead by extending her hands to both of us as she pulled us into the shop. The bell above the glass door rang, announcing our slightly off-balance entrance to the owner, who recognised and greeted us from the cashier.

'I can tell both of you have a lot to spill!'

She stood ahead of us in the queue, facing us with her full attention. Mila's hair was neatly tucked under a knit beanie that matched her thick wool coat and winter joggers. I made direct eye contact before starting off with my version of events.

'Oh, you have no idea. It seems your dress brought me some good luck. The dry cleaners are dropping it off at your place, by the way. So, I met this cute guy—'

Allegra interrupted impatiently while putting her hand on my shoulder, sensing that I was pacing for the right words. I retreated, instead giving her the floor to share first as she typically did. 'Seems to have even rubbed on me; it's been a while since a man has made me want to stay up all night.'

The elderly woman on the other side of the counter was clearly eavesdropping since she made a facial approval as she pointed at the different options of baguette fillings. There was an endearment about the fact that she probably knew far more about our lives in London than our families from the many morning runs, but none of us knew much about hers. I kept telling myself that one day, I'd take the time to ask her about her escapades, but given the famished hangover, my focus diverted back to getting to our designated park bench as soon as we could.

'So that's what happened when I left.' I quirked up an eyebrow before continuing.

'Not that I'm surprised, given how closely you two were dancing.'

Despite not being the topic of conversation, I instinctively looked around to see if there were any other known faces who could have heard us and spread the contents to undesired places. Taking notice of my concern, Allegra touched her credit card against the till, and we quickly regathered outside the shop to continue our chat with more privacy.

'Can we just take my driver up to the park?' Mila asked while examining the uphill walk that awaited us before we could reach the greener pastures of Hyde Park's Albert Gate.

'This is my cardio after consuming my weight in champagne last night,' Allegra retorted from behind her slightly tinted, circular glass frames. Nobody wears glasses in

London in the winter unless they're using them to hide the secrets of the previous night.

'I've got to side with Mila on this one. I've spent the last two days in heels for all sorts of varied reasons. I need to collapse into a seat and be peeled off near the grass.'

'Fine, fine. Boris can drive us up and drop us off by the spot.'

Allegra conceded as we all made our way into Mila's Rolls Royce Cullinan. My leg muscles relaxed as I placed my feet on the smooth wool carpets. Nobody broke the silence as we rested our heads against one another's on the short drive further uphill to the park entrance, where we'd be dropped off to find the bench we'd claimed as our very own.

The crisp autumn air made our cheeks rosy as we sat on the cold bench. The skies didn't have much light seeping through, but it still felt pleasant to stay outside. As a long-time Londoner, I'd come to learn to hold onto pleasant days for as long as I could before winters turned too damp for enjoying the outdoor air.

Allegra seemed eager to share her exploits as she turned her body slightly after placing her food on the bench.

'I'll start. So, Mila… You know we went down to the club last night?'

'Yes, I read from the warmth of my bed,' Mila said with an equal amount of eagerness to chime in despite her nonchalant exterior. From her perfectly coordinated maroon outfit to her fresh-looking skin, she looked out of place between both of us, with our dark circles crowning our faces.

'Well, I ended up in an unexpected entanglement with Georgie Carter,' Allegra said while giggling almost childishly.

With a look of complete surprise, Mila raised an eyebrow before responding to the admission of guilt. 'You can't be serious. Hasn't he been after you every time you're single but in the sleaziest ways?'

I jumped into the conversation after a sudden flashback of last night's dance floor advances that clearly left Allegra in a state of attraction.

'You could say his ways are a little… upfront.'

'Allegra, he's very brash and so unlike you.' Mila was clearly concerned about the revelation. It was very true; he was at the complete other end of the spectrum. It was something that often appealed to Allegra. She always thought men who were too proper couldn't be sexy.

'And very hot. Which is just what I was in the mood for last night,' Allegra continued while biting into her sandwich.

'I can't fault you for wanting a little action, but it does seem uncharacteristic.' Mila was still insistent on what realistically would be anyone's reaction listening to my best friend's new pairing.

'He proved his worth after putting Sara definitely in her place,' I added, providing the context that was so clearly missing about the turning point in last night's approach.

'I see, so this isn't about him at all,' Mila concluded, looking slightly disappointed.

'It is. I wanted him, and I had him. It has nothing to do with the entertaining way he made his point when she rudely tried to flirt with him in front of me. In all honesty, the night was surprisingly memorable. I might make this a recurring encounter,' Allegra clarified, looking at me straight on while pressing her lips firmly.

'I'm not sure what's more surprising, the fact that you're entertaining a pursuit of Georgie or that you think this isn't somehow connected to upstaging Sara.' I defended my position since I, too, was there and saw first-hand how things moved rather quickly after an initial lack of interest.

'It may seem that way, but I genuinely could not describe how satisfying the evening and early morning hours were.'

That was very atypical of Allegra; she often shied away from revealing any details of her pursuits. It was impossible not to assume there were secondary reasons at play here.

'So, can we expect to see Allegra off the market again soon?' Mila asked with a comical inflexion, shaking her head in disapproval.

'There was one thing that deeply bothered me about him; it's the only mishap that I can think of from it all.'

My curiosity was piqued as both Mila and I signalled our interest in further information. Up until then, it had been all praise despite the clear concerns about how mismatched it all seemed.

'It was all going well until he took off his shirt,' Allegra said.

'Was it that smell that reeks of alcohol and sweat that post-clubgoers seem to acquire?' Mila said while wrinkling her nose in disgust.

'No, I can live with that or at least bathe that,' Allegra said as we all broke into laughter while trying to maintain our food safely in our mouths.

'I can't imagine anything worse. I give up.' Mila looked genuinely perplexed.

'He has his ex-girlfriend's name tattooed on his chest, in gothic script of all things. I'm not even sure which part of it is most offensive to the eyes.' Her voice gave me the impression that there was, in fact, a part of him that may have put her off.

Mila gasped in horror. She had long remained an anti-tattoo enthusiast, which, according to her, came from the insistence of every man in her family on having questionable ink.

'It could only get worse if it was inside a heart design.' I couldn't help myself but add

'A red one,' she replied, laughing so loud that passing-by patrons of the park looked at us in curiosity.

The onset of hilarity and cringe was simultaneous. More confusing still, it didn't seem to deter her at all, as she had already declared an interest in continuing to see him.

'The lucky girl whose name is tattooed across this man's heart forever is… Alexandra. So naturally, I asked. Turns out, the heartbreaker was none other than Alexandra Wolf herself.'

Few things could have shocked me further at that point. The Bavarian might have had a vixen beneath all that coldness and proprietary. A man with a list of late-night delights as long as George would not easily decide to permanently mark his body with a female name. That had surely been a long-standing affair and most certainly a highly emotional one.

'I feel women need to be warned about him,' I said in a joking tone.

'Well, don't you have a column, Miss Paisley?' Allegra said in an equally funny manner.

In reality, she would have been horrified if any of it was shared outside the circle of trust. It was one thing for us to discuss things away from prying ears, but Allegra deeply disliked being at the centre of controversy where her name could be directly tied to scandal.

'Good thing he knows what he's doing once the lights are off. Besides, I did like how he stood up to Sara yesterday. He did what Axwell never would.'

Allegra was right. It must have exhausted her to have been consistently insulted in public, not to mention the emotional hurt from his frequent betrayals. There had been reputational damage to her otherwise pristine image, something equal in value to her as the sanctity of the relationship itself.

From where I sat in the middle, I turned to see Mila had finished her food and was patiently drinking Diet Coke. She seemed to be processing all that had happened before enquiring directly to Allegra.

'Are you thinking of seriously dating Georgie Carter?'

'What if I was? Would it really be that bad?'

Despite strongly defending her decision-making process, I could tell Allegra wasn't confident in what she was saying as she flicked her hair, twirling her hands around the roots in a self-soothing gesture.

I couldn't help pointing out the obvious situation, one for which we had already heavily judged many other women.

'His reputation aside, isn't he an ex-boyfriend of someone in your circle?

'She's more of an acquaintance than a friend.'

'Would that still be crossing some lines?'

'It only counts if it's people we actually care about.'

On that note, I took advantage of the closing of the discussion to make my way back home so I could rest enough to return to life as the only employed person in our circle. My body needed to recover before I could face another round of avoiding talking about my personal life with Nathan.

The post-fun slumber ended with the sudden arrival of a workday morning alarm, quickly followed by the disarming of my phone's silent mode. My heavy eyelids opened slowly to see a new message alert appear on the lock screen. I smiled back at the phone and rolled on my belly to respond.

Bex

> Is it cheesy to start the week off with a good morning message?

Me

> Well, good morning to you too! How's your week looking?

Bex

> Busy, but not too busy to meet up after work. Up for it?

Of course I was up for it. I had promised a twenty-four-hour detox that had firmly expired. I checked my phone's calendar before replying. A range of alerts I had set up appeared colourfully on the screen in front of me.

Monday was a fresh start to another week of work, but unlike any other, there was excitement brewing in town with the arrival of the world's most famous faces. It was beginning to look a lot like the annual Belgravia Charity Fashion Fair everywhere you looked. Our web team had started their regular countdown to the shows that should not be missed.

Equally, every influencer in town had their PR teams reach out to us to ensure they would be randomly spotted in a clearly not spontaneous encounter near the front rows. I had made sure to update my calendar with notes on events I was thinking of attending a few weeks back. Should I get my hands on these high-demand tickets, of course.

Me

> I might have a few events to attend, nothing confirmed yet, though. Keep you posted?

Bex

> Keep in mind I'm always up for an impromptu party.

That set, I quickly bolted out of my bed and started preparing for work. The unexpected messages from Bex had made my morning more exciting than I'd wish to give him credit for. I hurried through the morning motions to make my way out of the door quickly.

I made a special effort that morning to look like my fashionable evil twin. The office doors swung open, and I set foot inside wearing chunky-heeled military-style boots that hit my mid-calf, leaving a carefully curated space for a draping black jersey dress with ruched sides that extended to my lower thighs. Despite the chilly October air, my legs were warm beneath a thick layer of black wool stockings that gave my outfit an ode to the season. My body was wrapped in an oversized lava-stone-grey coat with a high collar and kept together by a thin black leather belt.

Nathan announced enthusiastically as soon as he saw me walk in that we would kickstart with our sprint meeting to run through the week's affairs. When I walked in, I instantly recognised there was not only a new face in the room, but it was one that I had seen on a few prior occasions.

Nathan gathered us around him like a primary school teacher about to kickstart an activity that was more fun in their head than out loud. We circulated around him like eager children would.

'Settle down, everyone. I've got some exciting news for you all. This week, it's all hand on deck for the Belgravia Charity Fashion Fair, and we've brought in another pair of hands to help us with coverage onsite. This is Caetano; he's a long-time Belgravia resident and applied to be a volunteer collaborator for the story.'

In fact, it had been my idea at one of our prior content sprints to open up our social media for local residents who wanted to collaborate. That sounded like a good way for us to diversify our usual pool of staffers. It did surprise me that he'd put himself up to the task, given that he already had the right connections in place.

Pointing his hands towards me, Nathan continued. 'Paze, since you already run our regular social column, it makes sense for you to tag team with Caetano onsite. He's more keen on doing fashion reviews, I hear, so you focus on who's who on the guest list.'

'Sounds like fun! I'm so ready to do this,' Caetano said with his deep voice and poshest accent.

'I've got press access to all the shows,' Nathan said while putting a lanyard on me that would be my gold ticket for the week.

'Now off you go to plan your schedules, my dream team.'

Making his way over to me, Caetano looked deeply into my eyes and said, 'Haven't I seen you before? I'm sure I have. You've got a very familiar face.'

'I'm friends with Allegra. We've been to a few things together.'

'Ah, of course, that makes sense. You look gorgeous, by the way. I was so worried about being placed with someone who was boringly mid.'

The most fascinating compliments were usually veiled with a layer of insult. Luckily, I had a doctorate in responding with deflection.

'I'm still looking into the rest of the week's outfits.'

'You know this goes, right? For some, it will be fashion weak. For others, it will be a fashion peak. And my job is to judge who goes where. Good thing you're now my teammate, so I can't cover you at all.'

Something inside told me that I should be relieved that I wasn't on the firing line of sharp comments. I was a fashion consumer, an average one at that. But I was by no means an insider, and that was going to be more of an experiment than a leadership opportunity for me.

When I walked back to my workstation, I caught Celine midway to Florence's office.

Putting her hand on my lanyard, she started, 'Look who's become the hot ticket in town.'

'Good news travels fast too, I guess?' I tried to inflect the end of that sentence with a smile.

'Remember that I summarise who's going to what key events for Florence's morning updates. You're representing her personally at these events as far as she's concerned.'

Nathan slipped an envelope discreetly on my desk. I peeked in to find a letter declaring I had passed my probation period. It also ended with a figure: the new salary for a full-time employee. I sighed with relief, thinking I could finally find a new place with a bit more space to breathe.

This is going to be my lucky week.

CHAPTER TWELVE

Bad luck, good luck

As with most things, it wasn't simply a matter of being at the event. That would be far too simplistic an approach to such an important point in the city's calendar. There were people specifically employed to know where to sit, down to the row and chair number. Every detail mattered terribly, and nothing would go unnoticed. As luck would have it, Caetano and I would be doing most of the noticing to report back to our readers.

There was too much on the line for me and I couldn't borrow outfits from Mila all week, particularly since she was busy with her own fittings ahead of the shows. Instead, I decided it was time for me to branch out on my own. I reached out to emerging designer Dalston Blues after hearing about them from our fashion team as the one to watch in our last team meeting. Surely, a press badge would give me some power to get at least one dress for free. An indie sample is always better than a cheap knock-off of something else.

Two days had already passed since my assignment was confirmed, which meant things were about to kick off after I picked up a few frocks at lunchtime. A selection had been made on my behalf after I sent in a series of selfies confirming my personal style. I peeked into the garment protectors and realised that the vibe I must have given was an indie rock fan with a vintage edge. It would do, particularly as I was only really beginning to discover my personal style.

It was quarter to five in the afternoon, and I was dressed as if I was about to head out to a party in the West End. Instead, I was about to descend from a cab next to Grosvenor Place. It may have seemed out of place anywhere else, but I also knew I would still manage to be underdressed for my assignment of covering one of the most traditional events of the autumn season.

As I emerged with my doll-like chunky heels on the pavement, I could already spot Caetano, impeccable in his black tweed jacket and jacquard trousers. An elegant antique white gold brooch with a family insignia on his left lapel caught my line of sight as I walked up to him. I'd have to pry into his heirloom later for more clues about his potentially aristocratic background.

As soon as I set foot in the main foyer, a well-adorned woman in a sheer black chiffon button-down shirt and a maxi-length silk skirt with exaggerated prints of cavalry paraphernalia headed our way. Her gait was like watching a big cat walk across the room in towering platform heels that added another twelve centimetres of height to her already generous stature. I recognised her from social columns. Clara Melo was Belgravia's beloved Brazilian social butterfly and legendary hostess across her several international mansions. She was well into her forties but didn't look a day over twenty-five and had the energy to match her unrelenting youthfulness. Those days, her energy was being channelled into the fashion brand she had co-founded with her daughter.

'Caetano, darling, are you here for my show?' she said after planting two kisses onto Caetano's cheeks and collecting him into an exaggerated embrace.

'Of course, mon amour. It's been on my calendar for months.' His tone of voice was equally over the top. He towered over both of us with his model heights, which made us look up to him while he added a loud laugh at the end of the sentence.

'Clara, this is Paisley. I'm spending the week with her at Sizzle Media as a special collaborator for the Fashion Fair. She's my work twin for the time being.'

'Pleasure to meet you!' I offered out my hand, but instead, Clara brought me in for a tight hug. I tried to place my hands around her, which most likely looked quite awkward to passing attendees.

Caetano had indirectly done me a huge favour by introducing me to one of the most talked about designers that season. I took advantage of the moment to ask a question that had been burning in my mind since researching the brands that would be showcasing at the event. Excitement grew in my stomach as I was about to uncover the first exclusive scoop of my career.

'If it's not too intrusive, I'd love to know you chose to name your brand London Republic.'

Clara seemed amused and let out an aristocratically pleased laugh to signal her satisfaction at my question.

'Darling, London will never be a republic. It's a utopia, much like everything about the brand.'

'You mean England will never be a people's republic.'

'No, I mean London. I can't speak for all of England, but this place—it eats people up with all the splendour of times past. This constant conflict inspires me.'

'That sounds so interesting. What's your current collection called?'

'If I was once Anne Boleyn, I am now Henry VIII.'

'Wow! That's even more fascinating. Is it an ode to the same societal criticism?'

'No, it's about my ex-husband and a warning to the next one in line.'

I wasn't sure if that was meant as a joke or seriously, so I decided it was a good time to exit the conversation. With the growing camaraderie that I had developed with Caetano, I grabbed his upper arm pull him away.

The next hours seemed to be an endless cycle of both interacting with people and avoiding people equally. Caetano turned out to be a phenomenal asset for my story-building with his endless knowledge of everyone's personal lives. He was generous with his contacts, introducing me to all the acquaintances he had accumulated while hotspot hopping throughout the year.

I was nearing social exhaustion when we finally reached the closing show of the evening. I had avoided spending too much time with my inner circle since I was officially on duty. My work etiquette was far more lenient as the evening was coming to a close, so I brought Caetano with me as I walked intently to where Mila and Mansour stood near the building exit.

'Well, well, well… if it isn't our resident social columnist,' Mansour said as I stood purposefully, closing off our small circle.

I feel like we haven't seen you at all in the shows!' Mila added in.

'I know, my bad! I've been trying to get the work bits out of the way so we could finally get some fun into the programme.'

Meanwhile, Caetano pulled in one of his model friends who walked past us and asked, 'Where's everyone headed to post-show tonight?

The tall brunette beauty in a distressed t-shirt dress and boots laughed as she replied, 'Le Chaise, of course, just call Skye when you're outside. They're running the club door tonight.'

We all listened, curiously awaiting our fate for the evening. I didn't know Skye personally, but their name was thrown around as one of London's top promoters, and someone in the group always had their number when needed. The very definition of nightlife for the high society folk was spontaneously arriving without any concern as to how one would get in since someone would always make sure it happened. I was sure that night wouldn't be much different.

Everyone in the group voted for us to head over to Le Chaise. It was one of the only places in town with no guest list; admission was strictly based on whether the hostess believed you had what it takes. The club was built on the side of a decaying old Victorian theatre, revamped with new decadent fittings that were reminiscent of a cabaret. The multistorey space still had the original features, including ivory balustrades that kept VIP guests secluded in viewing boxes looking down to the main dancefloor. I had heard rumours that music would stop to make way for erotic performances with bondage themes, but since phones were not allowed inside, I had no way of separating fact from fiction.

I discreetly pulled out my phone and sent a message to Bex.

> Me
> We're off to Le Chaise, up for it?

> Bex
> Never been but sounds wild. Meet you at the door?

> Me
> Same here, intrigued. See you outside in 30? xx

On the way there, we crammed all four of us into Mansour's chauffeured car. I sat next to Mila, who held up her micro lizard skin Kelly and pulled out a small leather pouch. I watched as she poured out tiny white pills discreetly into her hand.

She whispered into my ear, 'Want some xanny?'

I wasn't one for illicit substances, but I did have a soft spot for recreational use of legal ones. After all, how bad could they be if every other house on our street growing up had a prescription?

I didn't speak but instead mimed a yes while quickly downing the tablet alongside water that I grabbed from the car door. One thing you could always count on with Middle Eastern cars was the water bottles for guests, although I was sure Mansour's parents would have flustered had they known what I used it for.

We all arrived in Soho around the same time. I could see Bex exit an Uber. He had on a light blue shirt beneath a grey thigh-length coat with dark denim trousers. His look was far more casual than the guys in my circle, and that was one of the most attractive things about it. His beaming smile when we locked eyes as I left the car made my stomach react despite my other senses feeling numbed by the pill.

'Hey, can't believe we're doing this tonight,' he said as he greeted me with a prolonged kiss on my right cheek.

I felt relieved that he reserved himself from a public kiss on the lips. That would have left me mortified. I wasn't quite ready for that kind of affectionate display yet. Instead, it gave me the chance to introduce Bex to my friends by name alone, without titles, not that it stopped Mansour from giving me a cheeky look to signal he knew what we were up to.

Noticing the absence of my only friend he had already met, Bex questioned, 'Where's Allegra?'

'Honestly, nobody saw her this whole week at the shows. We're getting ready to send search and rescue soon.'

And by that, I meant gathering our troops and arriving at hers unannounced. Typically, it was something she hated, but then again, she had been offline during a peak season event, which was very odd in itself.

The club entrance rope lifted faster than I could notice as Caetano greeted the tall, muscular blonde at the door dressed in a matte cape that gave them a villainous flare. Skye exclaimed loudly to all of us before any door was opened, 'Phones out where we can see them. You will be given stickers to cover your phone cameras. Should you remove them inside the premises, you will be escorted out and permanently banned from any door I oversee. Understood?'

We all nodded whilst we all passed our phones one by one to be offered sacrificially to the vampire-like figure who stood between us and the hottest party in town. Nobody argued. We obeyed and walked in, unsure of what was to come once we walked past the doors and into a labyrinth of infinity room lighting. It was disconcerting, but then again, I wasn't fully sentient.

Bex walked close to me, which allowed him to clearly see my struggle to contain my overstimulated senses. I walked straight into a mirror and broke down laughing at myself as the rest of the group walked on, leaving us a few seconds behind on our own.

'You're going to get a concussion before we get to the dancefloor.'

Instead of responding, I took advantage of my emboldened mood between the Xanax and the music blasting to kiss him against the lit-up wall. It felt right; nobody could see us, but it was also dangerously public. When I pulled away, smiling, he gave me a little peck on the forehead and walked ahead, holding my hand for safety.

We finally made it out of the psychedelic tunnel into the completely contrasting nightclub interior. In the reviews I read, nobody mentioned that the entrance was meant to discombobulate you before you time-travelled into a cabaret. A crowded dance floor appeared in front of us, with a gilded stage on the other side that had a large chaise lounge in the centre. I locked my free hand in Mila's, who stood a few steps ahead, already on the dancefloor.

I whispered over to her, 'Glad you've decided to join us mortals tonight and not stay home.'

She offered me a half hug and replied, 'I did finally feel like I may have thrown in the towel too soon after all the stories you all told me. Who knows, maybe there's an odd art geek out there for me, too.'

She was clearly referring to my present company. I smiled at Bex with that thought, but we were quickly interrupted by a loud percussion coming from the stage. All of our eyes shot in that direction to take in the sights that started to emerge from the sides of the lush green velvet curtains. The vaudeville-style show began with a half dozen dancers emerging in early 20th-century style attire and headpieces that evoked the belle époque. Then suddenly, it was all juxtaposed with bondage-dressed performers simulating an explicit interaction with the graceful dancers. I felt uneasy watching the stage, which seemed to get more grotesque by the minute.

At one point, all of us seemed to tilt our heads sideways at the sight of a vulgar rendition of a sexual act involving a liquor bottle. It was at that point that my eyes, tired of being visually challenged by unpleasantries, decided to wander to the ornate VIP boxes that stood elevated above the main areas of the club.

When I thought I had seen just about everything, a familiar backside propped up within view of where I was on the dancefloor. On the box nearest to me on the right side of the stage, Celine rested herself against the railing while an older man stood in front of her, caressing her face. The low lights made it impossible to focus on his face. I could only see his silver hair reflecting the occasional shimmer when hit by moving strobe effects.

Caetano saw me staring up and asked, 'Do you also know Lord T?'

I replied loud enough for him to hear through the music, 'You could say we've got some people in common.'

It had been a week since fashion week and the debacle at the strangest nightclub I had ever attended. Despite that, there were so many questions swirling around in my brain about what I had seen. In the late hours of the night, in a less-than-holy setting, I had seen none other than Lord

Thurrington himself in very close proximity to his ex-wife's closest employee. In theory, a single man in the city had every right to whichever woman was consenting to his advances, but that was no ordinary man, and his entanglement with Celine seemed far more complex than a sexual affair.

My column was far more socialite than gossip, but those often intertwined in ways that the audiences were not completely privy to from the front of the screens. A simple photograph on a night out was enough to raise concerns if the context was known. Sadly, the ideal picture from inside the club was off-limits due to their intense privacy policies, but that did not mean that I had forfeited the right to wait a little too long outside the exit. I was no paparazzi, but then again, I had been tasked with capturing the fashion week—which, as anyone knows, included the seedy after scenes.

Under the guise of snapping my glamorous posse in the nearby graffitied walls, I had the perfect excuse to pull out my phone and capture several photographs of the evening. Some of them would be for the official story, others for a use far more unclear to me at the moment. Without fail, the Lord emerged from the club, hurrying into a vintage Aston Martin in the company of three leggy brunettes in similar tight dresses and nearly identical faces. From the dancefloor, I had only seen one, but the low lighting made it difficult to see the depths of his booth.

Although horrified, I still managed to capture her exit in a clear enough photograph that made my phone even more valuable. There was a mole at Sizzle Media, and potentially much worse for Florence Moray. I had suspected that they had a secret relationship since the incident at Celine's apartment, but I tried to push the idea to the back of my mind in order to not obsess about things I had no control over.

Calling Nathan into proximity, I informed him, 'There are several angles from the Charity Show and after party for me to share with you. Can I get your opinion on these pictures?'

I pointed at the nearest quiet room, which, thankfully, Nathan understood as a need for discretion at whatever was coming his way. A sigh of relief came out of me, grateful that journalists were equally protective of information.

I started off once I heard the door click behind Nathan.

'This will be awkward, but I took some photos yesterday at the after-party that captured a scene I couldn't look away from all night.'

Nathan looked at the photographs on my phone for quite some time before telling me, 'We need to bury anything related to Lord Thurrington.' I hadn't yet shown him the image with Celine in it, of course, but I wanted to test the waters with the ones where he exited the club in dubious company first.

'Is this a hard rule here at Sizzle?' I asked, confused as I had always assumed Florence's stance was that no one was protected from bad press unequivocally.

'Not exactly, but the last thing you want to do is be caught in the middle of a war where you're the least powerful party involved. This is less about a Sizzle party and more personal advice for you.'

Nathan seemed seriously concerned as he looked me straight in the eyes while speaking to me. So, I tried to change topics quickly and offer a distraction.

'I'm actually thinking we could run a profile on Allegra. Everyone's always interested in what she has to say, and I think now, with her new business, it wouldn't be so focused on the social aspect."

Nathan didn't seem to run with the idea too much as he retorted within a few seconds, 'She does get clicks, but I want to make sure there's some meat behind this if we're profiling. It's one thing to cover the party, but we need to make sure that there's more to talk about than the brand of champagne she's buying for the next party.'

I felt the need to jump to her defence. Besides, I genuinely felt she could have given us quality content.

'There's so much more to her than meets the eye. There are multiple layers. She's one of the most complex people I know.'

It wasn't that I had exaggerated, but generally, people did only see Allegra's nobility title and frequent photographs of her at social events. A very eligible bachelorette, beautiful and rich, was the typical coverage that came around after every party. Behind all of that was my best friend—one of my only true friends.

'Well, prove it to me then. Pitch me the side of Allegra that nobody but Paisley would know about. Get her to sit down with you and a photographer. People love a good story about a rich woman who's running free.'

'She's very sharp. In school and university, she was always ten steps ahead of us. She's taking her new venture quite seriously; it means a lot for her to make her own name.'

'But you see, she won't ever have her own name unless she changes it. That's not how privilege works. You can't start from scratch if you're already ten steps ahead and not only because you're cleverest in the room.'

It would be hypocritical of me to say I never thought of things in those terms because it often crossed my mind. My home was built on hard work, so I had been raised to admire sweat, blood, and tears on the way to the top. The rugged road to success has also been idealised by many in British history as the only true, respectable way to go. Then, I met some of the most generous people of my life in an unexpected environment where I was meant to be a fish out of water. At Dainter, Allegra had made it clear that messing with me was messing with her.

Nathan interrupted my train of thought with another probe. 'Nevertheless, I am intrigued. What was it like to grow up in her shadow?'

It felt strange to hear that question asked in such a direct way.

'I didn't think of things in those terms, ever really. We were friends, and that was all.' Which was true, most of the time. There were other times when I wished people at least pretended to be interested in me without wanting to get to know Allegra.

'Yes, but as far as I know, your parents are working folk. Successful professionals in their own right, but they've built their own nest, right?'

'I could hardly claim to struggle; my parents run an ad agency. They've done major things for Sizzle. I can't complain too much.'

There were definite negative aspects of their relationship with my employer, like the fact that Nathan and many of the team had direct access to my parents. It was uncomfortable to be around people who knew this much about my backstory.

'Ah, the intricacies of the British class system. You can both be statistically affluent but not upper class, while some are financially dwindling but hereditarily advantaged into a higher standing. If you're so inclined to these archaic notions, of course.'

'I'm really not. I just find all of it so fascinating because there is a constant sense of needing to be a part of something and status is never permanent. One wrong word, and you're out. It's quite stressful, really.'

I tried not to sound whiny while still highlighting that there was much to consider out of what would otherwise be a simple interaction. Sadly, I was very aware of how many living hours I had dedicated to fitting in perfectly.

Nathan took a pause before shifting his body to a more comfortable standing position.

'This sounds like something you've given quite a bit of thought to. Is it something you'd like to explore in the future in a piece?'

'I'm not sure I'd be allowed to circulate freely around my friends if I did,' I said with a slight but honest chuckle.

'It wouldn't have to be about them necessarily. In fact, it would be better if it wasn't about a person. These invisible barriers meant to keep us all in our place go far beyond a person or even a place.'

Nathan made a valid point, but I also knew while I was given laissez-passer to the upper echelon ambience, it was a right that could be revoked at any moment. Not to mention, high society had a penchant for protecting their own once under attack, even if moments before, they had fought over some other topic. For a group of people who shunned working-class practices, they sure knew how to unionise against any outside threat.

I formed my next words with some care so as to not seem to aggressively oppose my manager.

'You'd think so, but I've never seen it as loudly expressed as it is in Knightsbridge. It's usual for it to never really be said, but everyone seems to know their exact place. Everyone's always preoccupied with ensuring that their only mobility is ever upwards.'

'How do people even have the time to worry about such things when we have bills to pay?'

It was a very valid point, and perhaps if I hadn't met the people who were now my closest friends, I, too, would think like him. However, I was all too aware that most of them did not have to worry about such trivial things. I was convinced some of them had no idea that bills existed at all outside of shopping. Then, an idea came into my mind: something that could tie all of that together.

'Depending on how far you're willing to go, it's more like who will pay the bills rather than how.' I could feel the invisible venom dripping from my mouth as I let out a breadcrumb of a quote intended to dial back Nathan into a mental corner.

'Spicy! I guess it's all about finding the right partner,' Nathan retorted.

'No matter whose husband that is.' It was mean, but I needed to shift attention.

'I guess someone's bad luck is someone else's good luck.'

That was a good point. In many ways, I was tempted to feel that Lord Thurrington had owed loyalty to Florence, but they had already split many years ago. In that time, her business had flourished, and she had proven herself more than capable of managing both her personal and professional life without him weighing her down. While Celine considered bagging him a win, it was far too early to tell what long-term consequences there would be for her, but we already knew Florence's trajectory was steadily holding at the top of the pyramid.

'There are many people who seem like your next-door neighbour, but in reality, their designer shades hide a lot of secrets. It should make sense; there is no math equation that can explain how a 50k a year salary buys Chanel.'

It was an observation that I had made multiple times, particularly since I lived just on the edge of the capital of glamour. Far too many of my bus companions were indiscriminately wearing items that would make more sense on an executive, and yet they could not even afford an underground fare.

'Funny you should say that. I always ask Celine how the hell she's always looking so designer! I make more than double what she does, and I can barely buy new shirts after the bank's taken my soul to pay off the monthly mortgage fee.' Nathan's segue was unexpected, almost as if he had read my mind.

I nervously laughed and felt my nose flare up with itchiness. There was not much I could do at that point to hide the fact that every symptom of discomfort was stamped across my face. The crowning jewel of which was the burning sensation that clearly signified a wave of redness coming up from the inner layers of skin to rouge my cheeks with embarrassment.

'You know something about Celine! Oh my gosh, and you've been hiding it from me. Spill the beans.'

'I don't think it's my place. Besides, I'm not even sure what it all means.'

'This sounds like the type of thing that I definitely need to hear immediately. I love a good office conspiracy theory.'

I knew that there was no way I could convince him to let it go at that point. Like a true journalist, he was going to continue digging, and all I could think of was Bex telling me how it could be my downfall.

'I went to her flat right off of Sloane Street for drinks, but it turns out while it was a beautiful place, it was definitely not her place.'

'You're kidding me. Celine lives on Sloane Street? Is it her parents' place?'

'I reckon it's a different sort of daddy.'

It felt dirty even uttering those words out loud, but I could see Nathan's face contorting in numerous ways, showcasing a clear interest.

'Go on. You can't leave it there.'

'I couldn't help but read the mail. It was just sitting there on the counter, calling my name. It was addressed to someone very close to home.'

'I'm on the edge of my seat. Tell me already!'

'It was Lord Thurrington's place; she lives there. I'm not sure he does, but she definitely stays permanently.'

'This is outrageous. You mean to tell me that she's working directly for Florence while going home to her archnemesis? What if she's telling him all her secrets?'

Something in me said she probably was. The arrangement wasn't just about sex.

'Do we tell Florence?'

'Not yet. We need to know everything before we do. This is as salacious as it is an opportunity—for both of us. You see, we can be the ones that unmask Florence's biggest threat. Speak to no one about this, but report back to me immediately after you know more.'

'I think Celine isn't afraid of speaking to me; she's trying to bring me into her world.'

'And into her world, you will go. Observe everything and do not let her know anyone else is aware. This is my—I mean our golden chance to move up a floor here.'

It was obvious what needed to happen next. I had to take Celine into a place of comfort where she could openly share her exploits. Perhaps it wasn't my preferred outcome, but the course had been set, and it was too late to worry about it now.

CHAPTER THIRTEEN

A fleshy trade-off

The anticipation for today had been brewing all week. I mustered the courage to invite Celine out for brunch over the weekend. Celine had chosen a Moroccan restaurant off Brompton Road that was dimly lit with demure satin panels behind tables as the decoration. I had walked past it many times but never sat for a meal before. The setting was not only apt for the conversation, but it was intimate enough to seem like you had walked into someone's boudoir.

I walked in and parked my umbrella at a stand by the door. My beige trench coat dripped with hints of the rain and wind that had cut through me as I walked from the bus stop to the restaurant. My top layer of clothing was quickly removed as rows of perfectly dry local influencers judged me with their eyes. Nobody who was dropped off ever arrived that wet anywhere.

With the drenched weather, I had opted for wellies that would allow me to comfortably walk on the soaked pavement without worrying that my nerves would send me crashing down. My eyes searched for Celine as I continued to walk into the increasingly darker ambience of the cave-like restaurant.

I reached the most secluded back area, where Celine looked relaxed in tight gym clothes with a significant designer label stamped across bright Lycra and fresh makeup. It was as if I was the only person in town concerned with the rain. The only hint of winter in her ensemble was a neatly folded sheepskin and fur-trimmed maxi coat placed next to a Hermès Toile Herbag in a deep magenta. We sat in the very last enclave, an area reserved as per the thin red ropes and signage around it. The sofa-style seating was against the white painting wall with colourful leather cushions offering our back a comfortable relief.

At a distance, a stranger would have probably wondered if I was Celine's assistant. I had stumbled in wearing a thick red knit jumper that I had inherited from my mom's 90s closet with some relaxed jeans tucked into my plastic boots. At first sight, we looked like we lived in different eras, maybe even different planets.

We exchanged the expected greetings as I shuffled nervously in my seat while going through the menu. I was so conscious of my nervousness that I kept staring at my hands holding the iPad containing the food selection. I ordered within a few minutes of arrival as I couldn't maintain the small talk for much longer.

'Paze, you seem a little off. Everything okay, love?'

'Look, Celine, there's no easy way to say this, so I'm going to get straight to the point. I know there's something between you and Lord Thurrington.'

I felt a slight relief at blurting out the phrase but remained tense at the potential response. In contrast, Celine continued serving herself olive tapenade on bread as if the comment had been the most trivial possible.

'And what is it that you think is going on?'

'I'm not entirely clear on the details, but I do know that you're close, and I don't want to get caught in something that may jeopardise my career by association.'

That wasn't completely the truth, but it was also not a lie. I was afraid, but I also had ulterior motives to find out more since I had involved Nathan. I would still try my best to tread the line of not deceiving anyone in the process.

'So you do know, or you don't?'

'I know you live at this place, that he's bought you a lot of things, but he's not officially with you, so I'm worried.'

As the words floated in the air, I reflected on how strange a way it was to put that two people may co-habituate, given their relationship was the exact opposite of public.

'It's not what you think,' Celine said as she briefly looked up to signal to the waiters as they brought over our cold appetisers and drinks.

'How is it not?'

'I'm not sleeping with him if that's what you want to know.'

'That's reassuring, but it's not the only thing I'm worried about. What is the arrangement between you two?'

'All I do is find him girls. What they do next is up to them. In return, I'm taken care of with all my needs met, but I don't need to do anything or anyone else.'

Those were not at all the words I expected to hear next from Celine. I tried to keep my hands rested under the table to conceal their movements.

'So you're a pimp?'

Celine laughed loudly as her entire face split wide with a smile, as though she couldn't believe the ridiculousness of my accusation. I cowered my posture in embarrassment as I looked around to ensure nobody could hear us. In the meantime, the waiters arrived with a sprawl of Middle Eastern mezze for us to feast on.

In between polite expressions of gratitude to the staff around us, Celine cheekily winked at the tall and handsome waiter with a gleaming smile. Contrary to anyone else in that position, she had not become at all flustered with the conversation.

'It's not like—I don't take a cut of what they get. All I do is match up girls who are willing to meet a rich, old man with an adequate sponsor. He and his friends are lonely; they want company, and the girls want things they can't afford.'

She noticed I hadn't yet served myself any of the food in the small individual clay dishes, so she proceeded to fill my plate with hummus and *kibbeh* as if we were having another casual lunch between colleagues.

Unable to contain myself, I continued.

'Isn't that what a madam does? This is so messed up.'

My frown must have been obvious since Celine turned her body to me and touched my forearm with her manicured hand in deep pink lacquer.

'How so, babe? Both parties are consenting adults who know exactly what kind of a situation this is. Plus, both sides need privacy to ensure they can carry on living as civil society expects them to live.'

'I fail to see how this is correct. Is it even legal?'

'I don't see how it could be anything but legal. I haven't seen money exchanging hands, but I have seen a lot of plane tickets, yachts, handbags, and smiling faces. Call it a trade-off, a fleshy trade-off.'

It was so out of my comfort zone that I found my brain reminding me to take a bite from one of the meat and bulgur wheat-fried delicacies in front of me. Putting aside my good manners, I spoke with half of my mouth still full.

'I'm in shock.'

I tried to gulp down some water to make up for the fact that this was being so casually discussed. It was by no means a new concept, nor one that I hadn't seen time and time again in tabloids. It was just odd to see how truly close it could be to you.

'Don't be. In the end, everyone is just getting what they want. The number of girls around Knightsbridge who look for my help know I can get them what they want, and I'm usually open to helping since I know I can come to them later whenever they can return the favour.'

I will admit that part intrigued me. Who else could be in her books?

'What kind of girls?'

'The types we always see around Knightsbridge, you know which ones. Walking up and down in their best clothes for no apparent reason. All the best bags, but nobody knows where they got them from; it's so obvious.'

In all honesty, it was, but at the same time, I was still curious to hear how it had gone from girls finding convenient dates to an actual formal arrangement.

Celine opened her phone and started scrolling through her other account on Instagram, one that I had no idea existed. As she scrolled, a woman with her face partially turned away, showcasing her impeccably toned abs, appeared with her arm perched around Celine at a turquoise-coloured beach. I blinked twice and found myself still staring at a photo of a grinning Sara Gram right next to Celine in a lineup of twenty-something-year-old girls in minuscule bikinis, presumably at some benefactor's expense.

'You're starting to sound like the mafia. This is scary.'

Everything I said bounced right off Celine, who seemed flattered at my comparison. I started to envy the level of self-assurance required to deflect criticism so seamlessly.

'Come on, Paze, don't be such a prude. Not everyone can be as clever as you, as rich as Allegra, or as content with life as Nathan. For the rest of us, we need to fend for ourselves, and I'll be damned if someone will take me for what I've got.'

'Aren't you scared that this is a road of no return?'

She lifted the thick, cream napkin that had been resting on her thighs to clear the nearly invisible smudging of her matte, nude-coloured lipstick. After a short pause to admire her reflection in a silver mirror suspended against the tapered fabric covering the walls, she responded.

'I'm scared to end up with nothing. I'm scared of spending years working on my feet and not having a place to live at the end of it all. I want to have what everyone else has, and I'm not going to be shamed for it. Besides, there's a position for me opening up in his art business. There's a legitimate job at the end of the tunnel.'

'Still, you're getting something out of this, I assume. Won't that land you in hot waters with someone? With Florence?'

'Yes, it's a calculated risk. I get to live the life I dreamed of, and I have one of the most powerful men in town at my behest. He needs me, and I know exactly how to make that work to my convenience.'

Admittedly, I had always associated this type of venture with a simple materialistic transaction. In my imagination, there wasn't an attractive young woman who ran any such scheme. This was much less possible to me without a clear monetary value. Before I could carry on processing, she continued.

'The girls entertain his guests, so they get distracted and invest in the business. He knows everything they do and like, which makes them more agreeable to his sales terms if you get the gist.'

Had she just confessed to being part of a sex blackmail scheme? I was honestly too afraid to ask more at that point. I had no interest in getting pulled into the logistics of it, particularly when everyone involved seemed far too affluent to withstand someone knowing too much.

'How far will you go with this madness?'

'As far as I need. You don't understand, do you? Men like him have always been on top of everything, but I have him on his knees. I have run his entire life, and I truly enjoy that.'

With fear clearly stamped on my face, I lowered my tone and asked her the most sincere question I could muster.

'Why did you tell me the truth?'

'You're not going to tell anyone; you're harmless. I can see it.'

Was I? A feeling of disgust came over my stomach like a sucker punch. I felt the food I had at the start of the meal rise up my throat. *Calm down, or she'll think you're even weaker than she already does.*

Noticing my nervousness, she moved her body closer to mine and tilted her head sideways as if she was trying to showcase that she wasn't the foe I had suggested.

'You're kind, and you always make me feel like I've got a friend. I trust you, and I have so much more respect for you now that you actually had the guts to confront me,' she said with a mild smile, her tongue against her teeth as her dimples showed.

There was something about her that was inviting, calming even. I felt more at ease knowing that she hadn't told me out of pity for my lack of potential for harm. She probably did view me as a friend, I convinced myself. People like Nathan had always talked at her, not to her. I felt a little guilty for viewing her solely as a gateway to Florence when she had been open with me.

'I don't know how to feel about this. I need some time to digest it all.'

'Of course you do, I don't blame you. How about we close it all off with some nice mint tea and baklava?'

'Kind of sounds like just what I need right now.'

I wasn't sure how we got there. I had come into the conversation convinced that I would leave victorious, but instead, I felt less sure than I had going into it. I didn't agree with the situation, of course. But could I really blame Celine? Surely not. She was very aware of her actions. She also had her reasons, only a few of which were discussed that evening. I couldn't let a sense of moral superiority get the best of me.

Sensing how tense the conversation with Celine was likely to be, I had already made plans to meet Bex after I finished. On my way, I picked up all the things that would soothe my mood later: a bottle of moderately good wine and some chocolate-coated marshmallows. There wasn't a possibility to process all the new information by myself, and I felt there was a lesser chance of information leakage with him, which was ironic considering we had only recently met.

Upon arriving at his, we immediately sunk into his inviting dark brown leather sofa. After pouring both of us glasses of wine, I repeated to him all that I heard, and his face mirrored the shock that was probably apparent on mine earlier in the day.

'Are you going to tell someone this?'

'Who can I tell? What can I tell? It's very surreal.'

'You should tell Nathan; he can get it to Florence's ear. This is quite serious. Besides, if it gets to her that you knew and said nothing, this could cost you your job. She could have you blacklisted from the industry.'

'Alright, alright—you've managed to catastrophise more than me.'

'True, but I'm not always wrong. You should listen to this one; it's not only awful on its own, but this will twist against you.'

Bex was right; I knew that. Regardless, it wasn't going to be easy. In the world of journalism, information is currency, and timing is everything. I had valuable information that involved generally well-known figures of society but also affected the very people between myself and a paycheque. I also had no other contacts in the industry yet, so one wrong move could be the end of a career that had only started to crawl.

He continued, 'One thing that I found interesting was this art business that Lord Thurrington seems to have. I thought he was just in the media sphere. He's tried to buy us out so many times that I thought that it was all he cared about.'

After he had mentioned it, I started to think how it was actually quite confusing. I had meticulously read through the biographies of the Sizzle co-founders before and had never heard of it. There wasn't much information on any ventures outside of the media, although art was the refuge of anyone rich enough to buy it.

'I guess I need to dig into that bit. It does sound odd that Celine is sticking around if she genuinely could just have a job elsewhere. Do you think she's at Sizzle deliberately?'

Bex took a thoughtful sip of wine before responding.

'As a journalist, that's where I'd start to dig. Everything else is scandalous, but this is where it could be criminal.'

CHAPTER FOURTEEN

What's a story worth?

The unsettling feeling of knowing something explosive but also, not having any idea who would safely keep that information had plagued me for two weeks. I had the growing sensation that I was nearer than ever to coming across the story that would allow me to reach my true potential. At the same time, I never could have imagined the adrenaline involved in the stages before all the elements had neatly aligned.

After distracting myself for too long between mundane work tasks and date nights with Bex, I decided it was time to confront the truth. I arrived at work in a jumpy state, fearing that it was clear to anyone on my path that I hadn't slept well in days. Between the futile effort to cover dark circles with the wrong shade of concealer and my clumsiness in carrying an overflowing mug to my workstation, I created a backstory for my fellow content team colleagues. In case I was asked, I would be recovering from a bug. Sadly, the only infirmity that I suffered from was obsessive overthinking.

After I dropped off my latest jumbo Fendi bag, courtesy of a recent visit to my favourite vintage shop in Covent Garden, I hurried to the toilets at the edge of the office floor. I locked myself inside before taking a deep look at myself in the mirror. The tips of my hair escaped from the top of a clip that was placed on the highest point of my head. The signs of an upcoming season change were clearly reflected by how the summer blonde shades had darkened in hues. The monochromatic striped top I had chosen, in combination with a red lip stain and a mid-raise corduroy slack, gave me the confidence boost I needed. Inside, I could feel a stomach burn brewing, but at least I looked the part of a curious journalist.

It was too risky to discuss my intentions at the office, so I whisked Nathan away under the false pretence of buying him lunch, to which he obliged without suspicion. I figured we could walk over to the British Museum and sit in one of the touristy coffee shops nearby, free of any real Londoners whose precious ears might've recognised the names discussed.

We walked out at noon and found a coffee shop with a traditional green canopy at the door and a speck of resilient sun in the cooler months. I sat facing Nathan directly and started the inevitable conversation once he took his first stab at his rocket salad.

'Lord Thurrington isn't just an older man with a young appetite. He's running an entire operation of questionable activities.' The words came out of my mouth, but my body remained numb with anxiety.

'Yes, but this is by no means something he invented, nor is it a new gig. Why do you care so much?'

Fair point. A good chunk of the upper-class men of his background could fall into either of those categories. This felt personal though, too close for us to ignore as a distant concept.

'I confronted Celine recently. She confessed that she's his… arranger.'

'Celine's a pimp?'

Nathan enunciated the last part of the sentence slowly as if trying to convince himself that it couldn't possibly be true.

'One could call it that. Either way, it's really suspect that she's Florence's office manager. He seems to have promised her a position in his business, so this could be much more than a sex thing.'

Nathan's hands moved wildly, giving away his growing nervousness. 'Honestly, I did not expect that. What do you reckon we do with that information?'

I reluctantly replied, 'We are going to Florence. She has to know.'

'And what exactly do you expect will happen? She'll give you a seat next to hers and give you the dream job? Forget about it.'

'No, but if it can help her keep her enemies far away, then I think I need to do it. I work for her, after all.'

Nathan remained silent.

'I suppose if we do nothing, we are complicit. Dammit, Paze, with all your poking around, you left us exposed without much of a choice.'

I silently agreed with a solemn head nod. Nathan jolted up from his seat, clearing up the disposables around him. He paced for a few seconds with his arms on his waist before announcing that we were heading upstairs together to break the news to our most senior boss as soon as we got back into the Sizzle offices. He continued to talk about the past gossip relating to Florence's divorce as my attention drifted to the incoming crowds around us. Mentally judging the ill-fated fashion choices of tourists helped keep my mind from conjuring more anxiety than was necessary at that moment.

Nathan led us straight through the main entrance and towards the lift that would take us into Florence's inner sanctum. The doors to the penthouse floor opened up, and I suddenly found myself hesitating to move towards the door of the shaft. It was one thing to have bravado in front of Nathan, my new co-conspirator, but it was a completely different ball game to take this directly to the woman herself.

The open-plan floor seemed to go on infinitely without interruption. There was so much emptiness that it was almost unsettling. My stomach growled fiercely as I tried to adjust my nerves in this never-ending march to the end of the room.

There she was, dressed in a vibrant red pants suit with a cream-coloured turtleneck underneath. Her ear-length platinum blonde hair was flowy, with enough thickness for her to have been cast as a model in the 90s. Florence's deep blue eyes stared at me from behind a large mahogany desk. She examined my movements, surely already deciding whether I could be trusted.

As soon as we reached the desk, she stood abruptly and offered a firm handshake as a welcoming gesture. There was an intimidating aura about her; this was by no means a meek woman.

'Florence, nice to meet you. Paisley, I believe, right? Please do sit, both of you.'

She knew my name? It was strange to think she was aware of my existence. Nathan must have messaged her while we were walking and I was too distracted with the herd of bum bag wearers.

Nathan offered a nervous smile as we both sat in matching chairs that reminded me of a Church confession booth.

'Paisley Taylor-Jones is one of our rising stars at Sizzle; she's an innately curious person.'

'A great quality for a journalist,' Florence replied gracefully.

'I must agree that, typically, that would be the case. However, she's stumbled across a story—or indeed, a situation—that's rather sensitive in nature.'

Her body language shifted in her seat, clearly curious as to what could possibly warrant a meeting with two staffers who weren't part of her directorship. Nathan looked at me, granting permission for me to pitch my story.

'It happens that I have come across a member of London's elite in continuously compromising situations involving an endless supply of young women being provided for gratification for himself and his friends by a strategically placed arranger. There seems to be some sort of secretive business behind it, but it's unclear how it all ties together as of yet.'

Florence jumped in, 'Not to cut you off, but these scandals are a dime a dozen nowadays. Is there any differentiator in the story?'

Nathan cued for me to jump in next with a direct stare. 'Unfortunately, yes. He's your ex-husband.'

'I'm not incredibly surprised. Some of these allegations I made myself as part of my divorce proceedings.'

I licked my lips for moisture before continuing. 'Were you aware that Celine is the arranger?'

Her eyes popped out of her head at hearing this, clearly for the first time. 'As in Celine Moulin, who has keys to my house, Celine?'

I nodded, careful not to showcase my satisfaction at being the first one to break the news to Florence. It shouldn't have even crossed my mind, but ultimately, I was there giving her the information that all the rest of the staff had failed to acquire. In my first few months on the job, I was already making moves to protect her.

'This is ludicrous. It can't be.'

I slowly pulled out the printed version of the picture I had taken from the club night, aware that I may need to resort to evidence. I passed it to Florence, who moved it close to her eyes, as if to be completely certain that what I said was true.

'Following this slightly public display, I made sure to confront her. After all, this could have been a casual encounter. However, it has come to my attention that he's promised her a position in a new art business which heavily relies on young girls obtaining intel on potential investors by unscrupulous means.'

After another long pause, Florence turned her body towards the window with her arms crossed at the chest. No longer facing me, she started to speak again.

'Write the story. It needs to be told. But I don't want it to be solely focused on Lord Thurrington. It would be a breach of our peace terms to attack him directly. This will be a story about London's elite and what they're willing to do to get where they want to.'

Nathan suddenly decided he would contribute his own ideas.

'How about if this becomes a series? A sort of Elitegate, where each article gets increasingly more serious and tangles him into a web where it's eventually inevitable that his name gets thrown in.'

Florence tilted her head slightly to the side as if she was imagining the words Nathan had said sprawling across headlines.

'I like that. We could start exploring the triviality with which very serious things are treated on the way to the top. Make it philosophical; let's explore the contrasts between our readers and them. With each part, we explore more of how their way of life affects us all. I want our audience to find themselves discussing at dinner parties whether these people have a conscience at all.'

I interjected, 'I never intended to antagonise people. I understand the focus can't be on the Lord himself, but we could perhaps open the scope further. We could showcase both the glamour and dirty, leaving it to the reader to decide if it's worth it.'

Florence turned around and moved closer to me again. As a woman with significant experience, she felt no rush to speak or make decisions, which made everything she uttered more significant.

'Who do you write for, Paisley?' A simple question at the surface but riddled with much meaning; I was unprepared to answer it.

'For the readers of Sizzle.'

She maintained firm, stern eye contact with me while speaking.

'That is a rookie mistake in many ways. When we write something, we always write first for ourselves. A meaningful story is something we can no longer afford to keep inside of us. It needs to come out, even if it will never be seen by another set of eyes.'

'I don't understand. Isn't the purpose always to garner the most readers?'

'Not at all. This isn't Instagram. We aren't here merely for clicks. Everything, no matter how shallow it may look at a distance, must serve a purpose. I don't include social columns in my publications because I'm interested in the pageantry. It's there to remind all of us that they exist, whether we think of them or not.'

There was so much depth to what she was saying that it was challenging to find fitting words to continue the conversation.

'So, you want me to remind people that these issues exist even if we don't see them?'

'Yes, I do. There are multiple worlds existing all at the same time and colliding all the time, and yet none of them seem to truly see the existence of the other. This story must be told because you felt the need to tell me about it; it bothered you. So, it should bother others as well.'

As if on cue, Florence's phone rang, pulling her attention away from us and onto the device now in her hand. Before going back to her desk, she held up her phone, about to answer, and said, 'Do it, get started. Tell no one.'

Both Nathan and I exchanged looks, understanding that our stay in her presence had expired. We walked in silence, side by side, until we reached the lift that would descend us once again to the level of our peers, but now with the added weight of responsibility suffocating us on the way down. Once the doors shut behind us, Nathan started to speak in a quiet tone, instinctively looking over his shoulder.

'You realise that exposing high society people may cascade into the circle you keep as company. People could come after you.'

It was a point I hadn't thought about thoroughly. Thus far, I hadn't thought of anyone involved as living, breathing humans but as parts of a story.

'I'm still in shock. I have no idea where to even start.'

'What's a breakthrough story worth to you, Paze? Are you ready for the aftermath?'

It would be everything I ever wanted for years. A breakthrough story at Sizzle with the potential to give me a break in my career. I had always assumed the content would be distant, a discovery of some sort where the subject wasn't known to me prior to an investigation. As fate would have it, the first meaningful piece would involve a complex jigsaw of people I knew, heard of, worked with, and most likely would utterly despise me by the end. Failing to perform would destroy any chance of future ascension inside Sizzle.

I was not even slightly ready for that.

CHAPTER FIFTEEN
Pizza and Boys

The best day of my professional career as a journalist thus far also marked the start of my greatest anxiety crisis. After the bombastic interaction with Florence and the assignment that ensued, I spent the rest of the workday in a zombified state between a hot desk and the bathroom. My smart watch notified me of an irregular increase in heart rate as I felt the warmth of elevated preoccupation dominate the rest of the evening.

I was far from confident in my ability to deliver an unbiased piece that would potentially evoke the wrath of many people around me. This wasn't any social column, though; this would be a main feature in both print and digital, co-signed by Nathan. That detail was confirmed in an email to him a few minutes after we arrived back in our section of the office.

Nathan had since reminded me several times that both of our reputations were on the line. There was no room for error whatsoever, and yet I had spent the last days of the week in a haze of stress-induced sleep deprivation. The undereye bags that my colleagues in the news section carried had finally made their way to my face. Had my career been a marriage, this would have been us officially departing the honeymoon stage.

I entered the research phase with near obsession. Hours became days, and days became the fastest two weeks of my life, filled with obsessive mapping out of potential parties to my story. My main job as a social columnist hadn't been put on hold in the meantime, either. I had covered a few restaurant and gallery openings to fill in the voids between returning to my storyboard. Ironically, I had started to enjoy the less emotionally consuming task of attending social events. In fact, they had become a refuge from the much darker themes in *Elitegate Project*.

One of the few things that kept my mind off the task was speaking to Bex. We had gone from casual texts to an everyday situation and spent as much of our free time together as possible. I had started to get accustomed to his warmth as an antithesis to the inevitable coldness I was forced to present at work in order to maintain the secrecy required for the main story.

I had decided I couldn't tell any of my friends so as to not compromise them in the process. As a result, I used work as an excuse far too frequently as to why I started to miss out on small group encounters where the truth about my state could be potentially elicited. Instead, I had opted for public encounters at social events I was covering, where fewer opportunities would arise for a cornering.

Unfortunately, I could only keep it up for so long. I had a notification from the group, and I couldn't hide from them forever.

> Allegra
>
> Pizzeria tonight for dinner? I've booked a table for six.

She didn't need to specify the place. Allegra only ever ate pizza at Knightsbridge's most well-known spot. Nestled in a basement in one of the liveliest streets in the area, it had been the place of choice for passing by Hollywood stars and oligarchs for over four decades. Oddly, it had never been known to anyone who didn't need to know and existed quietly in plain sight with a small sign with a graphic of a tomato on the door leading the way. Conveniently, the live music was always too loud to have any meaningful conversation.

> Me
>
> Can I bring Bex?

I thought the least I could do was bring some back to get me out of any sticky corner.

> Allegra
>
> I'm counting on it.

I messaged Bex to make sure he could make it, with a little side of drama about needing support. He quickly replied that he'd pass by in an Uber by eight. The relief of not having to do this alone was noticeable. There was a growing sense of reliability in me that he understood the way my social life operated without judgment.

The rest of the day was spent in desktop research that didn't seem to inch me any closer to the truth needed for my article. I had spent hours looking for a vestige of an art company that would tie to Lord Thurrington, but his financial discretion was far too elaborate for me to uncover online. It was becoming painstakingly clear that the information flow would be in-person, covertly. My chest tensed at the thought of it, but luckily, it was nearing time to get ready for dinner.

Knowing that the clientele of the place of choice tonight was a combination of models, visiting royalty, celebrities, sex professionals, London's elite, workers from nearby retail stores, and friendly regulars that propped around the bar staff, it was more important than ever to dress adequately so as to not be misidentified. There wasn't a place that better defined all that happened in Knightsbridge, where several different layers of people seemed to coexist in such close proximity. I opted for high-waisted jeans, a second-skin white turtleneck, and a black vest top. My signal was, "I'm here for the food and for the company."

The Uber drive over was only a few short minutes, but Bex and I still had the chance to quietly enjoy each other's company.

'I've never seen you this nervous to meet your friends.'

'I've never had to hide something this significant from them. Besides, we don't know yet how far Lord T's tentacles reach.'

Pulling me closer to rest my head on his chest, Bex spoke with a low voice. 'I'm sure you will make the right decisions when you need to. I believe in you.'

I closed my eyes momentarily and breathed in deeply. There was so much on the line with this opportunity, yet all the feelings of inadequacy that had plagued me in my social life now spilt into my professional one. However, at least I would try to have some fun before the responsibility became too heavy to bear.

As soon as we stepped onto the cobbled pavement, the lively ambience of Beauchamp Place lifted my mood. The street may have been small, but it was filled with social venues of the most different kinds, from an upscale restaurant that was the favourite spot of Princess Di to an unmarked door that locals all understood to operate as the local brothel. Our destination was underneath a discreet staircase that emerged between two shops. The only giveaway that it was indeed a place worth visiting was a robust security guard at the top of the stairs that ensured only those deemed worthy would make their way down.

When we walked in, Allegra had already arrived and taken her seat at a table near the small stage up front. The live music hadn't started, but a DJ played radio hits while people received buckets full of chilled champagne on the cramped tables. She was wearing a bronze halter dress that showed off her freckled shoulders and allowed her hair to settle neatly at her side. Most surprisingly, right next to her was Georgie. As I continued to walk down the final steps, I noticed how she seemed at ease talking to him. It made me smile deeply as I made my way towards her.

Our slow-paced walk finally reached the table as both Allegra and Georgie stood politely to greet us.

'I miss you so much, Paze. Can you not be such a seriously committed professional, please?' Allegra said while giving me a tight hug. I felt those words ring true in more ways than she could ever imagine.

'I miss you too! It's nice to see both of you again.' I said the last part with a small wink to my friend.

Just as the guys finished their firm handshake, Mansour emerged from the staircase and started navigating the tightly set tables. He waved at us, but I noticed he suddenly changed his expression and turned his head vigorously to avoid eye contact with someone. I scanned the room and found a profile that looked suspiciously like Ameerah's sat by on one of the back, more dimly-lit, tables. I didn't stare enough to identify her company, but I was sure Mansour would spend the next hours trying to figure it out.

For the time being, my attention turned to the diverse menu of sexually suggestive titled drinks. There was never a better way to forget a long week than with a round of Sex on the Beach shots. The whole crew cheered on my naughty selection, and spirits remained high as the blasting Hozier hit drifted through the speakers.

Mila appeared around the corner from the same portal we had come through earlier. She was the last one to come in and sat next to me in the empty space, removing her black leather trench coat to reveal a mid-thigh leather cut-out dress that showed off her arms. I always wondered if she had a second life as a late-night techno dominatrix since most of her casual eveningwear was leather, latex, or both.

'You're lucky you met someone who seems nice,' Mila whispered to me while looking at Bex. We hadn't spent much time together with friends yet, but it hadn't stopped me from dropping updates on how things were going.

'Thanks! I didn't really see it coming, but I'm liking how we're getting closer.'

'You know, my dad called me last week and said he didn't send me to university so I'd remain single. He threatened to cut me off if I don't take things seriously.'

I gasped at the surprising revelation. Mila didn't have a job or intentions of getting one, but that never seemed to preoccupy her before. Her parents had expected she would eventually be an eligible heir of similar lineage in London. She had previously told me that this had been openly discussed in her household, as had warnings to maintain an intact reputation.

'They have slightly antiquated views of womanhood and, most importantly, independence. Maybe I need a change of plans.'

'What do you have in mind?'

'Remember how Ava moved to Miami? I spoke to her at Allegra's party about her concierge business. Her customers are mostly Russian and Arabic-speaking. I could go work with her.'

Mila had never seen the need to rush into a relationship, and I always liked that about her. The idea of her moving away for work seemed farfetched, though, particularly considering the potential reality of her parents not backing her financially. There wasn't a salary substantial enough to sustain her level of couture addiction.

The restaurant around us became increasingly busy, mostly with seasonal visitors from overseas. The live band started promptly at nine with a loud rendition of Gypsy Kings that seamlessly switched into Arabic pop. None of us knew what the lyrics meant, but we could all sing along somehow, used to the melodic intonations that we'd heard so many times. Everyone got to dance in their seats, imitating the much more suave table neighbours who clapped to the melody while moving their hips like a belly dancer.

Mansour wasn't as amused at the lacklustre performance of his native rhythms.

'And on that note, I'm off to the bathroom.'

Pleased with our enthusiasm, a neighbouring table sent us gratification in the form of a lineup of shots. We smiled back at them as Allegra reciprocated by offering them a bottle of bubbly that included a sparkler on top to signal its elevated cost. Despite my initial doubts, the night had started to remind me of the many times we went out to have fun without much care for what was to come.

After a few more minutes, Mansour appeared at the table and huddled everyone closer to speak to all of us over the loud music.

'I was just in the bathroom minding my own business, and I overheard the funniest gossip.'

We all signalled for him to continue telling us about his latest discovery.

'Some guys in the men's bathroom dabbling into some sink talc, if you get the gist.'

Georgie laughed excessively loudly as he interrupted. 'I've never heard it described so delicately.'

Rolling his eyes at the interjection but equally enjoying the undivided attention, he continued.

'I'm a gentleman, and we are amongst ladies. Anyways, they were bragging about how this girl, Cece or something, always comes through with bringing over the hottest new girls to their table. There's not much they aren't willing to do for a flyout and yacht picture.'

'And what's new...' Allegra, keen to hear more, shouted across from her side of the table.

'So, one of them says, she hooked me up with Sara Gram. You know, the one with the super tight abs, cross-fit chick with the perfect tan and the tightest dress.'

Mila looked up from cutting a slice of pizza to give her two cents.

'Seems everyone's talking about her nowadays.'

'Oh, it doesn't end there. He says he flew her out twice already, but she wanted a credit card and for rent to be taken care of. She's not in it for a free tip.'

Mansour reached out for a scoop of the shared tiramisu dish on the table. Before biting in, he looked around to ensure he had everyone's attention as he spoke.

'So, she's officially looking for a full-time sponsor now?'

Georgie responded to Mansour, who still stood above us. 'She tried that on me as well. Said she wanted to be taken care of and get off the market. I don't pay to get attention, so it never enticed me.'

Allegra gawked at Georgie with a proud smile. They may not have been seeing each other for long, but he was certainly quickly learning how to say the things that she liked to hear.

I couldn't help participating in the conversation. 'I personally hate locker room chat. I find it in poor taste when people publicly shame previous affairs.'

Bex, sensing that I might get a reaction to not condemning the table's foe, continued from my comment. 'It definitely says more about them than it says anything about her.'

Visibly annoyed at any hint of defence of Sara, Allegra sat upright before speaking. 'Whatever, it doesn't change the facts. So, she's got some pimp now called Cece? Not classy at all.'

I had almost overlooked that detail. Celine had shown me Sara's photo as one of the girls she represented in her scheme. *Could Cece be her nickname in the game? Had her notoriety become so wide that she was being mentioned casually by people?* This made my mind return back to work and the urgency of uncovering what was happening before anyone else figured it out.

I had to conduct the topic better so as not to let anyone wonder about where my loyalties stood.

'You're right, Allegra. I had hoped that the pandemic would have confined these types forever to OnlyFans so we could live in peace out here.'

I felt a little guilty as that's not what I believed at all, but I wasn't in a position to defend my ideals whilst simultaneously trying to cover up my growing interest in the subject matter. Sara was officially a person of interest in my story, so I'd need to make sure I didn't seem too keen on her to avoid suspicions.

Mansour finally sat back on his chair, but not before giving a prolonged glance over to where Ameerah was dining. The low lights made it hard to make out specific features, but I could still see her open a wide smile in our direction. Perhaps things weren't completely lost for Mansour after all.

In the meantime, the free-flowing shots kept coming to our table as Georgie and Bex tried to outdrink each other without touching the glassware with their hands. The hazy figures around the room moved faster as the copious amounts of alcohol we were consuming affected our vision. The rest of us laughed hysterically at their antics while Mansour, the only non-drinker of our group, threatened to cut off our supply for our own reputation's sake.

When the lights went on at 1AM, signalling for us to leave, it felt like a personal attack on our fun. We reluctantly left the building along with other revellers who were all waiting on the side of the curb for a ride to the next hotspot.

The air felt intrudingly cold as we stood outside, all huddled together. One by one, our group dispersed as drivers began to arrive to whisk everyone away to their final destinations for the evening. I stood tall as Bex leaned against a storefront, holding me close with hands around my waist. He whispered discreetly into my ear, causing the skin around my neck to tingle.

'Come home with me.'

I bit my lip, even though he couldn't see it from where he stood behind me. I moved my head, signalling my approval as one of his hands let go of me to pull a phone and order a rideshare for us. My body warmed despite the cutting cold breeze.

The minutes passed slowly as a white Mercedes C-class finally approached the area we stood in. Right before we got into the car, Allegra hugged me tight.

'This was so nice! I'm so glad everything's fallen into a better place.'

I smiled and gave her a peck on the cheek. It was true, but I feared how she'd react when she found out I hadn't told her what I was working on. There were few things she hated more than surprises, but the biggest one was not knowing what her friends were up to.

When we made it into Bex's place, I collapsed into my new favourite comfort sofa. I was slightly buzzed and put some music on my phone so that the vibe from the evening wouldn't evaporate too quickly. I started arm dancing while lounging with my head on his lap, which Bex reciprocated by craning his neck down into a deep kiss. The night was just starting for us.

'Morning, beautiful.'

Those first few words made me squint while lying belly down. I slightly opened my eyes to see an already-dressed Bex by the side of his bed. His strong body was being tucked into chinos while I could still stare at his toned arms.

'Morning, hot stuff.'

'You never call me that while fully awake. I like it. Want some pancakes? I'll run out to get some.'

I communicated yes with a thumbs up and resumed cuddling the down pillow next to me. I had every intention of enjoying all the time I could in a bed that was firmly planted on the floor, unlike my own bunk concoction. After I heard the front door close, I started reassembling myself ahead of his return.

He returned just in time for me to look slightly more put together than when he left. We stood around the kitchen bar top, eating casually while sipping on much-needed strong coffees.

'So, I need your advice as a peer now. Forget the fact that we're seeing each other for a second.'

'Hard, but I'll try my best.' He smirked while cutting through a fluffy piece of berry pancake.

I held on tight to the coffee mug before dispelling what had been on my mind since the evening before. 'Based on yesterday's events, it's obvious that I needed to know more about Sara, but it was equally unlikely that she would ever trust me, given that my friendship with her greatest rival was well documented. I would need to bring in a neutral force to the table who could keep her interested but wasn't a party to the story.'

'That sounds sensible, something I'd advise my team.'

'Bex, you need to help me. Can you pose a suitor to her and see what she shares?'

'It wouldn't be ethical for me as a journalist. Plus, I've never done this honey-trapping type of sting.'

'Fine, but would you do it for me as my boyfriend?'

The words slipped out of my mind without me thinking about it. The silence in the room while I waited for a response made my heart throb, drop, and nearly stop in the millisecond intervals that dragged out infinitely.

'Am I your boyfriend?'

I tried desperately to read his face for clues. Without the ability to turn back what I said, the best I could do was make it look more deliberate than accidental. 'Yes, I think. I mean, if you'd like to be.'

'I would, I think, like to be your boyfriend, yes.' He responded, slowly breaking into a timid smile.

I looked at him possessively while taking a step closer so our hips touched.

'I'd like that too.'

'I like you. I'm not sure what I'm going to do with you and your story, but I still like you.'

My cheeks flushed into a warm sensation that made me let out a childish chuckle. 'Does that mean you'll do it?'

'Fine, but now that I'm your boyfriend, you're not going to get all jealous when I have to get close to her for this story, right?'

'No,' I said in the most unconvincing tone.

Truthfully, I was already jealous.

CHAPTER SIXTEEN

A Name or Two

It was typical for Allegra to message me at lunch for personal updates. Between our distracting group chats and the occasional private message, that was the usual expected hour that she would have concluded her morning routine at her atelier-turned-office before heading out to her social obligations. I had an unexpected text at 7:30AM with surprising content. Sat on the high stool in the kitchenette, I sipped on a morning brew in an elastic shorts pyjama ensemble while I unlocked the phone.

> Allegra
>
> Alexandra wants to meet for lunch to talk about urgent business. Any guesses?

Truth be told, she wasn't exactly close enough to Allegra for them to spend much time on a solo outing. They co-existed in the same social sphere, but their relationship was a slight rivalry if anything. Lunch was far too intimate for their lack of proximity. However, there was one factor that now connected the two: they had both entered into personal relationships with Georgie Carter.

Me

> Do you reckon it's about Georgie?

Allegra

> At this point, I'm intrigued. Keep you posted. Also, I'm having Mansour sit incognito at the table next to us so he can keep track of what's going on. I need backup.

Me

> Both of you are nuts, and I love it. Won't it look odd that he's sat so close to you alone?

Allegra

> He's roped in Loujain as a fake date. Stay tuned!

I skipped to take a shower and prepare for another day at Sizzle. It still haunted me that I was potentially throwing my new boyfriend into the realm of London's most feared seductress in order to develop a story, but it was the closest thing to a plan that I had at the moment. There was still the question of letting Nathan in on the plan, which would require me to admit how low I had sunk in the research to have decided this was the best course of action. In response to the growing stress, I quickly prepared my comfort breakfast wrap and dashed through the door.

As per the frequent updates in our group, Allegra was summoned to an unexpected meeting on neutral ground. She was due to make her way up Park Lane, turn left, and venture East towards Covent Garden. The location wouldn't be her first choice, but it served a purpose, nevertheless. There would be fewer prying eyes from potential frenemies. The choice was considered in itself; it showcased a need for discretion. Nobody but bankers and lawyers loitered in the area, and truthfully, we knew neither of those types of people.

I made sure to book myself a faux meeting during my lunch hour, which showed on my calendar as 'Content Research.' I found a discreet, private office where I could hide from my colleagues and savour the incoming live coverage on our very own clash of the social titans.

The first message to come through as I set myself up with my takeaway lunch, laptop, and chunky headphones was Mansour's selfie to reassure us that he had taken precautions. He was wearing a camel-coloured baseball cap from Loro Piana with rounded glasses that made him look like a tech investor on his way to lunch to get legal counsel about a merger. Meanwhile, his sister had a crisp suit and feline glasses on. They might've actually pulled off being the perfect spies as long as they timed their entrance perfectly to avoid a direct encounter. I questioned how he'd ensure they'd sit close enough to pry into the conversation.

Mansour

> I've already bribed the manager. I leave nothing to chance.

I covered my mouth in order to prevent a loud laugh that might have brought unwanted attention to my whereabouts. While I waited for any real action to start, I reverted back to the research I was meant to be solely focused on. Staring at the screen where I had drawn a spider web to keep track of the moving parts, I fixated my eyes on the question marks around the profile I started building on Lord Thurrington. Things weren't clear yet, but I knew he was closely connected to far too many people I knew, and that made me deeply uncomfortable.

After a few minutes of filling notes in a spider chart, the live commentary started streaming in from Mansour. Alexandra had arrived first, five minutes ahead of the scheduled time. A discreet photo taken by a Mansour as he pretended to scan a menu showed her dressed in a structured royal blue velvet pantsuit. I zoomed in to see a pin on her lapel; it was her signature accessory. The choice for that lunch was a floating crown bejewelled with stones, likely diamonds. She looked classically regal.

At the office, I waved out to colleagues as they passed by on their way to lunch. The amount of people I could see through the enclosed windows dwindled quickly while I balanced researching Lord Thurrington's old paparazzi photos with keeping an eye on my phone. A second photo came in at the precise minute the lunch was due to start, this time showcasing Allegra walking in wearing a black organza top revealing her pale, slim arms under the sheer material that tied into an oversized bow at the neck. Her shiny black slacks hugged her hips tightly; the mood of the day was clearly reserved with a hint of sensuality.

I took a bite of my light lunch as I stared at my split screen with headphones plugged in for the next part of the afternoon. The minutes seemed to drag like snails before the next updates started to roll in. In another part of town, Mansour was sending voice notes of the conversation happening at the table right next to his. I had warned him it was bordering on the illegal, but he seemed amused at the concept of being an incognito rapporteur.

Plates clacking in the background against wooden tables, silverware hitting porcelain, and every conceivable restaurant noise was even more noticeable in anticipation of that moment. Their polite introductions were as expected, albeit short-lived.

'I know you're seeing Georgie. You know we went out for a while at this point, or so I'm guessing. No hard feelings there. In fact, a part of me is relieved that he moved on with someone whose name I'm not ashamed to be associated with.'

Alexandra's raspy voice sounded low but was still clear enough for me to understand. She continued after a brief pause.

'My concern is that you may not be fully aware of the circumstances of our break up, and I believe you'd like to know, woman to woman.'

Allegra's higher pitch came through with her melodic, posh intonation. 'I'm curious, to say the least; he has told me a story or two.'

'That's precisely the problem. A story or two, a name or two.'

'You know his name is not Georgie, or George, in fact?'

I gasped on the other side of the phone. No, I did not, and most likely, neither did Allegra. It felt strange to imagine him being called anything else since we'd known him so long at that point.

'I did not. What is it then?'

'I can't be too sure. I've seen all sorts of documents when I got particularly paranoid and rifled through his night drawer on one of the few occasions he took me to his flat after a drunken night. Sometimes he's Georgie, sometimes he's Archie, and I've seen some papers under the name of Jasper. With him, it's best to believe nothing is ever true.'

I had expected that some drama could ensue, but a direct accusation of that gravity was not something I anticipated. A part of me felt bad for listening in to what was clearly meant to be a very private conversation. *Please don't stop, Mansour.*

The next voice note came through with minutes of delay; clearly, there had been something shared that wasn't meant to reach all of our ears.

'You can do as you wish, but you've been warned that he's a fraud. Keep your wallet closed; I can't dictate what you do with your legs.'

Alexandra's tone had changed to annoyed, and I could hear at the end what sounded like a chair being dragged and heels walking away at a distance. There wasn't a time I had wished more to be in a different place. I wished to comfort Allegra, of course, but also hear the complete story.

There was no clear course of action following the disclosure of the events. I thought I'd offer to meet Allegra after work and offer her a supportive listening ear. It had to have been slightly humiliating for her to hear, no matter how much we had already warned her that Georgie Carter wasn't exactly great for her personal brand.

> Allegra
>
> I need you, please come over after work for a coffee. Girls night in? Drop you off at work tomorrow morning by car.

> Me
>
> You can count on me, always!

I turned up to Allegra's house holding my trusty overnight canvas bag from my student days. In it, I had transported the same snacks that had so long given us absolute comfort in moments of despair. After no longer than five seconds at the door, Allegra's long-time housekeeper-turned-adult-nanny, Maria, opened the door. She quickly ushered me in while helping me disrobe from my thick outdoor clothes.

'Miss Allegra is very stressed. She's in the home cinema room waiting for you.'

Hearing that, I hurried my pace through the entrance lounge, went straight to the stairs, and headed down to the sprawling basement, where there was practically a second house. I walked into a graphite-coloured room with several individual loungers in black leather and headed to the front row, where Allegra was perched in a velvet pyjama ensemble with feathers on the wrists.

'Hey, I brought crisps and candy. How are you?'

I lowered to hug her while she sprawled on a seat. On top of her thigh, I could see her phone rested with the screen down.

'I'm a little confused, to be honest.'

'I heard a part of what happened; I guess there was more to it,' I said with both earnest concern for my friend and genuine curiosity about the parts of the conversation I wasn't privy to via our carefully placed spy.

'Indeed, I think Mansour got nervous at some point that she was onto him. Alexandra said that there had been a few oddities with Georgie that made her believe he was a fraudster.'

Now, sitting beside Allegra, I crossed my legs on the chair, removing my shoes in the process.

'Those are really strong accusations. What could have made her so sure of it?'

Allegra paused and looked up at the ceiling as if trying to remember the precise words from the earlier confrontation.

'She claims he would often walk out on bills that were left for her to pay—forgetfulness was often the excuse—but then, things went missing from her home in Munich. Valuable art, which was then spotted again in London.' The expression on my face must have matched the shock that swept through my body. 'I know, Paze, I'm really surprised, too. Do you think… could it be true?'

The response needed a moment to ponder. I'd been around London long enough to know that anything could be true. There had been so many discoveries in the last months alone that made me think that not much was as it seemed in that part of town.

'It could be, Allegra, but it could genuinely just be an attempt to split you two up. I mean, let's not forget she showed up to your party with Sara. How do they even know each other?'

Hearing that, Allegra flipped the hair that had been falling down her clavicle to her back and shifted in her seat.

'I almost forgot about that, good thing you brought it up. I hadn't made the connection, but now that you say it, it is suspicious.'

I was pleased I had picked the right choice of words. Ultimately, Allegra had always been one for believing nothing was a coincidence, so any chance of connecting actions would be preferred rather than leaving things down to fate.

'If Alexandra wanted to catch my attention, she has it in full. Can't you use your journalist skills to dig up what connects them?'

I smiled at my friend for acknowledging that if someone were to figure out a connection, it would certainly be me. It could've been an interesting segue into approximation to Sara, particularly since I needed a way to get closer to her for my main story.

'I may be able to help. I've got a few tricks up my sleeve.' By tricks, I meant having my boyfriend serve as bait, and it was about time to get him on the field.

CHAPTER SEVENTEEN
Enemy of My Enemy

On the first day of the operation, Bex kicked off at five o'clock in the afternoon in Harrods. If there was one thing that was certain, it was that people in search of a sponsor would find themselves amidst wealth. Their moves were formulaic yet still well thought-out. There was no place in London that attracted more deliberately intended ambition than Harrods. Then, there was the question of timing. The latter part of the afternoon and early evening saw the arrival of the well-primed crowd, who walked the hallways of the store like lions seeking prey in an open savannah.

I had spent the last week educating Bex on the intricacies of the Knightsbridge crowd's rules of civility and how he should act if he wanted to yield any meaningful approach. The vintage watch he borrowed from his stepfather's cabinet, a classic loafer, and a well-cut designer jacket from a charity shop were handpicked for the day. I even went as far as sacrificing a splash of the expensive oud perfume Mansour brought me back from his last escapade to the Middle East. Nothing says money quite like the intensity of a sophisticated oud.

Bex had protested at the enormous amount of information I drowned him in over the course of a few days. However, it was no easy task, as I had carefully learned every mannerism and etiquette rule over two decades, which he would have to replicate in a few hours.

'Do people really go through this effort? It sounds like a lot.'

'You'd be surprised, Bex. People are willing to go very far to be a part of the crowd.'

Besides that, he had to be prepared to make it all look effortless. We planned to have him randomly stumble upon Sara during her daily visit to Harrods. It would take some convincing for the interaction to go far since her sensors were heightened to spot a middle-class man who didn't match the minimum income requirement to court her.

The plan was that I would stroll around the handbag section in search of a supposed work tote from where I could distantly observe the interaction. I dressed up in the suit that Allegra had gifted me for my first day at the office and combined it with a convincing blow-dry that I invested in as a part of my covert act. At the same time, Bex would unceremoniously walk in search of a custom man pouch.

Once the culprit was spotted, he would ask in a louder than necessary decibel for an item that was clearly special order. An exotic leather, difficult to find, and obscenely expensive.

'That sounds like a good plan, except how can you guarantee she will show up at Harrods at that time?'

'You're funny! What else does she have to do except attend daily to the golden brick crowd of a sponsored life? This is her job, basically. Harrods is her office.'

'That's kind of sad. I guess it makes sense since it's happy hour.'

The comment proved Bex still had much to learn, making me laugh while patting his shoulder. 'She's not looking for a man who works till five; she's looking for one who has breakfast at five.'

His face pulled into an expression of further surprise. I could tell Bex was horrified at the fact that people lived like that, and truly, I probably would, too, if I hadn't seen the destruction it caused with my own eyes. There were several people roaming the same halls daily, exclusively looking to transact but not for clothes or bags. There were those looking to flaunt their wealth and, thus, buy admiration. There were others looking for far more tactile interactions. For the normal shopper looking to buy an item from the shop, the subtly exchanged lustful looks and smiles could be overlooked. It took a seasoned frequenter to appreciate the art of openly looking for what you want without descending into reputational decline.

The mission was a covert one, even from my closest friends. I wasn't particularly proud of how far I was willing to go to uncover the story. Till then, all people knew of my interest in Sara was as a doting friend of Allegra who was ready to go the extra mile for her best friend. There was no doubt that any information I could share with her, I would, as long as it didn't compromise my main purpose for setting this up. It was a proverbial killing of two birds with one stone.

My part was to maintain a healthy distance while observing the interaction discreetly. I could avoid being seen by sticking to the maze-like brand concessions, which included wall-facing areas where I could hide in plain sight. With that in mind, we walked in from separate sides of the ground floor, spending a carefully timed number of minutes browsing while waiting for the first sighting. I looked with interest at the latest beauty launch on the Chanel stand while remaining aware of my whereabouts.

While waiting for a sales assistant to bring over samples of the season's red lipsticks for me to try, I felt a tap on my right shoulder. I would have jumped out of tension if the conversation hadn't opened with a slight apology.

'Hey, sorry, Paze, right?'

'Yes! Ameerah, good to see you.'

'Same, for what it's worth, I did think you were nice. Mansour was the one who was kind of an ass to me.'

'Don't tell him I said this, but I do agree.'

She cracked a smile before continuing. 'It's not like we're currently in touch, so don't worry.'

'I know, he's gutted that he blew it with you.' I knew I was probably overstepping, but given that I was already on one takedown mission, I thought I could karmically compensate by trying to bring those two back on talking terms. It felt like the right thing to do.

'I'm just tired of guys like him, who think because they have the right last name, they can just judge everything about you.'

'I'm not going to try to convince you he's not judgy or snarky sometimes, but behind it all is one of the best friends I've ever had and one of the most loyal people I know.'

My comment seemed to catch her by surprise, as most likely that wasn't the person she had come to know. Unfortunately, with people like Mansour, it was so easy to just write them off without getting to know the complex person beneath the glamour.

'If you say so. He'd need to prove it to me before I could believe any of it.'

From my right peripheral, I saw Sara walk in with another similarly dressed woman. It was time to untie myself from the current conversation and officially go into stakeout mode. I decided before Ameerah showed up that I would buy an affordable item and carry the iconic green bag to give my cover more credibility on. I signalled to the well-groomed sales assistant that I wanted to pay.

'I need to run, but it was good of you to come say hi; let's do coffee or something.'

'Cool, will find you on Instagram later.'

We said goodbyes with customary air kisses, and I hastily made my way to pay for my decoy purchase. I pulled up my phone to quickly warn Bex.

>   Me
> S incoming. Bad news, there's two of them.

> Bex
> Not my idea of a threesome, but I can make it work, I think.

I felt my cheeks burn slightly as I increased my pace and raced through the corridors that led through perfumery to the central escalators, which got me to the luxury accessories hall without looking like I was following them. The escalating stress probably made me look frantic as I attempted to reach a vantage point before my carefully orchestrated encounter would take place. I finally slowed my pace when I entered the brighter lights of the handbag displays.

At an opposite door, Bex came in with a confident stride that made me smile discreetly. I maintained a distracted demeanour as if scanning shelves for bags rather than the shop floor for two incoming social climbers. Within a few more minutes, the well-groomed duo strolled in from another corner with a catwalk-like stride. They made their way around the concessions before I spotted Bex giving Sara an inviting stare, just like I had taught him to do.

He stopped at Loro Piana a few seconds after passing her and asked the sales assistant, 'By any chance, do you have the cardholder in alligator?'

I was close enough that I could hear the interaction while pretending to inspect a leather bag mounted on a nearby shelf. In her seductive, raspy voice, Sara spoke to the same employee as she was about to head towards the trays of small goods hidden under the main table. 'If you've got the Extra Bag in the off-white alligator, I'd also be interested.'

It was a challenge not to break character and laugh at the outrageous request from Sara. That bag was clearly incompatible with any sort of budget she could be on but equally difficult to get a hold of, which meant that the only purpose was a conversation starter. Everything seemed so deliberate when you knew what to look for.

Bex took the bait to start a conversation with her directly.

'That's a beautiful choice; it's one of the classiest bags a woman can have.'

'Why, thank you. It's been difficult with LP and stock levels recently. I tried to get it in Monaco a few weeks ago, and it was completely sold out,' she said, flipping her smooth hair above her left shoulder.

'You're better off heading early to Gstaad; they have the best variety this time of year. But you need to get there right before everyone else.'

The funniest part of the interaction was that, most likely, not one of us had ever been to Gstaad, but it lived in our collective consciousness of status, which is why I felt it the optimal name-drop to coach Bex on during his training.

'That's a hot take; I will keep that in mind. Are you heading out there soon?'

'Probably, I'm a last-minute kind of guy.'

Good, Bex. He had listened when we discussed the optics of planning being something that rich people simply didn't do. It's much easier to be spontaneous when backed by a trust fund. In the meantime, the shop assistant pulled out the wallet that had kick-started the entire conversation.

'Sir, I've got your wallet in mauve if you're interested. It costs—'

'I'll take it,' Bex replied before she could finish.

That wasn't originally part of the plan. Every inch of my body wanted to run over to him to warn him that this tiny article was more expensive than my monthly rent. It took serious restraint to continue averting my eyes.

'Ma'am, we don't have the bag here, but we can keep your details in the system.'

Instead of a defeat, the opportunity crafted by Sara was aligned with her intentions of leaving the interaction open. She waited for the woman to depart towards the cashier with Bex's purchase before addressing him directly.

'This might sound weird, but can you take my number in case you see the bag in Gstaad? I've been looking for a while and will jump on a flight if I can finally get my hands on it.'

Truly, it was an Oscar-worthy performance. Every word perfectly led to the next set of seemingly innocent interactions that would weave a web around the prospect before leaving them trapped in her net.

'Sure. I'm Philip, by the way.'

'Sara, nice to meet you. Let's make a deal out of it. If you give me a hand finding the bag, I buy you a drink.'

There it was, the bold moves that had made Sara a well-known seductress in that part of town. I had to admit that there was much we could learn from her obstinacy in converting every lead into a sealed deal before walking away. I would probably never confess it to my friends, but there was a part of me that envied her uninhibited confidence.

Bex locked his phone quickly after saving her details and finishing paying for his new purchase. They waved each other off as he promised to do his best to help her find her coveted piece and walked off towards the main entrance. I took a few more seconds in my state of pretend browsing before walking off unscathed from the evening encounter towards another front-facing exit. As agreed, we met near the valet car park, where we both quickly jumped together once the vehicle emerged from underground.

'That was something. I was super nervous that we'd get caught out.'

'I was more worried about you buying a super expensive wallet without checking the price.'

'There's a fourteen-day refund policy at Harrods, so we're good. Plus, I think it gave our alias a little more authenticity.'

I leaned over to give him a peck of approval while he drove off towards Earl's Court. He had done well—too well. The jealousy started to simmer up again, reminding me that next to Sara, I might as well have been a school kid playing in the professional league.

Back at work, I worried about the inevitable deadlines that would soon be imposed on my research work. The collected intel was slowly forming a better understanding in mind of the inner workings of the silent web that ubiquitously connected so much of the elite. There was so much that didn't materialise linearly but, nevertheless, ended at the exact same place. I still didn't have a story in place, only fragments of rumours thus far.

My tactics of avoiding eye contact whenever I walked through the building failed as I heard a loud call for my name from a too-familiar voice. I turned around to face a gesticulating Nathan, urging me to make my way over to his desk.

'The editors want to see how your special project is coming along.' He winked, emphasising the secrecy of what I was tasked with. 'Any updates for me to pass over to them?'

There were many things I had already uncovered but was far from ready to share. I had to quickly think of a distraction that would keep Nathan away from me for a little while longer so that I could focus on making sense of what would be less likely to completely end my social life.

'There's an angle I'm working at the moment, not concrete yet, but I have some good leads.'

'And that is…' He wasn't going to back off anytime soon. I couldn't blame him either; he was a part of the team that was about to blow out one of the biggest scandals in town.

'Do you remember how at Allegra di Pienza's party she emerged with a man?'

'Sure, the messy, long-haired guy who looked like Jared Leto?'

'Yup, Axwell. So, they're no longer together, but she's seeing someone else. Turns out, he used to date Alexandra.'

Nathan looked at me, puzzled as to why I had decided to share all this information with him. Truthfully, it would be hard to keep up without all the details available, and I intended to have him help find stories where none existed concretely as of yet.

'Wait, Alexandra that we profiled?'

'Correct. So, she says to Allegra that he's stolen from her and goes by several different names.'

'All these high society relationships seem a little too close for comfort.'

He wasn't wrong; endogamy had been endemic within the upper classes for as long as money and rank existed.

'Your dating pool does decrease if your criteria is being a part of the 1%. Heck, in their case, it's more like the 0.1% of people who meet the long list of requirements.'

Nathan was tapping his foot against the carpeted floor. I supposed I was pushing it a bit by stalling with nothing more than moderately interesting gossip.

'I guess, but what does he have to do with your assignment?'

'Both Axwell and Alexandra are inexplicably connected to Sara Gram, Knightsbridge's most hated upwardly mobile figure. She was the pivot that caused many break-ups, including Allegra's own.'

'This is salacious, but what does that have to do with the story we're pursuing?'

I pulled Nathan closer by signalling to him with my fingers that I was about to reveal something truly significant. He looked around us to ensure no other ears could hear the secret meant for him only before standing very close to me.

'She's in Celine's books as one of her girls, if you know what I mean.'

He pulled away with an exaggerated expression akin to a real-life jaw drop. The information wasn't life-changing, but considering the names involved, it was, at the very least, entertaining.

'How about we start your series with a spicy little account of how a Knightsbridge high society princess lost out to a well-sought-out sugar baby? No names, just a little sauce to preview what's coming.'

I stood there reactionless, realising that I had just exposed my best friend to becoming the subject of gossip.

'She'll know it's about her; I can't do that. Not to mention, it will close off that channel for both of us.'

It wasn't the best response, but in the moment, I thought at least if it wasn't about me, then perhaps he would be more understanding.

'So, make it about this Sara girl.' He waved his hand flippantly before carrying on.

'Notorious sugar baby offending the rigid elite of Knightsbridge. I expect a draft in two days; we can post it anonymously to the website.'

Nathan didn't give me time to retort before walking off. There was no room to negotiate; it was decided, and I had to comply. I thought of it for a few seconds and realised that I could write in a way that appeased Allegra and gave her proof that I could be a key piece in a social takedown. It was about time I finally had a chance to be more than a mere observer.

CHAPTER EIGHTEEN

Galerist Schmalerist

The winter aesthetic had converted Hyde Park into a commotion of lights and smells emanating from the Bavarian village installed at its core ahead of the Christmas season. It felt like the market was gradually moving sooner into November, giving us residents of West London far more time to relish in the picturesque sights of Winter Wonderland. A sudden invite from Allegra to attend a midweek seasonal food and drink feast was met with my immediate acceptance.

The last interaction with Nathan had left me ruminating on the right way to bring up to Allegra that her golden rule of discretion should be put aside once again, this time far more drastically than a simple coverage of her last event. I felt it was the ideal setting to convince Allegra that the story about to be released by my employer was, in fact, in her favour. Nothing is quite as disarming to potential resistance as the cosy ambience of a Christmas market.

We met at the entrance to the Lanesborough Hotel and made our way across the road, walking past through the grandiose gates next to Apsely House. Away from the inevitable encounters of familiar faces inside the funfair, we could have a moment alone to chat about the recent occurrences.

Allegra wore a thickly padded Moncler coat, which fit more like a rainproof trench coat than a jacket. It was firmly belted around her slim waist while her hair practically dripped from a high ponytail, showcasing large diamond studs on her ears. Her seasonal wardrobe further enhanced her pale skin tone against the shiny black fabric.

Soon after our greetings and informalities, I kicked off the conversation, delving straight into one of the main matters at hand.

'You know how you asked me to look into the Sara and Alexandra situation?'

'Yes. Have you managed to find out anything?'

'Not quite, but I've planted someone into her life who will be reporting back to us.'

Allegra stopped to look at me with an expression of satisfaction with my update. There was a clear sign of approval even before she spoke. 'I'll admit, I'm impressed with your effort. I always thought social espionage was more Mansour's gig, but I like that you've taken my request seriously.'

In reality, it wasn't strictly her request that pushed me into action. I couldn't fault Allegra for believing that the story pivoted around her; most things usually did. It didn't feel right to keep so much from her, but in order to protect the integrity of my work, she would be strictly on a need-to-know basis about the details of the operation.

'How are things going with Georgie since the revelations by Alexandra?'

'I haven't said anything to him. Things are good; I don't want to believe any of it is true. He just gives me such a confidence boost. It's the first time I've felt so secure as a woman in my own skin.'

The choice of strong words made me realise in that moment that Allegra was truly falling for Georgie. She had never used any depth to describe her relationship with Axwell, which always felt like temporary entertainment to keep her from boredom. Beneath the surface, I knew Allegra had always felt the pressure of needing to be socially perfect. Her distant parents had kept her from ever feeling whole with constant half-compliments that were intended to challenge her to outperform herself. Ironically, whilst it was a major cause of her ongoing trauma, it was also one of the few things we could both relate to.

'Funny enough, I feel the same with Bex. He makes me feel at peace with all the things that made me uneasy before.'

'Looks like cuddle season will be different for us this year.' I smiled at the comment and at the pleasant mental image. *Except we can't do double dates until Georgie is in the clear.*

'Not to pick on what Alexandra said, but did she mention what happened to the artwork she claimed to disappear?'

My voice cracked slightly when I asked that, both due to the discomfort of the topic and my general lack of fitness in light of the brisk walk we were on. Allegra stopped to answer me as we waited ahead of a zebra crossing near the entrance to the gravel promenade of the park.

'She said that the items were a unique installation by Damien Hirst and turned out at this art gallery in Mayfair called *Trésor*. Her art acquisitions team at the business spotted them and inquired; the business said it was a gift to the seller obtained during their relationship. What's to say it's not true, that she didn't gift them and then change her mind post break-up?'

I could see in her nervous movements how Allegra's mind was contorting to ignore the obvious red flags in favour of an explanation that would exonerate her new beau from any wrongdoing. I had to tread lightly in my line of questioning to avoid resistance.

'Surely, if he had stolen the items, there would have been a police report filed? Even the most civilly mannered wouldn't have let that slip.'

'Yes! Exactly. She didn't mention anything of the sort. Never underestimate an ex-girlfriend scorned.'

In all fairness to Allegra, stranger things had happened in high society relationships. It didn't mean Georgie was innocent, but it did mean I had a gallery name and a starting point to investigate further. As we approached the fairy lights that illuminated the centre of Hyde Park, we refocused our conversation on our immediate surroundings.

'Allegra, do you think there's anywhere else in the world where people dress up in more designer clothes to come to a Christmas market in a park than to a fashion show?'

'But Paze, as you know, this isn't just any Christmas market. This is Winter Wonderland, and everyone comes to be seen. It's a continuation of everything else that happens at Harrods, just outdoors and with a ton of alcohol.'

I laughed loudly, thinking of all the winters spent in the delicate balance of looking put together while enjoying German beers without judgment. Walking past the stalls where fresh frankfurters and freshly baked pretzels were, the seasonal smells invaded our nostrils, making my stomach grumble with desire. Around us, well-groomed Knightsbridge folk blended in with tourists who could be identified easily by their scarves too tightly wound around their necks. In that part of town, winter wear was always elegantly draped and never uncoordinated.

Georgie greeted us at the entrance of a temporary wooden restaurant that had both indoor and outdoor seating fenced off from the rest of the funfair. Dressed in a Dior Homme winter puffer, his masculine woody cologne arrived to us before the rest of his body. He met Allegra with a long peck on the lips while tipping her sideways like an old movie star would with his leading lady. It took him a few seconds to acknowledge my presence.

'Hi Paze, good to see you. Is Bex coming?'

'No, he isn't today. He's buried beneath a ton of work that's overdue.'

It wasn't the truth; I couldn't risk being seen with Bex in this close proximity to the potential targets of our investigation. I kept the excuse simple enough to avoid too many follow-up questions that could lead to the lie being unmasked.

'Shame, I've got all my school buddies with me today. I'm sorry, ladies, but you're outnumbered.'

'No worries, Allegra and I can still outdrink all of you.'

Instead of retorting, Georgie laughed and took Allegra's hand so we could make our way over to our table. I walked behind the duo, focusing on not losing my footing amidst a crowd so dense I had to wait for the incoming traffic of people to pass before I could get closer to where they had walked ahead. When I finally reached our final destination, I stood next to Allegra, where she was being introduced to the row of rowdy men we were meant to sit with for the evening.

The first impression I had was that Georgie was a clone of all the people he socialised with and kept around. He was the leader at the head of the table, of course, but they all mimicked similar dress sense with their coats left intentionally unbuttoned at the top, revealing short chains around their dully veined necks acquired through vigorous exercise. Their mannerisms differed very little from one to another, with similar perfected smiles and discreetly peeking tattoos near their exposed hands that signalled their rebel streak without compromising an inheritance from old-fashioned parents. They were perfectly polite, but still, I missed Bex and his far more original demeanour.

As we finished introductions and settled into our seats, I fixated on a table we had passed on the way in but hadn't had a clear view of in the middle of the herd. My eyes readjusted, then, upon realising what I had seen, I turned to Allegra, who held an open-mouthed expression. She pulled me in closer to express herself in words now.

'Is Axwell with Sara in public as an actual couple? Not that I care, but it's insulting.'

It was the first time I had seen him make such a move with her. Traditionally, every other spotting had been more discreet, or at least overseas, where there was a chance to blame it on the substances consumed prior. He sat in open view of all of them with an arm around her. Things must not have been that serious, though, considering she had been all too keen on offering her number to my boyfriend in recent days.

Nevertheless, an opportunity presented itself, and I decided to take it.

'You know I could run a slightly derogatory article that alludes to them on Sizzle. I can't name names for legal reasons, but we can make sure everyone knows what they've done.'

Caught off guard by my atypical stance, one which would usually be far more befitting of bolder members of our brew, Allegra pulled away and looked at me with horror. I started to panic that my approach was perhaps too straightforward when I suddenly saw her lips discreetly move upwards, showcasing a clear delight in the devious plan.

'Do it. Socially annihilate them. Both of them.'

I arrived at the office to report back to work after an early evening packed with too many drinks, my head pounding with disdain for my decisions. The live music that had blasted from the amp system placed too close to our table still rang in my ears when I made my way to the co-working section, where I intended to set myself up for the day. When I placed my bag down, I instantly stalled my work by wandering off to the nearby kitchen for a lifesaving coffee.

In the galley, I nearly collided head-first with Celine, who, at nine in the morning, was already in a full face of glamour makeup and high heels.

'Excuse you, you seem to have rolled straight out of bed half woken up.'

'Sorry, Celine, I think I'm not even half awake at this point. I was at Winter Wonderland with some friends last night.'

She took a step backwards to lean against the countertop, clearly keen to hear more rather than escape the conversation. Always keen, Celine.

'Sounds like hell to me. I can't imagine why people are interested in being jam-packed into a cold park surrounded by drunk rich people acting like college kids.'

'You're not wrong, but it is fun. I like how we can act silly without being judged.'

At that point, Celine crossed her arms around her chest with her long cherry red acrylic nails gripping the sides of her monochromatic striped button-down silk shirt. Her smile broke out as she started to speak.

'Oh, you think they aren't judging you? That's cute! Everyone's always being judged.'

'It didn't feel like that at all. I think you're just a bit grumpy, Celine.'

'Let's see how they act the day you make a mistake in their books.'

The comment made the hairs on the back stand while I shivered. There were many things I was doing that could be objectively viewed by my friends as a transgression. At the same time, I was being careful enough to ensure that it wasn't solely self-motivated.

'You need to loosen up a bit, get to enjoy some time off with good friends.'

'Let me know when, Paze. You know where to find me.'

With that, she pushed herself away from the counter and walked off back into the main office area. In truth, I could have made plans with Celine, but after uncovering her activities, it made me nervous to be seen with her and potentially mistaken as one of her collaborators. The only place I would see her now was somewhere completely secluded from public eyes. It wasn't a question of judgment anymore in her case; she had really brought it unto herself. I couldn't be burdened to bear the consequences of her decisions as well as mine.

Feeling decidedly more awake after the encounter, I made my way to the corner from where I decided to kick-start my de facto work. There was much to do at that point, including a snarky article to bring down a foe of my friends. In an ideal scenario, it would see her upset enough to contact

Sizzle, which would give me an opportunity to pry further into Sara's connections.

I was also unclear as to how Alexandra tied into all of it; after all, they had arrived together at the beginning of the season party. Which reminded me I still had an art gallery to visit. Perhaps the day would be more interesting if I started with that before anything else. I was truly curious to understand who Georgie really was at that point.

There was only one way to find out more, and it wasn't going to happen from behind a desk. I took off in an Uber, paid for by my employer. As far as Nathan needed to know, it was all a part of my secret task. In many ways, it could very well be.

The Mayfair townhouse, where I was headed, was located off Curzon Street, tucked into a corner with large windows that displayed precious items hidden inside glass mounts. The lettering upfront was discrete, almost unnoticeable to anyone who wasn't specifically looking for it. A small sign above the white framed door had five letters in an elegant gold cursive 3D font, spelling out *Trésor*. I walked from the car with purpose, posing as someone who had every business being there.

Luckily, I had dressed in an elegant all-black ensemble that could conceal from any curious eyes the fact I could not afford a single thing at the art gallery. When in doubt, the simplest cuts in a monochromatic block were less likely to elicit suspicions, so I blended in with the environment. Funnily, I noticed right away that I was the only one in the store apart from a sales assistant who quickly hovered over to me in tall leather stiletto heels and a short black tweed dress.

'Can I help you?'

'I'm just having a look, thanks. I'm buying on behalf of a client.'

My voice sounded convinced when the words came out of my mouth, probably from hyping myself up in the car ride. I was here representing Allegra, technically speaking. If I could believe that, then I could convince her it was legitimate.

'Well in that case, what does your client look for typically?'

'Contemporary British, big names, something that could turn a higher profit for our fund.'

'Is this your first purchase?'

I smiled nervously, mimicking my first day at Sizzle in order to channel that same energy. I wasn't actually nervous, but I needed to make a connection with this woman. If she saw me as an equal rather than a threat, she might open up to me. It scared me how much I sounded like my parents, who, after years in marketing and advertising, had tried to pass down the art of capturing and maintaining attention.

'Can you tell? I just managed to get this job, and I don't want to mess it up. I'm a recent art history grad, so it means a lot to me.'

'No worries, I can help you out. I'm Anita, by the way. I have worked in this industry for around twelve years. It's not as scary as it all looks. I can send you a catalogue of our current offering.'

She sounded sweet enough; I almost felt guilt rising for putting the woman through a ruse, but I bottled that sentiment before it made me stumble on a plan that was going well thus far.

'I'm Paisley. That sounds good. Out of curiosity, why are there only jewels on display at the entrance?'

'It triggers more walk-ins. I will tell you a secret, though: most of the watches and jewellery we get from young women reselling gifts, if you know what I mean.'

The last bit of the sentence was uttered in a lower tone as if it was meant to truly be a secret, even though it was only the two of us in the gallery. Maybe she was testing me as well, in case I had something to offer her. I had to continue feigning ignorance to get her to explain better.

'What do you mean gifts they receive?'

'You could say that they get paid in rare objects, which they exchange for some sort of favour. Some of them keep the gifts, but more often than not, they want a quick turnaround for cash. I always think they'd be better off just charging money for what they do, but then again, they probably get more out of it than the per-hour girls.'

I had to keep my cover and emphasise that I wasn't there to sell anything. It didn't feel like she was fully convinced yet, so the next part needed to be unnecessarily aggressive.

'Not to mention they can continue to pretend they don't work in prostitution.'

'That's right! I guess there's a difference somewhere. On the artwork, though, there's a large private collector coming tomorrow with his family-held pieces. He's looking to hold a private viewing via us; I'll get you on the distribution list.' After she finished speaking, she pulled a form from behind a counter that would record my details as a customer. I started to fill in my details, or at least the ones I was willing to share.

'That sounds great! Do you know when it will be?'

'Not yet, but look out for a message about Lord Thurrington's viewing.'

I tried not to display my recognition of the name. Of all the galleries to have his private collection shown and sold in London, why would he choose this obscure one that didn't have the same prestige as one of the major auction houses? In particular, he was a man who regularly surrounded himself with women of a similar ambition to the ones selling gifts here. There had to be a more direct reason for it.

'Thanks; you can just reach me at the number I put on the form. It's always on.'

I turned my back after a short wave goodbye and made it to the door, where I was about to push outwards before Anita cried out to me. A tingling feeling hit my cheek, unsure of what she was about to ask.

'Paisley, you forgot to fill in your surname. We need them for all event attendees for compliance reasons.'

'Oh, it's Paisley Bex.'

I had no idea why I said that, but it was the only name that came to mind that wasn't my own in that split second. It was the one part of the plan that hadn't been properly conceived, so I could only hope it wouldn't be my downfall. Before regret could make me panic into an unintentional verbal confession, I exited the door as quickly as I could without looking like I was actively running away.

My legs carried the weight of my processing brain as I continued to think over all that had been uncovered. I walked along the uneven pavement in a small street full of mews houses until I had successfully distanced myself from the more bustling parts of Mayfair in favour of a quietly nestled residential block. From there, I pulled my phone out to call Nathan.

'So I tracked this lead about an allegedly stolen art piece and found out there's a whole other side of gifting and favours that I had no idea existed.'

Nathan audibly closed a door behind on the other side of the line.

'Oh, hi, Paze. Thanks for keeping me updated on your whereabouts.'

'Sorry, but there are more important things happening now. The art gallery was informed originally that the pieces were gifts from an ex-girlfriend. They returned the stolen items, of course. I went to visit them and find out more. Turns out, it's not quite a gallery but sort of an elite pawn shop where people exchange "gifts" for cash.'

I must have shared the words with increased speed, as it took a few long seconds for Nathan to comprehend.

'That seems like some sort of criminal activity.'

'Yes, it seems many people in London arrive there with items from benefactors that get bought back by the store and then resold for a profit.'

Now speaking in a lower tone, Nathan continued. 'It's not yet the main story, but if we can get them to share their perspective, it could be a start to the series. We start explaining how this flesh-for-currency business runs so closely to high society.'

It felt reassuring to hear that from my manager; after all, he was one of the current main gatekeepers of my upcoming journalist ascension. I felt proud that I had followed my gut, and it led me right into the heart of a story worth telling.

'And also, Paze, I need the little spicy piece on that love triangle or square involving everyone we deem worth photographing at functions. We're a little short of society coverage this week, and I don't want people clicking away.'

'Don't worry, it's coming your way.'

I hung up with a full smile on display. Things were good, things were happening at Sizzle, and I was at the centre of it all.

CHAPTER NINETEEN
Judge, Jury, and Executioner

The day that I would inflict my first piece of genuine malice into the world began with me staring at my laptop screen from the comfort of my bed. I feigned a stomach bug that would allow me to work from home, from where I could hide from the live reactions I would get from Nathan after I pressed send on the email. It was equally important to shield my own emotions, which would give away my lack of confidence at that moment.

I sat against the cold wall of the top layer of my bunk bed, dressed in my university hoodie and faded black joggers. My legs were crossed to prop up the laptop while the duvet was bunched up around me. I had spent the night working on the story that would expose Sara and Axwell to the wider world. Knightsbridge was about to go digital and, more importantly, borderless.

At the top of the email, bold letters spelt out the article title I had decided to submit:

High society's main bad boy, Axwell Mortimer, seen with a scandalous new interest

It was direct, to the point, and, I hoped, salacious enough to garner the right number of clicks to keep Nathan satisfied. I reread the title multiple times until I successfully made myself anxious enough to feel stomach pain. The very first story that could have me take centre-stage as a journalist could come to fruition.

My phone started to ring; Mansour seemed to have a sixth sense for when drama was about to ensue.

'So, have you sent it yet?'

'Good morning, Mansour. Or should I refer to you as a close source instead?'

Mansour laughed loudly from the other side of the line. I could tell he had enjoyed the process far too much since I decided to bring him in for backup as I powered through the draft article after the night at Winter Wonderland.

'I couldn't do it. Can we read through it one last time?'

'*Tammam*, read it back to me but with a confident tone like you're ready to publicly shame someone this time.'

'Alright, let's go through the opener. Well-known heir to the Mortimer industrial dynasty, often more seen stumbling out of clubs, is seen with a new love interest after being dropped by high society darling Allegra di Pienza.'

I knew Mansour wanted me to skip through the less interesting points and reach the part he had most closely collaborated on. It had been mentioned by Nathan that adding sources, even if anonymous to the public, would prevent litigious contestation.

'Sources close to the duo confirm concerns about the reputation held by new interest, Sara Gram. According to them, she is notorious for dating exclusively wealthy and well-connected men.'

'Can we get to the best part, please?'

I chuckled at his impatience and took a deliberately long pause, increasing the suspense.

'A close friend within the same circle reports that Sara is persona non grata in high society circles for notoriously having no regard for pre-existing relationships. Meanwhile, the same source claims Axwell has continuously cheated on his previous partners. Can they keep each other entertained for long enough? Only time will tell.'

None of what was said was a lie, but it would be hard to prove. At the same time, Axwell relied on his family's wealth, and in the typical blue blood approach, their response would be silence to allow it to simmer down quietly.

'Paze, you're about to finally create some enemies of your own. I was getting tired of having to share mine with you.'

I couldn't help laughing at Mansour's comment. It was a mixture of excitement and nervousness for putting myself out there to be criticised. There was also the fact that it was a far more open attack than anyone had ever done in our crowd. Of that fact, I felt quite proud.

'I'm sending it off then lying under my covers for a while. I can't bear to think of when it will be online and how everyone will react.'

'Remember, *habibi*, that you wanted this.'

The line went silent as I hung up and stared at my screen for a few more seconds. I squinted quickly, pressing send and eyeing the laptop for a short minute to ensure it had gone through before I could hide. My inner voice told me that it would become normal, stories would become easier, and I wouldn't get nervous anymore. That might have been completely true, but that day, I was going to numb myself with daytime hibernation. The scandalous content was already in Nathan's inbox, leaving me depleted.

Within a few hours, my phone started to go off with the alerts I had set up to notify me of publication. Shortly after, messages started piling in from different sources. My eyes were fixated on the most important names appearing on the locked screen as I dismissed different notifications in order without responding to any.

> Mansour
>
> Can we pick the next victim already?

THE KNIGHTSBRIDGE CROWD

Allegra

Thank you, I owe you one.

Bex

I'm here for you. Late lunch at my place?

The last message from Bex was the only one that warranted an immediate response. Seeing his name come up on the screen sent a warmness through my body. I was hungry—no food had entered my body in several hours, and the added stress was making me nauseous.

A quick response to him triggered a countdown of tasks that I needed to do before I could be seen in public and, more importantly, by my boyfriend. I laid out an outfit with a taupe knitted jumper and high-waisted dark wash jeans tucked into ankle boots. As I saw my reflection in the small bathroom mirror, I noticed the dark circles marring my complexion. These last few weeks had taken a toll on me, which I could temporarily conceal with makeup, but sooner or later, they would be impossible to mask.

Upon arrival, Bex met me at the door of his apartment building in a relaxed white t-shirt and jeans that looked out of place for the winter season. He had been working from the cosiness of his home, oblivious to the biting cold weather outside that I had encountered walking in between bus rides over to his place.

He held the door open as I hurried inside, planting a long kiss while moving his hands down to my waist. I felt his body temperature slowly defrost the coldness of my skin. In those seconds, with my eyes closed, any preoccupation with the outside world departed, leaving room only to enjoy that moment. When it was finally time to pull away, I bit my lower lip as we walked while side-hugging to his door. I really needed that; I really needed him.

When we got into his flat, I smelled the rich species coming through from the dinner table. He had gone to the effort of ordering from my favourite Indian restaurant in South Kensington. My stomach grumbled as we went straight for the food.

Bex started opening up packs for curries and naan as I poured Coke Zero into a glass.

'So I've managed to find out some things for you about Sara.'

'Are you talking to her regularly?'

My voice sounded annoyed but I reminded myself that this was my own doing for research's sake. There was likely a hint of jealousy flowing through, although I'd hate to admit it.

'Yes, stay focused,' he said with a laugh before carrying on.

'There's something shady, you were right.'

I took one of the serving spoons and poured a generous amount of butter chicken onto a plate while maintaining eye contact with Bex. He continued as I dipped bread into the sauce and started to eat.

'She was at that gallery you mentioned, Trésor. I had messaged her about whether she'd found the bag she was looking for, and she said no. We got into talking about plans for the weekend. She mentioned a private art sale at the gallery.'

I'd never been much of an art enthusiast myself, which made it even more ironic that my first investigative journalism piece was so heavily centred around an art gallery turned centre of all things seedy. Truth be told, everyone pretended to know art, but very few actually cared for it. There was a flare around gallery owners that made them immune to the normal social critique. They could get away with outfits most would not be caught dead in but were rather celebrating for their quirkiness. I needed to know more about who owned Trésor.

'I've got an email to join the viewing ahead of the sale. Obviously, we can't go together as it would blow our cover. But it would be good for you to suss out the place; I'm sure both of us can pick up more clues if we exchange notes at the event.'

I needed a pretence to contact Lord Thurrington about his painting, and it couldn't be related to Sizzle. He would figure me out in an instant, and it would not end well. I also had Bex currently chasing up another story on my behalf, so there wasn't a situation where it wasn't that obvious. Perhaps I could convince Allegra to participate. I could sell it to her that it would be a good way to see if Alexandra was lying to separate her from Georgie lover boy.

'Bex, I think you should go with Sara, and I'll convince Allegra that I could present myself as her representative. She wouldn't want to go anyways, but I think I can sell it to her.'

'You know something I don't understand about your friend is why she's entertaining a relationship with someone she's secretly investigating. Besides, wasn't it her idea to do an article on her ex-boyfriend?'

'Something like that. It helped me to create buzz internally at Sizzle, so I can't say it's all her.'

For a few seconds, Bex played with the last bit of food remaining on his dish before looking at me with serious eyes. 'Isn't this mixing work with personal life getting a bit uncomfortable for you? I say this as an editor: I think there are other stories you can pursue that perhaps have more real substance.'

There was a twinge of judgment in the way he expressed it that hit me like a hard slap. While I knew that Bex didn't enjoy the intricacies of the Knightsbridge crowd as much as I did, this was the first time he exposed harsher feelings.

'It isn't without substance. This article was a significant stepping stone for me. Not everyone has an interest in financial news like you do. Besides, it was a question of principles. I merely highlighted what everyone knows.'

'Paze, not everyone knows any of this or cares about all of these rules. You're starting to sound like Allegra.'

I went from frustrated with his initial response to upset by the condescension in his voice at the mention of her name.

'What's so wrong about sounding like her?'

'She's uptight and controlling of everything around her. These old-school high society rules just foment so much toxic behaviour where people believe they need to do the most to just fit in. It's sad, really.'

As he spoke, I couldn't stop looking straight at him, my jaw clenched tight. I had let my arms cross with my elbows on the table whilst my back slouched into a protective position. I took a deep breath before responding.

'I understand how it looks from the outside. However, she is a really good person who's been there for all of her friends. Also, people always want to be on top in any circle. If anything, the media is much more to blame for that. We're both journalists; shouldn't we uphold standards?'

'I just write about money, not what you can do with it, so I think I'm not contributing too much. I didn't mean to offend you; I just don't get why you care about this stuff.'

His face didn't show any hints of wanting to continue the discussion, so I receded into a more relaxed position with my arms dropping down next to me as I sank into the chair.

'I'm not offended; I guess it will take time for you to see the more real parts of my friends. Once you do, trust me, you'll like them just as much as I do.'

Bex smiled at me, although his raised brow told me he was still sceptical. We started to clean off the table together as the tension melted away slowly but not completely. The conversation shifted to planning for the next few days as I prepared to head out so that we could both carry on our remote working from the quiet of our respective homes. I said goodbye with a short peck as I headed back out into midwinter season London.

My mind filed the notion that I had seen a side of him that could be problematic in the long term. He had never criticised me so openly, and it had hurt. I could have fought back more vigorously, but I feared coming across as defensive, particularly when I did believe the words I told him. In time, I was sure he'd come to see my side.

I was lost in thoughts when my phone alerted me to a new message from an unknown number.

Unknown

> Paze, right? This is Sara. Caetano gave me your number. Loved the coverage, babe. I think we could do more together, coffee? Xx

CHAPTER TWENTY
Fame and Infamy

There had been many scenarios that crossed my mind before I published my first scandal, but none of them had been that the object of criticism would actually enjoy it. I hadn't given Sara's feelings much thought before pressing submit; I was partly relieved that she hadn't been crushed by my actions. After an evening of avoiding giving in to the varying reactions to my article, I succumbed to the exhaustion that had replaced the other emotions raging inside me before the release.

Awakening the morning after felt eerie. I wasn't the same as the day before, but I couldn't tell what it was that felt so different. The light creeping in between blinds kickstarted a bolt of cortisol in my body that had me jump out of bed without hesitation. There was an energy expanding through my core that made it impossible to waste another minute idly.

The last image from the earlier evening was Sara's unexpected cheerful message. There had never been an opportunity for me to engage directly with her, particularly given the animosity between her and every single person in my social circle. Having a direct relationship with her was so off the table that I had offered my boyfriend as bait to be able to get close enough to her for my work investigation. Surely, I couldn't just reply; it would be poorly perceived by those whose opinions actually mattered to me. Unless, of course, they were convinced it was purely work. Which it was, of course.

I was intrigued, and curiosity has notoriously gotten the best of me. So there wasn't much of a point to delay it further. Placing myself on my breakfast stool, I dialled her number while cradling an oversized coffee mug.

'Hi, is this Sara?'

'Hola! Thought you'd left me on two ticks there!'

Despite her voice having a particularly sensual dial, there was a girly cheerfulness in her words that reminded me of school days.

'Sorry about that, I had an early night. Also, I just realised it's really early now.'

'It's no bother honey, I've already run ten kilometres this morning. You've done me a great favour with this article of yours; everyone wants a piece of me.' There was a thin line between fame and infamy, although, for some people, it didn't seem to matter as long as it served as a stepping stone for their next move. Still, it was good that I was closer to Sara ahead of the art viewing.

'I am sorry I didn't know you very well before this, so I didn't have a chance to reach out.'

This was not the truth; I knew more about her than I cared to admit. Still, I needed to protect myself from opening up more than necessary.

'Did I misread your article? From my perspective, I'm a hot ticket, and every rich man in town wants me. In fact, I think we could work something out where I can help you get information.'

From the comfort of my flat, where she couldn't see me, I put her on speaker and played with my hair, gathering the strands into a messy bun. Had she seen me, surely my arched eyebrows would signal interest in counting this conversation further.

'I do keep my sources open. If you ever have anything to share, you know how to reach me.'

'I'm sure our paths will cross again soon. Although, as you can imagine, I'd rather our conversations not happen over text. Until then, take care, Paisley.'

With that, the line went silent, and I stared down at my phone, where I proceeded to save her number simply under her first initial. The last thing I needed was for her to contact me at a less-than-opportune time and cause an uproar in my circle. I hadn't yet decided if I would consider her a reliable source since everything seemed to have self-interest at its core, but perhaps having her side of the unfolding story would bring more insight than simply ignoring her. That was just what ethical journalists did, and I always sought to have integrity.

Time had not stopped to wait for my mind to process the earlier conversation with Sara. There was still a much bigger, more important story I was chasing that required my full attention. The upcoming private art sale at Trésor was finally happening, and I had made plans to attend.

In order to look like a convincing buyer for a socialite, I had to dress the part. I wasn't the principal buyer, so my look didn't need to be outwardly ostentatious. Au contraire, the idea was to appear to belong in a sea of connoisseurs who typically aimed to look effortless. In my experience, effortless to the fashion crowd was a code word for oversized and even slightly mismatched. I paired a pair of dark denim wide-legged trousers with an oversized denim buttoned shirt in the same shade and accessorised with a triple set of vintage pearls I bought off an auction website after too much wine. The look was completed with merlot-coloured leather ballerinas that cheekily showed only a sliver of toe cleavage.

On the way out of my building, I saw my gleaming reflection. The locks of my hair were loose on my shoulders while a rose gold shimmer sparkled on the tip of my nose. In the months since I started working at Sizzle, I had begun noticing more of my features and how I had finally achieved comfort in my own skin. I smiled proudly back at myself. I was surrounded socially by beautiful people, but I had started to feel as though I was becoming one of them.

The self-adoration was interrupted by a notification from the car share app on my phone letting me know that the driver had arrived. The cold winter air fogged up the glass at the door of my building, contrasting with the warmth emanating from the ground floor flats. I swung open the door and rushed into the black car waiting next to the dimly lit streetlight and the steps at the entrance of my doorway. Thankfully, with the full signal during my ride, I had enough time to investigate on Instagram who was arriving at the event.

An unanswered message lingered on the locked screen of the phone. I had intentionally left it there, avoiding the two blue ticks that would betray the fact that I knew the content.

Bex

> Hey! Haven't heard from you, are we okay?

The question had two different, equally true responses. I had realised that there was an uncomfortable twinge of judgment brewing in Bex that surely one day would become a much bigger problem. I also had no intention of confronting it yet, so I hid behind the screen and dealt with work instead. The slowdown in exchanging memes several times an hour, though, was a dead giveaway that something was amiss. I had taken too long in my attempt to let things blow over, inadvertently making it awkward. It was time to fix things before it got out of hand, particularly considering how important tonight was for me.

> **Me**
> I'm sorry, my phone was blowing up and I had to disappear to avoid an anxiety crisis. Make it up to later? Shawarma and chill?

> **Bex**
> It's not fair that you know all my weak points ;) Going to the gallery tonight?

> **Me**
> On my way, how about you?

> **Bex**
> Sara got me on the list, incognito remember?

> **Me**
> I can still check you out at a distance.

> **Bex**
> Kinda hot, flirting undercover.

I smiled genuinely in the car as my body relaxed into the warm seats. Things were back on track, and in a way, I would have Bex there watching over me as I went into the most significant mission of my reporting thus far. It felt safer having him there—like he could rescue me if I went in over my head. He was nearly ten years older than me, which, in the current phase we were living in, felt like I could lean on his much vaster experience when needed.

It was obvious we had arrived at the gallery when we approached a queue of cars ahead of a red carpet set up at the entrance. I exited before we approached closer, walking a short distance from the street corner as the cold wind hit firmly against my cheeks. I hurried my pace until I was met at the door by two large security guards in matching black suits.

'Good evening, are you on the list?'

I looked around quickly to ensure nobody could hear me since I knew the words that came next would confuse a possible acquaintance.

'Yes, I am. Paisley Bex.'

'I can see you here, on Anita's list. Enjoy your evening.'

The polite grin that overtook my face was mismatched internally by annoyance with myself for not having come up with a better alias when caught off-guard on my first mission. The door opened, giving me access to the foyer, which was nearly at full capacity. It was a great opportunity to blend into the crowd while I scanned the room for familiar faces.

I stood in front of an acrylic pill installation with small glistening crystals that reflected the lighting in the gallery. A grey-haired man appeared next to me, towering above my shoulders. His tobacco and wood-infused perfume was strong enough for me to take notice of his presence.

'I'm going to miss this one.'

'Is it yours?'

'No, I'm just the buyer. I work for Lord Thurrington; everything showcased today is his.'

My heart sped up slightly at the mention of his name, which I disguised by placing a hand under my chin and tilting my head like a focused buyer would do.

'I'm also here on behalf of a client. I hope I can find something that fits her bill.'

I could feel his eyes on my body even though my head was focused solely on the piece in front of me. His body had moved closer to mine, breaching my personal space with intimidation.

'If there's anything that you'd like to see privately later, I can ask Celine to call you for more details.'

'Celine? No, please don't.' I wanted to instinctively cover my mouth after having blurted out the damming sentence. The edges of my cheeks burned quickly, probably redder than a gala apple.

'Oh, so you know about her? You wouldn't if you were really here for the art.'

Before I could answer, I heard the familiar voice of Lord Thurrington, which I recognised from previous interviews I'd watched. The years of smoking cigars had given him a particular tone that echoed in the gravel of his voice.

'Blake, there you are! Trust him to be next to the pretty girl.'

He squeezed in between us, his shoulders close enough to touch mine. I moved sideways with a closed smile plastered on my face as if it had been artificially installed. This time, I took a good look at him and noticed he clutched a full whiskey glass in one hand while the other embraced his employee around the shoulder. He was in his mid-fifties but looked much younger at this distance. He had a few visible lines around his eyes but a youthful complexion. The aristocratic strong nose stood out as a key feature. His shirt was unbuttoned, showcasing the fading fake tan that kept his skin tone warm despite the cold weather.

Blake started speaking again as I watched them both closely.

'So you were about to tell me how you know Celine.'

I took a deep breath and decided it was time to play his game or lose everything. 'Was I? Regardless of how I know her, I know better than to hang out with you two.'

Lord Thurrington chuckled loudly, seemingly proud that his reputation had spread to younger crowds.

'I'm not even offended, but I do enjoy a little challenge. Tell me, what's your name?'

Offering him a smile with a slight lip bite, I raised my shoulder up to my chin while turning around towards the crowd and responded.

'Well then, I'm not going to make it easy for you.'

I walked off, hearing the two men laugh and fall back into a whisper behind me. I was adamant about losing myself in the large pool of people so that I could escape his advances for the time being. I spotted Bex in a corner, briefly meeting his gaze before walking off, keeping my eyes on the ground and smiling to myself. I found a quiet corner on the right side of the doorway, from where I could observe better without being seen.

Anita appeared from the back and came towards where I stood near the entrance of the gallery.

'Hey, how's the evening going?'

I asked her as we greeted with two cheek kisses.

'It's a good turnout; the client is happy. It's much better than our usual resale crowd.'

Her comment was a great segue for me to explore more of the unusual business model that had been wracking my brain for the weeks since we first met.

'Do you ever worry that the items that are resold might be claimed by the buyers?'

'They're usually too shamed or too married to admit they gave anything to a partner of questionable repute. There was one time that a bloke came around with things, and then his ex-girlfriend came around asking for them back.'

'Did she get it back?'

'She had cameras all over her estate; she showed us footage of him stealing, so we had to give it back. She didn't want a scandal, so the police weren't involved.

I looked at Anita with an expression of mild shock. Of course, this implicated Georgie in a very serious offence, but I still needed more information on the overall scheme. I spotted Lord Thurrington moving towards our side of the gallery and decided I needed to make a run for it.

'Got to go; I'm at work tomorrow super early. How about we have lunch one of these days?'

'Sure! Bonsoir!'

Before long, I managed to step outside the packed space and into the quietness of Mayfair in the evening. I placed my hands into my coat's pocket, only to feel the vibration of a message alert.

Bex

> Saw you leave, meet me at South Audley Street. Next to the modern building, my car is there.

The tension of having had Lord Thurrington's attention started to melt into the comfort of soon seeing my actual boyfriend. I had managed to maintain my story all evening, but I was sure he'd be pressing Celine for an answer on who I was and where he could reach me. The strangest part was that it felt good to think he'd lose sleep thinking of little old me.

CHAPTER TWENTY-ONE

Not my story

Waking up surrounded by Bex's lingering perfume had become my favourite morning ritual. His sprawling king-size mattress felt enormous when contrasted with the restriction of the bunk bed in my studio flat. I kicked off the soft sheets from my side of the bed before my alarm rang. In the stillness of the room, I sat up against the deep brown leather headboard and took in the sight of an undressed Bex. His facial expression was relaxed into a deep sleep with a hand behind his head.

At any other time, the moment would have felt blissful. My mind raced past the quiet room we were in and into the looming information at hand. Since Lord Thurrington knew my face, it would become harder to navigate unnoticed in his proximity. There were still cards to be played, of course. With some luck, Celine had yet to figure out what I had been doing in the shadows, and Sara still hadn't linked me to Bex. I silently analysed the situation while holding my bare knees close to my chest.

The most intrusive thought was that Allegra was dating some sort of conman. We may have been reluctant to trust Alexandra's version of facts, but there was outside confirmation that was unrelated. What if I didn't tell her directly? A plan started to materialise as I searched for my phone on the nightstand.

Me

> Morning Nathan! Might have some more scoop on last night's gallery event but it can't come from me.

Nathan

> Oh my... that good?

Me

> You want the story? It can't be tied to my name, or it will blow my cover with richies.

Nathan

> Make it worth my time and it's a deal.

A jolt of energy entered my body as I silenced my phone's alarm. Bex turned onto his side, towards me, as his eyes slowly opened in response to the melodic noise that had ceased a few seconds prior. He broke into a sleepy smile as I caressed his neck gently.

'You're up early.'

'No rest for the wicked.'

'And here I was thinking you were a good girl.'

I smiled, not at his joke but at how being in bed with him made me feel. The smile came naturally when I was this close to him. It had never been as fitting as in that moment; there wasn't much room in my schedule to cuddle with a story weighing heavy on my shoulders.

'I need to run to the office, but maybe we can do something cute later?'

'I'm not planning on moving much. Come back anytime you need more of me.'

It was tempting to spend the rest of the day between sheets and the warm touch of Bex's body. The contour of a muscled abdomen was an open invitation to skip through obligations for far more enjoyable pursuits. Fighting every instinct, I gave Bex a short peck on the lips before jumping out of bed.

As I left the room, I grabbed one of his blue button shirts that hung neatly on a matte black rack. I figured I could pull off a new style with yesterday's clothes if I added an oversized boyfriend shirt to the equation. The added advantage was a hint of his cologne, which would remind me of my morning view throughout the day.

On the way out, I passed by the ensuite toilet to fix my face with the basic utensils I had fit into my evening bag. The black eye pencil I used around my waterline the night before had left its vestige, but instead of removing it, I further emphasised the morning-after look with my fingers. I ran a creamy blush-pink lipstick on my lips as I stared at my reflection. I pressed my lips on the mirror, leaving a cheeky kiss behind for Bex to find later once he woke up properly. It may not have been the time for morning action, but I had every intention of making him think about my mouth throughout the day. It was only fair since I'd be fighting memories of his flexed obliques from the previous night.

Between the messy hair bun, the slightly smudged makeup look, and the men's shirt thrown on top of my all-black look, I actually pulled off the cool journalist aesthetic. I held onto the two sides of his sink and lowered my head—the weight of what I had to do next physically dragging me down. My eyes closed of their own volition while my breathing sped up to an erratic rhythm.

I forced my lids to open against their will as if that would help me remain in control of my body. The dark wood cabinets hoisted above the sink were directly in front of me. As I tried to decrease my heartbeat via paced short breaths, I pulled open the cabinet door in search of something that could soothe my nerves. After a quick scan, a small white cardboard box stood out with just the five letters I needed that morning: X-A-N-A-X.

Crossing two underground zones was far more pleasant as the chemicals freely flowed into my body and calmed the noise out of my head. The warm air of bodies occupying the same space that would typically be bothersome felt cosy instead. Station after station passed in a blur until I arrived at my stop.

I rushed into the office, stomping straight to where Nathan stood holding a cartoonishly large mint coffee mug with a slogan that had been half washed off. His winter wardrobe choices had proven to remain within a range of different shades of grey knit cardigans and dark denim. His smile widened as I approached, knowing well that I was a key pawn in his checkmate for promotion.

'Good morning, Miss Paisley. I've booked a meeting room for us.'

'Right, shall we get straight into it?'

With a nod, he started walking slightly ahead of me towards the corner meeting room. The soundproof glass door opened with a groan, much like my stomach was starting to sound, already punishing me for not eating before I was about to make one of the boldest manoeuvres to stay afloat in all my social circles. Instead of giving my growing appetite further attention, I sat neatly in an empty chair. Any emotion other than hunger still felt muted from the earlier pill as my hands rested calmly on the table.

Sat across from me, Nathan gasped loudly after hearing the carefully selected pieces of information I had decided to share with him.

'So if I've got this right, Allegra's boyfriend is a bonafide criminal.'

'Well, we can't say that since he hasn't been charged. Can we say "alleged con man" without a lawsuit coming through?'

My rationale for bringing up its legality wasn't coincidental. On the ride to work, I had remembered a particular lecture from university on how we must always self-preserve as journalists. Publications take the risk, not us. We cover our backs, which is what I intended to do by way of a sharply worded summary of meeting points later to ensure nobody could come after me.

'There are a few sources, plus you've got a recording from one of his victims. It's a grey area that I'm happy to tread on. This story will break the internet.'

It was true that I had a recording, but the consent of how it was obtained was not openly discussed. There were details that weren't particularly relevant at the moment. Although, I had every intention of eventually obtaining the necessary approvals needed to make it all square with the law. One problem at a time, Paze, one at a time.

'That's true; we do have a witness statement from someone at the shop who confirmed the theft. It brings a lot of our subjects in the wider story even closer to Lord T.'

The possibility that art was indeed a cover for a scandal that was about to crumble the very core of the Knightsbridge crowd had been very remote. However, the revelations from the Trésor event had made these worlds intertwined in a way that was increasingly difficult to separate. There were many moving parts that remained unresolved; everyone around me seemed to connect to the scheme. Above all, my best friend was in a relationship with a dangerous man. What else could he have been hiding from us?

Admittedly, I never believed that Georgie could be intelligent enough to put together such an elaborate scheme. I had misjudged him as another playboy melting away generational wealth like ice cubes in a midsummer pitcher of Pimms. Behind the immaculately greased hair was an even more well-oiled organisation, one that I was tasked with unmasking as a part of my Elitegate reportage.

'I can agree to pen this story under my name, but there is one condition.'

Of course there was. It was nearly unthinkable for Nathan not to have an angle, particularly when I had brought him an exclusive society scandal.

'You will need to mention that Georgie is Allegra di Pienza's boyfriend.'

'That's not relevant to the story.'

'It is, and you know it. He's nobody without her name attached.'

The intention behind my plan was precisely to spare Allegra the heartache of her questionable dating choices. There I was, handing the publication a blue-blooded scandal on a silver platter, but Nathan always wanted more.

'She's not involved in any of this; we would spoil her reputation by including her in something she doesn't condone. Besides, he's a regular on social pages. Doesn't that mean the story could stand on its own?'

'Allegra is a major socialite. Her life is open to public scrutiny, and she should have made a decision the second she had questions about her boyfriend.'

'This will crush her.'

She will never forgive me.

'Welcome to the real world of journalism, Paze. You will need to decide if you want to be taken seriously in this industry or stand beside your friend.'

'What if I decide not to include this in the story?'

'I will need to remove you from the assignment and hand it over to a more senior journalist to conclude a more thorough research process.'

In my head, I had thought that a number of scenarios could happen. None of them included an outright threat from Nathan. I could anger Allegra beyond repair this time, but what was the alternative? Confronting her directly with the truth was futile. With the story run by someone else, I would feign a lack of control over what transpired. It could look cowardly, but ultimately, it would make her gracefully exit the relationship before it was too late. I was giving her the perfect way out, even if it may not look like that from the onset.

'I'm here to write stories; I can always console my friend afterwards.'

Nathan broke out into a full smile that was disconcerting. He was enjoying this for some odd reason.

'I knew you had what it takes to make it in this industry. Can't wait to move you up to a more prominent space on the ink.'

His reassurance was bittersweet. Before I had time to change my mind, I took my leave by quietly exiting his proximity in favour of the office's open area. I marched towards the coffee station for a desperately needed mug of liquid warmth. The mellowness I needed for the meeting had served its purpose; it was time to reignite my body with some caffeine.

The Nespresso station at the centre of the eatery released rich smells of coffee beans that started to reawaken my senses. Simultaneously, my brain recommenced its usual ruminating activities. The story could be my biggest failure, and I could still lose all my friends. The legality remained ambiguous even if Nathan was confident. Sizzle Media was running my story both online and in print, with a sprinkle of social media. There was no turning back at that point, so the second part of the plan needed to kick into action immediately.

Phone in hand and earphones in place, I leaned against a wall, waiting for the coffee machine to work its magic.

'Allegra! Can you talk? I've got something urgent to tell you.'

'Paze? Is everything okay?'

'Yes and no, I'm good, but there's something going on that will upset you.'

I paused and looked around at my work colleagues around the office to ensure I wasn't within clear hearing distance of anyone in particular. There could be no mistakes with what was about to happen next.

'What's going on, Paisley?'

'Well, remember how you told me to look into the Georgie story?'

The background on her side went completely silent. I imagined how she'd walked away from everyone to hear the news from the privacy of a reserved corner. She only mumbled a response that was enough for me to know I should carry on.

'Well, I was at an art gallery opening this week for work, and it turns out the stolen pieces belonging to Alexandra did turn up there. Unfortunately, this was uncovered by a colleague and they're running a story on it.'

'Pardon me? You mean to say that I'm meant to deal with this discovery, and everyone will also know about it?'

Guilt started truly setting in upon hearing her voice slightly crack on the other side of the line. Everything was snowballing fast out of my control.

'Yes, Allegra, I tried to stop it from happening. The very least I thought I'd do is let you know.'

'Gosh, thank you for that. I don't know what I'd do if I didn't have you as a best friend right now. I've got to run. Kisses!'

The dead line tone hit my ears like a sting. This didn't feel like the right thing to do; it was just the only thing I could do. I robotically picked up a carton of milk to mix into a soothing latte. My eyes wandered around the office while I slipped into my drink. This place was a dream, this was everything I ever wanted. *It's all worth it in the end.*

CHAPTER TWENTY-TWO
Gossip Never Sleeps

For a full week, I was engrossed in a never-ending spiral of writing, editing, and several rounds of conversations with our legal department. The spinning wheel of pre-publication tasks had only favoured a crescendo of nerves that had settled in as a permanent state. At the same time, I had to constantly fend off my friends with excuses that decreased in believability. I had avoided Mansour the most since his senses were the strongest in catching lies. It didn't help that Bex had left town for an impromptu ski trip while I had been immersed in writing.

The growing list of reasons for my noticeable absence from my friend circle was running thin. I needed time and space away from them in order to convince the real victim of Georgie thus far. The only way to legally present the story without it seeming like a tabloid was for Alexandra to present her own version of events of the lunch encounter with Allegra. Perceived distance from the story was necessary for my own protection.

The notes loosely scattered around the desk I was working out of the office included a selection of verbatim quotes collected from a conversation Nathan had with Alexandra midweek. She had come into our office dressed in her characteristic power suit, with only a thicker Barbour coat as an indication that we were indeed in the cold season. I had observed at a distance, maintaining my unknown presence from behind a darkened glass room that allowed me to see out but ensured the passerby couldn't see me. In many ways, it was no different from my position in polite society.

'He specifically only dates heiresses, nepos, and hedge fund babies. Georgie is a fortune hunter that's nice to look at but equally deceptive.'

She had agreed to the quote being published as long as she was solely mentioned as an ex-partner and victim of his. It was a fair exchange in return for having a credible source, one that would really make the story fit to run past the corporates. Most importantly, I continued to maintain my cover story for all those who mattered.

According to our editorial team, the story was so piping hot that they pushed the online teasers ahead of the morning publishing. Fearing the information wouldn't be fresh for long, there was a sense of urgency to get it out immediately. It was also a jab at Lord Thurrington, with his connections to an establishment of contested repute.

The team at Sizzle had been waiting for that moment; the staff onsite had taken Florence's side in the divorce and company split. It was a small win for us, a major loss for those on the Thurrington side of the fence.

I refreshed the Sizzle page repeatedly until I stared at the headline I had written:

Knightsbridge's baddest boy: alleged conman boyfriend of society darling caught in stolen art scandal

A chill went down my spine when I finished reading the text. I had read the words many times since writing them, but this time, they would be flashing across several other devices at the same time. The story was no longer mine to protect; it was cascading into different people's consciousness and becoming the topic of conversation across town. The most fascinating part of the job had always been imagining how each person could be impacted by the very same set of words, of which all had been typed up in the sardine box I called an apartment. There, between plain walls, sharp-edged sentences were conjured in a direct attack on one of society's most popular boys. It was equally frightening and thrilling to have obtained the power to do so.

Without my earphones in my ears, the noises around the office were far more noticeable as the staff on the floor had all been waiting for the day's big story release. I looked around, waiting to make eye contact with someone from my team who could offer the real-life validation for my work that

I so intensely required to feel less anxious. I locked eyes with another featured journalist sitting a few rows back as she smiled and air clapped without actually emitting any sound. Her blue eyes narrowed behind a rounded glass frame rose with a raised blonde eyebrow to show she had been positively impressed. I beamed back with a nod; it fed my soul in that moment.

Meanwhile, passing through the corridors, the unmistakable firm footsteps that were so characteristic of Celine sounded against the wood floors. Her disposition looked particularly rested, which was confusing as surely she would have seen the headlines that linked Georgie's thieving activities to Lord Thurrington's gallery. She walked straight towards me in a dark teal dress that was clenched at the waist with a cream python skin belt. She came close enough that for a second, I thought she might hug me in the middle of the office, but instead, she whispered into my ear.

'I've resigned from Sizzle officially. Walk with me; we need to talk.'

I picked up my wallet from inside my work bag to create a faux pretence of heading away from the epicentre of the content team floor. The midi, hooded camel trench coat that hung from the back of the chair found itself on my back in less than a second.

'What's happened? When are you leaving?'

The chunky, heeled boots I had on seemed too heavy to follow Celine despite her heels being significantly taller than mine. Her sashay was unwavering in a moment that would have been nerve-wracking for mere mortals.

'I'm leaving immediately; I can't be seen here any longer. I know about the exposé that's coming up, so I'm jumping ship to where I will be better protected.'

'You're going to work with Thurrington?'

'Of course. You should consider a move. You're on the wrong side, Paze. The people here are just using you.'

Her hushed tone was barely audible despite walking next to her, but the content of the conversation made me look around nevertheless to see if anyone had heard us. A few whispering colleagues eyed us from the corner of the house, but on the publishing floor, where information is currency, they could have been keeping secrets of their own.

'And he wouldn't be using me?'

'Once you learn how to play the cards you clearly have in hand, nobody will use you.'

'How did you find out?'

'Don't you know that gossip never sleeps?' Celine gave me a large smile as she brought me in for a friendly embrace that emanated her musky, floral perfume straight into my nose. I took a breath while holding on to what felt like my closest friend at work till now.

As she pulled away from me to leave through the building entrance doors, I called out. 'Just before you go, I just want you to know the story wasn't going to be about you. I've avoided directly bringing you into the centre stage.'

Celine released an amused snicker while tilting her head slightly to the side in reaction to my comment.

'I know, Paze. We are insignificant in this power game. How far do you need to go before you realise that you'll never be one of them?'

Taken aback, I frowned as I raised my shoulders in confusion. 'If I wanted to be a part of the elite, why would I be exposing them?'

As she prepared to turn her back, flicking her hair above the oversized deep purple coat that covered her dress, Celine's face turned more stoic than I had ever seen her.

'You're exposing them because they don't let you in the door. Take care of yourself, nobody else will.'

I stood like a statue, staring at the back of the doors as they shut firmly with a bout of wind that came in behind Celine as she evaporated into the car on the street. Her words lingered in my ears as if they continued to sound in the echo of my inner thoughts. I didn't think she was completely right, but a part of me wondered if the ease of running stories on the subjects I selected had come from a disconnection to feeling any empathy for them. On the other hand, they all had it coming.

The side pocket of my trench coat vibrated furiously, forcing me to start walking outdoors to seek a nearby eat-out venue for my lunch break. A surprising name appeared on the locked screen, one that I hadn't noticed slip out of my group's regular encounters in the last few months. I answered while continuing to walk away from the office.

'Mila, it's been forever! What have you been up to?'

'It's snow season, darling; I'm obviously in Courchevel until I go back to Marbella for Christmas.'

Of course she was. Every change of season was a reminder that we vacation in different tax brackets. I, on the other hand, had only the awkward family season in Surrey to look forward to in the coming weeks.

'Anything exciting happening while trying to avoid the Instagram models?'

'Yes, Caetano and Sara are here together.'

No surprise there, either. Wherever there was a chance of champagne sparklers, those two would spontaneously appear. His high cheekbones and her toned abs were a society regular in more foreign destinations than I'd probably ever visit in a lifetime.

'Even with them around, I'd still rather be there than here.'

'How could you not? Everyone's talking about Georgie. How has Allegra taken the news?

I had yet to call her. There had just been so much happening today that I just did not find the right time to dedicate to her. 'She's Allegra, she's always fine.'

'True, which brings me to what I really wanted to discuss. Your boyfriend is here; I don't take him for a *Le Royale* kind of guy.'

Neither had I. In fact, he typically rolled his eyes anytime someone mentioned a nightlife hotspot like *Le Royale*. I had tagged along once with Allegra and her family, only to discover the club made every London member's only joint look shabby by comparison. The club, as the name suggested, was a who's who of every royal family looking for a quaint five-star snowy escape. The drinks were listed by vintage, not by price, and nobody would be caught dead with a visible brand logo. It was luxury so quiet that only those with a superbly well-established taste would appreciate it.

'Funny, I'm fairly certain he said he was going to Gstaad.'

'He's definitely here. I'm sure he probably just does the season in different places. I haven't seen him misbehave… yet.'

A sudden knot was felt in the centre of my stomach at Mila's words. Had he deliberately lied to me about where he was going? Surely, there was a misunderstanding somewhere.

'Can't wait to see you when you're back. Call me if anything scandalous happens.'

The line cut, and I still wasn't ready to put my phone away before one last message that had to be urgently sent.

Me

Hi babe! How's Gstaad?

Bex

As packed as ever, wish you were here :)

The worst part about catching someone in a lie is that you then need to do something about it. It hadn't been a part of my plan to suddenly need to concern myself that in unmasking someone else's boyfriend, I would simultaneously need to do the same in my own home. The message from Bex had left me feeling physically ill to the point that I needed to take a breather for the rest of the day. I had discreetly collected my belongings from the office before retreating to the sanctity of my studio flat.

As soon as I left the bus station on Gloucester Road, I spotted a familiar luxury car double parked in front of the restaurants. I walked across as the tinted window opened, relieving the anticipated rich Oud perfume that came from the inside.

'Hi Mansour. You could have just texted, you know?'

'And spare the theatrics? Not a chance. Besides, I've started to believe that you're deliberately avoiding me.'

In order to hide the growing nervousness that shot down to my hands, I opened the car door and gestured for him to shuffle across to the other seat. The custom leather seats adjusted to my body as I sank into the car.

'So where are we off to anyways?'

I looked at Mansour, taking in his ostrich leather jacket in deep mocha brown and oval-shaped, slightly tinted glasses. His neck was neatly wrapped in a nude cashmere turtleneck that complemented his tan skin tone. The edges of Mansour's shallow beard were meticulously shaved by his barber, giving him an appearance of constant primness.

'We're going off the grid for a very important chat.'

'We're leaving London?'

'No, what? We're going to Westfield.'

I started to laugh at the fact that going to the busiest mall in London was considered to be off the grid. The only context in which that could be applicable was if the only grid that mattered was within a five-mile radius of Knightsbridge.

Noticing that I was laughing alone, a very serious Mansour instructed his driver on our next destination. His full gaze then turned to me.

'Paze, I don't know what's going on with you and your work at Sizzle, but they just exposed your best friend's boyfriend. You do realise how this looks to us.'

'What do you mean by us? I gave Allegra a tip-off that it was coming.'

'Yes, to her, that may be enough, but I actually read the story. There were details there that only you could have known. I'm onto you.'

'What do you mean? We've got an extensive research team looking into stories all the time.'

'Yes, except the only one of them that knew about Alexandra and Georgie was you. Clearly, she's the unnamed ex-girlfriend. They were never public; we all found out together about his hideous tattoo that revealed their connection.'

My mind raced across every word in the article as I cross-referenced the source of each piece of information in seconds. There wasn't much margin for a wrong comment; everything I said next would be carefully analysed by the sharpest mind on that side of town. There was no room for error. One misplaced syllable or facial expression could instantly end any real prospect of belonging.

'You're not wrong that Alexandra was the source, but in reality, she came to Sizzle. The story is all from her perspective. I was not involved in the unmasking of Georgie.'

'You mean to say one of Europe's most discreet heiresses just spontaneously came to you with information that could potentially be trailed back to her?'

'It wasn't completely spontaneous. If you recall, we recently published the first public outing of Allegra and Georgie. Could it be jealousy?'

Mansour placed his hand on his body and relaxed on the oak panel of the door on his side.

'I supposed it could be that, *habibi*, but I still don't like you working for them.'

'Who knows how long I will be there… I don't feel anything is set in stone nowadays.'

Never before had I spoken truer words. The sense of security I had in my friendships, my place in the world, my future career, and even my new-found relationship with Bex all seemed to hang by a delicate thread. What would survive past the growing storm that I had inevitably found myself inside of while trying to simply secure the life I had long dreamed of having? I could drive myself into another panic attack thinking of that answer, or I could focus on a drive in a quarter-of-a-million-pound car through the most beautiful streets of London on my way to numb the pain with retail, gossip, and calories. I smiled at Mansour as he looked out his window onto the passing shops of High Street Kensington. For now, I was still there, taking in every drop of the lifestyle.

CHAPTER TWENTY-THREE
Order in the house

After a full week, the items acquired during the excursion to the mall sat still untouched in a melange of bags on the small couch in my flat. I sat there, enjoying the final day of the weekend with a homemade brew that kept me company in an otherwise stale apartment overflowing with notes about the next steps in my investigative story. I looked over to the combination of shiny and matte designer logos staring back at me while I sat in a stained university hoodie and sports shorts. That day had been filled with ludicrous shopping where Mansour tried to persuade me to buy dozens of things I couldn't afford, only to be so frustrated that I hadn't subdued that he gifted them to me.

While I appreciated every curated item he selected, I started to notice that apart from the boredom that usually motivated his spending rampages, there had also been a loneliness in his voice. This had been particularly pronounced in his constant reminder mid-conversation of how our once inner sanctum group had started to feel more and more distant. I thought of how, after several mentions of wishing things could go back to how they had been at university, I finally sat down on a velvet round inside the Versace store for a comical but truthful chat.

'Mansour, I never thought I'd say this, but your parents may be right in trying to find you a wife. That would probably be a much better use for your money at this point.'

Ever since we graduated from university, the pressure was on for Mansour to settle down back home. He had masterfully avoided the issue by enrolling in an endless cycle of postgraduate courses, which he had intended to maintain until his parents grew tired of asking him about his personal life.

'Whose side are you on Paze?' Mansour placed his hands on his hips while shaking his head in disapproval.

'I'm just saying, you could have all this fun with someone who appreciates your impeccable taste on a long-term basis.'

Mansour's eyes had remained firmly planted on a metallic jacquard tuxedo blazer displayed on a mannequin next to us. He then looked back at me, his eyes squinted slowly as he took in a deep breath.

'True, but if I'm honest, I can't stop thinking of Ameerah. I can't really focus on anyone else if I can't get her out of my mind.'

'Well, that's a name I haven't heard in a while.'

'I'm good at hiding my feelings behind a carefully tailored suit.'

I knew when to push and when to let go of things, particularly with Mansour's more serious subjects. His personal life was closely guarded, even from us. His way of showing appreciation was with lavish generosity. While it typically would feel great in any other situation, lying to him tainted the way I felt.

Back in my studio flat, a white-lettered Versace logo on the bag hiding a gifted turquoise latex cocktail dress gave a visual reminder that I was deceiving the only people who had ever shown me true friendship. I didn't feel worthy of them, not the dress and certainly not the friends.

Instead of dwelling further on self-criticism, I thought I'd do something more productive, so I pulled out my work laptop from the leather bag on the stool opposite me. I took a long sip of coffee just as the first email of the day caught me off-guard. Allegra contacted Sizzle with an official statement from her publicist. The only problem was she never had one until now. It took me a minute to scroll down past the response to find the answer I was looking for as to what it all meant. There was no clear indication of who her team was, and I remained intrigued at the approach of bringing in an external professional since she had long avoided any unnecessary exposure—which she deemed to be beneath her well-bred discretion.

She agreed to a follow-up article as long as she could control the narrative. In their strategy, it was decided that she would be answering questions around Georgie as long as she could decide which ones. Also, she wanted me to write the story personally and not anyone else. Nathan had already agreed on my behalf while including me as a mere carbon copy in the trail.

Allegra had decided to share details of her relationship with a con man. It most likely meant she had now decided to officially eliminate Georgie from her circle. It wasn't unusual for her to execute with a clean social blade, but it was without a precedent for Allegra to go to the press in order to control the narrative around her. For as long as I'd known her, the approach had always been a dignified aristocratic silence in the face of intrusive media. This time, though, she was going on the offence. I felt my heartbeat accelerate as guilt started spreading through my body like a cold spear.

Just then, a notification invaded the upper part of my phone screen.

Bex

> Guess who's back? Dinner tonight at mine?

Regardless of the fact that I knew he had lied to me, I missed him. I had also avoided bringing up any confrontation over the phone. I didn't want to seem as if I was jealous, pacing the last few days, but I also had no bandwidth to deal with a potential negation from his side.

> Me
>
> Would love to see you at 7.

Much preparation was needed before facing Bex with a mixture of longing and disdain for the compounding evidence of his untruthfulness. The outfit choice would have to be precise enough to make him stumble and, ideally, regret his dubious ski trip. But before then, there was a far more important relationship that also needed my attention for it to be nurtured.

> Me
>
> Allegra, I miss you. I got the message from your team. Can I see you first?

> Allegra
>
> The V&A, Tea Room, 4PM.

Very few people knew that Victoria & Albert had one of the most spectacular tea rooms in London. Even fewer people understood that behind the gold features and stained glass windows, many of London's most indecent secrets were shared while unsuspecting tourists admired the views. The only acceptable public locations for discreet conversations were those held where the surrounding attendees would be unsuspecting of the gravity of the content.

In anticipation of an evening of confronting the two most significant stressors, I had to decide on a convertible outfit that could satisfy the discretion of the meeting with Allegra and also assure Bex that I was very much not worth lying to. The pre-Christmas air was colder than usual; it chilled the windows of my flat as the heating fought bravely against the external winter.

I laid out the bodycon nude turtleneck knit dress that I had picked up recently as a part of a designer high street collab. The material was slightly thinner on the chest area, where the knitted material gave way to a mesh. I collected my hair into a messy ponytail with some strands left to frame my face. My tresses had grown without a regular haircut, while the lack of sunlight had darkened the roots from the usual lighter tones of summer. On my eyes, I used a chunky gold liner on the bottom lid that lit up my eyes in contrast to an attempted feline eyeliner flick on the top lid. I couldn't perfect it quite like Allegra, but I could perhaps elongate my shape into a more sultry look for later. Over the top of my outfit, I added my winter beige trench with a chunky crimson scarf that I had been gifted last Christmas by my parents.

While I completed my outfit with a pair of Timberland boots that had spent far too long in the back of my closet, I looked at the web diagram on my desk containing all the impending stories to be solved ahead of the centrepiece article in the exposé. There was so much to uncover still, and the story had already taken a toll on my life. A shiver shot down my spine at the thought of what else was to come.

The alert vibrated on my phone, signalling that the Uber driver had arrived. I figured it was worth a short drive in the name of longevity of the evening's look. The door to the building revealed a gush of coldness that entered from the edge of the dress's seam.

I entered the tea room and scanned the area for the obviously glamorous visitor. It took a few seconds to find Allegra had sat in the corner, on the far right side, wearing a black beanie with a dramatic black veil attached down to her nose. She had on a black tinted lambskin winter jacket and still wore her thin leather gloves as her hands remained poised gently on the stone table top. We gave each other air kisses before I sat in front of her.

'Paze, it's really good to see you. It's been tough, your absence has been noticed.'

Her gaze looked far more distant. I looked at her directly and could see the heavy colour correction employed under the eyes, most likely to hide evidence of sleeplessness.

'I'm sorry, I truly didn't know if you needed space. I assumed it was good to let you figure things out on how to terminate Georgie.'

'I'm not planning on breaking things off with him.'

This was an unexpected turn. I raised my eyebrows naturally in a mixture of confusion and concern for my friend's mental health state. Clearly, she needed to be reminded of what the situation truly entailed.

'Hmm… I'm not going to pretend that I understand. He's exposed you and your family name; besides, he's clearly a criminal.'

Allegra took a sip of her double espresso in a slowed cadence. She broke into a coy smile before continuing to speak.

'Do you know why I use my mother's surname?'

'I guess it sounds more exotic than Pembroke, I suppose.'

'It did set me apart, but also, we adopted our new names when my father went to jail when I was ten.'

For the second time in less than five minutes, I was left speechless. I had been friends with Allegra for as long as I could remember, and I never knew anything about her family's legal troubles. Clearly, any mention of it had been scrubbed away from where anyone could see. Still, I felt a little hurt by the lack of trust when she knew every intricate detail of my life.

'After all these years, you never told me about this.'

'It's not something to be proud of, particularly with my mother remarrying before I could come to grips with the situation. It was very painful for me to live with this reality…'

I held out both hands to touch hers; it was the most vulnerable I had ever seen her. The guilt of having benefited from a story that had led her to relive these moments bubbled up into an incoming bout of anxiety. As I tried to find the right words to make it slightly better, Allegra continued speaking.

'I'm not like her. I won't leave the man I love standing alone just because he's made some mistakes trying to make a better life for himself.'

She loved him. It couldn't be true, surely. It felt too fresh, and their pairing was far too odd. It felt as if my sensible, manicured best friend was trying to fix a childhood trauma with a vapid and eternally-in-college boy. I had to make it stop; I wouldn't let her throw away her reputation for him. For the time being, the situation required tact to avoid becoming the antagonist.

'You're one of the kindest people I know; you're nothing like her. I should warn you there will be more to come. Sizzle is still investigating leads and stories.'

She gracefully removed her headpiece while her eyes changed from sad to a much more intense gaze. She placed the beanie on the table without any sense of hurry. Her movements were planned, which only intimated me further.

After the pause, she spoke while maintaining eye contact. 'I'm going to need you to step up and put some order in the house. I may not be keen to break up the relationship, but I will not see our lives become a media mockery.'

I gulped nervously, realising I had yet to order any beverage that could be used as a prop to hide my feelings.

'Of course, I'm your insider there. Speaking of which, you wanted to share your side of the story?'

Allegra sighed deeply in annoyance before pushing her cup to the side.

'The only thing I hate about this place is needing to physically fetch my own coffee refill. Anyways, Alexandra is a lying little bitch. She just wanted to get back at Georgie for not giving back things she gifted him.'

I seldom heard Allegra use curse words, but when I did, it generally meant someone would soon be on the receiving end of her wrath.

'For such an accusation, you know I'll need evidence.'

'How can someone prove one's ex is obviously jealous of their upgraded romantic life?'

'I don't know, honestly, but maybe there's a bigger story that will overpower this one. Maybe Georgie knows something that can be useful to us.'

Allegra took in the words as if a breath of fresh air had entered her lungs. Her body readjusted back in the seat as her shoulders fell back, giving her smooth neck a chance to appear. A slow, asymmetrical smile appeared on her face, showcasing that she knew the exact story to plant to distract from her own entanglement.

'My father's lawyer once told him that there's this Lord Something-or-another who secretly runs all of Knightsbridge. He nearly owns as much property here as our friends from the Gulf.'

'I'm going to need a little more meat than that to sell it.'

'Here's the thing, people don't question his wealth because of his family's name, but apparently, he's got this crazy scheme where he dishes out young women who get expensive things from the rich men around which he resells for a profit. It's pretty slimy.'

'Did his lawyer just openly talk about this?'

'He was trying to get my father to be more positive about early release. He was right; nobody keeps a lord in jail.

That was his point; this guy apparently has dirt on everyone in town, so he's untouchable.'

That was the most uncomfortable truth in London. Accountability was only for those lacking in access and surname. Far too often, nothing could hurt the upper crust.

'Do you think the lawyer would speak to me about it?'

'I don't think I've got Blake's number—that was his name. But I'm sure I can get it off my father's assistant.'

I had heard the name recently, and since most of my friends don't have old-sounding names, it should have been easy enough to remember. Blake, Blake… I had to think quickly. I looked down at the table, which was still laid bare without any order on my side.

'I need to go grab something to drink, maybe some scones? Do you want some?'

Allegra negated my offering with a head shake and dived into her phone, giving me the chance to head over to the ordering counter. As soon as my body was completely turned away from our table, it hit me. I slowed my pace as the information dripped internally through the memory pathways in my brain. Lord Thurrington's lawyer was called Blake; could it possibly be the same person who looked after Allegra's father?

After ordering, I headed back to the table, taking in the environment as I made my way across the eatery packed with a mixture of tourists and older local residents. The number of international visitors across Knightsbridge and Kensington hadn't dwindled with the cold. A plethora of languages could be heard, filling the air above us with what was surely much lighter conversation than what weighed on my mind.

I passed by a group of Italian teenagers snacking away while their trip chaperone inspected maps. Next to them, a young family sipped on the Christmas-themed drinks from the counter while laughing at each other's jokes. At the left side, as I approached Allegra's table, an elderly woman dressed in an elegant navy turtleneck that reached up to where her thin, white hair ended enjoyed her tea whilst keeping a firm eye on her copy of the Sunday Times. I envied their peaceful existence, leagues away from the restlessness of the Knightsbridge crowd.

I finally sat down again, clutching my drink and a plate of scones with cream and jam. Allegra looked at me and my food choice with a mixture of judgment and envy for willingly partaking in a carbohydrate loading. Little did she know I was mentally preparing for an emotional marathon later to decode what was happening with Bex. I broke the silence while preparing to gobble on my sweet escape.

After a few seconds of silent snares at my plate, I responded verbally.

'What? I needed the treat. I've been very stressed lately.'

'Is that so? I'm so sorry. I haven't even asked much about you with everything happening on my end.'

'Well, I've been working quite a bit of research for a special task that Florence Massey herself asked me to do. It's one of those make-it-or-break-it career moments, but the further I search, the more nebulous it comes.'

Placing her focus now entirely on reading between the lines on my face, she smiled one of those warm smiles that comforts you like a mother would, or should.

'Paze, you're the smartest person I know. Heck, you're the smartest person anyone in our circle knows. If someone can crack a story, it's going to be you. Besides, since when are you besties with Florence? Hasn't she been your idol since school?'

Her words made me feel even better than the smile. I'd missed that part of our friendship since we had slipped into the never-ending busyness of professional life.

'Yes, she was and still is, quite frankly. I wouldn't say we're besties, but she's put some trust in me after my boss made sure I got a chance to show her what I can do. They say "don't meet your idols", but I feel like she's exactly how she's meant to be.'

'Let's hope she lives up to the hype. Can't wait to see what major story this will be.'

A sense of dread surfaced from the depths of my stomach, thinking about how this story could intertwine with Allegra in ways that she was not prepared for at all. Despite my recent lack of support for her, she had been as kind as always and even willing to give me information that could help further my career. I had to be wiser on how to protect her from the freefall that would ensue soon.

As we finished and I started my way out towards South Kensington station, my phone vibrated with a notification.

> Bex
>
> Change of plans, meet on Walton Street for food? I'm in the area anyways.

Odd, the self-professed Knightsbridge avoider was in one of the quintessential streets for local shenanigans. It was where the great migration post Harrods closing hours occurred; herds of the same people previously engaged in the intricacies of the social play happening in London's most exclusive department store would descend into the dimly lit bars and eateries of the adjacent street.

As the night sky appeared, so did the characters who came to the area looking for a chance encounter that could lead to an evening of pleasure. It wasn't an assumption that you only went there looking for a plus one to end the night with, but there was a connotation that the vast majority were single, well-dressed, and only dated rich. I was intrigued by the choice and slightly worried about what it meant for us.

Bex was waiting for me at the door of Dane's, a laid-back deli-turned-nightclub in the later hours. The cue that it wasn't your average neighbourhood eatery should've been the fact that two robust security guards stood outside at all hours of the day. Inside, a mix of smoky-eyed women in the tightest possible winter dresses and men dressed in logo-clad long-sleeved tops while metallic ski jackets that were too heavy for London rested on the sofas. We made our way to a table near the wall, from where the food display and door remained visible.

He had greeted me with a shy kiss at the door but hadn't grabbed my hand to guide me inside. It felt distant, even if his body was physically very close to mine. We sat opposite each other with an artificial candle providing some additional lighting in an otherwise very dark ambience of strategic lights only over the ordering counter. I looked him straight on, taking in every inch of his sexier-than-ever face with three-day stubble. Why did he choose to wear a V-neck that showed just the right amount of clavicle? It was going to be very difficult to stay mad at him when I could already sense arousal tingling between my highs. I needed to stay on track with something that wasn't sensual at all.

'So how's your trip? Tell me everything!'

'It was strange, actually; the snow wasn't great, so at some point, we moved to a different place that I hadn't been before.'

Instead of mere relief, there could have been a legitimate reason, after all, for him not being in Gstaad the whole time, I mentally patted myself on the back for not having engaged in any accusatory behaviour that would have imploded the whole relationship. I twirled the piece of hair that stuck out on the side of my face, trying to redirect the evening's mood to flirtation.

'Had no clue you weren't in Gstaad. Where else did you go?'

'Stepdad drove us to France, actually, and ended up in Courchevel. You won't believe who was there.'

A waiter interrupted with a timely distraction so I had more space to act on my surprised reaction face. Luckily, the lights were so dimmed it would be hard for Bex to pick up on what was likely to be overacting since I've always been a terrible liar.

'I'll have a negroni as well… so you were about to tell me who was there. Super curious.'

'Your friend Mila, total coincidence. I saw her coming out of this wild club there, don't even know how I recognised her, considering I had probably downed a full bottle of Grey Goose.'

I wondered why he had only mentioned her when it was highly unlikely that he hadn't seen Sara in the only flashy nightclub in a remote ski town. Considering she followed the trail of money, that was probably where she spent every night of her trip trying to recover the significant investment to get there in the first place. Then again, maybe he genuinely didn't think it was worth a mention—after all, those weren't people he showed much interest in before I asked him to trail her for a story.

'Anything naughty happen on the trip?'

Bex broke into childish laughter, probably sensing that my sentence had a twinge of possessiveness in the choice of wording.

'Behave, I've got a hot girlfriend, and I'm planning on taking her home tonight.'

His words melted away the building resentment that had been brewing since Mila's call. He took a sip of his drink, licking his lips to take in the residue of the bitter licoricey taste. My eyes went directly to his mouth, which he noticed and reciprocated by getting up slightly off his chair. He slid his hand behind my neck, pulling me closer to his face until we locked into a deep kiss. I could feel the drink on him still as he held on passionately for a few seconds.

When we both fell back into our chairs, I looked at him with eyes partially squinting with desire. 'Let's get a takeaway at yours; there are too many people here, and we're wearing too many clothes.'

Bex smiled with his lips locked while signalling to the waiter for the bill. He placed his hand over mine on the table, bringing me in closer again, but that time to whisper in my ear.

'I missed this version of you. Don't let her go anywhere.'

CHAPTER TWENTY-FOUR

If you can't beat them

The morning after a great night of making up for time lost is always the worst way to start off a work week. Before we slumbered off, I managed to make Bex a naked promise to wake up earlier than usual and drive me to my cubicle-like flat so I could turn up to the office with a fresh outfit. I figured it was enough arriving at the office particularly cheerful without needing the spectacle of clothes from the night prior.

With automated motions, I managed to reorganise myself into the corporate version that people at work were more accustomed to seeing. A takeaway smoothie and almond croissant on the way were as much as I could muster without delaying my entry beyond the time I was paid to appear at Sizzle Media. Within a short while of arriving at the office in a dressed-down jogger with a blue striped button shirt combo underneath my coat, an unfamiliar face approached me as I unpacked the items from my vintage Fendi bag.

She held a tablet close to her chest, sported gold-rimmed round glasses and shoulder-length curly blonde hair that trickled onto the upper part of a plain black blazer. There was an intern-ish air about her that gave off nervousness.

'Florence wants to see you upstairs. I'm Jessa, her new assistant.'

'Oh, okay. Nice to meet you.'

'She doesn't have much of a window, so I suggest you hurry up.'

Despite her intimidating nature, I missed Celine. Her small talk would have been far less transactional and far more interesting. Instead, Jessa's body language was robotic as she quietly guided me to the lift so we could make our way over to the higher-ups. It dawned on me that I was still caffeine-deprived and at an additional disadvantage of wit next to what was awaiting on the upper floor.

When I walked in that time, it did not have the same connotation as the first time I saw the expansiveness of the office. I was walking in with far more confidence, knowing that I was at least useful to Sizzle Media. The hangover from the drinks I gobbled down at Bex's flat probably helped numb my nerves. My brain diverted all energy to preparing coherent phrases which would be needed for when I would inevitably need to interact with my ultimate boss.

My legs halted of their own will next to Florence's table, where Nathan stood next to her, intently discussing something inaudible. Her maroon power suit with a delicate gold snakeskin belt exuded a powerful presence.

'Ah, welcome back, Paisley. I've been following your progress.'

'Thanks. Not going to lie, it's been pretty wild to go from columnist to having a feature story.'

I smiled genuinely, looking at Nathan to silently suggest that my success was his success, too. I hoped he understood my silent nod to his membership. Florence, in the meantime, pulled her chair out to take a seat before continuing.

'Speaking of which, I still haven't seen the anvil.'

'What do you mean?'

'The heavy hitter that drags everything down with it.'

I instinctively crossed my arms at the mention of the most uncomfortable topic currently looming over me. I regretted the reaction but tried to compensate by raising one hand up to my face into an awkward pseudo-intellectual pose. It was better, at least, than standing in front of my ideal journalist like a whiny child.

'I'm working on it, I promise. I've just had an important break from a source who potentially knows Lord Thurrington's lawyer.'

'The only thing is… Celine knows what we're doing. She will be a major nuisance, but as an infiltrator, I want her to be the one who takes the fall. It's what she deserves.'

Nathan had remained quiet until that point, observing our exchange without offering any word to the conversation.

His gaze remained mostly on the floor, which told me he wasn't necessarily agreeing with something, and I'd need to deduce what that could be.

He locked eyes with Florence, showing that he was ready to contribute to the course of action.

'I presume so since she left. But that isn't a bad thing. You should get close to her.'

Florence nodded her head as she started to smirk.

'Yes, Nathan is right. Make her believe you're on her team. I want you to go undercover.'

I took a step back, unconsciously distancing the two of them. I replied, 'I'm not sure if I have enough information yet. Besides, you know Celine studied law, right? She will certainly sue us if there isn't enough to go on.'

Florence moved from where she stood to stand in front of her desk, closer to me. She crossed her arms but maintained a subtle smirk.

'Which is why there's no room for error. You need to convince her that you really want to be like her. What do they usually say? If you can't beat them, join them? That's what you need to convince them of now.'

'But won't someone see me here and tell her? We don't know who's on their side.'

'You won't come to the office at all. For all intents and purposes, you don't work here anymore. Given the risk, we will offer a bonus for this with a double salary until the feature drops. Even your social media needs to be distanced from Sizzle. Every precaution must be taken.'

The shock of how significant the request was hit my veins like a shot of coffee and sent my brain into overdrive. I could feel the edges of my fingers numb with anxiety, so I moved them to a resting interlocked position in front of my stomach.

'I'm a little out of my depth, but I will work with Nathan to get this right.'

Florence took a deep breath before turning her back to me and returning to her work chair. She sat at once, making the metals holding it together sound audibly.

'There isn't room for error, Paisley. I need this story concluded before they have time to regroup, and I need Celine to go down for this. As for my ex-husband, he can only be tied to the scandal if there's indisputable proof. Both you and Nathan are on the line for this. Any mistakes will have grave consequences.'

Finally, Nathan started moving away from where he had stood on the powerful side of the room. He signalled with his head for us to leave before adding his final reassurance to our boss.

'There won't be any, Florence. We will deliver a scandal worthy of your trust.'

As soon as his words came out, Florence refocused her attention on the laptop open on her desk. We turned around and walked quickly as the peripheral view of the surrounding imposing decor faded away.

In the privacy of the lift, with just the two of us, Nathan finally addressed me directly. 'I can't believe I supported this madness. Now both of our asses are on the line.'

I stood silently as he moved his hands up to his head before continuing his rant. 'I'm going to need you to pull this off perfectly.'

'How is this my fault? You sanctioned this; in fact, you encouraged it!'

I could no longer hide my annoyance at feeling cornered by everyone who should have my back. It wouldn't suit me to showcase that yet, though, so I worked hard to push it back down before Nathan noticed anything.

'Paze, this isn't a joke. We could both be fired if this doesn't go well. I just got a mortgage for a new place in Islington. How can I explain this to my partner? Ugh, we need to put together a plan.'

The lift opened, releasing us from the discomfort that filled the tiny space between us. I went to the desk where I had dropped my things earlier, but before I could settle in, I saw Nathan gathering our team.

'It pains me to say that our lovely Paze will be leaving us for a sabbatical from journalism to pursue a personal project. Isn't that right, Paze? We will miss you here in the office.'

I had barely had enough time to process, so I packed my things quickly, trying to fend off any uncomfortable questions. The best excuse I could come up with was that I had been offered a unique study opportunity that I simply couldn't pass on. In many ways, it wasn't untrue, given that I would be tasked with observing egregious behaviour in the wild and writing a report on it, much like a study.

Nathan walked me out with a big, fake smile to showcase that he was, in fact, happy about my journey. It was discombobulating to see his capacity for feigning in front of the wider team. It made me wonder what else he could have been faking all along.

At the large doors to the outside of the building, much like I had done with Celine, he saw me off with a quiet whisper. 'Start putting an action plan together. Let's meet after work somewhere with some privacy to discuss. For now, don't do anything silly, Paze. I do trust you.'

I smiled disingenuously back at Nathan before replying in a slightly louder timbre. 'I trust you too.'

Note to self: Nathan was very self-serving. But if there was one thing I was used to, it was doing all the hard work in order for him to save himself and get the glory in the process. His time, too, would come, but right that moment, he wasn't a priority.

Without any other place to be in the early morning hours, I walked down Charlotte Street towards the student cafes nearby, where the youngsters of Fitzrovia could be seen on their laptops over a large bucket of liquid encouragement. Hints of Christmas surrounded the place with red and green decorations around the counter. There was some irony in pretending to be studying and finding a place amongst actual students to lounge while I thought of my next steps.

Once I was comfortably sitting and warmed up to a dark mocha, I pulled my mobile to kickstart the engine of covert reporting.

Me

Celine, I thought about what you said and I want in.

THE KNIGHTSBRIDGE CROWD

Celine

> Perfecto, but first, I need to see if you're ready for this. I will share the location, Saturday night at 8PM. Dress well.

I didn't know how ready I was, but the strong desire to make my mark at Sizzle had my blood boiling to show Nathan what I was finally made of. It was going to be more fun than I originally had thought, so I decided that it was time to enjoy the process of holding all the secrets that none of the London elite wanted to divulge.

The holiday season had never been my favourite. Apart from the food, there wasn't much I looked forward to that time of year. I was fresh-faced after spending Christmas and Boxing Day at home in Surrey, toasting myself in the warmth of my family home and indulging in countryside treats. The other positive was catching up on silent sleep in the comfort of my childhood home, but not before the reality of life in the city came crawling through the messages that made the walls of our detached chalet seem like a barrier to the action of Knightsbridge.

I got back in time to make Celine's appointment with some space to spare for a full skincare routine while catching up with all my favourite humans over the phone. I had missed my friends and Bex. They were the people I would have spent every moment with if it were acceptable to avoid your ageing parents for the holidays. It wasn't, though, so I put on a good face and braved the countryside for a few days away from all that mattered.

The first day of my new role as an undercover reporter started like any other in my daily life. I made my signature home meal wrap with caramelised onion and chunks of turkey, took a nearly scalding hot shower, and dressed myself in the correct outfit for the person I needed to convince everyone I was currently passing as on any given day. As hours passed, I slowly morphed back into my city self, leaving Surrey girl behind for the time being.

By the time evening finally came, I was re-energised with enough strength to face the initiation ritual that Celine had prepared for me. It was as if I was the newest recruit for a cult that would steal my innocence in the process. Except Celine was more of a madam than a cult leader, and I had barely innocence left to spare, anyways.

I met Celine in an Italian restaurant off Brompton Road. The neatly manicured houses around the square were like a movie set, where the prompt required affluent neighbourhoods with perfect facades, both for people and houses. I walked in and found Celine sitting near the entrance in a tight-fit turtleneck blue jumper mini dress with Gucci monograms printed on it. Her shiny hair was freshly blow-dried straight down, which elongated it further towards her waist.

As soon as I arrived, she stood to greet me, and I noticed how tall she stood on her stiletto-heeled mocha over-the-knee boots. It was the most impractical outfit for winter in London, but she looked every inch a Bond girl at a fancy ski resort.

We sat next to each other, and she complimented me on my choice of a plunge top leopard print bodycon dress. It wasn't something I was used to wearing; it was far more overtly sexy than anything I'd pick out on a normal day. But it wasn't a normal day or a normal occasion, and after a few hours of research, I settled on the fast fashion knockoff of Dolce & Gabbana's most iconic seductress outfit.

Soon after pleasantries and ordering a carpaccio each, Celine pulled me closer so she could tell me information that was intended for my ears only. 'Look at the tables around you.'

'What am I looking at?'

All I could see when I scanned the area were tables of people in varying states of ordering or eating food. There was a large mix of what seemed like seasonal visitors and perhaps some local residents. I tried to squint to see what details I could be overlooking.

'Observe and tell me what you see.'

'People eating, some of them are watching football. I don't know what you want me to say.'

'I want you to understand what happens around you all the time, and you don't notice.'

My eyes focused closely on a table near the entrance. The restaurant had many tables with one single man sitting down. One older man with a thick beard wrote down on a piece of paper and set it down. He looked to the side, making eye contact with the waiter, who proceeded to pick it up and then do the same to other tables. It was indeed odd, particularly because I hadn't seen it before.

'You get it now?'

'The waiter is picking up something written on all these tables. That's unusual.'

'Very good, Paze. They're bidding.'

'Bidding on what?'

Celine signalled with her eyes to an area behind her where a table with two university-aged girls sat together. One of them had shiny black hair that was perfectly straightened down to her waist. Her glossy brown eyes were highlighted with contrasted eyeshadow in tones of burnt gold. The corseted top she wore pushed her bust upwards near her chin. At her side sat a blonde with shoulder-length locks that nested onto a tight white turtleneck with a transparent mesh fabric exposing a generous bosom.

I felt disgusted, but my face remained placid. By that point, I had trained myself not to react externally to Celine's loose morality.

'They set an offer; the girls can accept or decline.'

'This is a sex auction, Celine.'

'Uh, that's kinky. Not quite; they just set out an invite and what's up for offer if they agree. Sex is always optional.'

'But it always happens, right?'

'It can happen if everyone's in the mood, I guess. I'm not in the room with them.'

'What if the girls aren't in the mood? Or if they change their mind at some point? They look a little young to have good sense.'

'I'm not about to mother them. They'll learn eventually to look after themselves, or they'll get a nine to five that chains them to a simple life. For now, my main concern is that the people who matter are entertained. The girls are not my concern.'

It shouldn't have surprised me how transactional the situation was for Celine, given that her past responses on the flesh trade had shown little concern for the morality of it all. And yet, her complete lack of preoccupation with the girls, who looked barely above eighteen, still made me physically sick. Florence was right; she needed to go down. For the time being, though, I had to hide my true feelings a bit better before she thought I was getting cold feet.

'I guess you're right. You're giving them a better chance of at least getting something out of it. How many uni girls are giving it away for free, anyways?'

Celine looked at me with a smirk; I had impressed her with my comment. I needed to keep that tone if I had a chance of succeeding with the infiltration.

'Very well, you're starting to understand me. Now, with your intelligence and mannerisms, I wouldn't put you up for this type of public display. I need you for one of the high rollers tonight. We're going to the casino tower to meet with some very distinguished folk.'

With that, Celine gesticulated at the restaurant manager, who was clearly a part of the scheme since he didn't bring us any bill for our consumption. Instead, Celine was helped by a staff member into a black and blue feathered coat that engulfed her entirely. She took the lead as I dressed into my beige coat, trailing behind her to the pavement outside where a Mercedes S Class awaited us with a driver opening the passenger door.

The drive to our next stop was short, a few minutes down the road, and we disembarked at a five-star hotel opposite one of the squares in Knightsbridge. We arrived at the hotel lobby, where the concierge greeted Celine like they were close friends. He slipped a discreet envelope into her top-opened bag. She led the way, but I trailed next to her as we made our way to the room lifts. She pulled a magnetic key card from the envelope and pressed the top floor.

The lift ascended directly to the penthouse suite, which opened up behind thick oak doors. A security guard stood on each side of the door while a tall, suited, muscular man asked for our phones. He produced two clear acrylic boxes with a security lock on top, which he opened to deposit our phones. He then placed them in a cupboard until exit time. I had no way of documenting what was going on, and more frighteningly, I had no way to ask for external help.

In the room, a mixed group of men of all ages mingled with other girls in carefully selected outfits that delineated every curve in their bodies. On the table, two Murano bowls full of white and pink powdery substances were visible, as were stacks of pills in hues of white and blue. A thick smoke floated in the air from a combination of cigarettes, cigars, and vapes, while open bottles of every brand of alcohol above one hundred pounds lined the side tables around silk fabric sofas. The scene was not at all what I was ready to encounter, yet I was reassured that the quantum of people present made it less intimidating.

In a corner, I spotted a DJ who presumably was responsible for the sensual lounge beats echoing to all walls of the large penthouse. From a distance, I saw Lord Thurrington walking from where the speakers were placed with a drink in his hand. As he approached, I noticed a vestige of white powder on his shirt lapel.

Celine forced laughter out of nowhere, pulling me into whisper range, pretending to tell me a joke.

'He doesn't know you were a journalist; he wouldn't let you in otherwise, but I think I can make good money with a girl like you, so I'm taking a risk.'

He came to where we stood, kissing Celine on the cheek for a good twenty seconds before turning towards me.

'You're new around here, but I remember seeing you somewhere before. Such a pretty girl.'

His hand ran down the side of my waist, and strangely, instead of disgusted, I felt slightly aroused. There was so much power in those hands that they didn't repulse me in the least. Instead, all I could think of was how, either way, he would have something to do with what would happen next in my career.

I asked to go find the bathroom. It was a good decoy to cool down the situation. The suite was so large it had a full-sized kitchen that separated the living area from the bedrooms on the other side of the floor. I got into a bedroom with an ensuite; it didn't look big enough to be the master, so I figured there was no harm.

As I was about to hit the flush, I heard two recognisable voices come into the room. A man and a woman spoke increasingly louder as they slammed the door behind them and walked closer to where I stood, partitioned by a wood door. I looked around the bathroom and found an empty glass nestled on the nearby sink. I pressed it to my ear and attached myself to the door to listen in as closely as I could.

'He's really angry with you. You need to be more careful about getting bad press. You know how it works; we need to keep the girls working and the drugs moving so we can keep expanding the family wealth. You shouldn't have brought your stolen crap to the store we use to launder the money. It's dumb, and he's right to be pissed at you.'

It was clearly Celine; her voice was easily distinguishable.

'Of course you're going to be on his side; he's your meal ticket. Unlike with you, he's never given me anything I deserve… Even though I'm his…'

Even though I was listening through the glass, I could clearly hear Georgie's deep voice. I wondered what he was doing there; clearly, he knew Celine and more about Lord Thurrington than he'd admitted to Allegra.

The conversation fell short with a knock on the main door of the bedroom. *Crap.* I couldn't believe I nearly uncovered crucial information. Nevertheless, there was a lot to unpack there. But before that, I needed to get out without getting caught.

I prayed every word from a childhood prayer that I could remember from my catechism days as a child. I needed both people on the other side of the room to leave without coming towards the bathroom. Given what they did for a living and the seriousness of the confession, I could have been in real danger.

Luckily, I heard their footsteps distance themselves from me as the door eventually slammed closed. I took a couple of minutes to ensure I heard nothing else so that I could finally exit the bathroom.

The door creaked loudly as it opened while my heart raced as if I was running in an actual physical activity. I peeked with just the tip of my head showing, and sighed with relief that the room was de facto empty.

When I finally made it to the door, I opened it and left with my eyes so focused on the way back that I missed the tall figure on the other side of the hall. I could only tell someone else was there when I heard a commanding voice sound from behind me.

'Going back to the party so soon? Stay a bit, it's more intimate here.'

I turned around to find Lord Thurrington standing quite close. His musky perfume mixed perfectly with the cigar residue that remained on his white, slightly unbuttoned shirt. It was the smell of peril; it was completely intoxicating. He stood there, leaning with one arm against the dusty pink wallpaper between the dark wood panels of the hallway.

Our eyes locked for a minute as I tried to find the right words to say. Instead, he quickly ate the space between us, grabbing my waist with his full hands and placing his open mouth on my neck. I growled without thinking of it, still in shock at his action, while my body acted of its own accord. He quickly moved his hands around my upper body. I gasped for air to begin processing what was going on. In a blurry few seconds, I found myself being taken into the room I had just exited with my lips firmly locked on his.

He locked the door before lifting my legs around his waist to throw me onto the guest bed. The dress I wore rode upwards on the sides, revealing exactly what he wanted to see. Our clothes flew off in a matter of seconds, his confident strokes motivating a reaction in every part of my body. He had barely seen me twice, but somehow, he seemed to read within milliseconds what brought me into loud moans. Our bodies merged into a rhythm cadence that I wished never to end.

When it finally did, after he made my body quiver with climax four times over, he pulled my hand out, offering a little kiss on the wrist. The reality of what just happened dawned on me at the sight of the plastic evidence thrown on the bed next to me. Without an exchange of words, he paced off to the bathroom where I had previously been to refresh himself while I started to collect my things from the floor.

Coming out of the bathroom, still undressed, I could see that he had maintained an athletic physique intact despite the signs of ageing on his skin. He was no doubt an attractive man, and I found myself wondering what he had looked like when he was my age rather than double it.

As he dressed in front of me, he spoke while staring at the mess he made of me, still sitting on the edge of the bed. 'I'm glad Celine brought you to me tonight. I want to see you again around here. You're not doing this with anyone else, though; those are my rules. We're going to have a lot of fun together.'

I wasn't sure what the correct response to his declaration was. I had never imagined being in this situation, but alas, there I was, sitting in a post-sex haze in front of the man I was meant to be investigating, who incidentally happened to be the ex-husband of my boss and idol. Starting with a smile, I leaned back slightly before speaking.

'You sure do know how to make a girl have fun. Can I assume things will be... discreet?'

He laughed as he finished measuring the folds of his shirt on his forearm to millimetric precision. 'You're adorable. Of course, darling, nothing that happens while you're with me ever gets out. I have a lot of people who make sure that my privacy is maintained at any cost. So don't worry, babe, you're safe if you're with me.'

It was clear he liked to have the final word as he instantly left the room without even a glance back to see my reaction. At any cost? What did that mean? A shiver ran down my spine knowing that I was there to do the precise thing he vowed never would happen.

My mind raced over to Bex and what he would think if he never knew what had happened. I didn't think it was cheating. I was on assignment; it was all for the story. Yes, my body had reacted to everything that happened. The process didn't change that; it was just a way to get closer to his side of the story. There wasn't any other way to get close enough to him to have substance for my article. Everything that happened in that room was purely a physiological response with no greater meaning outside of that. Besides, nobody had to know it ever happened, so, in many ways, it never happened at all.

As long as I could seamlessly exit, collect my phone, and make a note of all that I had learned, it had all been worth it. I left the room cautiously, taking measured steps while watching from the corner all the developments in the main living room in the time I had been gone. With no concept of time, I had no clue how long I had been gone for, but I noticed that the substances floating around must have taken effect as dancing became grinding and clothes started to slip off. I couldn't spot Celine anywhere, so I took the opportunity to walk close to the wall towards the entrance and back out.

The bodyguard at the door handed back my phone and coat, which I collected while hurrying towards the lifts. The doors closed, and I sighed in relief, taking in my reflection on the mirrored wall. I may have looked the same as before, but within me, everything felt very dissimilar.

CHAPTER TWENTY-FIVE
New Year Resolutions

The worst kind of hangover is not one caused by alcohol or even hard drugs. It's the moral hangover, the anxiety after doing something dubious at a party that could have consequences for the future. That type of post-party suffering can take several days to recover from, its length equating to the gravity of the act committed. In the time between the penthouse at the hotel tower and when I finally emerged from my cloister for outside air, I had spent time both reminiscing about the act but also pushing away, at times successfully, the guilt of the secret.

Since then, I had received a special delivery from Harrods containing an elegant package from Chanel. Inside was the epic 22 bag that I had seen in our section and wondered how anyone could afford it on a salary. The card had only an initial, just enough to decipher how it got to my apartment, not that there was any other way it would have made it to my possession. The only solace to my already crumbling with guilt was that the encounter that led me to owning the season's most wanted bag had, in fact, been one of the most satisfying of my life.

That fact, of course, did nothing to help the contradictory feelings I had around the boundaries of pursuing a career-changing story, my existing relationship that now bordered on stable, and the knowledge that nothing would remain the same once everything I knew made its way to printed paper. I had managed to avoid seeing Bex. I hadn't felt ready to face him without processing all my new, unfamiliar feelings.

Meanwhile, another, much more contentious relationship was far more difficult to avoid. A message had come through in the early hours, forcing me to confront the looming reality.

Nathan

> Meet me for an early lunch, 11:30 AM at Borough Market.

Well, at least he chose somewhere neither of us was likely to see anyone who knew what we were doing. I felt like a movie spy, meeting my boss at a busy marketplace eatery away where mostly serious city people would lunch. It also meant I could easily blend in with an uncomplicated outfit and winter coat.

I left home bundled up comfortably for a conversation where fashion was not a required attendee. The journey into the city on the underground on a workday reminded me of the normalcy involved in going out to an office for work. I missed so many aspects of mundane life that I would even take the cramped underground in good spirits.

At the entrance of the market, Nathan stood waiting in a thick black windbreaker and a lowered baseball cap. If I hadn't worked next to him for months, it would be hard to recognise his presence. He greeted me with a gloved handshake and guided me towards a stall selling hotdogs close to communal seats. We both ordered meals before sitting next to each other. I started off the conversation while Nathan bit into his lunch.

'I'm in. I managed to get very close to James... Lord Thurrington.'

He swallowed a large chunk of food before responding while preparing the food in his hand for another nibble. 'Good, now what's the angle with the story?'

'He's deeply entrenched in trading people. The store is a money laundering scheme. He throws these parties with drugs and girls. The people who attend invest in his businesses. It's the classic rich man doing shady things.'

I tried to be blasé about what I had seen, but truthfully, no matter how many times you heard about stories, it's different being faced with them in real life. Nothing prepares you for being in that situation, and I wanted to disclose how it was in detail. But I didn't; I couldn't come across like an impressionable young journalist who hadn't seen much of anything yet. So, instead, I played it cool.

'Yes, and it needs to be enough to warrant an arrest. This story needs to lead to good things for us, for Florence, for society. It can't be a lukewarm scandal; I need depth from you, Paze.'

His probing was expected. What wasn't on the cards was my heartbeat increasing as he pushed harder. I had to give him something more than just a random headline.

'I went to the last party; it was pretty intimidating. Although not as bad as this whole escort auction thing that Celine has going on in restaurants in Knightsbridge.'

Nathan's eyes opened wide as he finally scrunched up the foil that had been holding the hotdog together into a ball. He pointed at me while he spoke. 'Now this is something. This is seedy and illegal.'

'It's exactly what you heard. The most disturbing thing I've ever seen. Seems James is a kingpin with tentacles in everything that's wrong.'

He looked around to see who else was within audible distance before telling me in a hushed tone, 'You need to stay safe. People like this aren't going to let their guard down easily. I know a police inspector who works with us on the news side often; I will inform him of what's going on for your own safety.'

Despite the cold air coming in through the open sides of the market, I could feel the temperature rising around my wrists and neck. The pulses in my chest became so strong that I thought they might soon become visible through the clothes I wore. I took a deep breath before responding.

'Wow, I never agreed to any police matter. Besides, who's to say he isn't on their side already?'

'I vouch for him; you've got to trust me a little here.'

I did not, and as more time passed, the less I knew who to trust at all. Nathan had been so irate in our last conversation but seemed genuinely concerned all of a sudden. It was very confusing for me to comprehend.

'I'm not sure I can be involved in this if the police are getting involved; it sounds way too intense.'

'News flash, Paze, you're already involved. You got yourself into this by poking around Celine, remember? I'm just trying to keep you safe at this point. I don't want to have to find your body in a ditch because you went to the wrong party and got caught out.'

His words stung my ears while my body flinched backwards in disbelief. Did he really believe my life was in danger? It was just meant to be a little assignment on how hypocritical high society was, and now I was expected to cooperate with the police. How did things escalate to this point without me seeing it happen? I started to feel uneasy and moved my hands up towards my throat as my body seemed to choke on the words I was hearing.

Nathan noticed the quick onset of anxiety as it began manifesting physically. He stood up from the metal barstool he sat on the edge of to come over to my side of the oak-barrel-turned-lunch-table. He looked at me for consent before gently placing a hand on my shoulder.

'Are you okay?'

For the first time in as far back as I could remember, I felt a rush of wetness reaching my eyes involuntarily. The tears started to drip onto my cheeks whilst, on the other end, emotions bubbled up close in on my neck.

'I'm scared. I don't know how I will pull this off, let alone write a story about it. I... slept with Thurrington. What happens now with me?'

The words that had been choking me all along finally came out. I felt the same relief of having regurgitated a poorly digested meal. I looked at Nathan, who was holding his open palm over his mouth.

'You did what? He's a criminal, he's dangerous... Paze, he's Florence's ex-husband. We hate him; we're bringing him down with a hit piece, remember?'

'It wasn't like that. I was there listening behind a door I had no business being behind at all. It all happened so quickly, I didn't have time to think about it, and he was quite... abrasive.'

Nathan covered his mouth with his hand in shock; he lowered his tone again into a semi-whisper. 'Wait, Paze, did he rape you?'

'No, it wasn't like that. I wasn't necessarily against it, but it was so intense that I only realised what I was doing when it was over. I needed to stay in character.'

His expression changed as his eyes moved upwards into a surprised look. He moved one hand under his chin like he was digesting all the unexpected updates I was throwing at him. 'Well, if that was the reason, I've got to say you're committed. And probably more ready for this than you give yourself credit for.'

I paused to let those words sink in. I couldn't tell if Nathan truly believed in them or simply wanted to keep me calm so I wouldn't blow the operation, further imploding his career in the process.

'Do you think I'll be alright?'

'You will if you cooperate with the police. It's more crucial now that you've had an intimate relationship with the kingpin. They can ensure you're protected.'

'Fine, when do I meet the elusive policeman that will make sure I live to see another season?

'It's New Year's Eve, so I'm guessing in a couple of days once he's back on duty.'

The whole situation clouded my notion of public holidays, particularly since I now worked incognito from home and the occasional cafe. I guessed until I had protection, I'd stick to safer territories.

'Since I'm sure we've both got better places to be tonight, I'm heading back home. Planning on being at Allegra's tonight, so I should be safe enough.'

'When am I getting back on her guest list?'

I looked at him in disbelief that, in the midst of the situation, that preoccupation was still on his mind.

'You were never on it. You were my plus one, remember? Let's see how things go with keeping me protected, and I can get you another invite.'

'She's got claws! I have to say, I do like this Paze. Keep it up, and you'll have my job in no time.'

With that, he offered a cheek and then another for air kisses. I waited a few minutes until Nathan's back disappeared into a crowd of suits and jackets. As I turned in the opposite direction to make my way towards the nearby bus stop, I gently pushed AirPods into my ears before pulling out my phone to select the journey's soundtrack.

A blocked number text appeared on my screen with no information on who it could be, so I opened it quickly.

Unknown

> I'm in the mood for some more of you.

I instinctively looked around me to see if there was anyone watching me. The city moved around me, but no one seemed to look at me directly. A cold shiver made my forearm hair stand as fear entered my bloodstream. Nathan was right; I could be in real danger, and there was no one looking after me.

Every year, Allegra di Pienza had the most sought-out invitation of any season. However, this season was completely different. The invitations had been carefully curated to a very select few, posted, and responded to weeks in advance. In the middle of the complete upheaval of my life due to a story that had taken larger dimensions than I had ever planned for, I confirmed that I would be attending alongside Bex. After arriving home and barricading the flat entrance with the sofa for extra safety, I sat on the stool in my kitchenette, staring down at the invitation in front of me.

In a normal year, I would have spent the afternoon priming my hair and doing a face mask to avoid pores in our usual group photo. Instead, this time, I was sitting still in a wet coat from the walk back from the bus, stunned at what had happened earlier. I rested my head on my hands while enjoying a moment of stillness. Instead of silence, all I could hear within my thoughts was Florence's voice saying, 'What is a story worth?'

After a few moments, I could feel a vibration on the tabletop coming from my phone. I reluctantly looked, hoping it wasn't anything triggering.

Bex

> Pick you up at 8? Can't wait for our first new year's eve.

He was so sweet, and I didn't deserve him. I had to make it up for him after the story ended. Maybe we could finally go away together on our very first vacation.

Bex

> By the way, Sara is messaging me asking where I am. Do you still need me to play along?

Ah, yes, the unresolved matter with Sara. She was an important piece of the puzzle, one I had no idea how I'd use to get to the bottom of what I needed. I wasn't about to discard her after all the effort we went through to reel her in.

Me

> Yes, keep her busy please! I feel she's important, maybe you can help me figure out what to do with her. See you soon xx

I missed the days when the biggest concern in our friend group was if Sara would turn up, messing with our social feng shui. The problems we faced now made it all seem so petty, immature even. The world beyond our inner circle of friends and foes seemed too dangerous, too cruel. I looked around the starter flat, where adulthood had barely begun for me, and yet, it already seemed so very overwhelming. At least with the extra money I'd be making from the current work situation, I could afford to move somewhere nicer, perhaps with a real kitchen and a separate bedroom. It would all be worth it, in the end, I hoped.

For the last event of the year, I decided to wear the latex Versace dress gifted by Mansour. I meticulously curled the ends of my hair and left the volume they created to naturally land on my back. I smudged a dark, smoky look onto my eyelids with precision to emulate the runway look of the dress. On my lips, a satin finish nude tone contoured the natural line around my mouth. The process took several hours, between sips of prosecco, which no doubt made getting ready longer but far more enjoyable.

In the reflection, looking back at me on the mirrored doors of the closet, I watched as my foot slipped into a pair of beige heels. I covered myself with my usual beige winter trench coat, concealing the parts of my body that the dress so closely stuck to. With a chunky scarf loosely thrown around for extra warmth for those short-lived minutes between car and door, I walked out of the building to find Bex leaning against his car in full formalwear.

'You look absolutely beautiful,' he said, reaching over to kiss me while the unforgiving cold battered against my legs. The skin-coloured stockings I wore did nothing to prevent me from shivering while he held me, which ended our kiss far sooner than I desired. 'You're so cold; let's get into the car before you catch something.'

From behind the warmth of his car glass, the seasonal lights moved by quickly and meshed into one consistent gold streak. I looked at Bex, his muscles flexing as he gripped the steering wheel firmly. The car stopped at a red light opposite Harrods. He took a break in driving to look at me and smiled.

'I got really lucky with you.'

My words made him turn his attention for a short second towards me with an expression between a laugh and raising his brows up in disbelief.

'Paze, are you really getting sentimental here?'

'I can be emotional… if the right occasion arises.'

It was a white lie, but one I thought he wanted to hear. I had really felt the need to tell him how special he was to me, and indeed, he was quite special. But beyond that, emotions were not really my forte.

We arrived at Allegra's house with some delay caused by building up traffic along Knightsbridge as people made their way into town for fireworks. A few cars lined up ahead of us, searching for a single yellow line to park over. The lush gardens at the middle of the square overlooked us as we squeezed into a spot between a Porsche and a Lamborghini. With my hand firmly planted into Bex's palm, we walked into the party, my heels clicking against the stone floors.

Right at the entrance, a uniformed waiter offered us both champagne in a thick crystal coupe. I looked around and noticed that the foyer had been covered in greenery, creating the sense of walking into a greenhouse. A centrepiece with tropical flowers in tones of oranges and deep reds adorned the middle of the room atop an antique wood table. Meanwhile, the adjacent formal dining room had been set up with floral arrangements and long candlesticks while the room lights were switched off for a more intimate feel.

As we acclimated to the environment around us, a sequin-clad tuxedo-wearing Mansour emerged from the door that opened to the back garden. He carried a lit cigar in one hand while vigorously waving at us with the other. His eyes captured my look while a grin highlighted his approval of my choice of outfit.

'You're finally wearing the dress!'

The air kisses came midair before Mansour moved on to greet Bex separately. Seeing Mansour's glamorous getup, Bex asked him a question that had been on my mind upon seeing all the effort in getting the house ready.

'Do you know who's coming tonight?'

'It's strictly an inner circle affair tonight.'

Just as he finished, Mila made her way back in from outside, putting out her cigarette on a self-standing elevated gold ashtray. She wore a long red velvet dress with a unique silhouette reminiscent of a 1970s ballad performer.

'My lovelies! Looking fabulous, as always!'

Almost immediately behind her, Allegra and Georgie returned inside with rouged cheeks from the cold. Allegra had on a multi-coloured boucle Chanel dress with sequined details and a bow adorning her hair, which was up in a pinup style that bode perfectly with her signature eyeliner. Meanwhile, Georgie donned a double-breasted houndstooth print jacket with a sleek black button-down shirt underneath. Their styles had matured, matched even. The unlikely couple now looked perfectly synced.

'Paze! Bex! We can finally start off with dinner now that you've made it.'

I hugged her, careful not to pull on her perfectly arranged hair. I then turned to face my friends, who were starting to select seats around the lacquered mahogany wood table. The comfort of having them around allowed me to speak frankly.

'I'm really glad we did something so private this year; I'm done with people who aren't you guys around this table.'

Mansour broke out in laughter, finding my comment absurd. I looked at Allegra, and she shook her head in agreement with my thoughts. The last few months had been so action-filled that one night of complete comfort and privacy was exactly what we both yearned for.

'On that note, who's ready for the carefully curated tasting menu for tonight? And, yes, Mansour, you can have it all before you ask.'

Our laughter, in unison, reverberated off the tall, panelled walls. A parade of dishes entered the room, brought by the staff hired especially for this evening. The feast included fresh caviar from Mila's insider, Allegra's governess signature beef Wellington, Mansour's must-have richly spiced rice, and my favourite dessert, mille-feuille. Every course had been thought out to please one of us. Every part of the evening was designed to make her friends feel welcomed and treasured.

Once we finished dining, Allegra stood from her seat at the edge of the table with a glass in hand. She waited for us to give her our undivided attention before sharing her thoughts with a large smile.

'What's everyone's New Year's resolution? Let's go around the circle, you share, and then we toast. Mila, you start first.'

'This year, I want to find a passion. Something that keeps me up at night.'

We clapped for Mila as we all took a sip from our different choices of drinks.

'You next, Mansour.'

'Hmmm… I want to live a big love story.'

I looked at him, fully cognisant of what he meant by it but also keen like a sibling to tease him about his crush. 'Anyone in particular that you'd like to live that story with?'

Instead of responding, Mansour grabbed his water glass from the table and winked at me, knowing well that I was perfectly aware of who had captured his heart. I truly hoped that his wish would come true.

Allegra turned her head towards us, sitting towards her left side. 'Bex? What's your resolution?'

He smiled while pulling his cloth napkin from his lap onto the table, giving him some additional time to think about his answer. 'I want to move away from London… at some point.'

His answer caught me completely off-guard. That was not something we ever discussed in private, which probably should have been as we had become quite close in the months we'd been officially dating. I looked at him, my face clearly giving off the surprise I was caught in as he grabbed my hand under the table to comfort me.

Sensing the tension, Mansour quickly stood up with his empty water cup in hand as he searched with his eyes for nearby staff. Once he waved down the closest waiter, Mansour scoffed at Bex's comment. 'You wouldn't want to leave all of this behind? Where would you even go that comes close to what we've got here? Especially in Knightsbridge, it's the whole world inside of it.'

Allegra giggled, moving her gaze back to me.

'Paze, what have you set your eyes on for the year?'

I paused, looking around the table as all eyes focused on what I was about to say next. My back fell into the chair as I started to form words from the many thoughts crossing my mind at once, only a few appropriate to be shared out loud at the moment.

'I want to do something really meaningful that people know me by.'

My desire probably meant something different to each person on the table, depending on what they knew or thought they knew about what was currently happening in my life. Either way, it was the plainest truth.

'That's very honourable, also the most Paze response possible. Last, but not least, Georgie?'

He hadn't been as interested in our contributions, opting instead to alternate between topping up his drink and checking his phone frequently.

'I think things are pretty good; not much I can think of is missing.'

I couldn't tell if it was arrogance or keeping guarded secrets down, but once again, Georgie had avoided telling us anything with any substance. I still couldn't understand the efforts Allegra probably went through to maintain intelligible conversations with this man.

Seeing as he wasn't going to add anything further, I chimed in with a redirect. 'Allegra, aren't you going to share with us what you're looking forward to next year?'

I could see her appreciative smile open up with my recognition that she, as the polite hostess, had self-censored to last in an act of humility but had every desire to participate in the conversation if elicited.

'Now that you ask, I do have a resolution of my own. Seeing as my business is starting to crawl, bit by bit, I want to be on the thirty under thirty list.'

'That's my best friend, I believe in you. If I worked for Forbes, I'd certainly put you up there.'

Georgie finally offered us his full attention, rising to stand over her with his hands on her shoulders.

'And she's my girlfriend, not letting go of this little bright one.'

There was something about his tone that came across as less endearing than he intended. In order to not let the bad vibration linger, I encouraged us all to head out to the garden so we could hear the distant noises of the fireworks that would soon go off around London.

We huddled near the external heaters that projected warmth around a sitting pit. The year turned as bottles of champagne opened in commemoration of new beginnings. Bex and I kissed longingly under the clouded dark sky as Mansour and Mila cheered us on with loud claps. When we opened our eyes, we noticed that Allegra and Georgie lingered on their kiss still a few steps away from us. Mansour declared khalas khalas while pushing their two shoulders, much like a younger brother would censor their siblings until they pulled away laughing.

After everyone had finished their first smoke of the new year, the evening came to a close, and the group headed out towards the main entrance of the house. Another benefit of a small party was an earlier finale that would allow Bex and I to continue enjoying the rest of the night without an audience at his house.

I covered myself with the coat that previously had been deposited in the cloakroom on arrival. Allegra and Georgie stood embracing each other, waiting for the last guests to depart. When I was heading towards the door, I leaned in to give Georgie a goodbye hug. He welcomed the motion with a smile, and just as I was about to pull away, he spoke quietly into my ear.

'You looked hotter the other night, much prefer leopard spots on you.'

CHAPTER TWENTY-SIX

Power in Numbers

A new year is generally a new beginning for most people, with hopes and wishes that could come true in the next twelve months. No one really expected things to change, but our need for traditions has kept the ritual alive for most people. Of course, most people aren't actively involved in a journalistic investigation against some of the most powerful people in the city.

The year had started for me with the unshakable thought that my best friend's criminally inclined boyfriend had seen me at a seedy party while he himself had no good reason for being there. If I previously had reason to wish him completely gone from the vicinity of my friends, I had reached the point of no doubt that his presence was a threat to our peace. It was particularly problematic for me given that he knew my true identity and the people he surrounded himself with had both money and influence to make me go away.

I had been sitting in my flat going through these self-torturing thoughts in an endless spiral for the last few days until the city around me resumed work. Equally, I had been staring at a message from Nathan with the details of the police inspector that I was supposed to speak to about my predicament. I took one prolonged sip of my homemade oat latte before the dial started to ring.

'Inspector Oswin speaking.'

'Hi, this is… hm… Paisley. I think my boss, Nathan, may have spoken to you about a risky situation we've come across.'

'Miss Taylor-Jones, from Sizzle Media. Your lawyers have also been in touch; I'm expecting you to come by to the station with them for a chat. How does 2PM sound?'

I never had lawyers, so I could only assume these were Sizzle's legal team that Nathan had conjured without my knowledge.

'I'll be there. Please text me the address.'

'Will do, miss.'

The line cut sharply, leaving me back in the silence of the flat to process the fact that I was going to be at a police station. The suits accompanying me would doubtlessly offer directives, but ultimately, I had to be clever enough to understand that everyone would have their own agenda. It was time for me to figure out what mine needed to be.

I started to put together the ensemble for what I would wear to the police station when my phone rang again, this time making the hairs on my arm tingle. I answered without delay with my full curiosity engaged.

'Hi, Celine. How are you?'

'I'm good, but I also need a plus one for a private event tomorrow night at Scarlett's. Lord Thurrington specifically asked for you.'

A shiver quickly spread down my spine. It was a dangerous invitation, given that I was about to head over to a police station precisely to provide information that may have been valuable. At the same time, a warmth crept over my gut as I felt the cortisone flood my body with a mixture of fear and excitement.

'I'll be there.'

In all the years I had hung out with my friends, Scarlett's was the only place I had yet to enter. It was always the holy grail of London's high society, a member's club so exclusive that even the richest people in town waited years on the list before gaining admission. Allegra had dominated all other facets of elite living but never Scarlett's. She scoffed at it as if it were somewhere we'd worry about when the right age came, but everyone found it odd when she didn't celebrate her 21st there like every other socialite in her circle. Perhaps her father's criminal past had tainted her odds of becoming a member, given their strict morality clause and equal hypocrisy in allowing those who had yet to be caught.

If there was ever a place to get the missing information that I needed for the story, it would be there. I had to come in prepared, confident, and ready to not miss a beat. The story had consumed everything in my life, so I was ready to find the final piece to nail it shut once and for all. It had started as an opportunity to gain some favour with Florence, but it gradually had become so much more. The new goal was to survive with most of my reputation intact and, hopefully, with new-gained respect as a professional journalist.

My train of thought was interrupted by a vibration from my phone that also lit up the screen with a new message.

Nathan

> Oswin confirmed that you're coming in, will be there with you. Bringing the lawyers. Don't worry Paze, you're not alone on this.

When the time came, I headed to the police station, armed only with the sense of protection that came with knowing that Sizzle's legal team and Nathan would be accompanying me. I had dressed in the power suit I had worn on the first day at work, repurposed as the official costume that would hide any insecurities while faced with the consequences of my choices.

The plain grey entrance to the building looked even less inviting in real life than it had on the police shows I'd seen. There were splatters of the typical police blue in panels that served as a reminder that it wasn't a hospital lobby. Walls with varying posters of community programmes carried on until I spotted Nathan and two suited women speaking near a door. Two suited women speaking near a door, who seemed to have been anticipating my arrival. They waved at me as I made my way past a reception desk.

From inside the room, a middle-aged man emerged in uniform. He extended a hand as soon as I reached the group.

'Inspector Oswin, good to meet you. Now shall we head inside for a chat?'

I returned the handshake with one hand while keeping the other firmly planted on the underarm handbag I was clutching.

'Of course, let's get it started.'

As I entered the room, so did one of the women who had stood next to Nathan.

'I will be legally representing Miss Paisley Taylor-Jones as an employed journalist of the Sizzle Media publication.'

The inspector nodded silently and extended his arms towards the empty seats opposite him. We sat in near synchrony as Oswin passed two glasses of water to our side before taking his own seat.

'Nathan gave me a statement already about what you guys are up to with the story. I know Lord Thurrington's reputation; everyone does. But what do you want me to bring him in under?'

Before speaking, I took a deep breath, searching inwards for strength.

'He has some sort of operation that involves selling sex and taking commissions. I'm not sure the women fully understand or consent to what's going on. He also seems to own this gallery where people sell goods obtained from the punters, although not always legally. There's probably more that I don't even know yet. A lot of people seem strangely connected to him.'

I looked to the side. The lawyer took note of every word I said but did not look up from her Moleskine notebook. Without any connection made, I diverted my eyes across to Inspector Oswin, who finally realised I was done speaking.

'I'm going to be brutally honest with you, kid. Rich people get away with stuff all the time. We try to nail them, their legal finds a way out.'

His reaction didn't surprise me. Nobody would run an elaborate scheme if they didn't think it would be relatively easy to get away with it.

'So what do you suggest I do? Run a story and wait for him to come after me personally?'

'Let me cut it straight. The best thing you can do is have power in numbers. Get victims to talk to you, disgruntled employees, anyone. One person coming out is a rumour, two is a conspiracy… but ten? Fifteen? That's an investigation.'

The lawyer next to me finally stopped writing and seemed to silently agree with his statements by moving her head. It would have been nice to have more support, but I guessed it was better than nothing.

'How do I get them to talk?'

'Offer them anonymity. If this operation is as big as you say, more will come out. That will get them to come to us.'

The room had started to feel hotter than when I first entered. I slipped my jacket off before crossing my arms, using the table to support them.

'And then what? How will I be protected? These people could come after me.'

'Miss Paisley, they will come after you either way. Differently to everyone else, you've got the media protecting you.'

His statement was terrifying. It was also true that backing out peacefully was no longer a possibility when Celine thought she was winning me over. Perhaps the inspector was right, and I had underestimated the power of the media. It was more important than ever to get the final story out.

'So you're not giving me a security detail?'

'No, miss, you're not the Prime Minister. We need a credible threat against you to assign resources, and even then, it would be related to a high-profile investigation.'

Where previously I had been feeling brewing anxiety, I started to feel a quickening of my heartbeat as a jolt of heat hit my face. The vein on my neck pulsated as he remained calm despite my increasingly visible distress.

'I thought you were going to help me. I'll bring you a big fish to arrest, and you're having me run all the risk.'

Instead of reacting to my elevating voice, he remained perfectly calm, sitting relaxed on his chair with both hands firmly planted on the table.

'Is there a reason for you to believe you're at particular risk? You don't seem to have a direct relationship with the subject. He probably doesn't even know who you are yet.'

At that moment, I realised that I hadn't made a bad decision at the party after all. My face morphed into a slight smile as I imitated Oswin's pose, falling back into my chair. I looked at the lawyer next to me before carrying on.

'I'd like to waive my right to have you here for the next few minutes and have a direct conversation with the Inspector.'

Her face demonstrated surprise as she nervously flicked her ash blonde hair back from above her shoulder. 'I wouldn't recommend that you do that.'

Instead of cowering, I maintained my eyes firmly on her. 'I insist, I would like to speak without legal representation.'

She closed her notes with annoyance, quickly collecting her handbag from the floor under the chair. Since she hadn't provided much help, I thought I might as well eject her so she, too, wouldn't become a liability. The door closed behind her, and I waited a few seconds before returning to the conversation.

'He does know who I am. We've slept together, and he sends me gifts. I'm seeing him shortly. Does that change things?'

Oswin broke into a smile. I suspected he was pleased to hear that after years, there might've been a chance to catch an elusive criminal. 'That changes everything. You're now an insider witness with a personal relationship to the culprit. I can offer you proper protection.'

'What should I do next?'

'How comfortable are you with wearing a wire? It will help you with the story, but will definitely help me keep you safe.'

Finally, the words I wanted to hear. I'd wear a camera if I needed to; I was ready for the entire ordeal to be finished so

I could move on with my life. It felt like a small price to pay to finally have freedom again. At least, at that moment, it did.

In twenty-four hours, I had gone from a mere civilian journalist to a fully equipped undercover insider about to bring down a kingpin. The irony was that I had waited for years for the opportunity to enter Scarlett's, and all I could think of now was how I was about to lead an incognito operation, probably diminishing any chance of coming back. Still, I had every intention of making the night one to remember. Every detail inside the walls of the Mayfair mansion that housed the club would be etched in my mind forever and captured in my secret recording device for posterity.

Within my chest, I felt a pronounced pounce all day, which made the evening of danger and debauchery even more exciting. I had convinced Allegra that I needed a dress for the occasion, which had led to a flurry of questions about how I was getting in. It was enough for her to know that I was on an assignment and work had facilitated the entry. Once the excuse was fully accepted, I was given access to the adequately formal side of Allegra's closet. The club notoriously had the strictest dress code in London. We had tried several different iterations before settling on a halter-topped vivid red silk dress with a hemline that skimmed my calves. The dress was sized for Allegra's thinner body, which made it cling to mine, revealing a much more pronounced silhouette than intended by the owner. On her, the dress was chic. On me, the dress was sensual.

THE KNIGHTSBRIDGE CROWD

I had pulled out from my closet a white gold necklace with a single fiery red opal in the middle surrounded by tiny micro pave diamonds. It had been an heirloom passed down by my mother and reset for a modern look. That evening, it would drive attention down to my chest and, equally, conceal the microscopic camera given to me by Inspector Oswin. I had my hair professionally blow-dried into elegant waves at the bottom that framed the decolletage enhanced by the strategically draped silk. The makeup I selected was in varying tones of brown and nude with a double-lined lip for additional plumpness. A pair of flirty Mach & Mach bow heels had also made their way to me courtesy of Mila, who, in helping to put together the outfit, pointed out that I had nothing suitable to finish off the look that would fit the venue.

In the mirror, alone in my flat, I twirled to observe the finished product. Everything externally reflected the many changes of the last few months. I was presenting as a well-groomed, sexy, confident woman nearing her mid-twenties, with more excitement than uncertainty. There was a part of me that was scared. It was all very dangerous, but then again, how many women my age wouldn't wish to be in my position? I supposed that a little peril was necessary to feel alive.

I pulled out a clutch from my closet. It had been a rare find from a charity on Kensington High Street. The square black leather clutch, a non-designer item, would serve as a little reminder that I was still not one of them. I may have been dressed like them, spoke like them, and had tastes similar to them. Yet, I was still just an invited guest who could easily be removed from sight.

A message appeared on my phone screen as I began packing my makeup and keys into the bag.

Bex

> Good luck at the work do! You'll be amazing. Love you.

I read it again and again several times. The night's success could lead me back to this, to us. It was obvious that I should be fully available to build the relationship with Bex he deserved and I needed.

Clothed in a thick black winter coat on top of my outfit, I headed out to the taxi that waited to take me to Celine's flat. The low lighting in the back streets that connect South Kensington and Knightsbridge offered a relaxing ride as I sat, silently enjoying the calmness. When we finally pulled into Sloane Street, I walked out into the bitter cold that made my underdressed legs shiver. I hurried into Celine's building reception to wait for her to descend from a warm enclave. While waiting, I pulled out my phone for what was likely to be the last moments of tranquillity that evening.

Me

> I love you too, promise that things will be better soon.

I smiled at the screen before tucking it away safely into my handbag. Just as I did, Celine emerged in a corseted mini dress with sheer black lace, showing a nude-coloured slip underneath that was practically spray-painted onto her body. She carried in hand a cape-like black coat with feathered trims, and her platform heels gave her an additional fourteen centimetres of height, compounded with a tall ponytail that elongated her even further.

Celine walked with her signature stomp towards me while her floral perfume engulfed the air around her with intoxicating strength. Her eyes had fox-like features thanks to the dark, upward design of her makeup. She greeted me with air kisses while grabbing my hand for us to move outside together. As we did, I spotted a parked Lamborghini Urus right on the curb of the building entrance.

Before we stepped inside, Celine turned to me and said, 'Are you ready to have the most memorable night of your life?'

CHAPTER TWENTY-SEVEN

*Private Members,
Private Bathrooms*

There I was, standing in front of the most imposing mansion block in Mayfair. The name of the club was discreetly etched on the deep red awning that stuck out of the large glass windows of the building. I entered behind Celine, who walked arm in arm with Lord Thurrington in a full suit. I preferred to take in every part of the facade, a multi-million-pound improvement from the previous version that had been a far more elusive front of the house for nearly half a century.

Inside, the entrance was manned by a butler who knew each member by name. The entrance had wallpaper panels in tones of green and red with accents in mahogany wood. A few steps inside revealed a check-in table mimicking a hotel lobby, from behind which two receptionists enforced the rules requiring a signature in an antique-looking yellow book full of titles, names, and numbers. That book had more of the Tatler Social Power Index than any other place in London.

I watched in fascination as access was granted, and we passed through an intricately sculpted double door into a whimsically decorated ballroom with real green foliage and details of gold. On the ceiling, dimly lit amber chandeliers hung above foliage placed to cover most of the Victorian accents. Tables were situated around a sunken dancefloor where guests walked past between different areas of the venue. There must have been over three hundred well-dressed attendees moving around the various groups formed around sections of the room.

Celine spotted another acquaintance and moved towards her on the left while Lord Thurrington looked back to me, giving implicit authorisation for me to step up to the main female company role. He squeezed my arm, abruptly moving me closer to his side.

'You look exquisite tonight.'

'Thank you. What kind of event is happening here tonight?'

He stopped walking and turned his head close to mine, pointing to the crowd around us.

'It's a private gathering for all my different investments. Over there are the television executives for my channels and the editors of the publications I still own post-divorce. Those over there on the right side run the art part of the group. Those on the left are from the real estate company.'

I looked around, taking in how truly affluent he was, given the large groups of employees covering the elaborate banquet-style set-up. At the edge of a row of tables near a grand marble fireplace, I spotted Georgie sitting surrounded by a group of bodyguards, his face illuminated by a screen that he was fixated on.

'What business do they come from?' I said while pointing at Georgie's table.

'Oh, that's not business. That's my troublemaking son that never gives me a day of rest.'

Disturbed by the revelation, I let my mouth drop instead of restraining an external reaction. It didn't go unnoticed, unfortunately.

'I know, it's probably shocking to imagine I'm someone's father. I never married his mother; he grew up a little feral and lies about his name in order to not be linked to me. I'm trying to get him into the family business, but it's nonstop fuck ups with that one.'

Still in complete shock that Georgie's mysterious parentage was the man I was both about to expose and had felt strangely attracted to, I continued to contort my face while digesting the information. At a closer look, there were traits on his face that were undoubtedly similar to Georgie's. My eyes moved between the two of them; their noses and face shapes were the same. *Maybe Allegra and I had similar taste after all.*

'That's enough time spent on him. Can we get back to how stunning you look and how much I'm ready to take off that dress? I can see every inch of your body in it; it's driving me crazy.'

I looked at him in disbelief that he'd sneak in such a comment in, diverting attention from his son. At the same time, I blushed at the thought of him noticing the curves I had so intently decided to highlight. Looking him up and down, I took in his presence in an impeccably tailored suit that favoured his strong frame. His eyes watched me intently like a hawk. I squeezed his arm, bringing him closer to me to gain some more confidence.

'I am genuinely interested in your businesses, but maybe we could discuss in a quieter setting.'

He raised one eyebrow while moving his eyes up and down my torso. I needed to catch him in a place with limited noise to get it on camera. If I could distract him with entertainment, there was a good chance to make him spill the truth about his more criminal endeavours.

With a quick scan, he made sense of the layout of the room and started to pace towards a door frame. He looked back at me every few steps to ensure I was following behind without making it explicit that we were walking together. Despite the debaucherous acts of his other party, there was some decorum enforced in front of his more civil employees.

He opened a gold, painted door and held it open while I made my way through the frame seconds later. Inside, the soundproofing isolated all noise from reaching into the small foyer, which remained empty. Three separate doors lead to male, female, and private restrooms. He finally took my hand and hurried me through the door, signed with large letters for private, reaching straight for the elaborate lock on the door behind him. *Too high to function properly.*

Before he had the time to plant his hands on me, I took a few steps back till I leaned against a flamingo pink marble sink. I stood with one leg slightly in front of the other, leaving my hip tilted while I nested both palms by my sides on the cold stone. I watched him turn around and stumble while trying to straighten himself up. I maintained steady eye contact, looking at him from a lower angle, my chin slightly lowered towards my chest. To his senses, I must have stimulated an arousal as he responded by kissing me. I parted my lips slowly, as if I was actually enjoying it.

I stopped for air, moving up my hands to make space between us for my question.

'So, what does Celine exactly do with you?'

He took two steps closer to me while he broke out into a pleased grin. 'Are you getting a bit jealous? No need, darling… I much prefer a natural without all those fillers that make her look forty.'

Such a sexist pig. I fought hard to continue the seduction act and subsequent confession.

'Not at all. I'm just curious, given how she handled our introduction.'

'Celine brings the girls, and the girls bring wealthy men who, with a little blackmail, bring me real estate investments.

I've got the publications that my bitch of an ex-wife didn't get in the divorce, those I use to control what gets said about me. And the world goes round and round. Can we go back to the part where we were about to have sex?'

He was falling for the act and moving in closer. I made sure to fondle his belt before speaking any more. His eyes followed every movement I took as I made sure not to break eye contact while alluding to what would happen next.

'I'm just curious; I'm looking for a job, you know. How does that art gallery fit into it if I said I wanted a job there?'

'I could look into a place for you, somewhere I could keep you at my disposal anytime I wanted. I quite like that idea, actually. The gallery is where the dim-witted girls sell things to me that they don't fully understand the price of while turning it around to the right buyers.'

It was fascinating that despite being seasoned at this game, he was still spilling more than he probably thought he was as I kept his mind racing between reason and pleasurable strokes.

'Don't you already make money off of them?'

'Yeah, I mean, it's not my fault they can't manage themselves. They're pretty, young, and stupid. Makes it easier for them to just shut up and do what they're told.'

'That doesn't sound like they understand too well what they're signing up for.'

'Did you expect them to? They're just asking to be used, really. Don't get a wrinkle on your pretty face thinking about girls who barely think about themselves. I can get you a nice gallery manager gig that suits your pedigree.'

I'm not a dog, but he certainly is some kind of animal. Can't believe I found him even remotely attractive. He ran two fingers down my cheek, eventually inserting them into my mouth as I tried not to flinch at the aggressiveness with which he simulated a sensual movement. I had no desire to have him come even within a centimetre of me, and it probably showed as my body remained stiff. He didn't seem to care, lifting me up onto the cold marble of the sink.

This second time we'd been together, it all felt completely different; my body couldn't relax, and the feeling of lips against my neck caused a reflex that made me look in the opposite direction. It felt like a duty, an obligation, a means to an end. I tried to focus on the patterns of the wallpaper while he employed his energy in removing my lingerie.

He took a step back again, analysing my body as if he owned it.

'On second thought, let's see you from another angle today. Turn around, darling.'

I obliged, taking the opportunity to close my eyes, feigning satisfaction in his performance. Instead, my mind moved between all the things I would accuse him of in the story while he continued to enter my body as if mutual enjoyment was no longer a concern.

Luckily, the session was as short-lived, as was any attraction I'd previously had for him. Relieving himself of the latex that separated us, he patted me on the backside before readjusting his outfit. I turned on the tap to quickly wash his presence off me.

Once our looks were reassembled, we stood next to each other, looking back at the mirror reflection. He walked behind me, putting one hand around my hip and resting his head on my shoulder. With his other hand, he gently caressed my clavicle.

'Nice little chat we had here, but you do know if you tell anyone about any of this, I'll have to kill you, right? And that would be a shame; you're a great shag and look like you'd be fun company. So be a good girl for me.'

I felt his hand move up to my neck in a split second, grabbing it strongly and then quickly releasing me as I gasped and panicked for air. Upon his release, I choked as my eyes watered in relief. I started petting the area he had squeezed as my breathing remained in irregular, long inhales.

He laughed and kissed me with a peck on the cheek as I remained in the same position. My mind tried to calculate whether he had really just issued a direct threat on tape. I mustered an understanding nod as he left me. Instead of leaving me with my thoughts, he walked back to the door, where he held it open and used the other hand to signal for me to walk out before him.

As soon as I exited into the dark foyer, I gasped as my body froze in position. My legs remained planted while my eyes readjusted to see if guilt hadn't conjured someone who wasn't really there.

'Bex! What are you doing here?'

He looked straight past me to where Lord Thurrington emerged from the restroom behind and walked nonchalantly past both of us, but not before squeezing my waist so I could make some space for him. Bex didn't say a word; the context of proximity implied in his touch was enough to paint the picture.

'Bex, I know how this looks, but it's… it's a little bit more complicated.'

He grabbed his hips in distress before starting to speak again.

'You know what? Never mind, I don't even want to know. You've been absent and weird; I guess this is what you've been up to.'

I had to get close enough to whisper to him. The only explanation I could offer needed to stay between us. He signalled with his hand for me to stay away, so I had to resort to just projecting my voice and hoping for the best.

'Bex, I swear it's not as bad as you think. I mean, it kind of is… but I was trying to get the final bit of information for my article.'

'With all due respect, I'm an editor, and I've never had to fuck anyone to get that job.'

'It's not like that, it's just… I saw an opportunity to get the scoop I needed. It was the only way.'

'It's exactly like that. You think you're better than everyone when you're just another pretty girl screwing to get a story. You know what? At least Sara is honest about who she is. You're a fraud, Paze.'

I felt two tears drop across my cheeks, now burning with heat. The dress I wore suddenly felt too revealing as Bex looked at me in disgust, eyes scanning my body for evidence of another man's touch. His words hurt, but I knew deep inside that pain was because, on some level, he was correct. Before turning back to the main ballroom, he made one last comment.

'Oh, and I'm here because I work for that asshole now. Our partners sold out to him, so thanks for making things even more awkward. I'm done with you.'

The anger at how the evening transpired was the exact motivation I needed to finish the story. I stood alone in the dark as tears continued to roll down my face before quickly wetting the upper part of the silk, leaving little stains on my dress. I remained there for several minutes, alone, in darkness and with the faint sound of music coming in from under the closed door. I cleaned the smudge off my face using my index fingers to ensure makeup integrity would remain. With a deep breath in, I opened the door and made my way towards the building exit.

Every step I took clamped angrily against the old floors of the ballroom. I lost the ability to recognise anyone as all facial features merged with the ambience into shades of colour and light. All I could think of was getting home as soon as possible, dismantling the wire, and making people finally pay for what they'd made me do. *I would show them what a story was worth, what my story was worth.*

CHAPTER TWENTY-EIGHT
When Reality Calls

'It's time, everyone. The alerts are about to go off on the Sizzle app,' I shared out loud as Mansour and Mila grabbed their phones from the pale embroidered silk sofa. From a nearby blue chaise, Allegra took a sip from a wide porcelain teacup.

'I've added in some Baileys since I figured I'd need to digest whatever is hitting the rest of the world before I've had a chance to see it.'

In the three weeks following the eventful evening at Scarlett's, I had painstakingly laboured to both finish the article and keep my friends from discovering the content. Inspector Oswin emphasised daily the importance of secrecy ahead of publishing as a means to ensure it would go ahead without intervention from Lord Thurrington's influence. As a result, my closest friends would have to find out the most shameful acts of the last months alongside everyone else. At the very least, I had them around me for support.

Mansour stood up and stationed himself in the middle of Allegra's formal reading room. Clearly, he had volunteered to be the speaker of the house.

'Young girls, stolen goods, blackmail, property: everything's for sale in Knightsbridge, and this is the villain behind it all. Wait, and that's just the headline!'

I lowered my head, with eyes now fixated to the side on a Chinese dynastic vase that sat ethereally on a console table next to our sofa. Mansour continued as he now paced the perimeter.

'Despite a threat to her life following a brief personal relationship with Lord James Thurrington, Sizzle journalist Paisley Taylor-Jones chose to expose the exploitation and criminality behind one of London's most revered fortunes. She wore a hidden camera that captured extensive footage of the disgraced peer confessing his crimes.'

Allegra sat up, placing her warm drink on an oak side table. I looked at her and saw the expression of concern in her eyes.

'Since when did you have a relationship with him? He threatened your life? You should have come to us.'

'I went to the police; it was a complicated situation. I wanted to expose him and all the people around him. It just took an unexpected turn, at which point I was in too deep.'

I also knew that Mansour hadn't reached a key part of the article, one which would perhaps change Allegra's sympathy for me. I lowered my gaze once again to await my fate.

'I'm skipping down to the pictures; there's a lot of detail here about the nature of your encounters, and I'm not interested in visualising you in any compromising situation. Wait a second, isn't this—'

Mansour stopped and made visual contact with Allegra, who stood within sight of his screen. She asked the words I had dreaded would come up eventually.

'Why is Georgie's picture in this?'

I remained silent but looked up at Allegra with a mixture of embarrassment and sorrow in my eyes for what she was about to find out.

Mansour continued, 'Please don't get angry at me. I didn't write the article; I'm just the voice. *Georgie Carter, known high-society playboy, is Lord Thurrington's illegitimate son and heir apparent to his seedy empire with recent controversies including an accusation from an ex-girlfriend of theft and regular presence at his father's sex-fuelled orgies with young girls.*'

Now turned towards me, Allegra stared angrily as my eyes started to feel heavy.

'Excuse me? You knew this was coming out about my boyfriend, and you kept it from me?'

Mila sensed a confrontation oncoming and walked to stand between the two of us.

'I'm sure there's some good reason as to why this happened. It seems Paze was being threatened in this complicated situation she was in.'

Mansour had continued scrolling down and stopped to interject with another line of questioning.

'So if you had a hidden camera that recorded these, shall we say parties… that means that you attended? I need to know who else was there that I'd recognise, although I've got a couple of guesses for you.'

Allegra snapped back, 'Mansour, not the time. I'm still trying to figure out what else Paisley has been hiding from us.'

She hadn't referred to me by my government name in years. It felt like being called out by a disappointed parent.

'You were cheating on Bex with my boyfriend's father? Then you knew what he was doing and waited for it to blow up on national news? Who the hell are you?'

Mila and Mansour both stood by Allegra as her outburst turned to tears. She audibly sobbed as I recoiled into the corner of where I sat, accepting that she was right to be upset but also confident that I had no other choice. I closed my eyes, unable to face the reality of the aftermath, while my feet curled inwards like they had all the times I was bullied at school.

Pausing her crying, Allegra breathed deeply. It alerted my brain to open my eyes, only to see her approaching me.

'I would like you to go now. I need some space with my friends to figure out what happens next. Please leave, Paisley.'

It would certainly hurt to be excluded from Allegra's house and potentially her life in the imminent future, but the reality was there wasn't much of a chance of another outcome. I quietly let my legs fall off the sofa, put on my trainers, and exited the room, still in silence. At the door, I put on my coat while looking around at the detailing on the ceiling that so frequently welcomed my presence as a regular visitor.

From the other room, Mansour came rushing through and silently opened the front door. He stepped outside with me without any winter coverings.

'I've got a minute before they notice I didn't come to close the door. I'm sorry this had to happen to you. We all knew Georgie was trash; you were just the one who figured out how large a scale it really was. Take care, Paze.'

I smiled at him, grateful that at least one of my friends didn't despise everything I did. He responded with a bearlike hug that comforted the cold reality of what had just happened. With the sound of the door locking behind me, I disappeared onto the icy road on my way to the nearest bus station. A loud vibration came from inside my handbag, forcing the removal of my hands from my warm pockets.

New message from Blake, Lord Thurrington's lawyer. I had saved his contact after Allegra dug it out but never contacted it out of fear that it would be restricted by client privilege to divulge anything of interest.

Blake

> We'd like to offer a privacy deal to kill the story and your distance from the cops. It will be worth your time, trust me.

How bold. I hadn't imagined he would be thrilled with being exposed, but I hadn't thought he'd try to pay me off, either. That was not my reason for any of this; I had wanted recognition for my work, and I had wanted revenge. I evaded a response as other messages poured in, causing my phone's system to slow down.

The rest of the day was spent fielding questions from my colleagues at Sizzle, now fully aware of where my sabbatical had been spent. Florence had personally sent a long, thoughtful message welcoming me back officially and congratulating the personal sacrifices I had taken to courageously stand up in a world where powerful men always got away with it. Some other messages of support and admiration from my dedicated friends came in amidst others with confusion and consolation. I also noticed a notification that had come through while I was on my way home.

You've been removed from the Whatsapp Friends Group and can no longer send messages.

I called Mila straight away, as I thought she was the most likely to offer a straightforward answer.

'Hi, Paze…'

'Hey, so I was kicked out of our friend group, apparently.'

I could tell she had walked into a toilet, based on the echo, probably to be afforded more privacy.

'Allegra called for a crisis meeting. It was decided that you could no longer be a part of our private chat, given the circumstances.'

'That's a bit of an overaction, don't you think?'

'The gist of it was that Mansour was going to handle a single stream of communications in and out of the group. It makes it easier to navigate things for the time being.'

Despite being a victim of the situation, too, the people closest to me wanted distance. It was on the cards previously, but it still felt hurtful at that moment.

'Do you agree with this?'

'Look, I obviously care about you, and you're my friend, but you're also a journalist whose loyalties lie in your career ascension. There's nothing wrong with that, but we need to protect our private lives now. From you.'

They may no longer accept me as a friend, but it's clear that they also fear me. I suppose, on some level, that meant I had established some ground for myself as a formidable opponent. Still, the loneliness of not having close friends hit me alongside the painful reminder that Bex was also no longer in my life. The story had cost everything I had, everyone I had.

Instead of confronting Mila, I concurred that it was the best course of action and let her go. I melted into my simple couch, hyper-aware that the silence around me would not subside anytime soon. My eyes closed, lids resting gently as my neck fell to find the furniture's arm. While my body felt limp, my brain was as awake as ever, occupied with the events that unfolded in the first weeks of the year.

I was beating myself down, but in fact, I had achieved the story of the year. The piece I worked on was a success; everyone was either interested or haunted by my work. A lucrative settlement could be on the cards. I had influential men afraid of how my words and testimony could affect their livelihoods, even their manhood. My inner voice repeated in a loop until I voiced it aloud audibly. 'You aren't in the shadows anymore, Paze. This is good for you.'

THE KNIGHTSBRIDGE CROWD

The next day started uncomfortably, following a night of sleeping on a cramped couch surrounded by the partially eaten pizza that had kept me company during the first night in a while, with no one to speak to. With some liquored courage, I had messaged Bex again. And again. There hadn't been a response nor an acknowledgement of any sort that he had read the story. I eventually cut off my access to a connection in hopes that he'd see my apologies while I slept.

I checked my phone as my eyes adjusted to the light that had been on and now shown straight into my pupils. A headache that now pounded at my temples had awakened me to darken the room so I could ride out the hangover in peace.

With darkness assured, I finally removed my phone from airplane mode in hope that a flurry of texts from the people I missed would come through. *I wasn't entirely wrong in my reasoning.*

Allegra

> Meet me at the gym. 1PM.

The message was enough to encourage a reaction. To the trash went the food residue while I quickly selected an outfit. Sports leggings, an Alo baseball cap, and thermals that wouldn't look odd in a gym underneath the thick camel winter coat that had carried me through winter thus far. A warm shower and a slap of makeup later, I looked like a presentable version of myself.

On the way to visit Allegra in her most secluded sanctuary, the empty gym with views looking down at the rest of Knightsbridge, I passed the off-licence on Brompton Road, where printed copies of Sizzle lined the door. The story had broken online, and now I had officially been immortalised in real life as the young journalist who took on the powerful aristocrat. I asked for a copy, protected under the brim of my cap as if it were an invisibility cloak.

The clerk didn't recognise my image on the front page, the frozen moment in which both Lord Thurrington and I stared into the mirror at the bathroom at Scarlett's with his hand firmly wrapped around my neck. On the printed paper, the look of terror in my sunken eyes and half-opened lips was more vivid than I remembered that night. I instinctively touched my neck again, in the same place he had. I choked the same way I had that evening, forgetting for a second where I was and that I had an audience.

In front of me, the older woman who had sold me the copy examined my face before speaking while pointing at my photo.

'She looks a little like you. Must be more or less your same age, if not a bit younger. Can you imagine how scary? He could have killed her there and then.'

I swallowed, hyperaware that any outward display of anxiety could give away my true identity.

'I guess she does. Well done her for standing up for what's right.'

The woman now opened her own newspaper, turned to me and pointed at the middle paragraph on the second page of the spread.

'The naughty bits are there. It seems there was a lot of sex and a lot of girls. Not many pictures of the other ones, though, especially not any of the ones doing all the pimping.'

Celine, the unnamed co-conspirator. The Sizzle legal team banned Nathan and me from adding her name, her photo, or any mention of her likeness. Despite her role in the scheme, her knowledge of undisclosed private information acquired while in Florence's employment was deemed too much of a risk. It was decided she'd live to see another day in anonymity, at that time at least.

'Clearly, I need to read the rest of the story. Good day!'

I headed out again, this time with my own face stamped across a newspaper I held tightly under one arm and my vintage handbag in the other. If there was one thing I had learned from Allegra, it was to always enter a confrontation with the weapons you need. I had to make her see I was truly the victim in all that happened.

CHAPTER TWENTY-NINE

Great Burning Ambush

The porter held a large glass door open for me to pass, which I proceeded through, noticing my heart racing faster than the steps I was taking. During the walk, I had rehearsed in my head several of the words I intended to say, but they started to erode into more dispersed thoughts. Instead of welcoming, as it had been previously, the gilded décor now felt like the cage of a trap. I maintained some apparent composure as I walked towards the lifts, passing in front of a group of guests sitting at a lunch table reading Sizzle. *I was everywhere, and it was bittersweet.*

With the opening of the lift, the muted winter light shining through large windows illuminated the tropical-looking pool area of the hotel. I spotted Allegra sitting on a deck lounger wearing a plum kaftan and caramel tinted sunglasses, even though we were in winter and indoors. I walked while removing my outer layers, which had started to suffocate me with the intense heating used to artificially simulate perennial summer.

'Hi, Allegra.'

'You may sit, Paisley.'

I winced at the harshness of her tone and obliged without questioning.

'I have called you here because I thought I at least owed it to you to hear your side of the story.'

As she spoke, she lifted her legs, reclining onto the lounger. I noticed a discreet tremor as she lifted her water bottle from a console table next to her. The stern façade was perhaps not as stone cold as it may have seemed.

I looked at her straight on and started making my case. 'I wasn't thinking straight. I was under pressure to do something I wasn't sure I could, and things happened far too quickly.'

Allegra remained in the same position, her eyes concealed by sunglasses while waiting for me to continue speaking.

'There were so many moments when all I wanted to do was to tell you everything I was feeling, what I was going through. It was really hard for me.'

At that moment, Allegra moved her body back, creating more distance between us. She moved up her hands while shrugging her shoulders.

'It was hard for you, Paze? You don't think a second about anyone else, do you? You've exposed me at all times, you lied to me, you used information that was confidential to build your story. But, of course, tell me more about how difficult life is for you.'

I covered my mouth with one hand. *Surely, I didn't do all that.*

'Allegra, seriously, I don't think that's how I remember things. Besides, it doesn't change the fact that I was threatened in a private bathroom by one of the most powerful men in town just for exposing his crimes.'

Moving closer to the edge of where she sat, I pulled out the printed article and pointed to my face on it.

'Does this look to you like someone who's as scheming as you've described?'

'Paze, you never looked like someone who'd end up in a private bathroom having sex with my boyfriend's unsavoury father. Yet, there you were. I feel sorry for what you've gone through, but surely you can see some of your actions may have put you in that position.'

I shook my head as my eyes rolled to the ceiling, fighting back any display of uncontrolled emotion that attempted to sabotage the conversation.

'Wait, you still refer to Georgie as your boyfriend?'

The comment finally stirred up a physical reaction as Allegra sat herself up straight to answer me.

'The article complicated things, and it opened my eyes to the fact that I should know him better, but it didn't change my willingness to fight for us.'

I retorted, without thinking through my response. 'He doesn't belong with you, in your world.'

She removed her sunglasses, placing them next to her thighs. She looked at me directly and said, 'Neither did you and yet I was willing to accept you, too. Much like with him, all I expected was loyalty, and yet it was too expensive a request for someone who's willing to do anything to get ahead.'

The words stung in my ears, giving a sudden onset of pressure around my temples. Meanwhile, Allegra slipped on her poolside slippers and grabbed her locker keys.

'I've heard what I needed to hear from you, Paze. Now please go before I need to remind security that you're not a member of this club.'

I stood up quickly, knowing too well that she meant everything she said. Without a word, I turned around and walked away from my longest friendship. I walked at a fast pace, avoiding any further interactions.

Across the road from the hotel, I used a metal gate to support myself as I looked around at the red, gold and white buildings that surrounded me. *I did belong here, more than any of them.*

I had studied every mannerism, I learned to talk like them, to dream like them. It didn't come naturally to me, but I learned to be the ultimate Knightsbridge girl through effort. From the curated group of close friends I had created to the days spent observing how people there lived. The only thing I didn't have was their money; this was clear by the way Allegra was far more willing to forgive Georgie than me despite the fact that we both hadn't been fully transparent. *The only thing I didn't have was their money. The only thing I didn't have...*

I smiled while pulling out my phone from my handbag.

> Me
>
> Hi Blake, I'd like to entertain the proposal. Send me your office address.

The next day, I made my way to Saint Paul's underground station. The requested meeting would take place at his larger office in the presence of his wide team of associates, paralegals, and secretaries. It felt safe to keep things professional rather than personal, given the previous direct threat. I walked into a building near the old city wall and the cathedral, rife with black pea coats and foreign tourists wrapped in layers that were more suited for the Arctic.

A very sophisticated security system set up at the reception of the building safely guarded London's most expensive hourly workers. The building headquartered many of the city's most sought-after legal experts with a waiting list of millionaires and billionaires in need of cleaning up after their mess. On my side, there wasn't anyone accompanying me but the certainty that I had nothing else to lose. And the nervousness around potentially seeing the man who had grabbed my neck and threatened to kill me.

The office was minimalistic, with elegantly placed lighting that emphasised the dimensions of the area. I spotted Lord Thurrington, Blake, and an entourage of staff in suits sitting around a large conference table inside an aquarium-like meeting room. At the sight of him, the steps I took became increasingly more laboured as my body reacted in self-preservation. Each time my feet touched the ground again, I felt an increase in the tightness growing inside my chest.

I finally slid in, disrobing the outer layers to reveal a far more conservative look than the one Lord Thurrington was accustomed to seeing me in. I wore a simple, black suit that was bought off the high street for the occasion. From inside my handbag, I pulled out a notebook and a pen, where I had prepared talking points to be used as needed during the negotiations. On the other side of the table, Lord Thurrington looked at my bag and outfit with an eyebrow raised. I couldn't tell if it was suspicion or the disappointment of seeing me fully clothed. Either way, the thought made me giggle, removing some of the heaviness that had weighed upon my entrance.

'Thank you for coming, Ms Paisley. We would like to start off with an obvious condemnation of the deception used to entrap my client, The Honourable Lord James Thurrington, a successful businessman who's contributed tremendously to society and was evidently taken with your youth and attractiveness at the expense of his better judgment.'

It was anticipated that, like every other lawyer comfortable working for a super predator, Blake would attempt to transfer guilt onto the weaker party. The only problem was I didn't feel particularly weak.

'Must be quite embarrassing to be challenged by someone as young and attractive as me. A bit of a blow to the ego, isn't it?'

In response, he coughed an uncomfortable sound, using it to conceal any hint of real emotion. Instead, Blake continued to speak.

'James has made a generous offer for you to retract your personal commentary, remain silent, and stop cooperating with the police. He would like to offer you ten million pounds in cash.'

That was more money than I would ever see as a journalist. It was far more than my parents had ever saved in a lifetime of work, and all within less than a year of my professional career. Perhaps there was some logic to Celine's thought process; there was a slightly easier way to comfort. I brushed that thought off, afraid of what opening that door could lead to in the future. I told myself to stay focused; it was too late for internal ethical dilemmas.

'Are there any further conditions I need to be aware of?'

'Yes, he wants you to leave the city. You will need to start a new life elsewhere.'

Surely, we could exist in a city as large as London without ever crossing paths again. Pressure in my lower back compounded as the muscles irradiated the stress flowing from my veins.

'I can't really imagine myself on a daily Surrey commute. That's a tough sell.'

Lord Thurrington struck the table with a loud thump that made the paralegals jump in their seats. I closed my eyes for a few seconds before staring at him directly like a schoolmaster would with an unruly child. He remained defiant, gurgling words out like he had started the day with a few too many whiskeys.

'No, you don't understand, darling. I want you out of the country. I will leave you in peace, but you get the hell out of here, and you quit working for my ex-wife for good. Given who I am, I could get you to agree to this for free, but I'd rather pay for my problems to go away.'

His voice was grave with the obvious threat seeping through his offer. It was clear that he was serious enough to be visibly upset in front of a wider audience. At the same time, he was afraid of the damage I could cause to him and his business. I could leverage his fear just as much as he could mine.

'I want twenty million, and we're game.'

He laughed nervously as the multiple suits in the room all looked at each other, likely wondering if he'd break the glass table next in anger or subside. I could feel my heart speeding, anticipating another aggressive reaction from his side.

'That's a lot of money for a little girl like you. Don't get greedy.'

His reaction was exactly as I imagined in my head, which made it easier to exaggerate the counter-action I needed to take. I placed both one hand across and used the other as a prop to put one finger across my cheek, mimicking a thinking statue. I arched my back and slowly broke into a relaxed smile.

'It's not as much as I'd be saving your ass from jail. That's a really tough place for a privileged man like you.'

The anger shot up to his eyes, which contracted an additional carmine tone to them. His nose flared as he stared at Blake, both silent and clearly calculating the counteroffer.

'Fine, just get the hell out of my life for good.'

I smiled with full teeth showing and extended a cordial but ironic hand to shake with him. He left it hanging, got up in a rush, and exited the room, quickly followed by some of his staff.

Before doing the same, Blake politely shook my hand, concluding our dealings on the matter. He moved towards my side of the table to escort me off the premises before finishing off our day with a final consideration.

'I'll have the NDA sent across to you later with the terms. Obviously, once signed, this will never be spoken of again. Hope you enjoy your hard-earned wealth.'

Oh, trust me, I would definitely be enjoying never having to be told I didn't belong.

CHAPTER THIRTY
A Social Exile

I opened my eyes to see the floral curtains of my childhood bedroom gently hitting the antique glass windows. A cold breeze was seeping in between the black iron frame that sustained the bottle glass feature. In the days that followed the legalities, I successfully forfeited my London sardine can of a flat and returned to Surrey as a temporary landing. The money would only become accessible to me when I was out of the country. In the meantime, I had to formally resign and use my own funds to reorganise my life. It gave me a chance to hold on to old Paze for just a little while longer before I buried her on my way out of the country.

Every door that was closed to me recently felt bittersweet, from the flat that had been rented to be my first *pied a terre* in the city to the emotional resignation letter that I had submitted to Nathan blaming my mental health for leaving the dream job behind instead of the truth that it was a combination of fear and money that made me walk away. His guilty look after reading the letter followed by words that I'd never forget.

'I'm sorry for pushing you too hard, Paze. You clearly weren't ready yet, and I should have protected you as your manager.'

Perhaps he wasn't the monster that I had concocted in my head. He seemed sincere in his regrets, making sure that Florence personally wrote me a recommendation letter and a very personalised thank you note for my short-lived services. The article had quickly become the number one topic on Sizzle's pages, with print copies that sold in droves. I hadn't let them down, and even if it came at a huge cost to my own personal life, that truly mattered to me. However limited in time it had been, I knew I had made my mark, and nobody could take that away from me.

Back in my room, I took in the decor around me. There was the familiarity of the space, albeit one that I never liked very much. It was full of my mother's stylistic choices that were imposed on me when the room had been last redecorated while I was still a teenager. My parents had wanted to raise a proper upper-class girl with traditional values. Instead, I had grown to be an ambitious, socially mobile journalist with a pending payday that would eclipse their life earnings. Their encapsulated countryside life was so far away from the Knightsbridge crowd that I had managed to avoid them reading about the scandal I was embroiled in.

When I finally picked up my phone from the nightstand to see how long I had hibernated, instead of the typical messages from my closest friends, there was a single notification from the most unlikely of senders.

Celine

> For whatever it's worth, I'm proud of you. You've become exactly who I always thought you could be.

What did it say about me if the only person who knew me and was proud of what I'd done was a heartless malefactor? She was not someone I cared about impressing; quite the opposite. Her words lingered like the stench of dubiously acquired money that would soon follow me in life. Would monetary compensation ever make up for the lack of friends? Or the self-loathing that crept in between bouts of pride in the article? There were far too many questions spinning in my head without the right amount of coffee to help me unpack them.

The constant questions from my family as to the reasons that had led me back there had me in a state of emotional exhaustion. Nevertheless, it was a small price to pay for a free spot to stay for a few more days until I figured out where to go more permanently. I could understand their confusion at the sudden change of plans after spending years talking about working for Sizzle and finally moving close enough to

Knightsbridge to catch a whiff of the same air. If it wasn't for the adrenaline, I, too, would be questioning how things would end once the dust had settled.

Perhaps I had unconsciously wanted to do this. I had grown tired of the never-ending superficial pettiness that seemed disconnected from the grittiness of the real world. I remembered all the conversations with Bex trying to defend a way of life that I both criticised but was equally enamoured with at the same time. Damn it, my mind had moved back to Bex and the grieving of another relationship. I missed him intensely, and it was perhaps one of my biggest regrets not to have included him more. Could things have been salvaged had he known my side of events? I supposed I would never know, given his radio silence after the fateful night. Ever since, I had reminded Mansour that he was morally obligated to listen to my relationship mourning after the Ameerah debacle.

He had also been my conduit back and forth with Allegra, who had not forgiven me, and Mila, who had morally reprimanded my actions by siding with her. It wouldn't be long before I would have to consolidate plans for life after Sizzle, but it was unlikely I'd manage to reconcile with them beforehand. I had never known a life without Allegra living alongside me, cheering at every success and consoling every heartbreak. There was an unshakable emptiness in not having her as a constant anymore; it was the most frightening part of being forced to move on.

Before I condemned myself to pillow screaming, I heard a knock on my door with a cadence that I knew too well. It sent me all the way back to my school days.

'Paisley, honey, I've got you all the ingredients to your stress-curing wrap for breakfast. Come down for breakfast with us?'

It was a sweet touch from my mother. We haven't been close since college years when boarding drifted us apart sooner than it would've had I stayed home. Still, we occasionally shared moments that helped me feel slightly more loved than usual. I was in no position to be picky about the source of affection; I just knew I needed it.

'Coming, I'm just going to brush my teeth.'

Moments later, with my hair in a messy ponytail and a sweatshirt pyjama, I walked down the noisy staircase outside my room that led into the naturally lit kitchen glistening with bronze-coloured shiny pots over the stove—neither really used aside from being decor. I grabbed all the essentials for my wrapping activities in the fridge and mounted them onto a plate, creating a tower of foods to be taken to the dining table. My mother had set a table for three, which seemed odd, but I also couldn't spot her anywhere.

Through the wooden archway, I heard several footsteps coming in and overheard my mother saying, 'She's right in there; I'll go out for a coffee so you guys can have some privacy.'

Curious, I stuck my head out to catch a glimpse as the steps got closer. I readjusted my eyes to ensure I wasn't having a stress-induced hallucination.

'Mansour? Bex? What are you guys doing here?'

Looking at me up and down, Mansour stood in front of the table in his head-to-toe YSL suede jacket and smart trousers combo with leather ankle boots. In contrast, I must have seemed like an alien species sequestered to a country life.

'Oh, God, this is critical; you look ridiculously unwell. I'm arranging for appointments immediately. Do you know an IV drip?'

I laughed genuinely and loudly at the absurdity that it was Mansour to have a normal, human breakdown. Bex chuckled, more shyly than I had, but still warm enough for me to feel instantly better.

'I'm so glad you're here, Bex.'

Mansour moved ahead of him, taking a seat next to me at the table, leaving us in locked eye contact.

'You're glad he's here? Do you know how much effort I put into this operation? I can be very irritating when someone tells me no. I could no longer tolerate the moping, especially when we need to be planning your exit from the country immediately.'

There were so many words that needed to be said at that moment. Instead, I looked at Bex, begging him to just feel what I was going through so I'd be spared further humiliation. He must have noticed, breaking the awkwardness before I had to speak.

'I'm sorry that I haven't responded to your messages. I didn't know what to say. I was upset and, quite frankly, a bit judgemental. I owe you an apology, and I wanted it to be in person.'

'You shouldn't be. I really didn't consider how this story would affect us. I didn't think far ahead; I just wanted to do well. I never thought we were at risk, and things happened so fast.'

Bex took the seat in front of me, making the wood on it creak as he sat down. He looked like himself, dressed in a blue button shirt and navy blue trousers. The feeling of his shirt on my skin, just thinking about it, made me wish we weren't meeting in these circumstances.

'I'm sure there are things we could have both done better. When Mansour said you were leaving for good, I knew I couldn't leave things like this with you. I meant it when I said I love you; even if we aren't together, I don't wish you harm.'

Not the words I had fantasised about hearing from him. I wanted him to say it would be fine and that we could give it another go. At least he didn't hate me fully. I'd take that.

'I'm glad you're here. I really didn't want to leave without seeing you first.'

'I don't know what happens from here onwards, but I'd think we can stay in each other's lives in one capacity or another.'

One of the most singular realisations hit me, sitting there between two people who had meant so much to me in different ways. People can outgrow a friendship, a relationship, a situation. In fact, you can outgrow an entire crowd. I made peace with the fact that our lives were evolving differently. The self-admission was both frightening and exciting.

I smiled sincerely and started making my breakfast wrap. Mansour poured himself a coffee while Bex tucked into toast and jam. It was quiet, peaceful, and everything I needed in that moment.

'I really need to move out. Surrey is consuming every part of my personality. I almost cooked myself a meal from scratch last night.'

Mansour covered his mouth in horror at the scene. He knew me well; I was always more of a takeaway girl than a domestic goddess. The countryside felt strangely claustrophobic despite the open fields.

Bex finished his breakfast, placing the knife he had used to spread jam across his plate.

'What do you think you'll do next? Go on a working holiday somewhere? I was really surprised to see that you're leaving Knightsbridge.'

Of course, I was bound by a non-disclosure agreement that forbade mention of the action reasons I had to suddenly uproot everything. Different people had heard different segments of the story I had fabricated, with some threads of truth woven in between. A mental breakdown after my first hit piece, burnout, and a need to find myself were all a part of each version. Missing was any connection directly to what had happened or the money that had been placed into an international account under my name.

'I want to be somewhere near the seaside, maybe some warm weather to change the sombre mood?'

Mansour chimed in, restless in his seat.

'I've got a place in Marbella that my parents bought back in the 80's. I wouldn't be caught dead there, and they've migrated to Como summers, so if you want the place, it's yours if you need a place to crash.'

'Marbella? What the hell am I going to do in Marbella?'

'What you do best, Paze. Pretend to fit in.'

BOOK TWO IN THE SERIES IS COMING SOON.

The Marbella Crowd

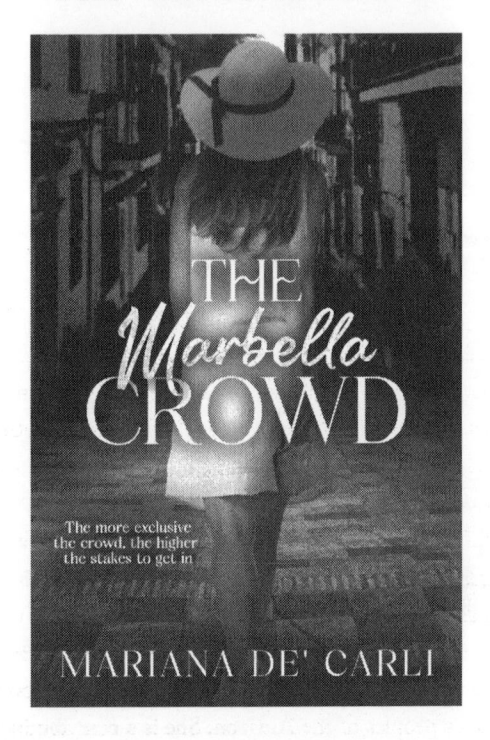

Register for updates

www.marianadecarli.com

ABOUT THE AUTHOR

Mariana Fonseca De' Carli Orti is a Brazil-born author, linguist, and public speaker. She's published works in both Portuguese and English after graduating from King's College London in Modern Languages. Her postgraduate studies focused on Law, and later, Marketing at Rome Business School in Italy. In 2025, she's due to complete a Master's in Applied Neuroscience from King's.

In the last years, Mariana has owned a successful fashion brand, worked as an exhibition organiser for major events companies worldwide and consulted for international organisations. Currently serving as a Trade & Commercial Advisor for a government agency, Mariana continues to write both contemporary fiction and nonfiction focused on the Indigenous peoples of the Amazon. She is a contributing columnist for several publications globally, covering topics around travel, arts, and cultural trends.

FOLLOW ME ON SOCIAL MEDIA
FOR BOOK UPDATES:

@londonrepublic

https://goodreads.com/marianadecarli

ACKNOWLEDGEMENTS

As a debut novelist, writing this book has been a very personal experience. There are many great people who have played a pivotal role in how this story came to be, and ultimately, resulted in the book it is today.

Firstly, I'd like to thank my family for taking a huge gamble on a dreamy eighteen year old high school student's decision to uproot her whole life in Miami and move across the pond to study in London. Without my mother's support for my wildest dreams, the encounters and life experiences that led me to Knightsbridge, would have never happened. I thank my loving husband, Daniel, for his constant encouragement to transform memories into stories with their own characters that have long lived only in my imaginarium. Gabriel, my younger brother who so often lived out the most incredible adventures with me in Knightsbridge and beyond. I acknowledge the endless belief in me that my grandmother Maria do Carmo has always had, and most significantly, her spirit of courage to reach for what seems unattainable without fear.

I have been very fortunate to come across supporters of my writing in the many stages of life that were also significant in making the jump from book aficionado to professional writer. I show my sincere gratitude to Celio Said, who gave me my first writing gig at sixteen years old, and continues to be a great supporter of my work. I've been unbelievably lucky to grow to also have the guidance of distinguished authors who have generously given me their time and professional tips in the last years. Thank you to my published peers who've been inspirational to my journey throughout the years including Gracia Cantanhede and Monther Kabbani.

It would have been impossible to leave out the collection of brilliant minds that keep me motivated. Kingdom Creatives and Writer's in Riyadh are both wonderful local communities that enrich our lives. Brandie Janow and Lubna Ahmed Haque, respective founders of the groups have been an immense part of my work.

I acknowledge the phenomenal help I received from beta readers who provided great feedback on the story: Brandie, Lubna, Samar Jaafar, AG Danish, Rita Abi Rached, and Jody Odowick.

Thank you to Dani Edwards of Scott Editorial and the wider editorial team for their fabulous work. Najla and Nada Qamber, the brilliant book cover designer who captured the essence of the story in breathtaking design.

Finally, I am deeply grateful to you, the reader, for coming this far alongside Paze and her eye-opening account of London's elite. Her story will continue to develop, as she too discovers that you can escape a city but not the power game to the top. I hope you come along with her to warmer climates and higher stakes.